COUNT LEO TOLSTOY was born on September 9, 1828, in Yasnaya Polyana, Russia. Orphaned at nine, he was brought up by an elderly aunt and educated by French tutors until he matriculated at Kazan University in 1844. In 1847, he gave up his studies and, after several aimless years, volunteered for military duty in the Army, serving as a junior officer in the Crimean War before retiring in 1857. In 1862, Tolstoy married Sophie Behrs, a marriage that was to become, for him, bitterly unhappy. His diary, started in 1847, was used for self-study and self-criticism, and it served as the source from which he drew much of the material that appeared not only in his great novels *War and Peace* (1869) and *Anna Karenina* (1877), but also in his shorter works. Seeking religious justification for his life, Tolstoy evolved a new Christianity based upon his own interpretation of the Gospels. Yasnaya Polyana became a Mecca for his many converts. At the age of eighty-two, while away from home, the writer's health broke down in Astapovo, Riazan, and he died there on November 20, 1910.

Resurrection

by

Leo Tolstoy

Translated by Vera Traill
With a Foreword by Alan Hodge

A SIGNET CLASSIC from
NEW AMERICAN LIBRARY
TIMES MIRROR
New York and Scarborough, Ontario
The New English Library Limited, London

Published by arrangement with Hamish Hamilton, Ltd.

SIGNET CLASSIC TRADEMARK REG. U.S. PAT. OFF. AND FOREIGN COUNTRIES
REGISTERED TRADEMARK—MARCA REGISTRADA
HECHO EN CHICAGO, U.S.A.

SIGNET, SIGNET CLASSICS, MENTOR, PLUME AND MERIDIAN BOOKS
are published *in the United States* by
The New American Library, Inc.,
1301 Avenue of the Americas, New York, New York 10019,
in Canada by The New American Library of Canada Limited,
81 Mack Avenue, Scarborough, 704, Ontario,
in the United Kingdom by The New English Library Limited,
Barnard's Inn, Holborn, London, E.C. 1, England.

First Printing, June, 1961

5 6 7 8 9 10 11 12 13

PRINTED IN THE UNITED STATES OF AMERICA

FOREWORD

❧

NOBODY reading *Resurrection* and knowing nothing of its author's life would guess that Tolstoy was seventy-one years old when he wrote it, nor that it was his first full-length novel for over twenty years. For *Resurrection* is one of Tolstoy's greatest books. "A remarkable work of art," Chekhov called it, singling out for special praise the scenes in which Tolstoy portrays princes, generals, lawyers, aunts, peasants, convicts, and government inspectors. The personalities of these characters and the atmosphere of the houses, offices, jails, and country estates in which they move are rendered with the same unsurpassed skill that Tolstoy showed in his longer and more ambitious masterpieces.

The vitality of *Resurrection* is not wholly due to the fact that Tolstoy's extraordinary genius and tremendous energy had suffered no decline. What moved him afresh was the desire to put into the form of a novel the spiritual "conversion" he underwent after finishing *Anna Karenina* in 1876. This crisis of mind he had already described in several autobiographical and didactic works, but it was by no means over and done with twenty years later. Indeed, all Tolstoy's life is a history of spiritual strife. As early as the Crimean war, when he was a young officer and the promising author of a number of stories, he was wrestling with the problems of human egotism. He felt the need to realize in himself the good, the pure, the simple life, and his diary of the time is full of self-reproach for frequently transgressing his ideals. The conflict in him was not only a matter of striving after harmony in his own nature. At the age of twenty-seven he declared his hope of becoming the founder of "a new religion corresponding with the present state of mankind; the religion of Christ, but purged of dogmas and mysticism—a practical religion, not promising future bliss, but bliss on earth." His conversion in 1876 marked his final resolve to set aside other pursuits for the sake of this aim.

All Tolstoy's books have a strong autobiographical flavor. In *Resurrection*, Prince Nekhludov's realization that he can only redeem his self-respect by renouncing his property and his position in the world is founded on one of Tolstoy's deepest convictions. Likewise the self-questioning of Pierre Bezukhov in *War and Peace*, and the development of Kostya Levin's philosophy in *Anna Karenina*, reflect Tolstoy's own preoccupations. While writing those two books he was living on his property at Yasnaya Polyana in the province of Orel, bringing up a large family, ploughing his own fields, cobbling his own shoes, running a school for the children of his peasants, deliberately shunning the pleasures of sophisticated society in Moscow and Petersburg, and cutting himself off also from all the political and literary movements that were agitating the leading minds of Russia. Tolstoy was working out his own way of salvation, and after 1876 he believed he had found it. Though he wrote several stories in the twenty years that followed, he used his energies principally for preaching his new creed. Turgenev reproached him with abandoning literature: "I am writing to you," he appealed from Paris, "specially to say how glad I am to have been your contemporary, and to express my last and sincere wish. My friend, return to literary work!" But Tolstoy did not heed this deathbed supplication. He was out of sympathy with the idea held by Turgenev and most of Turgenev's French friends that literature was purely a form of Art, and the novelist its dedicated hierophant. For Tolstoy, literature was pointless if it did not convey a moral lesson.

In one form and another, Tolstoy's novels contain most of the moral teaching which he also set forth in his didactic works: they celebrate the virtues of family life, chastity, pacifism, and the simple rounds of rural toil; more powerfully still, they show up the evils that arise from the ownership of property and from the subordination of man to political, social, and ecclesiastical institutions. These teachings had a wide influence. Many disciples came to visit the Sage and Saint at Yasnaya Polyana, and numerous Tolstoy colonies were founded on his principles. A terrible struggle thereupon broke out, and continued until Tolstoy's death, between him and his disciples on the one hand, and his wife and most of his children on the other: the story of it is one of the saddest passages in the biography of great men. In his own life Tolstoy's religion of anarchism proved ironically impracticable; it was also completely out of step with the historical processes that were leading to the Russian Revolution. But Tolstoy was not discouraged: he went on with the struggle according to his own lights until finally, at the age of eighty-two, he felt driven to quit and renounce his home. Ten days later he died in a wayside station hotel. So ended his own lifelong attempt at Spiritual Resurrection.

Tolstoy derived the idea for the plot of *Resurrection* from a newspaper report, according to which a nobleman, called to serve on a jury at the trial of a prostitute for murder, recognized her as a girl whom a long time since he had himself seduced. On the basis of this conscience-striking incident a tremendously powerful story is built up—indeed, its consequences can hardly be said to have an end. The problem of whether Prince Nekhludov should finally marry Katusha Maslova and settle down with her in Siberia is one which Tolstoy found extremely difficult to solve. He is said to have tried to make up his mind by playing a game of patience which did not come out. However that may be, the path that Prince Nekhludov's life takes after his spiritual regeneration is left to the reader's imagination. It could not be otherwise, since Tolstoy himself was never able to work out a satisfactory way of life for the Resurrected and Regenerate man.

Resurrection underwent an immense amount of rewriting. All the family were engaged in cross-copying Tolstoy's proof corrections. Louise Maude's English translation appeared shortly after the first Russian edition; Constance Garnett's version in 1904. Though *Resurrection* was banned in 1900 by two of the largest circulating libraries, it had a larger sale in Britain than any of Tolstoy's previous books; and the success of a dramatized version, put on at His Majesty's Theater, soon persuaded the libraries to revoke their ban. The royalties from sales were devoted by Tolstoy to assisting a fundamentalist and pacifist Russian sect, named Dukhobors, to emigrate to Canada, where they still flourish.

Tolstoy's life is very fully documented: his diaries, journals, and love letters have all been translated into English. Volumes of reminiscences are available in English by his wife and three of his children, also, by several of his disciples, and by Maxim Gorky.

—ALAN HODGE

RESURRECTION

BOOK I

CHAPTER ONE

No matter that men in their hundreds of thousands disfigured
the land on which they swarmed, paved the ground with stones
so that no green thing could grow, filled the air with the fumes
of coal and gas, lopped back all the trees, and drove away every
animal and every bird: spring was still spring, even in the town.
The sun shone warmly, the grass came to life again and showed
its green wherever it was not scraped away, between the paving
stones as well as on the lawns in the boulevards; the birches, the
wild cherries, and the poplars unfolded their sticky and fragrant
leaves, the swelling buds were bursting on the lime trees; the
jackdaws, the sparrows, and the pigeons were happy and busy
over their nests, and the flies, warmed by the sunshine, hummed
gaily along the walls. Plants, birds, insects, and children rejoiced. But men, adult men, never ceased to cheat and harass
their fellows and themselves. What men considered sacred and
important was not the spring morning, not the beauty of God's
world given for the enjoyment of all creatures, not the beauty
which inclines the heart to peace and love and concord. What
men considered sacred and important were their own devices
for wielding power over their fellow men.

So, the idea that every man and every living creature has a
sacred right to the gladness of the springtime had never penetrated into the office of the city's prison. But concerning the
sacred and important character of a certain sealed and numbered document received on the previous evening, ordering that
on this day, the twenty-eighth of April, at nine A.M., three
prisoners, two women and one man, should be summoned to
court—concerning this, no doubt whatever was entertained.
One of the women, the most important prisoner, was to have a

special escort. In conformity with this order, therefore, on the twenty-eighth day of April, at eight o'clock in the morning, the senior warder entered the foul and gloomy corridor of the women's ward. He was followed by a gaunt woman with gray curly hair, wearing a jacket with braided sleeves and caught at the waist by a belt with blue edging. She was the superintendent of the women's ward.

"It is Maslova you want?" she asked the warder on duty, following him toward the door of one of the cells that led from the corridor. The warder, clanking the padlock, opened the door of the cell, which let out a burst of air still fouler than that in the corridor.

"Maslova is required in court," he called out, and closed the door again while he waited.

The fresh, invigorating air of the fields had penetrated even into the prison yard. But the air in the corridor, heavy with the germs of typhoid, with the stench of sewage, tar, and putrefaction, was oppressive the moment one entered. The woman superintendent, coming from the yard, although familiar with the atmosphere, was affected by it. No sooner had she entered the corridor than she felt languid and drowsy.

A bustling could be heard inside the cell, the voices of women, and the patter of bare feet on the floor.

"Come along, Maslova! Get a move on, I tell you!" called the senior warder. After a minute or two a young woman, short in height and full-bosomed, came out and stood beside him; she was wearing a gray prison cloak thrown over a white blouse and skirt; on her feet were linen stockings and prison shoes.

A few dark ringlets had deliberately been allowed to escape from the white scarf tied around her head. Her skin had the curious pallor that comes from long imprisonment, the sort of hue which brings to mind the shoots springing out from potatoes kept in a cellar. The short, broad hands, and as much of the full neck as could be seen beneath the ample prison cloak, were the same color as her face. Her sparkling black eyes, one of which had a slight squint, sharply contrasted with her pale and puffy face.

She carried herself erect, her full bosom well forward, and her head thrown back; as she entered the corridor she looked straight into the eyes of the warder, ready to obey his orders whatever they might be. Just as he was about to lock the door of the cell, an elderly woman pushed forward a pale, stern, and wrinkled face. She started to say something to Maslova, but the warder slammed the door in her face. As the head disappeared, a peal of women's laughter rang out from the cell. Maslova smiled and turned toward the barred window. The old woman pressed her face against the grating and muttered in a hoarse voice: "Don't forget, you're to say as little as you can, and stick to it."

"If only the business could be settled one way or another. Nothing could make it worse," said Maslova, with a shake of her head.

"Yes, it'll be *one* way, not *two* ways," said the warder with a superior, official air, pleased at his own joke. "Come along, follow me."

The old woman's eye vanished as Maslova stepped forward into the middle of the corridor and swiftly followed the warder. They went down a flight of stone steps, passed the still fouler and noisier cells of the men's quarters, from which many eyes peered through the grated windows, and entered the office.

Two armed soldiers were waiting. A clerk handed one of them a document smelling of tobacco and, pointing to the prisoner, said: "Take her." The soldier, a peasant from Nizhni Novgorod, with a red, pock-marked face, tucked the document into his cuff and, nodding toward the woman, winked slyly at his comrade, a broad-cheeked Chuvash. The soldiers and prisoner descended the stairs leading toward the main exit. Here a small gate was opened, through which they passed, and turned into one of the paved streets of the town.

Cabbies, tradespeople, cooks, workers, clerks in the civil service, all paused to gaze at the prisoner; some shook their heads as though saying to themselves: "Such are the consequences of bad behavior—so different from ours!" Children looked at her terror-stricken, but when they saw that she was guarded by soldiers they knew she could do no harm. A peasant who had sold his charcoal and had just been drinking in a tavern, went up to her, crossed himself, and offered her a kopeck.

The prisoner blushed, bowed her head, and murmured something indistinct. She glanced out of the corner of her eye at the staring people and seemed to be amused by the attention she attracted. She took real pleasure in the pure spring air, so different from that of the jail; but walking was painful in heavy prison shoes and, picking her way over the cobblestones, she tried to step as lightly as possible. Passing by a corn merchant's, her foot nearly struck one of the pigeons strutting about unmolested on the road. It rose and, as it flew, fanned the air

close to her ear; she smiled, then heaved a deep sigh as the sense
of her present predicament came over her.

∗

CHAPTER TWO

THE story of Maslova, the prisoner, was a very common one.
She was the daughter of an unmarried serf, who lived on an
estate belonging to two maiden sisters, where her mother was a
dairymaid. This unmarried woman had a baby every year, and,
as often happens among village people, each one of these un-
welcome, unwanted babies, after being carefully baptized, was
left to starve by its mother, whom it hindered in her work.
Thus she disposed of five children. Each one was regularly
baptized, starved to death, and buried. The sixth child, whose
father was a gypsy, was a girl, and would have shared the fate
of the others had not one of the maiden ladies, while visiting the
farmyard to reprimand the old woman in charge of the dairy
for having sent up bad cream, happened to catch sight of the
mother with her pretty, healthy child. Having scolded the dairymaid about the cream and also for keeping a woman with a
newborn child on the premises, she was about to leave when
her eyes rested again on the child. Moved by pity, she offered
to be its godmother. The little girl was baptized, and, out of
compassion for the godchild, milk and money were sent to the
mother. This was how it happened that the girl lived, and forever after the old ladies called her "the rescued one."

The child was only three years old when her mother sickened
and died. As her grandmother, the dairymaid, showed that the
care of so young a child was too much of a burden, the old
ladies took her into the manor house.

The little girl, with her bright, black eyes, was unusually
attractive and a real comfort to the good ladies. The younger
and more kindly of the sisters, Sophia Ivanovna, was the child's
godmother. The disposition of the elder, Maria Ivanovna, was
more stern. Sophia Ivanovna dressed the little girl in nice
clothes, and taught her to read, intending to give her a good
education. Maria Ivanovna used to say that the girl must be
brought up to work and be trained for a housemaid; she was
exacting; if she happened to be out of sorts, she punished and
even beat the child. The result was that under two opposing

influences Katusha grew up half a servant and half a lady. She sewed, kept the rooms in order, polished the icons with chalk, roasted, ground, and served the coffee, did the small washing, and now and then read aloud to the ladies.

She had several offers of marriage, but was not inclined to accept any of them. She saw that the life she would be obliged to lead with the laboring men who offered marriage would be too hard for her, accustomed as she was to a life of comparative ease in the house of her mistresses.

She lived in the house in this way until, when she was sixteen, a rich young prince came on a visit; he was the nephew of the ladies of the manor, and at that time a student at the university. Katusha fell in love with him, though she did not dare acknowledge it to herself. Three years later, when he was about to join his regiment, he paid his aunts a four-day visit. On the eve of his departure he seduced Katusha, and when he bade her good-by handed her a hundred-ruble note. Within five months of this time it became clear to her that she was pregnant.

From that moment life became a burden to her. Absorbed in schemes for escaping the disgrace which threatened her, she went about her duties listlessly. One day, before she knew what she was saying, she had spoken insolently to her mistresses—bitterly she repented this in after days—and asked to be discharged.

The ladies, seriously displeased, let her go. She found a situation as housemaid in the family of a police officer, but stayed only three months because her master, who must have been about fifty years old, began to pester her with amorous advances. One day, when he was especially aggressive, she lost her temper, called him a fool and an old devil, and struck him a blow that fairly knocked him down. She was dismissed for impertinence. There was no chance for her now in domestic service as the time of her confinement was drawing near, and she took lodgings with a village midwife who also sold spirits. She was not very ill when the baby was born, but the midwife, who had previously delivered a peasant woman now lying ill with puerperal fever, infected Katusha. Meanwhile, the baby boy had been sent to the Foundling Hospital where, according to the story of the woman who took him there, he died on his arrival.

When Katusha came to the midwife's house she had a hundred and twenty-seven rubles—the hundred her seducer had given her and twenty-seven which she had earned. When she left she had only two. She had no faculty for saving money. She spent it on herself and gave to all who asked. The midwife charged her forty rubles for two months' board and lodging, including the tea she drank; she paid twenty-five for having her child taken away; she lent the midwife forty rubles to buy a cow, and twenty rubles were flung away on clothes and sweet things to eat; so that when she recovered she had no money and had to look for a place. She found one in the house of a government forester, a married man who, like the police officer, very soon began to importune her. She loathed him and did all she could to avoid him, but he was a man of experience and too crafty for her. Moreover, he was the master and could order her about as he liked. So one day, having chosen his time, he succeeded in overpowering her. Soon afterward his wife chanced to find him alone with Katusha, and in her rage threw herself upon the girl; Katusha resisted, there was a struggle, and the consequence was that she was turned out of the house without her wages. Then she went to her aunt in the city.

The aunt's husband was a bookbinder who formerly had a good business but, discouraged by losing his customers, took to drink and squandered everything he could lay hands on. The aunt kept a small laundry, by means of which she supported herself, the children, and her good-for-nothing husband. She offered to take in Maslova as a laundress, but, seeing the hard life of the other laundresses employed by her aunt, Maslova hesitated to accept the offer, visiting the employment agents meanwhile. At last a position was offered her with a lady who had two sons, pupils at a secondary school. Within a week the elder boy, who was in the sixth form and already had a mustache, was neglecting his studies and devoting all his time to Maslova. The mother laid all the blame upon the girl and sent her away.

She had no other place in view, but it so happened that just as she entered the employment office she met a lady decked out with rings and bracelets, who, when she learned that Maslova was looking for a situation, gave her an address and asked her to call. When Maslova called she was received hospitably; the woman offered her cakes and sweet wine, and immediately sent out her maid with a note. In the evening a tall, gray-haired man made his appearance; he took a seat beside Maslova and smilingly began to joke with her. The mistress of the house called him out into the next room, and Maslova heard her say: "fresh from the country." Then she took Maslova aside and told her that the man was a wealthy author who would treat her generously if he found her to his liking. She proved satisfactory, and received twenty-five rubles and the promise to be sent for again. The money was soon spent in repaying her aunt and buying a gown, a bonnet, and ribbons. A few days later the author sent for her, and she went. He gave her another twenty-five rubles and offered her a flat of her own.

While she was living in this flat, she fell in love with a cheerful shop assistant who lived in the same house. She announced this herself to the author and left him, taking another and smaller lodging. But the shop assistant, who had promised to marry her, left her one fine day and went to Nizhni Novgorod; and so she found herself alone. She would have liked to keep her lodging, but was not allowed to do so. The police told her that she could not live in that way unless she procured a yellow ticket[1] and submitted herself to regular medical examinations. She then returned to her aunt who, seeing her fashionable clothes, her gown, cape, and bonnet, received her respectfully and no longer dared to offer her employment as a laundress, for it was clear that Maslova had risen in the world. Indeed, it no longer occurred to Maslova herself that it was possible for her to be a laundress. She regarded with pity the hard lives of the laundresses: some already consumptive, with thin white arms, washing and ironing in a temperature of thirty degrees,[2] the steamy atmosphere redolent with soapsuds, windows open in winter and summer alike. She looked at them and was horrified to remember that she had once thought of accepting this life of torture. About this time, when she was especially short of money and no new protector had made his appearance, Maslova encountered a procuress who earned her living by providing women for houses of ill fame.

Maslova had long ago acquired the habit of smoking, but it was only during her liaison with the shop assistant, and especially after he left her, that she began to drink. Wine was consoling; not only was it pleasant to the taste, but it also made her forget all she had been through; it gave her abandon and self-confidence, which she never felt except under the influence of drink. Without drink she felt ashamed and sad.

The new-found friend, having invited first her aunt and then Maslova herself to drink some wine, offered to introduce her to the best establishments in town, speaking in glowing terms of the advantages of such a life. Maslova had to choose between the degrading position of a servant, with casual adultery

---

[1] License for prostitutes.—Tr.
[2] Tolstoy is using the Réaumur scale: 30° R. is about 90° F.—Tr.

—for she could not hope to avoid being pestered by men—and the position, countenanced by law, of legalized adultery, regarded as a financial transaction. She decided to accept the latter. She had the idea that by adopting this profession she could be revenged on her first betrayer, on the faithless shop assistant, and on all the men who had wronged her. Another allurement was the woman's promise to let her order every sort of gown: gowns of velvet and silk, ball gowns with short sleeves and cut low in the neck; the picture of herself arrayed in bright yellow silk trimmed with black velvet was irresistible, and she surrendered her passport. That night her new friend hired a cab and took her to the notorious house of Mme. Kitaeva.

Thus Maslova entered into a life of habitual sin against every commandment, divine and human—a life which is led by hundreds and thousands of women, not only with the consent but under the patronage of a government anxious to promote the welfare of its citizens, a life which ends for nine women out of ten in disease, premature decrepitude, and death.

The morning is spent sleeping off the effects of the night's carouse. At three or four o'clock in the afternoon they rise wearily from their dirty beds; seltzer water is taken to settle the stomach; this is followed by a cup of coffee and then, clad in loose wrappers, bed jackets or dressing gowns, they dawdle from room to room, exchanging idle visits, gazing out of the windows from behind the drawn curtains, squabbling half-heartedly with one another. Then comes the bath, the perfuming of the hair and body, the trying on of gowns, disputes with the proprietress, contemplation in the mirror, the painting of face and brows, the eating of fat, sweet food. Then, arrayed in resplendent silk gowns, cut to display the form to the greatest advantage, they come down into the decorated, brilliantly lighted hall. The guests arrive, and then come music, dancing, sweets, wine, smoking, and adultery with men of all conditions —young, middle-aged, and decrepit, married and unmarried, merchants and clerks, Armenians, Jews, and Tartars, rich and poor, healthy and diseased; adultery with men drunk and men sober, men tender and men brutal, soldiers and civilians, students and schoolboys, men of every rank, age, and character. Shouts, jests, squabbles, music, tobacco, and wine; wine, tobacco, and never-ceasing music till early dawn. At the end of the week there is a visit to one of the government offices where physicians in the employment of the government subject these women to a medical examination, sometimes with dignified gravity and sometimes with a playful jocularity, destroying the sense of shame bestowed by nature upon man and beast as a protection from their own wickedness; then they give them a written permission to continue in the sins they and their accomplices have been committing all the week. So it goes on, day after day, week after week, summer and winter, weekdays and holidays.

Thus Maslova spent seven years. During this period she was in two houses, and once had to go into hospital. In the seventh year of this life, and the eighth dating from her first sin, while she was yet only twenty-six years old, there occurred the incident for which she was arrested; now, after six months' detention among thieves and murderers, she was on her way to the court of justice to undergo her trial.

❖

CHAPTER THREE

WHILE Maslova, exhausted after the long walk with her guards, was drawing near the court, Prince Dmitri Ivanovich Nekhludov, the nephew of her patronesses, the man who had seduced her, was leaning back on the down mattress of his well-sprung bed; his immaculate, elaborately pleated linen shirt was open at the neck; he smoked a cigarette and gazed absently into space, thinking of his engagements and musing over the incidents of the day before.

He sighed as he reviewed the previous evening, which he had spent with the Korchagins—people of some wealth and social importance, whose daughter he was expected shortly to marry; he threw down his cigarette and was about to take another from his silver case, but, changing his mind, he put down his smooth white legs, thrust his feet into slippers, threw a dressing gown over his shoulders, and hurried heavily into the dressing room, where the air was oppressive with the scent of cologne, pomades, and perfumes. First he cleaned his teeth, many of which had gold fillings, with a special powder, and rinsed his mouth with scented water; then he proceeded to wash, drying himself with the help of several towels. Having washed his hands with scented soap, he carefully brushed his long nails; after washing his face and thick neck in the marble basin, he entered a third room, where a shower bath awaited him. He bathed his white, stout, vigorous, muscular body with cold water and dried it with a Turkish bath towel; he then put on fresh linen and shoes that shone like a mirror, and finally seated himself at the toilet table. Here, with a brush in each hand, he applied himself to his short, curly, black beard and to his hair, which was just beginning to grow thin at the temples.

Everything that he used for his toilet, as well as his linen and all his clothing, his shoes, neckties, tie pins, and studs, were of the finest quality, simple, durable, and costly.

Taking at random from among a dozen neckties and tie pins the first he happened to lay his hand on—for this affair of dressing, once so entertaining, had lost all its interest—he put on the carefully brushed clothes that lay upon the chair waiting for him; and now, clean and perfumed if not thoroughly refreshed, Nekhludov entered the oblong dining room, where three peasants the previous day had labored over the brilliant polish of the parquet floor. The room was furnished with a huge oak sideboard and a stately dining table of the same wood with four widely spaced legs carved like lion's paws.

On this table, covered with a fine, starched cloth embroidered with large monograms, stood a silver coffee pot filled with fragrant coffee, a silver sugar bowl, a cream jug with boiled cream, and a basket containing freshly baked rolls, rusks, and biscuits. Beside the plate lay the morning mail—letters, newspapers, and the last number of the *Revue des Deux Mondes*.

He was just about to open the letters when the door that led into the corridor was opened and a stout, elderly woman came into the room. She was dressed in mourning, and wore a lace fichu on her head to hide the thinness of her parting. This woman, Agrafena Petrovna, had been lady's maid to Nekhludov's mother, who had died not long before in this very apartment, and she continued to live with the son as a housekeeper.

Agrafena Petrovna had traveled abroad with his mother and had quite the air and manners of a lady. She had been with the Nekhludovs ever since she was a child, and had known Dmitri Ivanovich when they used to call him Mitenka.

"Good morning, Dmitri Ivanovich!"

"Good morning, Agrafena Petrovna! What's the news?" he asked in a jocular tone.

"A letter from the princess, or it may be from the young lady. The maid brought it some time ago and is waiting in my room," said Agrafena Petrovna, smiling significantly.

"Very well, I will see it now," said Nekhludov, taking the letter and frowning as he noticed Agrafena Petrovna's smile. The smile meant that she suspected the letter was from the young princess, whom Agrafena Petrovna believed he had made up his mind to marry; and this supposition annoyed Nekhludov.

"I will tell the girl to wait," she said, and, having restored to its proper place a crumb brush lying on the table, sailed out of the dining room.

Nekhludov opened the scented letter and began to read:

Having taken it upon myself to be your memory [thus ran the letter, written with a bold hand on a sheet of heavy gray paper with deckled edges], I hereby remind you that today, the twenty-eighth of April, you are summoned to appear in court as juryman, and therefore you will not be able to go with Kolossov and us to see the paintings, as in your usual reckless fashion you promised last night— *à moins que vous ne soyez disposé à payer à la cour d'assises les 300 roubles d'amende que vous refusez pour votre cheval* for not appearing in time. I thought of it last night after you left. Now, don't forget.

M. KORCHAGINA

On the other side of the sheet it said:

Maman vous fait dire que votre couvert vous attendra jusqu'à la nuit. Venez absolument à quelle heure que cela soit.

M. K.

Nekhludov frowned. This note was part of the skillful campaign the princess had been waging for nearly two months, aimed at chaining him to her side with invisible bonds. But besides the hesitation common to men who have passed their first youth and who are not deeply in love, there was another, more important reason which prevented Nekhludov from making an immediate offer of marriage. It was not that ten years ago he had seduced Katusha and then deserted her; that affair had quite gone out of his mind, nor would he have considered it any obstacle to his marriage. The reason was that he had a liaison with a married woman, the wife of a marshal of the nobility. So far as he was concerned, this affair was at an end, but he had not yet succeeded in persuading the lady to agree with him. Nekhludov was shy with women, and it was that very shyness which had tempted her to try and conquer him. She had drawn him into a liaison which grew daily more absorbing and at the same time more distasteful to him. At first he had not the strength to resist the temptation; then his feeling of guilt prevented him from forcing a break with her. And for this reason he felt that he had not the right, even had he been so inclined, to propose marriage to Mlle. Korchagina.

Among the letters on the table was one from this woman's husband. When Nekhludov recognized the writing and the postmark, his color heightened and instantly his spirit rose as it always did in dangerous situations. But his excitement was uncalled for. The man, who was marshal of the nobility in the district where Nekhludov's principal estates were situated, had written only to inform him that a special assembly of the *Zemstvo*[1] was to be held in the last days of May, and to ask him to be present *pour donner un coup d'épaule* in the discussion of important questions concerning schools and roads, as strong opposition was expected from the reactionary party.

The marshal of the nobility was a liberal-minded man, and together with a few friends who shared his views he struggled against the reaction which had set in during the reign of Tsar Alexander III; absorbed heart and soul in political activity, he was unaware of his domestic misfortune.

Nekhludov recalled the painful moments he had passed through in connection with this man. He remembered the time when he thought that he had learned the truth, and when he had consequently made all arrangements for a duel, deciding that he would fire in the air; then the shocking scene when she had rushed distraught into the garden to drown herself in the pond, and how he had gone out in search of her. "It is out of the question to engage myself in any commitment until I have heard from her," he thought. A week ago he had written her a decisive letter in which, taking the entire blame upon himself and declaring his readiness to suffer any penalty, he said that for her own sake it seemed best to consider their intimacy as an affair of the past. It was a reply to this letter that he was awaiting. That he had received none so far might possibly be a favorable sign: if she had not agreed to a breach she would by then either have written or appeared in person, as she had often done previously. He had heard a rumor that an army officer had fallen in love with her, and though it caused him some jealousy

---

[1] Rural local authority in pre-revolutionary Russia.—Tr.

it also encouraged him to hope for release from the dishonorable life he was leading.

Another of the letters was from his chief steward, who wrote that it would be necessary for the prince to visit his estate in order to take formal possession and to give instructions concerning its further management. Was it to be conducted as it had been during the lifetime of the princess, or would the young prince consider the proposal made by the steward to the princess and again now repeated—namely, to increase the stock and equipment and to cultivate themselves the land now rented by the peasants? The latter would certainly be the more profitable. He also apologized for not sending the three thousand rubles that were due on the first of the month. The money would be sent by the next post. The reason for the delay was that he had been unable to collect it from the peasants, who were so dishonest that he had been obliged to appeal to the authorities.

This letter was pleasing in some respects and displeasing in others. It was gratifying to feel himself the master of so large a property, but on the other hand it disturbed him to find that whereas in the first blush of youth he had been an ardent admirer of Herbert Spencer, now that he had become a great landowner he found himself shocked by the proposition (in *Social Statics*) that private ownership of land is unjust. At one time, burning with the enthusiasm of youth, he maintained that land ought not to be treated as private property, and while at the university he not only wrote a thesis on this subject, but actually surrendered to the peasants a small piece of land which he had inherited from his father. Now he was a great landowner and must make his choice between two courses: either give up his property as he had done ten years ago with the five hundred acres that came to him from his father, or else admit the error of his former convictions.

He could not repeat his earlier action, for the landed estates were his sole means of support. He was unwilling to re-enter the government service, and at the same time he had already contracted habits of self-indulgence and luxury which he considered impossible to break. Nor was there any need, since he had lost the desire to astonish the world just as completely as he had lost the convictions, the pride, and the courage of youth. The alternative was to deny Spencer's lucid and unanswerable arguments against private ownership of land (arguments later brilliantly confirmed by Henry George), but this was an alternative which he also refused to face.

All this made the steward's letter unpleasant.

AFTER Nekhludov had finished his coffee he went into his study to look up the summons and see at what hour he was to attend in the law court, and also to write a reply to the young princess.

In order to reach the study he had to pass through his studio. Here stood an easel with an unfinished portrait, its face turned to the wall where a few sketches were hanging. The sight of the picture, over which he had labored for two years, the sketches and, in fact, the very studio itself, increased his ever-growing suspicion that his painting was a failure. He had often told himself that this feeling was due to his taste's being too highly developed; nevertheless, the feeling was a very unpleasant one. Seven years ago he had left the government service feeling sure that he had a vocation for art; from the heights of his artistic being he viewed all other occupations with a certain scorn. Now he hated to recall his self-delusion. He looked at all the luxurious appointments of the studio with a heavy heart and went into his study.

The study was a large, spacious room decorated and fitted out with every luxury and convenience of the time. One of the drawers of the huge writing table was labeled "Immediate," and in it Nekhludov found the summons, which ordered him to appear in court at eleven o'clock. Sitting down at the table, he wrote a note to thank the princess for her invitation, saying he would endeavor to be with her at dinner. But he had no sooner written it than he tore it up: the note seemed too unconventional. He wrote another, but this one seemed too cold, almost rude. He destroyed it also. Then he pressed an electric bell on the wall, and his servant, a morose, elderly man, clean-shaven except for side whiskers, wearing an unbleached cotton apron, entered the room.

"Get me a cab, please."

"Certainly, sir."

"And isn't there someone waiting from Princess Korchagina? Tell her to present my thanks to her mistress and say that I shall try to come."

"Yes, sir."

"It isn't a very courteous way of replying, but I can't write. Never mind, I shall see her tonight," thought Nekhludov, and left the study to get his overcoat. When he came out of the house he found a familiar cabby with a rubber-tired cab waiting for him at the door.

"I was at Prince Korchagin's last night just after you left," said the cabby, turning toward him a strong, sunburned neck, set off by a white shirt collar. "The doorkeeper told me you had only left a minute before."

"Even the cabbies know about my visits to the Korchagins," thought Nekhludov, and the question of whether to marry Mlle. Korchagina or not, which had preoccupied him of late, rose in his mind once more; but like most of the questions that presented themselves to him, he could not decide it either one way or the other.

There was something to be said in favor of marriage. Besides the comforts of hearth and home it offered him, by regulating his sexual relations, the possibility of what he considered a moral life; and secondly a family of children, so he hoped, would give a meaning to his meaningless existence; such were his arguments in favor of marriage in general. The case against it rested, in the first place, on the fear, common among bachelors past their first youth, of losing his freedom and, secondly, on an unaccountable awe of that mysterious being, woman.

Among the arguments in favor of marrying Missy in particular (Mlle. Korchagina's name was Maria, but, as is usual among a certain set, she was called by a nickname) was first, that she was of good family and was different in every way from the ordinary people: in dress, carriage, manner of speaking and laughing. Not that she was eccentric—far from it. She was merely well bred, a qualification he prized above all others. Secondly, she held him in high esteem, therefore he was sure that she understood him. It was that understanding of him (in other words, her recognition of his superior worth) that testified in the eyes of Nekhludov to her intelligence and good judgment. On the other hand, when he thought over the arguments against marrying her, it seemed to him that a girl might yet be found with even higher qualities, and also that Missy was already twenty-seven and that he was hardly her first love. This was tormenting. His vanity revolted against the thought that there had been a time when she had not loved him. She could hardly be expected to have known beforehand that someday she might meet him, and yet the mere idea that she could have ever loved another was humiliating in the extreme.

So the arguments pro and con were fairly well balanced, or at least they were equally forcible; with an involuntary smile

Nekhludov recognized in himself the ass of the fable, unable to decide which bundle of hay to turn to:

"At any rate, until I get an answer from Maria Vassilyevna" (the wife of the marshal of the nobility) "and that affair is off my hands, I can pledge myself to nothing," he reflected, and the respite was not without its consolations.

"There will be time enough to think of all this later," he said to himself as the cab drew up noiselessly on the asphalt before the entrance to the court. "Now I must fulfill a public duty in my usual conscientious way. Besides, these things are often interesting."

He passed the doorkeeper and went into the hall of the court.

❖

CHAPTER FIVE

WHEN Nekhludov entered, the corridors of the court were already full of activity. The attendants were hurrying noiselessly to and fro, carrying messages and various papers; ushers, lawyers, and clerks went back and forth, plaintiffs and the defendants who were not in custody wandered about aimlessly or sat waiting.

Nekhludov asked one of the messengers: "Where is the courtroom?"

"Which do you mean? Civil or criminal?"

"I am one of the jury."

"The criminal court, then. Why didn't you say so? Turn to the right, and it's the second door on the left."

Nekhludov followed the directions. Two men stood waiting by the door. One, a tall, stout, kindly-looking merchant had clearly both dined and wined and was in the best of spirits. The other, a shop assistant, looked like a Jew. They were discussing the price of wool when Nekhludov approached them and inquired for the jury room.

"This way, sir, this way. Are you one of the jurymen, too?" asked the merchant, with a cheerful wink.

When Nekhludov replied that he was, the man went on, holding out his soft, broad hand: "Good, we shall be working together. My name is Baklashov, merchant of the Second Guild. Whom have I the pleasure of speaking to?"

Nekhludov gave his name and passed at once into the jury

room. There were about ten jurymen present, of every sort and condition. They had only just assembled; some were sitting, others were walking up and down inspecting each other and getting acquainted; there was a retired colonel in uniform, some men in frock coats and business suits, and one wearing a peasant's dress. Although some of them were heard protesting and complaining about the interruption to their work, every man among them was pleased at the idea of discharging an important public duty. They talked among themselves, discussing the weather, the early spring, and the prospects of business; some of them had already become acquainted and some had not. Those who did not know Nekhludov were in haste to be introduced, evidently considering it a great honor, and he, as always, accepted the homage as nothing less than his due. If he had been asked why he regarded himself as superior to the majority of men, he would have found it difficult to tell. His life certainly gave no evidence of special excellence. That he spoke English, French, and German with a good accent, and that his wardrobe was supplied by the best tailors, would hardly justify an assumption of superiority. He was quite well aware of that, yet he really seemed to think himself better than other men and not only accepted every manifestation of homage as his due but showed resentment if it were withheld. Just now he felt that he was not treated with sufficient respect in this jury room. There was one man he knew, Piotr Gerassimovich (Nekhludov prided himself on never remembering his surname), who had once taught his sister's children; since then he had become a teacher at a secondary school. Nekhludov could not endure his free-and-easy manner, his complacent laughter —in short, his vulgarity.

"Aha! So you've been caught too, have you? You didn't manage to wriggle out of it?" he shouted to Nekhludov.

"I had no wish to wriggle out of it," replied Nekhludov, in a forbidding tone.

"There's civic virtue for you! But you just wait, you'll sing a different tune when you feel hungry and sleepy," he shouted still more loudly.

"This confounded son of a priest will be slapping me on the back next," thought Nekhludov, and he assumed an expression of gloom which would have been natural only if he had just heard of the death of every member of his family.

He walked away and approached a group gathered around a tall, handsome, clean-shaven man who was talking with great animation about a trial now going on in the civil court, where he seemed to be familiar with the judges and fashionable lawyers whom he referred to by their Christian names. He was describing the remarkable way in which a famous lawyer had handled his case: he had succeeded in compelling an old lady who had the right on her side to pay his client, her adversary, a large sum of money.

"That man is a genius!" he exclaimed.

His hearers listened respectfully and occasionally attempted some observation, which he invariably interrupted with the air of one who is much better informed than the rest of the world.

In spite of his late arrival Nekhludov was obliged to wait after all, because one of the judges was delayed.

⚜

CHAPTER SIX

THE president of the court, a tall, portly man with gray whiskers, had arrived early. Although married, he led a loose life, and his wife did the same; they made a point of never interfering with each other. This morning he had received a note from the Swiss governess who had been in their employment the summer before and was now on her way from South Russia to Petersburg, telling him that she would be in the city that day and would expect him between three and six o'clock at the Hotel Italia. He was anxious, therefore, to begin the session as early as possible and to adjourn in time to call on the red-haired Clara, with whom he had had an intrigue at his country house during the summer.

Entering the judges' room, he locked the door, took from the lower shelf of the cupboard a pair of dumbbells, and stretched twenty times, up and down, forwards and sideways; then, holding the dumbbells above his head, he bent his knees three times.

"Nothing does a man so much good as exercises and a cold shower," he said to himself, feeling the biceps of his right arm with his left hand, on the third finger of which he wore a gold ring. There was still a twisting movement to be done (he always went through these two exercises before a sitting that threatened to be long), but someone tried the door. Hastily replacing the dumbbells, he opened the door, saying: "I beg your pardon."

One of the members of the court, a small man with high

shoulders, wearing gold spectacles, entered the room, frowning.

"Matvey Nikitich has not arrived yet," he said, in an irritated tone of voice.

"He's always late," said the president.

"He ought to be ashamed of himself," said the member, angrily; sitting down, he took out a cigarette.

This member, a very thrifty man, had had an unpleasant dispute with his wife that morning. Having spent her allowance before the end of the month, she had asked him to advance her some money. He said he would do nothing of the sort, and a quarrel ensued. The wife told him that if he was going to behave like this he needn't expect any dinner at home; whereupon he departed, very much afraid that she would keep her word as she was a woman from whom anything might be expected. "What's the good of leading a virtuous life?" he reflected, glancing at the beaming face of the jolly, vigorous president; with his elbows sticking out he was passing his handsome white hands through his long whiskers, arranging them on each side of his embroidered collar. "He's always contented and cheerful, while I am a martyr."

Just then the secretary came in bringing some documents.

"Thank you very much," said the president, and lighted a cigarette. "Which case shall we take first?"

"The poisoning case, I suppose," replied the secretary, with assumed carelessness.

"Very well," said the president, thinking to himself that he could get this case over by four o'clock and then get away. "Hasn't Matvey Nikitich come yet?"

"Not yet."

"Is Brewe here?"

"Yes."

"Then tell him if you see him that we shall begin with the poisoning case."

Brewe was the assistant public prosecutor, whose duty it was to read the indictments. The secretary met him in the corridor. He was hurrying along with a portfolio under his left arm and sawing the air with his right. His uniform was unbuttoned and his heels clattered as he walked.

"Mikhail Petrovich wants to know if you're ready," said the secretary.

"Ready? I am always ready," said the prosecutor. "Which case comes on first?"

"The poisoning case."

"Very well," said the prosecutor, but in his own mind he

thought it anything but well. He hadn't had a wink of sleep the previous night. He had been at a farewell party given by a friend; they had been drinking and gambling till two o'clock; then they had called at the brothel where Maslova was living six months before. Consequently he had had no time to read the poisoning case, and had meant to glance through it that morning. The secretary, who happened to know of this, had maliciously advised the president to take the poisoning case first. The secretary was of liberal, even radical views, while Brewe was a conservative and, like all Germans in the Russian government service, was devoted to orthodoxy. The secretary both disliked him personally and envied his position.

"And how about the *Skoptzi?*" [1] he asked.

"I told you it could not be heard for lack of witnesses," said the prosecutor. "I shall say so to the court."

"What does it matter?"

"It can't be done," replied the prosecutor and, still swinging his arm, ran into his private room. He had availed himself of the absence of an unimportant and unnecessary witness to postpone the case of the *Skoptzi* simply because if it were to be tried in a court where the jury was composed of educated men, the accused might be acquitted. He had, therefore, connived with the president to transfer the case to a provincial town, where most of the jurymen would be peasants and the chances of getting a conviction would be greater.

The commotion in the corridor was increasing. A large group of people gathered at the door of the civil court where the case mentioned previously by the good-looking juror was being heard. The old lady, who had been cheated out of her estate by the craftiness of a talented lawyer acting for a sharp dealer, came out during the recess. The judges were as well aware of the position as the plaintiff and his lawyer, but the presentment of the case was such that it was impossible not to take the old lady's property and give it to the sharp dealer.

The old lady was a stout person in a gaudy dress and a bonnet trimmed with enormous flowers. She stood at the door of the hall with her lawyer, waving her short, fat arms and saying over and over again: "Well, then, what are you going to do? What does it all mean?"

The lawyer gazed absently at the flowers on her bonnet, evidently not listening to her.

---

[1] Literally, "*eunuchs*"; a religious sect that practiced castration. —Tr.

Following the old lady out of the door of the civil court came the famous lawyer with his shining shirt front; his complacent countenance shone, too, for had he not succeeded in impoverishing the old lady with the gay bonnet, and enriching his client, who was to pay him ten thousand rubles out of the hundred thousand he had just won? He was conscious that every eye was fixed upon him and his whole bearing seemed to say: "There is no need of any expressions of devotion! I know what you are feeling." And he quickly passed through the crowd.

❧

CHAPTER SEVEN

MATVEY NIKITICH arrived at last, and the usher, a gaunt-faced man with a long neck and slightly protruding lower lip, entered the jury room with a sidling sort of gait. This man was an honest fellow who had a university education, but could never keep a position for any length of time because of his periodical bouts of drunkenness. Three months before, a countess who took an interest in his wife had obtained his present job for him, and he was pleased that he had succeeded in keeping it so long.

"Are all the gentlemen here?" he asked, putting on his glasses and looking around.

"I believe so," replied the jovial merchant.

"We will call the list," said the usher and, taking it from his pocket, began to read, looking at those whose names he called, sometimes over his spectacles and sometimes through them.

"Councilor of State, I. M. Nikiforov!"

"Present!" said the stately juror, who was so well versed in the ways of the law.

"Ex-Colonel Ivan Semionovich Ivanov!"

"Present!" replied the thin man in the uniform of a retired officer.

"Merchant of the Second Guild, Piotr Baklashov!"

"Ay, ay," said the good-humored merchant, grinning. "Ready!"

"Lieutenant of the Guards, Prince Dmitri Nekhludov!"

"I am here," said Nekhludov.

The usher glanced at him over his pince-nez and bowed with a pleasant and amiable expression, as though wishing to distinguish him from the others.

"Captain Yuri Dmitrievich Danchenko! Merchant Grigori Efimovich Kuleshov!"—and so on. All but two were present.

"Then, gentlemen, please proceed to the courtroom," said the usher, pointing toward the door with a courteous wave of his hand; pausing to make way for each other as they passed through the door, the jurors entered the courtroom.

This was a long and spacious hall. At one end three steps led up to a platform, on which stood a table covered with a fine green cloth with a fringe of darker shade. Three armchairs with high, carved oak backs were drawn up to it, and on the wall behind hung a life-sized portrait of the emperor in uniform, with a decoration on his breast; he stood with one foot advanced, grasping the hilt of his sword. In the right-hand corner of the hall was a shrine with the image of Christ crowned with thorns; a lectern stood beneath it, and further toward the right was the desk of the public prosecutor. On the left, opposite the desk, was the secretary's table, and beyond it an oak rail with the prisoners' bench behind it. On a platform toward the right there were two rows of high-backed chairs for the jurors, and underneath this platform the tables for the defense. All this was in the front part of the court, divided from the back by a railing. The back was all taken up by benches, rising tier after tier till they reached the wall. Four women were seated on the front benches—servants or factory girls—and two men, also working people, all evidently overawed by the imposing style of the hall and talking timidly in whispers.

Soon after the jurymen entered, the usher stepped forward in his sidling fashion and called out in a loud voice, as though he meant to terrify his listeners:

"The court is coming!"

Everyone rose, and the court entered. The president, with his powerful muscles and elegant side whiskers, came first, followed by the gloomy member in gold spectacles, whose former depression had grown a shade deeper, for just before entering the hall he had met his brother-in-law, a candidate for some position in the government legal department, who told him that he had just been to call on his sister and that she had declared there wasn't going to be any dinner in the house that day.

"It looks as if we shall have to go to an eating house," said the brother-in-law, laughing.

"I don't see anything funny in it!" replied the gloomy member, and grew gloomier than ever.

Last of all came the third member of the court, Matvey Nikitich, the one who was always late, a bearded man with

kind eyes, large and slanting. He suffered from a catarrhal affection of the stomach and had by the advice of his doctor begun that morning a new treatment, which was responsible for
keeping him at home even longer than usual. As he came up
the steps his face wore an expression of deep concentration. He
believed in some curious doctrine of chances and was in the
habit of speculating on all sorts of subjects. Just now he was
counting the number of steps from the door to the chairs, for
he had decided that if the number should turn out to be divisible
by three, the new treatment would cure his catarrh, and that if
not there was no chance for him. When he discovered that there
were twenty-six steps, he managed to get in a short one, just by
the chair, to make up twenty-seven.

The president and the members of the court, arrayed in uniforms with gold-embroidered collars, made an impressive picture as they stepped onto the platform. They seemed to
appreciate this themselves and, as though overcome by the
sense of their own grandeur, kept their eyes modestly cast down
and hurriedly took their seats behind the table covered with the
green cloth. On this table stood a three-cornered object sur-
mounted by an eagle, several of those glass jars commonly used
to hold sweets that one sees in refreshment rooms, an inkstand,
pens, clean paper, and newly sharpened pencils of various
sizes. The public prosecutor came in with the judges, swinging
his arm as usual; with the portfolio tucked under his arm, he
took his seat and instantly became absorbed in reading up the
case, taking advantage of every moment to prepare himself. It
was only his fourth indictment. He was very ambitious, and
determined to make his way, and his idea was that he must
obtain a conviction in every case in which he prosecuted. He
knew the general outline of the poisoning case and had the
skeleton of his speech sketched out, but he was still short of
a few facts and was hurriedly searching for them and taking
notes. The secretary sat at the opposite end of the platform
and, having prepared all the papers he was likely to require, was
reading over a newspaper article forbidden by the censor,
which he had obtained the day before. He meant to discuss it
with the bearded member of the court, who shared his views,
and wished to be thoroughly posted before he began the discussion.

CHAPTER EIGHT

THE president examined the papers, asked the usher a few questions and, receiving answers in the affirmative, ordered the prisoners to be brought in. The door behind the rail opened instantly, and there appeared two gendarmes wearing their caps and carrying unsheathed swords in their hands. They were followed by three prisoners: a red-haired, freckle-faced man and two women. The man wore a prison cloak that was too wide and too long for him; to prevent his long sleeves from slipping down, he kept his arms pressed to his sides with thumbs thrust out; his eyes were fixed on the bench he was approaching. Passing to the farther end, he took his seat on the very edge, carefully making room for the others; then he looked at the president, and his cheeks twitched as if he were muttering something. He was followed by an elderly woman with red eyes, also in prison dress, with a prison kerchief tied around her head. Her face with its red eyes was ashen gray and had neither eyebrows nor lashes. She seemed perfectly composed. Having caught her cloak against something, she detached it carefully, without haste, and sat down.

The third prisoner was Maslova.

As she came in, the gaze of every man in the courtroom turned toward her, attracted by her eyes shining black and brilliant in her white face, and by her full bosom swelling under the prison cloak. Even the gendarme, as she passed him, gazed after her until she was seated, and then with a guilty air turned away hastily and stared at the window in front of him.

The president waited until the prisoners were in their seats, and as soon as Maslova sat down he turned to the secretary. The court then proceeded to its regular business: the roll call of the jury, the discussions about those who had failed to appear, the imposition of fines, the allowances to be made for those who had claimed exemption, and the filling up of vacancies in the jury from the reserve list. After folding up some slips of paper, the president placed them in one of the glass jars; then with the gestures of a conjuror he proceeded to turn back his gold-embroidered sleeves, revealing his hairy arms; he took out the slips one by one, unfolding and reading each of them as he withdrew it from the jar. Then, letting down his sleeves, he requested the priest to swear in the jury.

The old priest, with his sallow, puffy face, his brown cassock, his gold cross hanging from his neck, and a trifling decoration pinned on one side of his chest, shuffled his swollen feet toward the lectern which stood beneath the icon.

The jurymen rose and crowded around the lectern.

"Come forward," he said, touching the cross on his chest with his fat hand as he stood awaiting the approach of the jurors.

He had been a priest for forty-seven years. In three years' time he would be celebrating the fiftieth anniversary of his consecration, just as the cathedral archpriest had recently celebrated his anniversary. He had served in the district court ever since it began, and was proud to have sworn in many thousands of men, and proud also that in his old age he was still able to labor for the prosperity of the church, of his country, and of his family, to whom he expected to leave thirty thousand rubles in interest-bearing securities, not to mention the house they lived in. That his labor in court, that is to say, the administration of the oath upon the Bible, in which all oaths are expressly forbidden, was not of a virtuous character, never once entered his head; and it was anything but irksome to him, for he loved it sincerely. It brought him into contact with men of wealth and influence. Just now he was pleased to have made the acquaintance of the famous lawyer who had won his respect by making ten thousand rubles out of the case of the old lady with the flowered bonnet. When the jury had mounted the platform the priest thrust his gray, bald head into the greasy opening of the stole and then, after rearranging his thin hair, addressed the jury.

"Raise your right hand and place your fingers like this," he said in a slow, tremulous voice, as he lifted his plump and dimpled hand and bent the first two fingers to the thumb. "Now repeat after me: 'I promise and swear by Almighty God, by His holy Gospels and by our Lord's life-giving Cross, that in this matter which . . .'" He paused after each sentence. "Don't lower your arm," he said, addressing a young juror who had dropped his arm, "'in this matter which. . . .'"

The stately gentleman with the side whiskers, the colonel, the merchant, and a few of the others held their hands aloft with the fingers together exactly as the priest required, and seemed quite enthusiastic; others were reluctant and indifferent. Some repeated the words loudly, and, so to speak, defiantly; others spoke hardly above their breath, too slowly at times and then with a rush as though fearing to be left behind. Some pressed their fingers tightly together as though they were afraid of dropping something; others held them loosely for a while, then suddenly compressed them. Everyone but the old priest felt more or less uncomfortable. He, however, had not a shadow of doubt that the function he was performing was useful and important.

After the oath had been received, the president requested the jurymen to select a foreman. They rose and, jostling one another, hurried into the jury room, where most of them instantly took out cigarettes and began to smoke. Somebody suggested that the stately gentleman would be a suitable foreman, to which all at once agreed; they extinguished and threw away their cigarettes and went back to the courtroom. The elected foreman notified the court of the choice that had been made, and they once more resumed their seats in the double row of high-backed chairs that had been prepared for them.

All went smoothly, quickly, and with a certain degree of solemnity; this exactitude and decorum evidently pleased the participants, confirming them in the belief that they were performing an important public function. Nekhludov himself was impressed.

After they were seated the president explained to them their rights, duties, and responsibilities. All the while he was addressing them he was in perpetual motion: now he leaned on his left elbow, now on his right, now he flung himself against the back of the chair; he straightened the papers in front of him, stroked the paper knife, and fingered the pencils.

They had the right, he said, of putting questions to the accused through the president himself, and they were allowed pencil and paper and the privilege of examining any articles of evidence. Their duty was to pronounce an honest verdict. They were responsible for preserving the secrecy of their deliberations, and any betrayal would render them amenable to the penalty of the law.

He was listened to with respectful attention. The merchant, diffusing around him a smell of spirits and trying in vain to suppress his hiccups, nodded his approval at every sentence.

✤

CHAPTER NINE

HAVING finished his speech, the president addressed the prisoners.

"Simon Kartinkin, rise!" he said.

Simon sprang to his feet, the muscles of his cheeks twitching with nervous excitement.

"Your name?"

"Simon Petrov Kartinkin," he answered loudly, as if he had been prepared for the questions and had his answers ready.

"What is your station in life?"

"I am a peasant."

"What province and district do you come from?"

"Province of Tula, district of Krapivensk, parish of Kupiansk, village of Borki."

"Your age?"

"Thirty-three; born in 18—."

"What religion?"

"Of the Russian religion. Orthodox."

"Married?"

"No, sir."

"What is your occupation?"

"I was a cleaner in the Hotel Mauretania."

"Have you ever been tried before?"

"Never! I have never been tried, because as we used to live . . ."

"You have not been tried before?"

"God forbid! Never."

"Have you received a copy of the indictment?"

"I have."

"Sit down. Efimia Ivanovna Bochkova," said the president, turning to the next prisoner.

But Simon remained standing, and consequently Bochkova was invisible to the judges.

"Sit down, Kartinkin!"

But Kartinkin did not sit down.

"Sit down, Kartinkin!"

Still Kartinkin continued to stand and was only induced to seat himself when the usher, his head on one side and his eyes

35

opened unnaturally wide, hurried to him and whispered in tragic tones:

"Sit down! Down!"

Kartinkin then sat down as swiftly as he had risen, and drew his prison cloak around him while the convulsive twitching of his cheeks began again.

"Your name?" said the president, with a weary sigh, examining a paper that lay before him and without so much as glancing toward the woman. All this was a mere matter of routine for him, and when it was necessary to expedite affairs he could do two things at a time.

Bochkova was forty-three years old, a *meshchanka*[1] of Kalomna, a chambermaid in the same Hotel Mauretania. She, likewise, had never been arrested before, and had also received a copy of the indictment. She answered boldly, and the tone of her voice seemed to say: "Yes, my name *is* Efimia Bochkova, and I *have* received a copy of the indictment, and I'm proud of it, and there's no cause for anyone to laugh about it." As soon as the questions had been answered, she sat down again without waiting to be told to do so.

The president addressed the third prisoner.

"Your name?" he inquired amiably, never proof against the charms of an attractive woman. "You should rise," he added softly and gently, noticing that Maslova still kept her seat.

Maslova rose, and throwing back her shoulders, fixed her smiling black eyes, with their barely perceptible squint, upon the president, but did not say a word.

"What is your name?"

"They call me Lubov," she said quickly.

Meanwhile Nekhludov had put on his pince-nez and, as the prisoners were examined, he scrutinized each one in turn. "Impossible!" he thought, fixing his eyes on the prisoner's face. How could it be possible? Lubov? He turned the name over in his mind.

The president was just going on to the next question, when the member in spectacles whispered impatiently in his ear. The president nodded and, turning to the criminal, "How can it be Lubov?" he asked. "That is not the name entered here."

The prisoner was silent.

"I am asking you for your real name."

"The one given you in baptism," added the surly member.

[1] One who belongs to the class of *Meshchane*—citizens of the lowest grade or class in a town, corresponding to the peasant in the country.—Tr.

"I used to be called Katerina."

"Impossible!" Nekhludov said to himself over and over again, yet he had no doubt that it was she: his aunts' half-ward and half-servant, the girl he had been in love with, truly in love with, and whom he had seduced, forsaken, and forgotten. It had been an episode painful to remember, and he never allowed himself to think of it: he, who so prided himself on his good breeding, had proved to be anything but a gentleman. He had played a contemptible part with that woman.

Yes, it was she. There was no mistaking the mysterious individuality that nature stamps on every human face and never repeats, setting it apart from every other in the world. Unhealthily pale and swollen though it was, her face retained the same fascinating peculiarities of mouth and eyes, the characteristic little squint, and the air of submission which seemed to belong to her whole personality.

"You should have said so at once." The voice of the president was very gentle. "What is your father's name?"

"I have no father."

"Well, then, tell us your godfather's name."

"Mikhail."

"What crime can she possibly have committed?" thought Nekhludov. He had difficulty in breathing.

"What is your family name—your surname?" continued the president.

"They called me Maslova, like my mother."

"What class do you belong to?"

"*Meshchanka.*"

"Of Orthodox religion?"

"Yes."

"And what is your occupation?"

Maslova made no reply.

"What was your occupation?" he repeated.

"I was in an institution," she said.

"What sort of institution?" the member in spectacles asked severely.

"You know what sort it was," said Maslova. She smiled, glanced quickly over her shoulder toward the public part of the court, and at once fixed her eyes again on the president.

There was something so extraordinary in the expression of her face, something so pathetic, so awful in the words she had just uttered, as well as in her smile and in the swift glance she cast toward the rear of the room, that the president lowered his eyes and a profound silence fell upon the hall.

This pause was suddenly broken by the sound of laughter; then someone said "Ssh!" and the president raised his head and continued:

"Were you ever on trial before?"

"No," said Maslova, softly, and sighed.

"Have you received a copy of the indictment?"

"I have."

"You may take your seat."

The prisoner arranged her skirt with the same movement that a well-dressed woman makes when she adjusts her train; when she had sat down she folded her small, white hands inside the sleeves of her prison cloak and resumed her intent gaze at the president.

The witnesses were called, then sent out of the courtroom; the physician who was to act as expert was sent for; then the secretary rose to read the indictment. He read loudly and distinctly, but so rapidly that his voice, which mispronounced *l* and *r*, was an uninterrupted, dreary monotone. The judges were restless. They sat now with their elbows on the table, leaning first on one arm, then on the other, now leaning against the back or the arms of their chairs; they closed their eyes and opened them again, and whispered to one another. Meanwhile, the gendarme was trying to repress the beginning of a yawn.

Kartinkin was twitching all the time. Bochkova sat still and occasionally thrust a finger under her kerchief to scratch her head.

Maslova was also quiet, listening to the reader with eyes fixed upon his face. Now and then she started, as though she were about to speak, then changed color, sighed, shifted the position of her hands, looked around, then again rested her eyes upon the secretary.

Nekhludov sat in his high-backed chair, the second from the end in the front row. He never took off his pince-nez, but sat staring hard at Maslova, while a painful, complicated struggle was taking place in his heart.

CHAPTER TEN

THE indictment read as follows: "On the seventeenth of January 188–, the proprietor of the Hotel Mauretania informed the police of the sudden death of a Second-Guild merchant from

Siberia, Ferapont Smelkov. The police doctor of the fourth district has certified that Smelkov's death was caused by a rupture of the heart, induced by an excessive use of alcohol. He was buried two days after his death, and on the subsequent day there arrived the Siberian merchant Timokhin who, learning of his friend's death and of the attendant circumstances, declared his suspicion that Smelkov's death did not proceed from natural causes. He felt sure that his friend had been poisoned by malefactors, who had stolen money and a diamond ring that could not be found when the inventory was taken; whereupon an investigation was ordered, bringing to light the following facts:

"I. That the proprietor of the Hotel Mauretania, as well as the clerk of a merchant—Starikov by name—with whom Smelkov had done some business, knew that he, Smelkov, had in his possession three thousand eight hundred rubles which he had received from the bank, whereas all that was found in his suitcase, which was sealed after his death, and in his wallet, was the sum of three hundred and twelve rubles and sixteen kopecks.

"II. That Smelkov had spent the day and the night previous to his death with the prostitute Lubov, who twice at different times had gone into his room.

"III. That the said prostitute had sold Smelkov's diamond ring to her mistress.

"IV. That on the day following Smelkov's death the chambermaid, Efimia Bochkova, carried to the Commercial bank, and deposited in her own name, the sum of eighteen hundred rubles.

"V. That from the examination of the said prostitute Lubov, it was discovered that the hotel servant Simon Kartinkin had given the said Lubov a certain powder, advising her to put it in Smelkov's wine; which, according to her confession, the said Lubov did.

"At the examination of the said Lubov, she testified that during the merchant Smelkov's stay in the brothel where she 'worked,' as she expressed it, he had sent her into the room which he was occupying in the aforementioned Hotel Mauretania to fetch him some money, and that, having unlocked his suitcase with the key he had given her, she opened it and took out forty rubles, as directed, but no more. Simon Kartinkin and Efimia Bochkova would both testify that what she said was true, at least in part, for it was in their presence that she had unlocked the suitcase, taken out the money, and locked the suitcase again.

"With regard to the poisoning of Smelkov, the said Lubov

testified that when she came to his room for the third time, she gave him, at the instigation of Simon Kartinkin, a glass of brandy into which she had put something, alleging that she thought it a powder to make him sleep and allow her to get away from him; but that she took no money whatever. She said that Smelkov gave her the ring when she threatened to leave him because he struck her.

"At the cross-examination of the other accused, Efimia Bochkova testified that she knew nothing whatever about the disappearance of the money, that she had never gone into Smelkov's room, and that the said Lubov had been busy there all by herself. If anything was stolen, the said Lubov must have been the one who did it when she went to the room to fetch the money and used the merchant's key."

When this was read, Maslova gave a start and gazed at Bochkova open-mouthed.

"When Efimia Bochkova was shown the bank receipt for the eighteen hundred rubles," the reader continued, "and asked how she had come by such a sum, she testified that it was what she and Simon had been saving for twelve years, and that she was going to marry him.

"At his first examination, the said Simon Kartinkin confessed that he and Bochkova had taken the money at the instigation of Maslova, and divided it between Maslova, Bochkova, and himself; he also confessed that he had given Maslova the sleeping powder which she was to use to put the merchant to sleep; but during the course of a second examination he denied that he had taken any part in the affair and accused Maslova as the sole culprit; concerning the money which Bochkova had deposited in the bank, he testified, just as she did, that the money was the fruit of their united earnings, chiefly tips received from guests during the eighteen years they had served in the hotel.

"For the elucidation of the circumstances, it was found necessary to exhume Smelkov's body and to make a post-mortem examination of his internal organs, and ascertain what chemical changes had taken place. The examination showed that the merchant Smelkov's death was caused by poisoning."

This was followed by an account of the preliminary examination of the witnesses and of their evidence. The indictment concluded as follows:

"Smelkov, merchant of the Second Guild, being addicted to drunkenness and an immoral way of life, had entered into relations with the prostitute commonly known as Lubov, in the house of Kitaeva, and, having become infatuated with her, sent the said Lubov, with the key of his suitcase, to the hotel room he occupied to fetch him forty rubles to pay for wine. The said Lubov, having entered the room, conspired with Bochkova and Kartinkin to steal and divide among the three of them all the money and valuables of the said merchant Smelkov. This design was accomplished."

Here Maslova again gave a start and even half rose to her feet, while a deep crimson color suffused her face.

"The diamond ring," continued the secretary, "and very likely a small sum of money, was given to Maslova, which she either lost, being intoxicated that night, or hid. Now, in order to conceal the traces of the crime, the accomplices decided to entice Smelkov back to his room in the hotel and there to poison him with arsenic. With that intention, the said Maslova returned to the brothel and there persuaded the said Smelkov to go back with her to his quarters in the hotel and then, having received the powder from the said Kartinkin, Maslova put it into the wine which she gave Smelkov and which was the direct cause of his death.

"In view of the aforesaid, Simon Kartinkin, peasant from the village of Borki, thirty-three years of age, the *meshchanka* Efimia Ivanovna Bochkova, forty-three years of age, and the *meshchanka* Katerina Mikhailovna Maslova, twenty-seven years of age, are accused of having, on the seventeenth day of January 188–, stolen money from the merchant Smelkov, to the amount of two thousand five hundred rubles, conspired to kill him in order to conceal all traces of their crime, and given him poison, from the effects of which he died.

"This crime is provided for in section 1455 of the penal code. Therefore, in accordance with article so-and-so of the code of criminal law, the peasant Simon Kartinkin and the *meshchanki* Efimia Bochkova and Katerina Maslova are to be tried by the judges of the district court and a jury."

Thus ended the monotonous reading of the long indictment. The secretary collected his papers and resumed his seat, mechanically smoothing his long hair. Everyone drew a long breath, and the sense of relief was followed by the even more pleasant anticipation of the trial, when, no doubt, all would be made clear and justice would be satisfied. Nekhludov was the sole exception: he did not share that feeling. He was completely overwhelmed with horror at the thought of what Maslova might have done—Katusha, the charming and innocent girl he had known ten years before.

WHEN the indictment was finished, the president, after consulting the other members of the court, turned toward Kartinkin with an expression that seemed to say: "Now we are going to get at the truth of the matter, down to the minutest detail."

"Peasant Simon Kartinkin," he said, turning to the left.

Kartinkin rose, let his arms fall along his sides, and stood leaning forward; his lips moved, but he made no sound.

"You are accused of having on the seventeenth of January 188–, conspired with Efimia Bochkova and Katerina Maslova to steal money from the baggage of the merchant Smelkov, and of having brought the poison and incited Katerina Maslova to give it to the merchant Smelkov in wine, causing his death. Do you plead guilty?"

"It's impossible! Our business is to serve the guests and—"

"You will have a chance to tell us about that later. Are you guilty or not guilty?"

"No, sir. I only—"

"You shall say all that later. Do you plead guilty?" the president repeated in calm but resolute accents.

"I can't do that, because—"

Here the usher again rushed to Simon Kartinkin and with a stage whisper reduced him to silence. The president, with an air of finality, changed the position of his arm and addressed Efimia Bochkova.

"Efimia Bochkova, you are accused of having stolen money and a ring from the baggage of the merchant Smelkov in the Hotel Mauretania on the seventeenth of January 188–, and, after dividing the stolen property with your accomplices, of poisoning the merchant Smelkov, from the effect of which poisoning he died. Do you plead guilty?"

"I am not guilty of anything," she said boldly. "I did not go into the room at all. That shameless hussy did the business when she came—"

"You may give those details afterward," repeated the president, as firmly and calmly as before. "So you plead not guilty?"

"It wasn't me who went into the room; I never persuaded him to drink the stuff; I wasn't there at all. If I had gone into the room I should have thrown that creature out."

"Then you do not plead guilty?"

"Never!"

"Very well."

"Katerina Maslova," began the president, addressing the third prisoner, "you are accused of having come from a brothel into one of the rooms in the Hotel Mauretania, of having the key of merchant Smelkov's suitcase in your possession, of stealing from that suitcase certain money and a ring." He uttered these words mechanically, leaning all the while toward the member on the left, who was telling him that from among the incriminating articles the glass flask was still missing—"of stealing money and a ring," repeated the president. "It is affirmed that, after dividing the stolen property, you and the merchant Smelkov came back to the Hotel Mauretania together, and that you introduced poison into his wine, thus causing his death. Do you plead guilty?"

"I plead guilty to nothing," Maslova began rapidly. "I repeat what I said all along: I have taken nothing, nothing—nothing whatever. He gave me the ring of his own accord."

"You plead not guilty to having stolen two thousand five hundred rubles?" said the president.

"I repeat that I took forty rubles and no more."

"And do you plead guilty to having given merchant Smelkov drugged wine? Do you plead guilty to that?"

"I do. I gave him the drugged wine, but I thought it was only sleeping powder; I was told that it would do him no harm; I never thought of such a thing as killing him; it never entered my head; I speak as if I were in the presence of my God. I never meant to do it," she said.

"So you do not plead guilty to the stealing of merchant Smelkov's money, but you plead guilty to having given him the powder?"

"Yes, I plead guilty to that; only I thought it was a sleeping powder; I gave it to him only to make him sleep. I never thought, I never wished—"

"Very well," said the president, evidently satisfied with the result he had obtained, "then tell us how it came about. You can improve your position by making a clean breast of it. Tell us all the circumstances," he said, leaning against the back of his chair and placing both hands on the table.

Maslova remained silent, looked straight into his eyes.

"Tell us how it all happened."

"How it happened?" She suddenly began to speak very fast. "I drove to the hotel. Someone showed me the way to his room.

He was there and even then, already, he was quite drunk." (She pronounced the word "he" with an indescribable accent of terror.) "I wanted to leave him, but he would not let me."

She relapsed into silence, as though she had suddenly lost the thread of her recollections and was thinking of something else.

"And what then?"

"What then? I remained for a while, and then I went home."

The assistant prosecutor half rose from his chair, leaning awkwardly on one elbow.

"You have a question to ask?" inquired the president, and, on receiving an affirmative reply, indicated by a gesture that he was at liberty to do so.

"I should like to ask if the prisoner has had any previous acquaintance with Simon Kartinkin?" he said, without looking at Maslova; having asked the question, he frowned and pursed his lips.

The president repeated the question. Maslova directed a glance of alarm at the assistant prosecutor.

"With Simon? Yes. I knew him before," she replied.

"I should like to know the nature of this acquaintance. Did they see each other often?"

"What sort of acquaintance? Why, he used to send for me for the guests. I wasn't an acquaintance at all," replied Maslova, glancing uneasily from the assistant prosecutor to the president.

"I should like to know why Kartinkin always sent for Maslova in preference to the other women?" said the assistant prosecutor, with a cunning Mephistophelian smile, his eyes half closed.

"I don't know. How should I know?" Maslova replied, casting an anxious look around the hall; her eyes rested for a moment on Nekhludov. "He sent for the one he wanted, I suppose."

"Does she recognize me?" thought Nekhludov, and felt the blood rushing from his face. But Maslova did not distinguish him from the others; her eyes again sought those of the assistant prosecutor with a frightened look.

"So the accused denies that she had any intimate relations with Kartinkin? Very well. I have nothing more to ask."

And the assistant prosecutor at once removed his elbow from his desk and began writing something. As a matter of fact, he did not write at all, but only traced over with his pen the words of his notes: he had observed how a prosecutor or a lawyer after a clever question would note down some remark to be embod'ed in the closing argument, which was supposed to confound his opponent.

Before resuming his examination, the president paused to ask the member in spectacles whether he was willing to continue the questions according to the order previously arranged.

"And what happened after that?" was his next question.

"I went home," continued Maslova, with more assurance, her gaze now concentrated on the president. "I gave the money to the mistress and went to bed. I had just fallen asleep when Bertha, one of our girls, woke me up and said: 'Get up, your merchant has come back again.' I did not want to go down, but madame made me. *He*" (she again articulated the word with evident terror), "he was treating the girls with wine and wanted to send for more, but he had no money in his pocket, and madame would not trust him. So he sent me to his room in the hotel, told me where the money was and how much to take, and I went."

The president was whispering something just then to the member on his left and did not hear what Maslova said, but he repeated her last words so as to make it appear that he had heard it all.

"You went, and then what happened?" he asked.

"I went and did what he had told me to do. I went into his room, but I did not go alone. I called Simon Mikhailovich and her too," she said, pointing to Bochkova.

"She's lying! I never went in—" interrupted Bochkova, but she was silenced.

"I took four ten-ruble notes with them in the room," continued Maslova, frowning; she did not look at Bochkova.

"Did the prisoner notice, when she was getting the money, how much there was left?" interrupted the prosecutor.

Maslova gave a start when he spoke to her. She did not know why it was, but she felt he wished her no good.

"I did not count them; I saw there were some hundred-ruble notes."

"The prisoner saw the hundred-ruble notes? That is all."

"Well, you brought back the money," continued the president, looking at his watch.

"Yes."

"And then?"

"Then he took me back to the hotel with him again," said Maslova.

"And how did you give him the powder in the wine?"

"How did I give it? I dropped it into the wine and handed him the glass."

"But what did you do it for?"

She sighed deeply.

"He wouldn't let me go," she said, after a pause. "I was dead tired. I went into the corridor and said to Simon Mikhailovich: 'I wish he'd let me go. I'm tired.' And Simon Mikhailovich said: 'We've had enough of him, too. We're thinking of giving him a sleeping powder, and then you can go.' 'Very well,' I said, thinking it was some harmless powder. So he gave me the powder. When I went back into the room, Smelkov was lying behind the partition and told me at once to give him some cognac. I took a bottle of *fine champagne* from the table, poured out two glasses, one for him and one for myself, and dropped the powder into his. If I'd known, how could I have given it to him?"

"Well, and how did you come by the ring?" inquired the president.

"He gave me the ring himself."

"When did he give it to you?"

"After we went back to his room. I was going to leave him, and he struck me on the head and broke my comb. Then I was angry and made up my mind to go. He took the ring off his finger and made me a present of it, to persuade me not to go," she said.

At that moment the assistant prosecutor rose again, and with his usual air of feigned simplicity inquired if he might ask a few more questions. Permission was granted, and he bent his head over his embroidered collar.

"I should like to know how long the prisoner remained in the merchant Smelkov's room?"

Again Maslova looked alarmed, and her eyes wandered anxiously from the president to the assistant prosecutor.

"I don't remember how long it was," she replied, hurriedly.

"And has the accused also forgotten whether she made any other calls in the hotel after she left the merchant Smelkov?"

Maslova reflected for a moment.

"Yes, I went into an empty room next to his," she said.

"What did you go in there for?" asked the prosecutor, forgetting himself and addressing the question directly to the prisoner.

"I went in to arrange my dress and wait for a cab."

"And did Kartinkin go into the room with the accused, or did he not?"

"He also dropped in for a moment."

"Why did he come in?"

"There was some of the merchant's cognac left and we drank it."

"Ah, you drank it, did you? Well and good! And did the prisoner talk to Simon, and if so, what about?"

Maslova immediately frowned, blushed, and said rapidly:

"What about? I didn't talk about anything. I have told you everything. You may do whatever you like with me. I am not guilty, that's all I can say."

"I have nothing more to ask," said the prosecutor, and, shrugging his shoulders, began to note down in the rough draft of his argument the admission of the accused that she had remained alone with Simon in the unoccupied room. There was a pause.

"You have nothing more to say?"

"I have told you everything," she said, with a sigh, and resumed her seat.

The president then noted down something, received a whispered communication from the member on his left, declared a recess of ten minutes, and hurriedly left the courtroom. The consultation between the president and the bearded, pleasant-looking member on the left was about the latter's trifling disorder of the stomach, for which he wished to do a little massage and take some drops. And this was why a recess was declared at his request.

Lawyers, jurymen, witnesses, all left their seats and walked about the courtroom, with the pleasant feeling of having accomplished a certain part of this important business. Nekhludov went into the jury room and took a seat by the window.

⚜

CHAPTER TWELVE

YES, it was Katusha. The relations between them had been these:

When Nekhludov first saw her he was a third-year undergraduate, and was staying with his two aunts preparing his thesis on land tenure.

Usually he spent the summer with his mother and sister on his mother's estate near Moscow. But that year his sister had married and his mother had gone to take the waters at some foreign spa; so, having his thesis to prepare, he decided to stay with his aunts. It was quiet on their remote estate, and there was no distraction. His aunts loved him tenderly, and he, for his part, liked their old-fashioned, simple way of living.

It was during the summer spent with his aunts that Nekhludov went through that period of exaltation when a young man first begins to grasp all the beauty and significance of life and the possibility of an unlimited advance toward perfection for himself and for the whole world, and vows himself faithfully and with confidence to achieving this perfection. That year he was reading Spencer's *Social Statics,* and the writer's theory of land tenure had made a strong impression on him, all the stronger because he was himself heir to large estates. His father had not been rich, but his mother had received 25,000 acres of land for her dowry. For the first time he understood all the cruelty and injustice of private ownership of land and, since he was one of those to whom a sacrifice to the demands of conscience means the greatest spiritual joy, he decided to relinquish his property rights and give up to the peasants the land he had inherited from his father. This was, in fact, the subject of his thesis.

His life on his aunts' estate was simple: he rose very early, sometimes as early as three o'clock, and took a swim before sunrise in the river that ran at the foot of the hill; often the morning mist had not yet lifted, and he would return while the dew still sparkled on the grass and flowers. Sometimes after his coffee he would work on his thesis or look up references, but very often he chose to leave the house again and walk in the woods and fields rather than read or write.

Before midday dinner he always took a nap in the garden. At dinner itself his exuberant spirits were a constant source of amusement and entertainment for his aunts. Then he would ride or row, and in the evening he either read in his room or sat with his aunts and played solitaire. Often at night, and on moonlit nights particularly, he could not sleep simply because he felt so intensely the all-pervading joy of life; instead of going to bed he would roam in the garden with his dreams and thoughts, sometimes till daybreak.

Thus, happily and peacefully, he spent the first month of his visit, never noticing his aunts' half-ward and half-servant, the black-eyed, quick-footed Katusha. Brought up under his mother's wing, Nekhludov, at nineteen, was still an innocent boy. If a woman figured in his dreams it was only as a wife. A woman who could not be his wife was, to him, quite neutral.

On Ascension Day that summer a neighbor came to spend the day; she brought her two young daughters and her son, and also an artist, a young man of peasant stock, who was staying with them at the time. After tea the party went to the newly mown meadow in front of the house to play a game of *gorelki*. They took Katusha with them, and presently she and Nekhludov were paired off together. Nekhludov was always pleased to see Katusha, but he had never thought of her and himself in any close relation.

"I'll never catch those two unless they slip and fall," said the painter, who was himself a good runner and whose part in the game was to prevent the pair from joining hands.

"Oh, yes, you'll catch them all right! Now then, one-two-three!"

They clapped hands three times. Katusha could hardly help laughing as she changed places with Nekhludov and, seizing his large hand with her own little rough one, she gave it a squeeze by way of a sign, then started toward the left, her starched skirts rustling as she ran.

Trying to escape from the painter, Nekhludov ran as fast as he could. When he looked back he saw the painter chasing Katusha, but her nimble young limbs stood her in good stead. She was running toward the left. Directly in front of them were some lilac bushes, forming a sort of boundary, beyond which they were not to run. Katusha, however, signaled to Nekhludov that this was the place where they were to join hands, and he ran behind the bushes. But he did not know that there was a narrow ditch there overgrown with nettles; he stumbled and fell into the nettles, already wet with dew, stinging his hands. Laughing at his mishap, he rose at once and gained an open space.

Katusha, with a shining smile, her eyes black as two gleaming blackberries, was flying to meet him. They came together and joined hands.

"You must have stung yourself," she said, panting and smiling, while with her free hand she adjusted her plaits.

"I didn't know the ditch was there," he said, also smiling and holding her hand clasped in his.

She drew nearer, and without knowing how it happened he stooped toward her. She did not draw back; he pressed her hand and kissed her on the mouth.

"Well, whatever in the world!" she cried, and quickly withdrawing her hand she ran away from him.

Running to a lilac bush, she broke off two clusters of white flowers which were already beginning to fade; she held them to her burning face and looked back at him over her shoulder; then she returned to the other players, walking briskly and swinging her arms.

From that moment the relationship between them was changed. It was the beginning of the state that exists for an innocent youth and maiden when they are attracted toward each other. Whenever Katusha came into the room, or even when Nekhludov caught a glimpse of her white apron in the distance, it was like a ray of the sun for him; things about took on a different air, became brighter, more interesting, more important; the whole of life became more joyful.

Katusha, too, was under the same spell. And this was dominant whether they were together or away from each other. The mere knowledge that there was a Nekhludov and a Katusha seemed to be a great joy to them. If his mother wrote him an unpleasant letter, or if he came upon difficulties in his thesis, or if he felt sad for no reason, he had only to remember that there was Katusha; all his troubles vanished when she came in sight.

Katusha had much work to do about the house, but she was very quick and had time to read in her leisure hours. Nekhludov gave her Dostoevsky and Turgenev, whom he had just been reading himself. Turgenev's *A Quiet Nook* was her favorite. They talked in snatches, when they met in a passage, on the veranda or in the yard, or in the room of his aunts' old attendant, Matryona Pavlovna, where Nekhludov sometimes came to drink a cup of tea.

Those conversations in the presence of Matryona Pavlovna were really the most pleasant. It was not easy to talk when they were alone; their eyes expressed something of more consequence than their lips could say; their mouths seemed shattered, and a strange, unaccountable fear made them part hurriedly.

Such was their relationship during this visit. The aunts noticed it, took alarm, and even wrote to his mother, who was abroad at the time.

Maria Ivanovna, the elder aunt, feared that Dmitri would form an illicit liaison with Katusha. But there was no danger of that, for, though he did not understand it himself, Nekhludov loved Katusha with an innocent love, and this love was a sword between them. Not only did he feel no desire to possess her physically, but the very thought made him afraid.

The more romantic fear of his aunt Sophia Ivanovna was that Dmitri, with his resolution of character, might determine to marry the girl without ever considering her birth or position;

and this had more foundation. If he had clearly understood his feelings for Katusha, especially if they had tried to argue and to dissuade him from making her his wife, this might very easily have happened. The directness of his mind would have probably led him to decide that there could be no reason against marrying a girl, no matter who she was, so long as he loved her. But his aunts did not speak of their fears, and he left them all still unaware of his love for Katusha. He was sure that his feeling for her was simply a manifestation of the joy that had enriched his life at that time, a joy shared by this charming, sunny-tempered girl.

But when the day came for him to go away, and he saw Katusha standing with his aunts on the porch, her black eyes filled with tears, he felt that he was leaving behind him a precious experience which could never be repeated. And he grew very sad.

"Good-by, Katusha. Thank you for everything," he said, looking over Sophia Ivanovna's bonnet as he seated himself in the droshky.

"Good-by, Dmitri Ivanovich," she replied, in her sweet, caressing voice, keeping back her tears, and then ran back into the hall where she could weep unheeded.

❦

CHAPTER THIRTEEN

AFTER that, Nekhludov did not see Katusha for three years. He had just been promoted to officer's rank and was on his way to join his regiment when he stopped to pay his aunts another visit. He was no longer the same man who had spent the summer there three years ago.

Then he was an honest, unselfish youth with a heart open to every good suggestion; now he was a depraved, accomplished egotist, who cared for nothing but his own pleasure. Then the world was God's, a mystery into which with excitement and delight he was striving to penetrate; now the whole of his life seemed a clear and simple matter regulated by the conditions of his own station. Then he needed communion with nature and with men who had lived, thought, and felt before his time, with poets and philosophers; all that interested him now were worldly affairs and good comradeship. Then women seemed mysterious and charming, charming because of their very mystery; now his idea of a woman, of any woman except the women of his own kin or the wives of his friends, was clearly defined: a woman was the means of repeating a familiar enjoyment. Then he did not care about money; he could have lived on a third of the allowance his mother gave him, and he gave up his paternal inheritance in favor of the peasants; now his monthly allowance of fifteen hundred rubles was insufficient, and he had already had some unpleasant interviews with his mother about money matters. Then he regarded his spiritual self as real; now the real was his healthy, vigorous, animal self.

And all this terrible change came about only because he had ceased to believe himself and placed all his confidence in others. He had ceased to believe himself and begun to believe other people because it was too difficult to go on living, believing oneself. If a man believes himself he often has to give judgment against his lower self, which seeks easy joys, but when he puts his trust in others, there is nothing to decide: everything has already been decided against the spiritual self, and in favor of the animal self. Moreover, when he trusted in his own judgment he was always blamed, whereas now, trusting others, he received nothing but the approval of those about him.

When Nekhludov thought, or read, or spoke of God, truth, wealth, poverty, everyone around him considered it ridiculous and out of place; his mother and his aunts, affectionately ironical, called him *"notre cher philosophe"*; but when he read novels, told questionable stories, went to see a French farce and recounted the plot amusingly, everybody admired and encouraged him. When he considered it his duty to wear an old coat and abstain from wine everyone thought it an oddity, a kind of ostentatious eccentricity; but when he spent money on hunting or on furnishing an unusually luxurious study, everyone praised his taste and gave him absurd, expensive presents. When he meant to preserve his chastity until his wedding day, his family were anxious about his health, and even his mother was rather pleased to hear that he had become a real man and had ousted one of his comrades in the heart of some Frenchwoman. So far as the episode with Katusha was concerned, the dowager princess could never think without horror that her son might possibly have married the girl.

It was the same when Nekhludov came of age and gave up the small estate he had inherited from his father to the peasants, because he considered ownership of land to be unjust; this scandalized his mother and relatives and was ever after a cause of reproach and sneering in the family.

He was continually told that the peasants, when they were given the land, were not only no better off, but became still more miserable, for they set up three drinking houses and gave up all idea of work. But when Nekhludov entered the Guards and, in the company of distinguished friends, squandered and gambled away so much money that his mother was forced to draw on her capital to pay his debts, she was hardly upset at all; to sow wild oats during youth, and in good society, was healthy and perfectly natural.

Nekhludov had at first made a fight for his principles; it was a hard struggle, because everything that seemed right to him seemed wrong to other people; and vice versa, all that he regarded as evil was applauded by his world. The struggle ended in his surrender; he gave up his own ideals and adopted those of other people. First the feeling of distrust in himself made him uncomfortable; but this wore off, and Nekhludov, who was beginning to smoke and drink about that time, soon forgot it and felt nothing but relief.

His intensely passionate nature inclined him toward this new life, which commanded the world's approval. The voice that called for other things was silenced. This transition, which began when he went to live in Petersburg, was completed on his entering the army.

Military service generally corrupts a man. It puts him in a position of complete idleness, that is to say it provides him with no rational or profitable occupation. It frees him from the common obligations of humanity, giving him in return only the conventional distinctions of the regiment, the uniform and the flag—autocratic power on the one hand, slavish submission on the other.

But when to the corruption common to all military service, with the glories of its uniform and its flag, its warrant for rapine and murder, is added the demoralization produced by wealth and by intimacy with the royal family—a privilege of the regiment of Guards, into which only wealthy and aristocratic officers were admitted—then this demoralization becomes a perfect mania of selfishness. And Nekhludov had been in that state of selfish madness ever since he entered the military service and began to share the life of his comrades.

Their only occupations were to wear a fine uniform, manufactured and taken care of by other men, with helmet and weapons also forged and kept bright by the labor of others; to ride a fine horse, schooled and fed by another; to take part in parades and reviews with men of similar rank, galloping to and fro, waving swords, firing guns, and teaching other men to fire them. There were no other occupations but these; and men of the highest rank, both young and old, the tsar and his court, not only approved of this mode of life, but extolled and rewarded the men who pursued it. To frequent an officers' club or an especially expensive restaurant in order to eat and drink (chiefly to drink), to spend money obtained from any unheeded source —this was regarded as excellent and important. Women, dancing, and the theater, relieved by the excitement of galloping and swordplay, followed by more squandering of money on women, drink, and cards—such was the life; all the more demoralizing because, where a civilian would be secretly ashamed of such conduct, a soldier considers all this quite proper and boasts of it and is proud of it, particularly in wartime. This was so with Nekhludov, who entered the army soon after war with Turkey was declared.

"We are prepared to sacrifice our lives in war, so we are justified in leading a gay, carefree existence; indeed, it is the only life possible for us, and therefore we lead it": in some such vague phrase as this Nekhludov would have expressed himself at that period of his life. What he felt was chiefly the delight of being free from the moral obligations which he had formerly set himself. In short, he lived under the spell of a dementia of selfishness.

Such was his state of mind when, after an absence of three years, he paid a visit to his aunts.

⚜

CHAPTER FOURTEEN

NEKHLUDOV decided to pay this visit partly because his aunts' estate was on the route which his regiment was following, partly because they had invited him, but principally because he wanted to see Katusha. It is possible that his passions, no longer constrained, may have already suggested the evil which he afterward brought to Katusha, but he was not aware of this, wishing only to revisit the places where he had been so happy, to see once more his slightly ridiculous but kindhearted aunts, who always surrounded him with an atmosphere of unobtrusive love and admiration, as well as to meet that nice Katusha whom he remembered so pleasantly.

He arrived toward the end of March, on Good Friday, over roads almost impassable, in a downpour of rain, cold and soaked through, but in the state of excitement that he usually enjoyed in those days. "I wonder whether she is still here," he thought, as he entered the familiar, old-fashioned courtyard, now filled with drifting snow and surrounded by its red-brick walls. He had hoped that the sound of his sleighbells might bring her out to greet him at the side entrance; but the only persons he met were two barefooted women, who seemed to have been scrubbing floors, for their skirts were tucked up and they both carried pails.

Neither did he find Katusha at the front entrance. Only Tikhon, the manservant, with his apron on, came out on to the porch.

His aunt, Sophia Ivanovna, attired in a silk gown and cap, met him in the hall. "How nice of you to come!" she exclaimed, embracing him. "Sister is a little tired from standing so long in church. We received the Sacrament this morning."

"My congratulations, Aunt Sonya," said Nekhludov, kissing her hand. "Ah, forgive me, I have wet your gown!"

"You must go directly to your room. You are really soaking wet. Why, you have a mustache! . . . Katusha, Katusha, make haste and bring him a cup of coffee!"

"I'm coming!" He heard the pleasant, well-remembered voice, and his heart beat with joy. She was there. It was as though the sun had emerged from a cloud. . . . Nekhludov, followed by Tikhon, walked happily to his old room and began to change his clothes.

He wanted to ask Tikhon about Katusha, how she was getting on, and whether she was engaged to be married. But Tikhon was so respectful and at the same time so severe, so very insistent about pouring the water out of the jug for him, that he hesitated to mention Katusha. Instead, he confined himself to questions about Tikhon's grandchildren, about his uncle's old horse (still referred to as "brother's horse"), and about the dog, Polkan. They were all alive and well, except Polkan, who had died of rabies the year before.

He had just taken off his wet clothes and begun to dress, when he heard a light footstep and a knock at the door. Nekhludov recognized the footstep and the knock. No one but she walked and knocked like that.

He threw on his wet greatcoat and went to the door.

"Come in."

It was she, Katusha—the same, but even more enchanting. Her naïve black eyes had the same smiling expression and fascinating little squint. She wore a clean white apron just like the one she used to wear. The aunts had told her to bring him a new piece of scented soap and a couple of towels: one of the Russian embroidered sort, the other a bath towel. The cake of soap with its embossed lettering, the towels, and their bearer, were all equally clean, fresh, unblemished, and pleasant. In her delight at seeing him, she gathered her charming bright-red lips into the sweet little pucker he remembered of old.

"Welcome to you, Dmitri Ivanovich." She brought out the words with an effort and blushed as she spoke.

"How art thou? How do you do?" He was not sure whether he ought to call her "you" or "thou," and discovered that he was also blushing. "Are you well?"

"Yes, the Lord be thanked. . . . Your aunt told me to bring your favorite rose soap," she continued, laying the soap on the table and spreading the towels over the arms of the easy chair.

"There is some soap here," said Tikhon, speaking up in defense of the dignity and independence of the guest and pointing with pride to a large dressing case fitted with silver boxes, bottles, brushes, pomades, perfumes, and many other toilet articles.

"Give my thanks to my aunt. How glad I am to be here!" said Nekhludov, feeling all of a sudden as light-hearted and tender as in the old days.

Her only answer was a smile as she left the room.

Nekhludov's aunts, who had always been devoted to him, welcomed him this time more warmly than ever. Dmitri was going to the war, where he might be wounded or even killed, and this affected them deeply.

Nekhludov had planned his journey with the intention of staying there only one day, but after he had seen Katusha he was very ready to remain over Easter Sunday, and telegraphed his friend and comrade, Schoenbock, whom he had promised to join in Odessa, to come and visit his aunts instead.

No sooner had Nekhludov seen Katusha than his feeling for her sprang up again. As it had been in the past, so it was now; he could not see her white apron without emotion; the very echo of her footfall, her voice, her joyous laughter, filled him with delight; he could not gaze calmly into her pretty eyes that looked like two black currants wet with the dew, or see without confusion how she blushed whenever she encountered him. He knew he was in love, but not in the same way as before, when love was mysterious and unconfessed even to himself, and when he had been sure that love came only once. Now he was in love, and he knew it and rejoiced in his knowledge; and although he still refused to admit it, he vaguely recognized the nature of his emotion and its probable results.

In Nekhludov, as in all people, there were two natures: one was spiritual, seeking only the kind of happiness which means happiness for everybody else as well, and the other was an animal nature, absorbed in self-gratification and seeking pleasure at the expense of the rest of the world. At this stage of his egotistical dementia, brought on by life in Petersburg and in the army, the animal nature seemed to have won the day. But at the sight of Katusha and the revival of his early love for her, his spiritual nature began to assert its rights, and unknown to himself, during the two days before Easter, it struggled to hold its own. His conscience told him to go away: there was no sound reason for prolonging his visit; he knew that no good could possibly come of it. Yet he was in such a happy frame of mind that he shut his eyes to the consequences, and stayed.

This Easter Eve, the priest and his deacon had driven over in a sledge to perform the midnight service. The aunts' estate was about two miles from the church. They said the road was in a bad state and, what with the thaw, they had had the greatest difficulty in driving their sledge.

Nekhludov, with his aunts and the servants, attended the service. He kept his eyes fixed on Katusha, who stood near the door and brought in the censers for the priest. After exchanging the Easter greeting with his aunts and the priest he was about to retire, when in the corridor outside he heard Matryona Pavlovna, his aunts' elderly maidservant, getting ready to go with Katusha to the village church for the traditional blessing of the Easter cakes and cream cheeses. "I will go too," he thought.

The road to the church was impassable, for either carriages or sledges; so Nekhludov, who felt perfectly at home at his aunts', gave orders to saddle the old stallion known as "brother's horse," and instead of going to bed he put on his brilliant uniform and close-fitting riding breeches, threw his greatcoat over his shoulders, and, mounting the heavy, overfed old horse, started for the church through darkness, slush, and snow.

❖

CHAPTER FIFTEEN

THIS midnight Easter service remained one of the happiest and most vivid recollections of Nekhludov's life.

When he rode into the churchyard out of the black night relieved by occasional white patches of snow, his horse splashing and pricking his ears at the sight of the row of lamps lighting up the church, the service had already begun.

Recognizing Maria Ivanovna's nephew, the peasants showed him a dry spot to dismount; they tethered his horse and led him into the church, which was filled with people.

On the right-hand side stood the men; old men in homespun coats, bast shoes, and clean white leg wrappers; the younger ones in new cloth coats with bright-colored belts around their waists, and top boots. On the left were the women, with red silk kerchiefs on their heads, wearing sleeveless velveteen jackets, bright-red blouses, many-colored skirts, and heavy, nailed shoes. Staid old women with white kerchiefs, gray jackets, and old-fashioned shoes of leather or new shoes of bast, stood behind them. Between the old and the younger women were the children, their hair greased, and dressed in their best clothes. The men made the sign of the cross, bowed to the altar, and, as they rose again, tossed back their long hair; the women, particularly the old ones, fastened their dull and faded eyes on one of the many icons, each with a circle of burning tapers, and made the sign of the cross, firmly pressing their bent fingers first to the kerchief on their foreheads, then to each shoulder, and finally to the waist, moving their lips all the while and bending to the floor in genuflections. The children imitated their elders, and prayed zealously whenever anyone was looking at them. The tall candles, decorated with golden spirals and surrounded by tapers, threw their light on the glittering, gilded cases of the icons. The lamp hanging in the middle of the church was bright with tapers; from the choir came the cheerful singing of amateur choristers, a combination of bass and treble voices.

Nekhludov walked to the front of the church. The local aristocracy stood in the center: a landowner with his wife and son, the boy wearing a sailor suit; the superintendent of police; the telegraph operator; a merchant in top boots; the village elder, a medal on his chest—while, to the right of the altar and directly behind the wife of the landowner, stood Matryona Pavlovna in a shot-silk lilac gown and white shawl, and Katusha in a white frock with a pleated bodice, a blue sash, and a little red bow in her black hair.

It was all festive, solemn, and bright: the priest in his silver-cloth vestments embroidered with gold crosses, the deacon and subdeacons in their gold and silver surplices, the choristers with oiled hair and holiday raiment, the lively, dancing melodies of the hymns, and the priests with their triple, flower-bedecked candles, constantly blessing the congregation and repeating the Easter salutation: "Christ is risen! Christ is risen!" It was all beautiful, but loveliest of all was Katusha in her white dress and blue sash, with the little red bow in her black hair and her eyes radiant with delight.

Nekhludov knew that she was conscious of him although she never turned her head. He felt it as he passed close by her going up to the altar. Though he had nothing in his mind, he tried to find something to say as he came near. "My aunts said they would break their fast after the service," he said.

Her charming face grew pink as it always did at the sight of him, and the look of joy deepened in her dark eyes. "I know," she answered with a smile.

At that moment the subdeacon, with a brass coffee pot[1] in his hands, was making his way through the crowd. Apparently impelled by respect for Nekhludov, he tried to avoid brushing past and, without noticing Katusha at all, he moved so close to her that his vestments touched her dress. Nekhludov wondered how the man could have so little perception; he should have understood that everything the world contained was created expressly for Katusha; that there was nothing in the world that might not be overlooked except Katusha, for she was the center of all. It was for her that the gold icons glittered, for her the tapers were burning in the sanctuary, for her the joyful chant rang out, "Behold, the Passover of the Lord, rejoice, O ye people!" All that was good in the world was for her. And Katusha, it seemed to him, knew that it was all for her. These were the thoughts in Nekhludov's mind as he gazed at her slender form and dainty, pleated, white dress; the rapture of her face showed him that the singing of his own heart found an echo in hers.

During the interval between early and late Mass, Nekhludov left the church. The people bowed and made way for him to

---

[1] Coffee pots were often used for holding holy water in Russian churches.—Tr.

pass. Some knew him, and others asked: "Who is he?" He stopped on the church steps. The beggars instantly gathered around him and, giving them all the change he had in his purse, he went down the steps.

It was near dawn, but the sun had not yet risen. The people were lingering in the churchyard, sitting down on the graves. Katusha was still in church, and Nekhludov waited for her. And still the congregation came pouring out, hobnailed shoes clattering down the stone steps, and, separating in different directions, the people wandered through the churchyard.

Maria Ivanovna's pastry cook, a very old man with a shaking head, stopped Nekhludov and gave him the Easter kiss, while his wife, an old woman whose silken kerchief did not hide the Adam's apple in her withered throat, drew a saffron-colored egg from her pocket handkerchief and gave it to him. A stalwart young peasant in a new sleeveless coat with a green sash came up to him.

"Christ is risen," he said, with smiling eyes, and as he drew nearer Nekhludov could preceive the peculiar, agreeable, peasant odor; then, tickling him with his curly beard, the youth kissed him squarely on the mouth with his firm, fresh lips. While Nekhludov was exchanging kisses with the peasant and accepting from him a dark brown egg, Matryona Pavlovna's lilac gown and the darling, dusky little head with its red bow came in sight.

She saw him at once over the heads of the people standing in front of her, and he noticed how her face lit up. She stopped with Matryona Pavlovna in the porch, distributing alms to the beggars. A beggar, with a red scar where his nose should have been, approached her. She took something from her handkerchief, gave it to him, and drawing still nearer, her eyes shining with happiness, exchanged three kisses with him without showing the slightest sign of disgust. And while she was kissing the beggar, her eyes met Nekhludov's with a questioning look, as though asking: "Am I doing right?"

"Yes, dear, yes; everything is just as it should be, everything is beautiful, and I love you." When she descended the steps and he went up to her, he had no intention of exchanging the Easter greeting. All he wanted was to be near her.

"Christ is risen!" said Matryona Pavlovna, bending her head, her face wreathed in smiles, while the tone of her voice said: "On this night we are all equal." She wiped her mouth with her handkerchief rolled into a ball and offered him her lips.

"He is risen indeed!" responded Nekhludov, exchanging three kisses with her.

He looked at Katusha. She blushed and instantly came toward him.

"Christ is risen, Dmitri Ivanovich."

"He is risen indeed!" he answered.

They kissed each other twice, then paused as if considering whether or not the third kiss were necessary and, having concluded that it was, kissed a third time and smiled.

"You are not going to the priest's?" asked Nekhludov.

"No, we shall stay here awhile, Dmitri Ivanovich," replied Katusha, breathing a deep sigh of content like one who is pleased with what she has done, and looking straight at him with an expression of maidenly purity and love.

In the love of men and women there is a moment when the zenith is reached, when their love has nothing in it that is self-conscious, or rational, or sensual. Such a moment came to Nekhludov on his joyous Easter night.

Katusha's small, glossy, black head, the white, pleated dress enclosing modestly her graceful body and small breasts, the blush, the tenderly shining black eyes, her whole being expressed the purity of virginal love: not only the love that he knew was for him, but love for everybody and everything; love not only for all that is good in the world, but also for the beggar she had kissed.

He discerned that love by the light of his own experience. The same love was in his heart, and he knew that she and he were one.

When he now thought of Katusha this was the moment he recalled above all others. Ah, if it could but have stopped there, with the feelings of that night! "Yes, all the shameful business began after that Easter Eve!" he said to himself, as he sat by the window in the jury room.

❖

CHAPTER SIXTEEN

ON his return from church Nekhludov broke the fast with his aunts; then he took a glass of wine and some vodka—a habit contracted in the regiment—and went directly to his room, where he fell asleep without undressing. He was roused by a knock at the door. Recognizing Katusha's knock he rose, rubbing his eyes and stretching himself.

"Is that you, Katusha? Come in."

She half-opened the door.

"Lunch is ready," she said.

She had not changed her white dress, but the knot of ribbon in her hair was gone. Her eyes were beaming as she looked into his, as though she had brought wonderfully happy news.

"I am coming," he said, taking up his comb to straighten his hair.

She stood still, and he, noticing it, dropped the comb and took a step toward her. At that instant, however, she turned and left the room. He heard her light footsteps on the carpet of the corridor.

"What a fool I am!" said Nekhludov to himself. "Why didn't I make her stay?"

He ran out into the corridor and overtook her.

He couldn't have told what he wanted her for, but while she was in his room he had felt there was something he ought to have done, something that was always done on such occasions, and that he had not done.

"Katusha, wait," he said.

She glanced at him and stopped.

"What is it?"

"Nothing, but—"

Then, with an effort, calling to mind how all the men he knew would have acted in the circumstances, he put his arm around her waist.

She looked him in the eyes.

"You mustn't, Dmitri Ivanovich, you mustn't," she murmured, blushing to the point of tears and pushing his arm away with her strong, rough little hand.

Nekhludov released her and for a moment he felt not only uncomfortable, but ashamed and disgusted with himself. He ought to have listened then to the voice of his conscience. But he did not understand that the discomfiture and shame came from his better nature claiming the right to be heard; on the contrary, he accused himself of stupidity and wondered why he was not more like other men.

He overtook her again and, clasping her waist, kissed her on the neck. This kiss was different from those he had given her before, the one behind the lilac bush, and the Easter kiss after church that day. This was a terrible kiss, and she felt it.

"Oh, what are you doing?" she cried, in a voice as though he had broken a priceless treasure. She turned quickly and ran away.

He went into the dining room. The aunts, elegantly dressed, the doctor, and some neighbors stood near the table where the side dishes were spread. Everything was quite as usual, but a wild storm was raging within Nekhludov. He understood nothing of what was being said to him, and answered at random; he thought only of Katusha, recalling the sensation of that last kiss when he caught her in the corridor. He could think of nothing else. Although he made an effort not to look at her when she entered the room, his whole being was aware of her presence.

After dinner he went at once to his room and, too much excited to sit, he walked up and down, listening to every sound in the house and expecting at any moment to hear her footsteps.

His animal nature had won the upper hand while his spiritual nature, which had been in control during his former visit and even that very morning in church, was now trampled underfoot. A dreadful beast had taken possession of his soul.

Throughout the rest of the day he watched for Katusha, but did not manage to meet her alone. Probably she was trying to avoid him. Toward evening, however, she had to go into the room adjoining his. The doctor was to stay the night, and Katusha had been sent to make up his bed.

Hearing her footsteps, Nekhludov followed her. Treading softly and holding his breath as if he were about to commit some crime, he entered the room. She had thrust both hands into a fresh pillow case and, holding the pillow by the corners, she looked at him over her shoulder and smiled, but not with the joyous smile he knew so well. It was a frightened, pitiable smile. It seemed to tell him that he was doing wrong. For a moment he paused; it was his last chance to vanquish temptation. The voice of his real love for her was speaking, and although it was but a feeble whisper, it bade him consider her, *her* feelings and *her* life.

And then the other voice broke in: "Are you going to let the opportunity slip by, and forfeit your own happiness, your own enjoyment?"

The second voice stifled the first. He was now the slave of a wild, ungovernable passion. Hesitating no longer, he strode across the room and, taking her in his arms, made her sit down on the bed; he sat down beside her, with the feeling that more remained to be done.

"Dear Dmitri Ivanovich, please let me go," she said, in a

faint and piteous voice. "I hear Matryona Pavlovna coming!" she suddenly cried, and indeed someone was coming to the door.

"Then I will come to you in the night. You'll be alone?" he whispered.

"No, no, you mustn't," she said, but the tremor and confusion of her whole being said something different.

It really was Matryona Pavlovna bringing a blanket. With a glance of reproach at Nekhludov, she began to scold Katusha for having taken the wrong blanket.

Nekhludov left the room without a word. He felt no shame. He could see from Matryona Pavlovna's face that she was angry, and knew that she was in the right; but the animal nature which had overcome his first feeling of love for Katusha was now dominant and left no room for anything else. He knew that his passion must be satisfied and was seeking only the opportunity.

He was restless all evening. First he went to his aunts' room, then to his own, then out on to the porch. He thought of one thing only: how to meet her alone. But she avoided him, and Matryona Pavlovna, for her part, tried not to let Katusha out of her sight.

❧

CHAPTER SEVENTEEN

THE evening wore away and the night came on. The doctor had gone to bed. The aunts were also preparing to retire. Nekhludov knew that Matryona Pavlovna was now with them and that Katusha was alone in the maids' room. He went out on the porch again.

It was dark, and the mild night air was damp and filled with white vapor born of the belated snows of spring and also serving to melt them away. Strange sounds rose from the river flowing at the foot of a steep bank, about a hundred paces from the house: it was the ice breaking up. Nekhludov went down the porch steps and, using patches of hard snow as stepping stones, made his way across the puddles to the window of the maids' room. His heart was beating so fiercely that he seemed to hear it. His breath now stopped, now burst out in heavy gasps.

The room was lighted by a small lamp. Katusha was sitting by the table plunged in thought, looking in front of her. Nekhludov watched her without moving; he wondered what she would do, believing herself unobserved. After a minute or two, she raised her eyes and shook her head in smiling reproof, so it seemed, of her own thoughts; then, with an impulsive gesture she leaned her arms on the table and again fell to gazing before her.

As he stood watching, he listened to the throbbing of his own heart and at the same time to the mysterious sounds arising from the river. There, in the fog, a slow and constant struggle was going on, a wheezing, a cracking, a falling. The thin ice tinkled like breaking glass.

Gazing at Katusha's face which showed the tormenting struggle going on within her, he pitied her but, strangely enough, this pity served only to increase his desire.

He tapped on the window. She started as though she had received an electric shock; she sprang from her seat terror-stricken, ran to the window, and, screening her eyes with her hands, pressed her face against the pane. She recognized him, but the terror did not go out of her face. She looked extraordinarily grave; he had never seen her like that before. She did not smile until he smiled, and then as though submitting to him. In her heart there was no smiling, only fear. He beckoned to her to come out into the yard, but she shook her head and remained standing by the window. Once more he bent toward the pane and was about to entreat her to come out, when she suddenly turned toward the door, as if someone had spoken to her from within. Nekhludov moved away from the window. The fog was so dense that all he could see five steps from the house was the light of the lamp shining red and huge out of a black, shapeless mass; and all the while the dreadful creaking, crackling, rustling, and hissing of the ice could be heard going on below. Suddenly nearby a cock crowed; then another; and presently, from far away, the village cocks joined in the chorus. It was the second time that night that the cocks had crowed.

After walking to and fro behind the corner of the house, stumbling into an occasional pool of water, Nekhludov went back to the window of the maids' room. The lamp was still burning, and Katusha was sitting at the table with the same look of indecision on her face. As he approached the window she looked toward him, and when she heard the knock, never pausing to ask who was there, ran quickly out of the room; he heard the outer door creak as she opened it. He was waiting for her by the porch, and put his arms around her without saying a word. She clung to him and, as she raised her head, he kissed her on the lips. They stood behind the corner of the porch on a spot where the snow had melted away and the ground was dry. He was filled with unsatisfied, tormenting desire. Then again, came the creak of the outer door, and the voice of Matryona Pavlovna called out angrily:

"Katusha!"

She slipped away from him and ran into the house. He heard the door latched, then all was still. The red light disappeared, and he was left alone with the fog and the turmoil of the river.

He went up to the window, but there was nobody to be seen. He knocked, but got no answer. Then he went into the house through the front door. Taking off his boots, he walked barefooted along the passage to her door, which was next to the room occupied by Matryona Pavlovna. He listened to the old woman's peaceful snoring, and was just going on when he heard her cough and turn over in her creaking bed. For several minutes he stood motionless. Then, when all was quiet and the steady snoring began again, he moved on, trying to avoid boards that creaked. He crept up to Katusha's room. It was very still inside, but he was sure she was awake because he could not hear her breathing. Very softly he called, "Katusha!" The moment she heard him she jumped up, came to the door and, angrily as it seemed to him, began to urge him to go away:

"What does this mean—how could you—your aunts will hear!"—but her whole being said: "I am yours," and it was only this that Nekhludov understood.

"Open the door just a minute, I entreat you!" He hardly knew what he was saying. She was silent, then he heard her hand fumbling with the latch. It rose with a click and he went in.

He caught hold of her just as she was—with arms bare in a coarse, stiff nightgown—lifted her, and carried her out. "Oh, what are you doing?" she whispered, but he paid no heed and went on.

"Let me go," she kept repeating, clinging closer to him all the while.

As she left him, trembling and silent, giving no answer to his words, he stepped out onto the porch and stood there trying to understand the meaning of what had happened.

It was almost daylight. The noise of the breaking ice in the river below had become even louder, and a new sound of gurgling water could be heard. The mist was settling and beyond it the newly risen moon shed a somber light on something black and menacing.

"What is the meaning of it all? Is it a great happiness or a great misfortune?" he asked himself, and then he thought: "It happens to everybody. Everybody does it." He went back to bed.

❖

CHAPTER EIGHTEEN

THE next day Schoenbock, gay and brilliant, made his appearance. The refinement and charm of his manner, his generosity and above all his devotion to Dmitri, captivated his aunts. But although his generosity was attractive, its utter recklessness amazed them. He gave a ruble to some blind beggars who came to the gate, and fifteen rubles in tips to the servants; and when Suzetka, Sophia Ivanovna's lap dog, happened to graze its leg, he instantly tore a strip from his hemstitched cambric handkerchief to make a bandage. Sophia Ivanovna knew that such handkerchiefs could not be bought for less than fifteen rubles a dozen. The aunts had never met a man like this. They had no idea that Schoenbock owed more than two hundred thousand rubles, which he knew he could never pay: what then were twenty rubles more or less?

Schoenbock stayed only one day. The following night, their leave having expired, he and Nekhludov departed together.

During that last day of Nekhludov's visit, when the events of the past night were still fresh in his mind, two conflicting emotions struggled in his heart: one was the ardent recollection of sensual love (whose realization, however, had fallen short of its promise) accompanied by a certain satisfaction of having accomplished his object; the other was a consciousness of a wrongdoing that had to be put right, not for her sake but for his own.

In his present condition of selfish madness, Nekhludov could think of nothing but himself. He wondered if his conduct would be blamed, if found out; but he gave no thought to Katusha's feelings or future welfare.

He sensed that Schoenbock suspected his relations with her, and this tickled his vanity.

"No wonder you grew so fond of your aunts all of a sudden that you had to stay a whole week," Schoenbock observed after seeing Katusha. "I should have done the same. She's a lovely little thing."

Nekhludov reflected that although it seemed a pity to leave before he had fully gratified his passion, it would be just as well to close at once a relationship which might grow irksome if continued. He was also thinking that he ought to give her some money, not because she was likely to need it but because it was customary in such cases, and it would be considered dishonorable if, having taken advantage of her, he didn't pay her. So he gave her a sum of money which he considered suitable for him to give and fitting for her to receive.

After dinner on the day of departure he lingered in the vestibule waiting for her. She blushed when she saw him and was about to pass on, but he stopped her.

"I wanted to say good-by," he said, crumpling in his hand an envelope containing a hundred-ruble note. "I—"

She guessed what he meant, and frowned as she shook her head and pushed away his hand.

"No, no, you must take it," he muttered, and thrust the envelope into her bodice; then he rushed back to his room, groaning aloud like a man who has burned himself playing with fire, and for some time he paced the floor in distress, gasping and moaning as though in physical pain.

But what else could he have done? It was the same old story. The same thing, he knew, had happened to Schoenbock and a governess; and to Uncle Grisha; and to his own father when he lived in the country and had that illegitimate child by a peasant woman, the same Mitinka who was still living. And if everybody did it how could it be helped? In this way he tried to comfort himself, but with no success.

At the bottom of his heart he knew that he had played a dastardly and cruel part. He knew that he had forfeited his self-respect and had lost all right to be considered the upright, noble-hearted, generous fellow he always meant to be. He could neither look an honest man in the eye nor blame a fellow sinner. And yet he had to keep up his self-respect if he wished to lead a pleasant life. There was only one way to do that: to forget the past. And after a while he succeeded. His new life and environment, his gay companions, and the war, each contributed its share toward this result, and the longer he lived the less he remembered, until at last he completely forgot it all.

Once only, after the war was ended, he went to his aunts again, hoping to see Katusha. His heart ached when he was told that shortly after his previous visit she had left the house to give birth to a child; his aunts had heard that she had in fact had a child, and afterward had gone from bad to worse. Judging by the time of its birth, the chances were that the child was his. His aunts said that the girl was as depraved as her mother. Nekhludov felt somewhat relieved by this view of her character, which seemed to offer an excuse for his own conduct. He had intended at first, nevertheless, to find her and the baby, but he never made the necessary effort, to begin with because the thought of her was mortifying and painful, and later because as time went on his sin faded from recollection until finally he ceased to think of it at all.

But now this surprising coincidence, bringing back the past, compelled him to acknowledge his own heartless cruelty and baseness, which had permitted him to live peacefully for ten years with this sin on his conscience. Still he had no intention of making a public confession; he feared only that the affair might be discovered and that she or her lawyer might denounce him and put him to shame before everybody.

❧

CHAPTER NINETEEN

IN this frame of mind Nekhludov left the courtroom and went into the jury room, where he took a seat near the window and smoked unceasingly while he listened to the talk that went around. The cheerful merchant was evidently in sympathy with the way Smelkov had passed his time.

"Well, sir, he had his fling in true Siberian fashion, that's what I say! He was no fool either, to choose a girl like that!"

The foreman was stating his views, to the effect that much depended on the experts. Piotr Gerassimovich and the Jewish clerk were laughing over some joke between themselves. Nekhludov answered all the questions addressed to him in monosyllables, desiring only to be left alone.

When the usher came with his sidling gait and called the jury back into the courtroom, Nekhludov was panic-stricken; he felt more like a culprit than a judge, for at the bottom of his heart he knew that he was a blackguard who ought to be ashamed to look a fellow being in the face. Yet by force of habit he stepped upon the platform with his usual self-possession; resuming his seat next but one to the foreman, he crossed his legs and toyed with his pince-nez.

The prisoners, who had also been taken out, now returned to their seats. There were some new faces in the room—the witnesses—and Nekhludov noticed that Maslova seemed unable to take her eyes off a portly woman who sat in the front row behind the rail. She was richly dressed in silk and velvet, and wore a high-crowned hat trimmed with a large bow; from her arm, bared to the elbow, hung an elegant bag. This woman, he was afterward informed, was the mistress of the establishment with which Maslova was connected.

The examination of the witnesses began; they were asked their names, religion, and so on. Then, after a short consultation about whether the witnesses should give evidence on oath or not, the old priest came shuffling in again and with the same gestures readjusted the gold cross on his breast, and with the same tranquil self-assurance, as though he were performing a most useful and important duty, swore in the expert and the witnesses. After the oath had been administered all the witnesses left the room under escort, except Kitaeva, the proprietress of the brothel. She was asked to tell what she knew of the case. Speaking with a strong German accent, but clearly and intelligently, emphasizing every sentence with an artificial smile and nodding her head at the same time, she gave her evidence as follows:

A rich Siberian merchant had sent Simon, the hotel servant, to her house for one of the girls, and she had sent him Lubasha. Later on Lubasha came back with the merchant. He was already somewhat "ecstatic"—here she smiled slightly—and went on drinking and treating the girls; but his money gave out and he sent this same Lubasha, to whom he had taken a great fancy, back to the room he occupied in the hotel. She glanced at the prisoner as she said this.

Nekhludov thought he saw Maslova smile too, and the sight of that smile filled him with a strange feeling of disgust mingled with pity.

The court had appointed as counsel to defend Maslova a young barrister who was also a candidate for a judicial post. "What is your opinion of Maslova?" he asked, coloring as he spoke.

"A ferry goot one," replied Kitaeva. "She is an etucated girl and with plenty of style about her. She was prought up in a goot family and can reat French. Sometime she a drop too much has taken, bot nefer has she herself forgotten. A ferry goot sort of girl."

Katusha, who was watching her mistress, suddenly turned to the jury; her gaze rested upon Nekhludov; her slightly squinting eyes were grave. Her whole face was grave, even stern. In spite of the terror that crept over him, Nekhludov could not detach his gaze from the strange, squinting eyes with their whites so bright and clear. They recalled that dreadful night, with its mist and breaking ice, and above all the waning moon with upturned horns that rose at daybreak and shed its light on something black and menacing. Those two black eyes, looking at him and at the same time beyond him, reminded him of that black and menacing something.

"She recognizes me," he thought, and flinched like one who expects a blow. But she had not recognized him. She drew her breath with a long sigh and turned her eyes to the president. Nekhludov sighed too.

"If it were only over!" he thought. It seemed as if he were out hunting and had a wounded bird to put out of its misery. He had experienced this same disgust and pity for the bird fluttering in the game bag; he wished to put an end to its suffering and forget it. These were the feelings that filled Nekhludov as he sat listening to the cross-examination.

❖

CHAPTER TWENTY

THE case dragged on, as if to spite him. After every witness, the expert included, had been examined in turn and asked all sorts of irrelevant questions by the assistant prosecutor and the lawyers with their usual air of importance, the president invited the jury to examine the exhibits brought into court as material evidence. There were two: an immense diamond-cluster ring evidently made for an exceedingly fat forefinger, and a test tube containing the poison which had been analyzed; both these articles were labeled and sealed.

Just as the jurors were about to look at them, the assistant prosecutor rose again and demanded that the medical examiner's report should be read before they proceeded further.

Although he very well knew that this document would be nothing but a bore (besides delaying the luncheon recess) and that the assistant prosecutor demanded it only to stand upon his rights, and although he was anxious to finish in time to meet his Swiss girl, the president had no alternative but to consent. The secretary took the document and in his lisping, monotonous voice, slurring all the *l*'s and *r*'s, began to read:

"The external examination proved that:

"1. Ferapont Smelkov's height was six feet five inches."

("What a size!" whispered the merchant in tones of awe into Nekhludov's ear.)

"2. Judging from outward appearances he was about forty years of age.

"3. The corpse presented a swollen appearance.

"4. The flesh was of a greenish hue and showed dark spots in places.

"5. The skin was blistered and had peeled off in large pieces.

"6. The hair was dark brown, thick, and easily detached from the skin.

"7. The eyeballs were protruding from their sockets, and the cornea looked dull.

"8. Serous fluid was oozing from the nostrils, ears, and partly open mouth.

"9. The face and chest were swollen to such an extent that the neck could no longer be seen. . . ."

The description of the enormous, fat, swollen, and putrefied corpse that had been the body of the jovial merchant, was detailed in twenty-seven items and occupied four pages. While the reading was going on Nekhludov was seized with indescribable disgust and loathing. Katusha's life, and that revolting corpse, the serum oozing from the nostrils, the eyes protruding from their sockets, and his own treatment of Katusha—all seemed to belong to the same order of things. He felt surrounded by horrors from which he would never escape.

When the reading of the external examination was finally concluded, the president raised his head with a sigh of relief, hoping it was all over; but the secretary at once proceeded to read the examination of the intestines. Again the head of the president drooped and, resting it on his elbow, he closed his eyes. The merchant who sat beside Nekhludov could hardly stay awake and kept nodding. The accused and the gendarmes remained motionless.

"The examination of the internal organs showed that:

"1. The covering of the skull was easily separated from the bones, and showed no sign of bruising.

"2. The bones of the skull were of average thickness and in perfect condition.

"3. There were two dark-colored spots on the cerebral membrane, each one measuring about four inches in diameter; the membrane itself was pale . . ."—and so on and so on for another thirteen paragraphs.

Then came the names and signatures of the assistants and finally the opinion of the medical examiner showing that the changes in the stomach (and to a lesser degree in the kidneys and bowels) revealed by the autopsy, lent great probability to the theory that Smelkov's death was caused by poison. Owing to the changes that had taken place in the stomach and bowels, it was difficult to state with certainty what kind of poison had been used, but the presence of a large quantity of alcohol in the stomach seemed to indicate that this poison had been introduced in wine.

"He certainly could drink!" whispered the merchant, who had just woken up.

But even the reading of this report, which lasted fully an hour, did not seem to satisfy the assistant prosecutor, for when the president turned toward him and said "I suppose it will be unnecessary to read the report on the intestines," he drew himself up in his chair and without glancing at the president said in a severe tone of voice: "I must request to have it read!" His manner was designed to show that a prosecutor's rights were not to be trifled with, that he would insist on having the report read and that a refusal would be regarded as a cause for appeal. Here the martyr to intestinal catarrh (the member with the beard and kindly eyes), feeling quite worn out, turned to the president and said:

"What's the use of reading all this stuff? It's only a waste of time. These new brooms don't sweep any cleaner—they take longer, that's all."

The member with the gold spectacles said nothing, but only looked in front of him with an air of gloomy fortitude as if he had ceased to expect anything good, from wife or life alike.

The reading began:

"On the fifteenth of February 188-, I, the undersigned, in compliance with an order from the Medical Department numbered 638," read the secretary, pitching his voice in such a key as to preclude any chance of slumber, "and in the presence of the assistant medical inspector, have made an examination of the following internal organs:

"1. The right lung and heart (contained in a six-pound glass jar).

"2. The contents of the stomach (in a six-pound glass jar).

"3. Of the stomach itself (in a six-pound glass jar).

"4. Of the liver, the spleen and the kidneys (in a three-pound glass jar).

"5. Of the intestines (in a six-pound earthenware jar). . . ."

As the reading began, the president leaned first toward one member and then toward another, whispering to each in turn; receiving an affirmative answer, he intervened:

"The court considers the reading of this report superfluous," he said. The secretary paused and gathered up his papers, while the assistant prosecutor with an angry look began to make notes.

"Gentlemen of the jury," said the president, "you may now examine the material evidence."

The foreman and several of the jurors, not quite knowing what to do with their hands, went up to the table and took turns in examining the ring, the glass jars, and the test tube. The merchant even tried on the ring.

"Ah! That was some finger!" he said, returning to his seat. "Like a cucumber," he added, as though gloating over the gigantic proportions of the deceased merchant.

⁕

CHAPTER TWENTY-ONE

WHEN the examination of the exhibits was over, the president announced that the investigation was concluded and, eager to finish the business as quickly as possible, took no recess, but called on the prosecutor to proceed, hoping that as he was but human after all, he might want to smoke and have some dinner himself and therefore show a little mercy to the rest of them. But the assistant prosecutor had no more idea of mercy for himself than for others. Very stupid by nature, he had had the misfortune to be awarded a gold medal while at school, and a prize for an essay on slavery at his university when studying Roman Law, and his conceit was extraordinary: helped by his success with women, it had become quite monumental. When called on to speak, he rose slowly from his seat, well aware of the graceful figure he made in his gold-embroidered uniform, leaned on the desk, and turned to look around the room, avoiding the eyes of the prisoners. He began:

"Gentlemen of the jury! The case now before you is, if I may so express myself, very typical."

He had been preparing his address during the reading of the reports of the medical investigation, and he fully expected that, like the famous speeches of famous lawyers, it would be of great public significance. True, his audience was four only: one cook, one dressmaker, Simon's sister, and a coachman. But what of that? Other celebrated lawyers had begun in the same way. His theory concerning the duties of his position was that a public prosecutor ought to penetrate into the depths of the psychological significance of crime and lay bare the diseases of society, and he intended to live up to his principles.

"You have before you, gentlemen of the jury, a crime of the *fin du siècle*, if I may so describe it, a crime possessing the specific features of the deplorable corruption to which those elements of our society that are subjected to the burning rays of this process, are particularly exposed . . ."

He spoke at length, trying to remember all the clever things he had thought of, and principally trying never to pause, but to make his speech flow smoothly for an hour and a quarter. He stopped only once to clear his throat; then, taking up the thread of his discourse, he made up for this brief pause with redoubled eloquence. He spoke, now in mellow, insinuating tones, balancing himself first on one foot and then on the other, and looking at the jury; now in quiet, businesslike tones, glancing into his notebook; now in loud, accusing tones, addressing in turn the public and the jury. But he never once looked at the prisoners, who were all three gazing fixedly at him.

His argument was a hodgepodge of everything that was (and is still) considered to be the last word in scientific wisdom. He talked of heredity and of congenital criminality, of Lombroso and Tarde, of evolution, of the struggle for existence, of hypnotism and hypnotic suggestion, of Charcot, and of decadence.

The merchant Smelkov, according to the definition of the assistant prosecutor, was a type of the genuine, vigorous Russian, generous to a fault and whose very generosity made him an easy prey for the profoundly depraved creatures into whose hands he had chanced to fall. Simon Kartinkin was the atavistic product of serfdom, timorous, illiterate, and unprincipled, who even had no religion. Efimia was his mistress and a victim of heredity; she showed every symptom of degeneration. But the chief instigator of this crime was Maslova, herself an example of the very lowest type of degenerate. "This woman," he went on, without looking at her, "has been educated—we have just heard the testimony of her mistress. Not only can she read and write, but she knows French. She is an orphan, and probably the germs of criminality are in her nature. Brought up in a cultured family of the nobility, she might have earned her living by honest work; but she forsook her benefactors and, in order to gratify her passions, became the inmate of a brothel, where she was the best educated among her companions. As, gentlemen of the jury, you have just been told, she possessed the power of gaining influence over her visitors—using that mysterious faculty recently investigated by scientists, by the school of Charcot in particular—the power of hypnotic suggestion. It was by means of that faculty that she gained control over Smelkov—kind, trusting, wealthy; she used her power without mercy, first to steal his money and then to take his life."

"He's going a little far, isn't he?" said the president, bending toward the serious member and smiling.

"A thorough fool!" said the serious member.

"Gentlemen of the jury!" the assistant prosecutor continued, gracefully swaying his body from side to side, "the fate of these criminals lies in your hands; but it is also in your power to control the fate of society, which will feel the effects of your verdict. You will consider the nature of this crime, the social menace of such pathological individuals as Maslova, and you will strive to guard the healthy elements of society from contagion, in some cases from actual destruction."

As though overcome by the importance of the verdict about to be returned, the assistant prosecutor, evidently delighted with his own eloquence, fell back into his chair. The gist of his argument, shorn of the flowers of rhetoric, was that Maslova hypnotized the merchant, insinuated herself into his confidence and, having been sent to his room with a key, intended to take all the money for herself; but, surprised by Simon and Efimia, she was forced to share it with them. To conceal the traces of her crime, she brought the merchant back to the hotel and poisoned him.

The argument of the assistant prosecutor was followed by that of a middle-aged lawyer in morning coat and low-cut waistcoat, which showed a semicircle of stiff white shirtfront. He glibly pleaded the cause of Kartinkin and Bochkova, who had paid him three hundred rubles, exonerating both and putting all the blame on Maslova.

He denied the assertion of Maslova that Bochkova and

Kartinkin were present when she took the money, insisting that the evidence of a poisoner could not be countenanced. The twenty-five hundred rubles, said the lawyer, might easily have been accumulated by two thrifty persons, who sometimes received between three and five rubles a day in tips. The merchant's money had been stolen by Maslova and had either been transmitted by her to some third party or else lost while she was in a state of intoxication. The poisoning was the act of Maslova alone.

Therefore he asked the jury to acquit Kartinkin and Bochkova of taking the money, but even if they should find them guilty of theft, he demanded their acquittal on all counts in the poisoning affair.

In conclusion he pointed out sarcastically that the brilliant remarks of the assistant prosecutor on the subject of heredity, though they might be true in general, could not apply to this case, as no one knew who Bochkova's parents were.

The assistant prosecutor shrugged his shoulders contemptuously and wrote something down in his notebook.

Then Maslova's counsel rose and in a timid and faltering manner began to speak in her defense. Without denying that she had taken part in the theft, he insisted only that she had no intention of poisoning Smelkov. When he took on himself to be eloquent and began to describe Maslova's youth and how she had been ruined by a man who had gone unpunished while she bore the consequences of her sin, this excursion into the domain of psychology was so unsuccessful that everybody felt embarrassed. While he was mumbling something about the cruelty of men and the defenselessness of women, the president, wishing to help him out, advised him to adhere more closely to facts.

When the lawyer ceased speaking, the assistant prosecutor rose again and took up the cause of heredity against the defending counsel who had spoken first. He began by saying that Bochkova's unknown parentage could in no way invalidate the doctrine of heredity. Science had established the law of heredity on so firm a basis that we could not only deduce crime from heredity, but heredity from crime. As to the hypothesis of the defense that Maslova had been ruined by an imaginary seducer (he pronounced the word "imaginary" with sarcastic emphasis), the facts rather tended to prove that it was she who had been the temptress—and not of one victim only. After these remarks he took his seat with an air of triumph.

Then the prisoners were permitted to speak in their own defense.

Efimia Bochkova kept repeating that she knew nothing whatever, that she had nothing at all to do with the affair, and stubbornly laid all the blame on Maslova.

Simon only said several times:

"Do as you please, but I am innocent—it's unjust."

Maslova said nothing. When the president told her she might speak in her own defense she only cast a look around the room, like a hunted animal, and then, dropping her head, broke into loud weeping.

"What's the matter?" said the merchant next to Nekhludov, for he had heard him utter a strange sound. It was a strangled sob.

Nekhludov did not even yet understand the full significance of his present position and attributed the sobs he could hardly repress to weakness of nerves. He put on his pince-nez to conceal his tears, then pulled out his handkerchief and blew his nose.

The dread of the disgrace which would befall him if all these people knew what he had done was stifling the remorse that struggled in his soul; for, at this stage of the affair, his strongest feeling was fear for himself.

❖

CHAPTER TWENTY-TWO

AFTER the last words of the prisoners, there was an argument lasting for some time about the form of the questions to be placed before the jury. This settled, the president began to sum up. Before stating the facts to the jury, he explained to them in a pleasant, informal tone of voice that burglary was burglary and theft was theft, that theft from a room that was locked was theft from a room that was locked, and that theft from an open room was theft from an open room. While offering these explanations, he looked repeatedly at Nekhludov, as though endeavoring to impress him with the importance of the information and in the hope that, understanding it, he would explain everything to the rest of the jury. Then he proceeded to elucidate another truth, namely that murder is a deed which aims at the death of a fellow creature, and that therefore poisoning is murder. When this truth also had, in his opinion, been sufficiently apprehended by the jury, he explained that if the crimes of theft and murder were committed simultaneously, this combination of crimes would be theft and murder.

Although anxious to get away to his appointment, he had become so completely a slave of routine that, having once begun to speak, he could not stop; so he explained to the jury that if they found the prisoners guilty, they had the right to say so, and if they found them not guilty they had the right to say that also. If they found them guilty of one crime and innocent of the other, they should declare them guilty of one and innocent of the other. Next he explained that, though granted this privilege, they should use it with discretion. He was also about to explain that if they made an affirmative answer to a question they would thereby agree to everything the question included, and that if they did not agree to the whole of the question, then they must state to which part they did not agree; but glancing at his watch and seeing that it was five minutes before three, he decided to begin his peroration:

"The circumstances of the case are as follows . . ." and then he repeated all that had been previously stated several times by the defense, by the assistant prosecutor, and by the witnesses.

During the president's address, the associate members, while listening to him with an air of profound attention, looked now and then at their watches, and although they approved of his speech or, in other words, considered it to be as it should be, they found it somewhat lengthy. This was the agreed opinion of all, from the assistant prosecutor to the last member of the bar, not to mention the other listeners. At last the president finished the summing up.

It seemed as if there could be nothing more to say, and yet, so pleased was he with the inspiring tones of his own voice, that he was reluctant to stop, and found it necessary to add a few words concerning the importance of a right which had been granted to the jury, and which they should beware of abusing: he reminded them that they had taken an oath, that they were the conscience of society, that the secrecy of their deliberations in the jury room should be held sacred, and so on and so on.

From the moment the president began to speak, Maslova never once took her eyes from his face, as though afraid of losing a single word; Nekhludov, therefore, set free from the dread of meeting her eyes, gazed at her intently. And his mind passed through that familiar sequence when first impressions are of the outward change that absence brings upon a face well loved but long unseen; then gradually the looks of former years return, the changes vanish, and there rises the characteristic expression of a singular, unique spiritual personality.

Indeed, neither the prison cloak, the heavy figure, nor the fullness of the chin, nor the lines on the forehead and around the temples, nor the swollen eyelids, could hide the truth. It was the same Katusha who on that Easter morning had gazed so innocently into the face of the man she loved, with tender, laughing eyes full of joy and life.

"And what a strange coincidence! That I should be on the jury in this particular case! That I, who have not seen her for ten years, should find her in the prisoners' dock! How will this all end? Oh, if it would only end quickly!"

He had not yet ceased to rebel against the feeling of repentance that had risen in his heart. He tried to think of the affair as a coincidence, which would pass from his memory and leave no trace behind. He was like a puppy when its master seizes it by the neck and rubs its nose in the mess it has made; the puppy yelps and tries to pull away from the consequences of its misbehavior and forget about it, but the implacable master will not let it go. So Nekhludov, appreciating the baseness of what he had done, now felt the weight of the master's hand; and yet failed to understand the significance of his deed or recognize the master. He did not want to believe that what he saw was the result of his own act. But the inexorable hand held him there, and he felt that he could never escape.

Outwardly he still preserved an air of indifference as he sat there in the second chair of the first row, with his usual air of careless ease, playing with his pince-nez—yet in his heart he saw all the cruelty, cowardice, and baseness not only of this one particular action, but of his idle, depraved, complacent, cruel life as a whole. The terrible veil, which for ten years had hung between him and the consequence of his crime, was beginning to waver, and now and again he caught a glimpse of what was hidden behind it.

CHAPTER TWENTY-THREE

His summing up ended, the president gracefully lifted the paper containing the list of questions and handed it to the foreman. The jurymen, glad of an opportunity to rest, rose awkwardly to their feet and made their way a little shame-facedly to the jury room. As soon as the door had closed behind them, a gendarme approached and, drawing his sword from its scabbard, raised it to his shoulder and took up a post by the door. The judges left the room to stretch their legs, and the prisoners were led away.

From habit, the jurymen at once brought out cigarettes, lit them, and presently the feeling of constraint caused by their false position in the courtroom wore off; as they smoked they felt relieved and began a lively conversation.

"That girl is innocent; she didn't know what she was about," said the kindhearted merchant; "we must let her down easily."

"That's what we are about to discuss," said the foreman. "We must not be guided by impulse."

"That was a good summing up by the president!" said the colonel.

"You call it good, do you? It almost put me to sleep."

"The chief point is that the servants couldn't have known about the money unless they had heard about it from Maslova," said the Jewish-looking clerk.

"Well, do you think that she stole the money?"

"You'll never make me believe it!" exclaimed the kind-hearted merchant. "I'm sure it's all the work of that red-eyed old witch!"

"They're a bad lot," said the colonel.

"But she says she never went into the room."

"And you believe her? I would never believe a wretch like that!"

"Whether you would believe her or not doesn't settle the matter," said the clerk.

"She was the one who had the key."

"What of that?" retorted the merchant.

"But what about the ring?"

"She told us about that, didn't she?" shouted the merchant. "The fellow was crazed with drink, he hit her—and then, naturally, he was sorry. 'Here,' says he, 'don't cry; here's a ring for you.' Think what a giant of a man he was, six foot five, they say; he must have weighed twenty stone."

"What has that to do with it?" interrupted Piotr Gerassimovich, the schoolteacher. "The question is: was she the chief instigator, or did the servants plan the crime?"

"The servants couldn't have done it alone. She had the key."

This random talk went on for some time. At last the foreman said: "Gentlemen, please! I propose that we seat ourselves around the table while we discuss the matter."

With these words he installed himself as chairman.

"Those girls are a bad lot," said the clerk, and to show that Maslova must have been the chief culprit he told how one of her kind had stolen a watch from a friend of his on the boulevard.

The colonel in his turn began another still more startling story about the theft of a silver samovar. Here the foreman called the jury to order by rapping the table with his pencil: "Now, gentlemen," he said, "please concentrate your attention on these questions."

All became silent. The questions were framed as follows:

1. Is the peasant of the village Borki in the district of Krapivansk, Simon Petrov Kartinkin, thirty-three years of age, guilty of having, on the seventeenth of January 188–, in the city of N——, conspired with certain other persons with intent to rob and murder the merchant Smelkov by giving him poisoned brandy, so causing his death, and of having stolen from him about twenty-five hundred rubles and a diamond ring?

2. Is the *meshchanka* Efimia Ivanovna Bochkova, forty-three years of age, guilty of the crimes described in the first question?

3. Is the *meshchanka* Katerina Mikhailovna Maslova guilty of the crimes described in the first question?

4. If the accused Efimia Bochkova is not guilty of the crimes set down in the first question, then is she guilty of having, while employed in the Hotel Mauretania, on the seventeenth day of January 188–, in the city of N——, stolen from a locked suitcase in a room occupied by a guest of the said hotel, the merchant Smelkov, the sum of twenty-five hundred rubles, for which purpose she unlocked the suitcase with a key which she had brought and fitted to the lock?

The foreman read the first question.

"Well, gentlemen, what do you say?"

The question was quickly answered; all agreed to say

"guilty," convinced that Simon had assisted in the poisoning as well as in the theft. An old *artelshchik*,[1] who voted for acquittal on all counts, was the only exception.

The foreman thought that he must be laboring under some error and proceeded to explain that there could be no reason for doubting the guilt of Kartinkin; but the *artelshchik* was not to be persuaded. "Never mind, it's better to be merciful," he said, adding, "we're none of us saints ourselves."

The second question concerning Bochkova was answered after much talk and discussion by "not guilty," because there was no clear proof of her share in the poisoning (a point upon which her counsel had strongly insisted).

The merchant, in his eagerness to acquit Maslova, insisted that Bochkova was the chief instigator. Many of the jurors agreed with him, but the foreman, wishing to keep within the limits of the law, said that there were no grounds for considering her an accomplice in the poisoning.

After much argument, the foreman won the day with his opinion.

To the fourth question, concerning Bochkova, the answer was "guilty" but, as a concession to the *artelshchik,* a rider was added recommending her to mercy.

The third question, concerning Maslova, raised a fierce dispute. The foreman insisted that she was guilty of both poisoning and theft, but the merchant disagreed and was supported by the colonel, the clerk, and the *artelshchik.* For a while the others seemed to be wavering, but at last the opinion of the foreman began to gain ground. In fact, the jurors were so tired that they were ready to join whichever side promised the speedier decision.

Not only from his former knowledge of Maslova, but from all that had passed during the trial, Nekhludov felt sure that she was innocent of both the robbery and the poisoning. At first he was confident that all the jurors would take this view, but when he saw how the merchant's clumsy defense of Maslova, evidently based on his personal fancy for the girl (which he took no pains to conceal), had aroused the opposition of the foreman, and how fatigue was making everyone so eager for a decision that he was ready to say "guilty," he felt that he must speak in her defense. Still he dared not venture. He had a horrible dread lest his former relations with her might be dis-

---

[1] A man who belongs to an *artel*; that is, a workmen's cooperative association.—Tr.

covered. And yet how could he leave the affair as it lay? Come what might, he must voice his objections.

With a face now flushed, now pale, he was about to open his lips to speak when Piotr Gerassimovich, who had been silent up to that moment, evidently exasperated by the arrogant manner of the foreman, began suddenly to argue with him and said in so many words precisely what Nekhludov was about to say.

"One moment, please," he began. "You argue that because she had the key she must have committed the theft, but couldn't the servants have unlocked the bag with a false key *after* she had gone?"

"Hear, hear!" said the merchant, approvingly.

"She couldn't have taken the money, because in her position she would hardly know what to do with it."

"That's just what I say!" exclaimed the merchant.

"But it's very likely that her visit to the room suggested all that business to the servants. They took their opportunity and then tried to throw all the blame on her."

Piotr Gerassimovich spoke in an irritable tone and his mood infected the foreman, who at once began an obstinate defense of his own views. But Piotr Gerassimovich's arguments were so convincing that the majority agreed with him in believing that Maslova had taken no part in stealing the money, and that the ring had been given to her by Smelkov.

When they passed on to the question of poisoning, her ardent champion the merchant remarked that she ought to be acquitted because she had no reason to murder Smelkov. To which the foreman replied that it was impossible to acquit her of that, since she confessed that she had given the powder.

"Yes, but she thought it was opium."

"Opium is a deadly poison, too," said the colonel, who was fond of digressions; he immediately began a rambling tale of how his brother-in-law's wife had once taken too much opium and would certainly have died if there had not been a doctor near by, who took instant measures for her relief. The colonel told his story so impressively and with such dignity that no one had the courage to interrupt him. Only the clerk, encouraged by his example, decided to break in with a little tale of his own.

"Some people get so used to it they can take forty drops at a time. I have a relative—"

But the colonel would tolerate no interruption; he went on describing the effects of opium on his brother-in-law's wife.

"It's gone four o'clock," said one of the jurors.

"Well, gentlemen, what is your decision?" asked the foreman. "Shall we consider her guilty without intent to rob and without intent to steal any property? Shall we say that?"

Piotr Gerassimovich, pleased with his victory, assented.

"But we strongly recommend her to mercy," added the merchant.

All agreed to this. The *artelshchik* was the only man to insist on a verdict of "not guilty."

"That's really what it amounts to," explained the foreman. "She had no intent to rob, and did not steal any property, therefore she is 'not guilty.' "

"Write that down, and add that we recommend her to mercy. Surely that should clear her," cried the merchant, in high good humor.

They were so worn out and so confused by all these discussions that no one thought of adding the clause, "but without intent to kill."

Nekhludov was so agitated that he, too, overlooked this point. It was in this way, therefore, that the answers to the questions were drawn up and taken back into the court.

Rabelais tells of a judge who was trying a case and who, after quoting all sorts of laws and reading some twenty pages of unintelligible Latin, proposed that the contending parties should throw dice, odds or even; if the number turned up even the plaintiff would be right; if odd—the defendant.

This was a similar case. That particular verdict was returned not because all were agreed but because first, the president, in spite of all the time he had wasted, had omitted his customary direction to the jury, namely, that if they answered "guilty" they had the privilege of adding "but without intent to kill"; secondly, because the colonel had told a stupid, long-winded story about his brother-in-law's wife; thirdly, because Nekhludov was so agitated that he did not notice the omission of the proviso "without intent to kill," thinking that the proviso "without premeditated intent" nullified the accusation; fourthly, because Piotr Gerassimovich happened to leave the room just as the foreman was reading over the questions and replies; and lastly, because everybody was tired and wanted to get away as quickly as possible and therefore thought it best to agree to any decision that would hurry matters on.

The foreman rang the bell. The gendarme standing with drawn sword in hand near the door put it back into its scabbard and moved aside. The judges took their seats, and the jury came filing in.

The foreman carried the paper with suitable solemnity and

presented it to the president, who, when he had read it, spread out his hands in surprise and turned to consult his companions. He was astonished that the jury, having put in the first proviso, "without intent to rob," should have omitted the second, "without intent to kill." According to the verdict of the jury Maslova had committed neither theft nor robbery, but she had poisoned a man without any apparent object.

"Just look at this absurd verdict!" he said, turning to the member on his left. "This means penal servitude, and the woman is innocent."

"Do you really think so?" asked the surly member.

"I am sure she is; I regard this as a case for applying Article 818."

(Article 818 says that if the court finds the accusation unjust, it may set the decision of the jury aside.)

"What is your opinion?" asked the president, turning toward the kindhearted member, who made no immediate reply. He glanced at the number on a paper before him and, hastily adding the figures together, found that he couldn't divide them by three. He had decided in his mind that if the number was divisible by three, he would agree with the president; but even though it was not, he was too kindly to dispute the point, so he agreed just the same.

"I think just as you do," he said.

"And you?" said the president, turning to the irritable member.

"By no means," he replied, decidedly. "The newspapers are forever repeating that the juries acquit criminals; what would they say if the court did the same thing? I would not consent to it on any account."

The president looked at his watch.

"Well, I am sorry," he said; "then nothing more can be done," and he handed the questions to the foreman to read aloud. Everyone rose, and the foreman, shifting his weight from one foot to the other and clearing his throat, read the questions and answers. The whole court, secretaries, lawyers, and even the prosecutor himself, expressed surprise.

The prisoners sat perfectly still; they did not seem to understand what the answers meant.

When all were again seated, the president asked the prosecutor to announce the punishments to be inflicted on the condemned.

The prosecutor, elated over his unexpected success in obtaining Maslova's conviction, and naturally ascribing it to his own eloquence, half-rose in his seat and, after consulting the Penal Code, said:

"Simon Kartinkin should be dealt with according to Article 1452 and paragraph 4 of 1453; Efimia Bochkova according to Article 1659, and Katerina Maslova according to Article 1454."

These punishments were the heaviest that the law allowed.

"The court will adjourn to consider the sentence," said the president, rising.

Everyone followed his example, and with that air of relief that springs from duty fulfilled, began to leave the hall or walk about.

"I say, my dear fellow, we made a bad blunder there," said Piotr Gerassimovich, coming up to Nekhludov, who was listening to the foreman's explanation of some matter. "Do you realize that we've sent her to Siberia?"

"What's that?" exclaimed Nekhludov, this time utterly regardless of the teacher's overfamiliarity.

"Certainly!" he replied. "We ought to have given the answer 'Guilty, but without intent to kill,' and we didn't. The secretary has just told me that the prosecutor wants her to be sentenced to fifteen years' penal servitude."

"But that's what was decided," said the foreman.

Piotr Gerassimovich began to dispute this, saying that as she had not taken the money it was the natural inference that she had no idea of committing the murder.

"I read the answers to you before we left the room," said the foreman, trying to defend himself, "and not one of you said a word against them."

"I was not in the room at that moment; but I can't imagine how you could have let it pass," said Piotr Gerassimovich, looking at Nekhludov.

"I never thought—" said Nekhludov.

"It's evident you didn't!"

"But we can make it right," said Nekhludov.

"Too late for that now."

Nekhludov looked at the prisoners. Their fate about to be decided, they sat behind the rail without moving. Maslova was smiling. An evil impulse stirred in his heart. Till then he had been anticipating her acquittal and, assuming her to be unlikely to leave the city, had been painfully uncertain how he would act toward her. It was a difficult position. But the prospect of Siberia settled at once the question of their future relationship. The wounded bird would cease by its struggling in the game bag to remind him of its existence.

CHAPTER TWENTY-FOUR

PIOTR GERASSIMOVICH'S guess proved true.

On his return from the judges' room, the president proceeded to read:

"On the twenty-eighth day of April, 188–, in compliance with the decree of His Imperial Majesty, the Criminal Court of N——, by virtue of the verdict of the jury, in accordance with Section 3 of the Penal Code, decrees that the peasant Simon Kartinkin, thirty-three years of age, and the *meshchanka* Katerina Maslova, twenty-seven years of age, be deprived of all special and personal rights and sentenced to hard labor: Kartinkin for eight and Maslova for four years, with the consequences stated in Article 25 of the said Code. The *meshchanka* Efimia Bochkova, forty-three years of age, after being first deprived of all special and personal rights and privileges, is to be imprisoned for the term of three years, in accordance with Article 42 of the said Code. The costs of the case shall be evenly divided between the prisoners and in the event of their inability to pay will be defrayed by the Treasury.

"The articles of material evidence shall be sold, the ring returned, and the glass jars destroyed."

Kartinkin stood with hands pressed against his sides and fingers bent upward; his lips twitched. Bochkova was apparently undisturbed. But Maslova on hearing the sentence blushed scarlet.

"I am not guilty, not guilty," she suddenly cried, in a loud voice. "This is wicked. I am not guilty. I never dreamed nor thought of such a thing. I speak the truth, and nothing but the truth!" And dropping down on the bench, she sobbed aloud.

When Kartinkin and Bochkova left the room she still sat weeping, so that the gendarme was obliged to touch the sleeve of her prison cloak.

"It is impossible to let this thing go on," said Nekhludov to himself, utterly forgetting his selfish thoughts; hardly conscious of what he was doing, he hurried out into the corridor to catch another glimpse of Maslova.

A lively crowd of jurymen and lawyers, pleased to have dispatched the case, were jostling in the doorway, so that he was detained for several moments. When at last he reached the corridor she was already some distance ahead of him. With quick steps, paying no heed to the attention he was rousing, he overtook her, walked on a little way, and stood waiting. She passed by without glancing toward him. Although she had stopped crying, and was wiping her flushed face with the end of her kerchief, she still drew her breath in convulsive sobs. After she was gone he turned hurriedly back to find the president. He had already left the court, but Nekhludov caught him in the cloakroom.

"Sir," he said, going up to him just as he was putting on his light-gray overcoat and taking his silver-headed cane from the hands of the doorkeeper. "May I have a word with you about the case which was decided just now? I am one of the jurors."

"Certainly! Prince Nekhludov, I believe? I shall be delighted. I think we have met before," said the president, shaking hands with him. He recalled with satisfaction the good time he had had on that particular occasion. He had not forgotten the evening of his meeting with Nekhludov, when he had danced better than all the young men. "What can I do for you?"

"There has been a misunderstanding about Maslova. She is innocent of the poisoning, and yet she has been condemned to penal servitude," said Nekhludov, with an anxious frown.

"The court gave its decision in accordance with the answers which you brought in," said the president, walking toward the entrance, "although these answers did seem inconsistent with the facts."

He now remembered that he had intended to explain to the jury that to answer "guilty" and omit to add "without the intent to kill," means guilty of intentional murder, but, being in a hurry, he had forgotten to do this.

"Yes, but is there no remedy for it?"

"A reason for appeal can always be found. You will have to consult a lawyer," replied the president, putting on his hat a little to one side and continuing to move toward the door.

"But this is terrible!"

"Yes; but you see, in Maslova's case there were just two alternatives," replied the president. He evidently wished to impress Nekhludov with his amiability, and so, after achieving a satisfactory arrangement of his whiskers over his coat collar, he placed his hand lightly under Nekhludov's elbow, remarking as he turned again in the direction of the door, "You're going out as well?"

"Yes," said Nekhludov, and, hastily putting on his overcoat, accompanied him out into the street. Here, standing in the bright sunlight, they had to raise their voices to be heard above the rattle of wheels on the cobbles.

"It is a curious situation," the president went on. "There were two possibilities: either a complete acquittal or, what would amount to the same thing, a nominal term of imprisonment—from which the days of her preliminary confinement would be deducted—or penal servitude. There was no *via media*. If you had only added the words 'without the intent to kill,' Maslova would have been acquitted."

"It was an unpardonable omission on my part," replied Nekhludov.

"That's where the trouble lies," said the president.

He had only three-quarters of an hour in which to see Clara.

"I should advise you to consult a lawyer," he said. "He will find you a case for appeal. There will be no trouble about that. To Dvorianskaya Street," he added, turning to the cabby. "Thirty kopecks—I never pay more."

"This way, Your Excellency!"

"Good day! If I can be of any use to you, my address is Dvorianskaya Street, Dvornikov House. It's easy to remember." And with a friendly bow he drove off.

❖

CHAPTER TWENTY-FIVE

THE talk with the president of the court, and the freshness of the air out of doors, had a calming effect on Nekhludov. He began to think that perhaps he had been overwrought by a morning spent in such unaccustomed mental excitement; it had been such a remarkable coincidence! He must do everything in his power to mitigate her fate, and as soon as possible. Yes, he must act at once.

The first step was to find out, before going any further, the address of Fanarin or Mikishin, two well-known lawyers. He returned to the courts of justice, took off his overcoat, and went upstairs. In the first corridor he met Fanarin himself; he stopped him and asked if he might consult him on a matter of business. Fanarin, who knew Nekhludov by sight, said that he would be very glad to be of service.

"I am rather tired just now, but if you will put the matter into a few words, I am at your disposal. Will you come in this way?" said Fanarin, and led him into a room, apparently the private room of one of the judges. They seated themselves at a table. "Now, if you will kindly state your business——"

Nekhludov began at once. "In the first place I shall have to ask you to regard this as strictly confidential. I should be sorry to have it known that I am taking any personal interest in this affair."

"That goes without saying. Please go on."

"I served on a jury today which condemned an innocent woman to penal servitude. This troubles me very much." Nekhludov was annoyed to find himself blushing and hesitating over his words.

Fanarin glanced at him sharply and lowered his eyes again. "Well?" he said.

"We have condemned an innocent woman, and I should like to carry the case to a higher court."

"You mean to the Senate," said Fanarin, correcting him.

"And I shall be glad if you will take up the case."

Nekhludov, in haste to get over the worst, went on hurriedly, the color again rising to his face.

"The fees and other expenses, whatever they may be, will be a charge on me."

"Oh, we shall settle that later," replied Fanarin, smiling condescendingly at Nekhludov's inexperience. "Now, what are the facts of the case?"

Nekhludov told the story.

"Very well. I will take the papers and look them over tomorrow. The day after tomorrow—or perhaps we had better say Thursday—if you come to my house at six o'clock in the evening, I will give you an answer. And now, if you will excuse me, I have a few inquiries to make here."

Nekhludov bade him good day, and went out.

The talk with the lawyer and the consciousness of having already taken steps for Maslova's defense relieved his mind. He went out into the courtyard. The weather was fine, and he drew in joyfully a deep breath of the sweet spring air. The cabbies vainly offered their services. He chose to walk. His mind was in a whirl; thinking of Katusha and the way he had treated her, he felt sad, and everything looked gloomy. "Well, there will be time to think it over; now I must try to throw off these painful feelings," he said to himself, and, glancing at his watch, remembered the Korchagins' dinner. It was not too late, and he could be there in time. He heard the ringing of a passing tram car, ran after it and caught it. When he reached the square he jumped off and hailed a cabby, who drove so rapidly that in ten minutes he was pulling up in front of the large house belonging to the Korchagins.

❖

CHAPTER TWENTY-SIX

"COME in, Your Excellency! You are expected," said the fat, friendly doorkeeper. The heavy oaken door swung noiselessly on its patent English hinges. "They are at dinner, but I was told to ask you in."

The doorkeeper went to the stairs and rang the bell.

"Any visitors?" asked Nekhludov, taking off his overcoat.

"Only Monsieur Kolossov and Mikhail Sergeyevich."

A handsome footman in a tail coat and white gloves looked over the balusters and said:

"Please come up; Your Excellency is expected."

Nekhludov mounted the stairs and, passing the familiar richly furnished ballroom, entered the dining room. All the family, with the exception of Princess Sophia Vassilyevna (who never left her own rooms) were seated at the dinner table. The aged Prince Korchagin sat at the head of the table with the doctor on his left and, on his right, Ivan Ivanovich Kolossov—formerly marshal of the nobility, now a bank director, Korchagin's friend and a liberal; beyond him on the left sat Miss Rayder, the governess of Missy's little sister, with the child herself, who was just four years old; opposite them on the right was Petya, Missy's brother and Korchagin's only son, a sixth-form schoolboy on whose account the whole family was staying in town to await the end of his examinations; next came the university student who was coaching him; on the left again, Katerina Alexeyevna, a maiden lady of forty, a rabid Slavophile; opposite her sat Missy's cousin, Mikhail Sergeyevich Telegin, familiarly called Misha; and at the foot of the table sat Missy herself. There was a vacant seat beside her.

"That's good! Sit down, we are only at the fish course," said Korchagin, chewing carefully with his false teeth and looking up at Nekhludov with bloodshot eyes that had no visible lids.

"Stepan!" he called to the stately butler, his mouth still full of food, indicating with his eyes the vacant seat. Although Nekhludov knew him intimately and had often seen him at the dinner table, today his red face and sensual mouth, the napkin tucked under the chin, the apoplectic neck, and the whole corpulent, overfed, typically officerlike figure struck him very unpleasantly.

Nekhludov's mind involuntarily reverted to what he had heard concerning the cruelty of this man who, during his terms of service as governor of several provinces, had had men flogged and hanged without the slightest reason. He could not have wanted to curry favor, for he already possessed all that high birth, wealth, and influence could bestow.

"Immediately, Your Excellency," said Stepan, in the act of taking a ladle from the sideboard loaded with silver. He made a sign to the handsome footman, who at once busied himself with the cover next to Missy, rearranging the cutlery and a starched napkin folded so as to show the family crest.

Nekhludov made his way around the table, shaking hands. Everyone rose to greet him except Korchagin and the ladies, and this hand-shaking with people to whom he had hardly spoken a word in his life struck him today as senseless and absurd. He apologized for being late, and was about to take the empty seat between Missy and Katerina Alexeyevna, when the old prince insisted that if he wouldn't take a glass of vodka, he must at least whet his appetite with a bit of something from the side table, on which stood lobster, caviar, cheese, and salted herrings. Nekhludov had not realized how hungry he was but, after the first bite of bread and cheese, went on eating greedily.

"Well, have you been undermining the foundations of society?" said Kolossov, derisively quoting the words of a conservative paper which had been campaigning against trial by jury. "I suppose you've been acquitting the guilty and condemning the innocent—isn't that so?"

"Undermining the foundations—undermining the foundations—" repeated the prince, chuckling. He had an unbounded admiration for the wit and learning of his liberal friend.

At the risk of seeming discourteous, Nekhludov made no reply to Kolossov and sat down to his steaming soup.

"Let him eat in peace," said Missy, smiling. She used the pronoun "him" deliberately, as a way of implying her intimacy with Nekhludov.

Meanwhile, in lively tones and with great fluency, Kolossov was giving an account of the article against trial by jury which had roused his indignation. Mikhail Sergeyevich, Korchagin's nephew, was agreeing with him, and repeated the gist of another article from the same paper.

Missy was very *distinguée* as usual, and well, unobtrusively well, dressed.

"You must be terribly tired and hungry," she said to Nekhludov, after letting him finish his soup.

"No, not particularly. And you? Did you go to see the paintings?" he asked.

"No, we put it off. We went to play tennis at the Salamatovs'. Mr. Crooks plays wonderfully well."

Nekhludov had come here to be entertained. He used to like being in this house because its air of luxury and good taste appealed to him, and because he was susceptible to the implied flattery and deference with which he was always surrounded. But today, strangely enough, everything he saw jarred on him: the doorkeeper, the broad, luxurious staircase, the flowers, the footmen, the table decorations, and even Missy herself, who seemed artificial and unattractive. Kolossov's self-satisfied tone of make-believe liberalism, the basic vulgarity of his talk, Korchagin's thickset neck and sensual face, the French phrases of the Slavophile lady Katerina Alexeyevna, the constrained faces of the governess and the university student, and above all that pronoun "him" on Missy's lips applied to himself—all this was annoying. He had not yet made up his mind about Missy. Sometimes he saw her dimly, as if by moonlight—pure, lovely, innocent, and good—seeing nothing but what was beautiful. Then again, as if the bright sun shone on her, he could not help noticing her imperfections. Today, for instance, he saw every tiny wrinkle on her face, how her hair was fluffed out, the sharpness of her elbows, and the size of her broad thumbnail, exactly like her father's.

"I call it deadly dull," said Kolossov—he was speaking of tennis. "We had ever so much more fun playing *lapta*, when we were young."

"Oh, but you haven't tried. It's awfully exciting," said Missy. Nekhludov found her drawling emphasis on "awfully" grossly affected.

A general discussion was started in which Mikhail Sergeyevich and Katerina Alexeyevna took part. Only the tutor, the governess, and the children sat silent and visibly bored.

"Oh, these interminable disputes!" exclaimed Prince Korchagin, with a loud laugh; he removed the napkin from his waistcoat and rose noisily from the table, pushing back his chair, which was at once set aside by the footman. The others followed his example; they all went up to a side table on which bowls were standing filled with scented water, and while they were rinsing their mouths they continued the same uninteresting conversation.

"Don't you think so?" said Missy to Nekhludov, appealing to him for confirmation of her statement that nothing betrays one's disposition more quickly than a game. But on his face she saw that look of disapproval which she always dreaded; she was puzzled to guess what could have caused it.

"I really couldn't say. I have never given the subject a thought," he said, in reply to her question.

"Shall we go to Mamma?" she asked.

"Certainly, if you wish," he said, in a tone which plainly showed that he did not want to go.

She looked at him without speaking, but her glance made him ashamed of himself. "Why should I go about making people uncomfortable?" he said to himself, and then, with an attempt to be more amiable, he declared that it would give him much pleasure if the princess would receive him.

"Certainly, Mamma will be very glad. You can smoke, too— and Ivan Ivanovich is there."

The mistress of the house, Princess Sophia Vassilyevna, was a chronic invalid who for eight years had been seen by her friends only in a reclining position, draped in silks and velvets with many frills of lace and ribbon and surrounded with flowers and all sorts of *objets d'art* in bronze, gilt, lacquer, and ivory. She never went out, and received only her "special friends," that is to say, those whom she regarded as superior persons. Nekhludov was thus distinguished for several reasons: he was considered clever, his mother had been an intimate friend of the family, and it would be a good thing if Missy were to marry him.

Princess Sophia Vassilyevna's room was on the farther side of a large and a small drawing room. When she reached the large drawing room, Missy, who was walking in front, paused with deliberation and, resting her hand on the back of a gilt chair, gazed fixedly at Nekhludov.

If Missy was anxious to marry Nekhludov because he was considered a desirable match, it didn't follow that she had no regard for him; she had grown accustomed, too, to the thought that he was going to be hers (not she his), and now, with the unintelligent but persistent cunning which has so often been observed in the insane, she was beginning to work her way toward the object in view. First she must persuade him to tell her what was the matter.

"Something has happened to you," she said. "Tell me about it."

The incident in the law courts came into his mind; he drew his brows together in a frown and changed color as he replied, impelled by a burst of candor:

"Yes, something has happened. Something serious and wholly unexpected."

"What is it? Can't you tell me what it is?"

"Not now. You must pardon my silence—I haven't had time yet to think it over myself," he said, blushing still more deeply.

"Then you won't tell me?" she asked. Her face quivered, and she pushed away the chair she had been holding.

"No. It is impossible," he replied, feeling that his words were also an answer to himself, acknowledging that indeed something very important had happened to him.

"Well, come along then," she said, shaking her head as if to chase away some unwanted thoughts, and went on with a quickened step. It seemed to him that she pressed her lips together to hold back her tears. He was sorry and ashamed to have hurt her feelings, but he knew that if he showed the smallest sign of weakness it would mean defeat for him, and he had no intention of committing himself. Today he feared this more than anything, and he followed her in silence to the door of the princess's boudoir.

❧

CHAPTER TWENTY-SEVEN

PRINCESS SOPHIA VASSILYEVNA had just finished an elaborate and hearty dinner. She took her meals in private so that no one should see her performing a function so very commonplace. On a small table drawn up beside the couch stood her coffee, and she was smoking a cigarette. Princess Sophia Vassilyevna was a tall thin woman with dark hair, large black eyes, prominent teeth, and a weakness for appearing younger than she really was.

The rumor had gone about fairly widely of her intimacy with her doctor, yet until this day Nekhludov had never admitted the thought; but this time, when he saw the doctor seated beside her, with his oily shining beard divided down the middle, a feeling of disgust came over him.

Kolossov was sitting in a soft low easy chair near Sophia Vassilyevna, stirring his coffee. On the table beside him stood a glass of liqueur.

Missy came in with Nekhludov, but she did not stay.

"You may come to me when Mamma gets tired of you and sends you away," she said to Nekhludov and Kolossov in an easy, friendly tone of voice that betrayed no sign of recent annoyance. Her light footfall on the soft carpet was quite inaudible as with a cheerful smile she left the room.

"How are you, my friend? Sit down and tell us everything," said Princess Sophia Vassilyevna, her careful smile displaying large white teeth—a perfect imitation of those that nature had formerly endowed her with. "They tell me that you came from the courts very much depressed. It must be an ordeal for a man of sensibility," she said in French.

"It is indeed," said Nekhludov. "It often makes one feel one's own lack of . . . that one has no right to judge."

"Comme c'est vrai! . ." she exclaimed, as though struck by the truth of his observation. "And how are you progressing with your painting? I am immensely interested in it, and if it were not for my poor health I certainly should have come to see it long ago."

"Oh, I have given that up," replied Nekhludov, drily. Today her flattery was as transparent to him as the little fiction about her age, which she tried so hard to conceal. He could hardly treat her with ordinary courtesy.

"Oh, how could you do that! And Repin himself told me," she said, turning to Kolossov, "that he had real talent! It does seem a pity!"

"How can she tell such lies," thought Nekhludov, frowning. When his mood became too unmistakably morose and Sophia Vassilyevna saw that all attempts to draw him into a witty and agreeable conversation were condemned to failure, she turned to Kolossov and asked him what he thought of the latest play, in a tone of voice that said: "Any opinion you may express will be accepted by me as final, for every word you utter deserves to be immortalized." Kolossov disapproved of the play, and took the opportunity to air his views on art in general. Princess Sophia Vassilyevna, confused between her enthusiasm for the justice of his criticism and her desire to defend the author all in one breath, alternately surrendered and tried to compromise.

Nekhludov looked and listened, but his perception went deep below the surface of what was before him. As he sat there he saw that neither Sophia Vassilyevna nor Kolossov felt any interest in the play or in each other, and that if they talked it was only to satisfy the physical need to exercise the muscles of the throat and tongue after eating; also that Kolossov, having drunk vodka, wine, and liqueur, was somewhat tipsy—not tipsy like the peasants, who drink seldom, but like men with whom the drinking of wine has become a habit: he did not reel about, nor talk nonsense, but he was in a state of self-satisfied excitement. He noticed, too, that Princess Sophia Vassilyevna, even during the conversation, was all the while casting uneasy glances at the window, through which a slanting sunbeam was moving toward her, a betrayer which might shed too bright a light on her wrinkled face.

"How true that is!" she said, in reply to some remark of Kolossov, and pressed the electric bell by her side.

The doctor, like an intimate friend of the house, left the room without speaking. Sophia Vassilyevna followed him with her eyes as she continued the conversation.

"Please lower that curtain, Philip," she said, with a glance at the window hangings as the handsome footman entered the room in answer to her bell. "No, I cannot agree with you, I shall always insist that he has a great deal of mysticism, and poetry cannot exist without mysticism." Angrily, one of her black eyes was following the man's movements as he adjusted the curtain. "Mysticism without poetry is superstition, and poetry without mysticism becomes prose," she said, with a sad smile, her eyes still fixed on the footman and the curtains. "Philip, that's not the one I meant; it's the one in the large window," she exclaimed, in the aggrieved tone of a sufferer, resentful of the effort spent on uttering words. And with her jewel-bedecked fingers she raised the fragrant cigarette to her lips to soothe her feelings.

The muscular, broad-chested, handsome Philip made a slight inclination of the head, as though begging her pardon; then, noiselessly stepping over the carpeted floor with his strong, thick-calved legs, he went silently and obediently to the other window and without taking his eyes from the face of the princess began to draw the other curtain, so that no shaft of light could possibly fall upon her. But he blundered again, and again the exhausted Sophia Vassilyevna was obliged to interrupt her conversation about mysticism to direct that idiotic and vexatious Philip. There was a gleam in his eye just for one instant. " 'It would puzzle the devil himself to find out what you want,' he's probably saying," thought Nekhludov, observing the byplay. But the handsome and athletic Philip brought his feelings instantly under control and quietly went on doing what his help-less and artificial creature of a mistress commanded him.

"Of course, there is much truth in Darwin's theory," said Kolossov, sprawling in a low chair and gazing at the princess with his sleepy eyes. "But he exaggerates."

"Do you believe in heredity?" asked the princess, addressing Nekhludov; she felt annoyed by his silence.

"In heredity?" he repeated. "No, I do not." His mind was filled with strange images. He seemed to see the superb figure of the footman Philip as an artist's model, and beside him Kolossov, stripped also of his garments, with a stomach like a melon, bald head, and scraggy, flabby arms. In the same dim way he imagined, as they must be in reality the shoulders of Sophia Vassilyevna, now covered with silk and velvet; but this picture was so hideous that he made haste to banish it from his mind.

Here Sophia Vassilyevna measured him with her eyes.

"Missy must be waiting for you," she said. "You had better go to her. She has a new thing by Grieg that she wanted to play for you. . . . A very interesting piece."

"Missy has nothing to play to me. I wonder why this woman never speaks the truth," thought Nekhludov, rising to clasp the transparent, bony, jeweled fingers.

He was met in the drawing room by Katerina Alexeyevna.

"The duties of a juryman seem to have made you melan-choly," she said, in French as usual.

"Yes. Forgive me, I am out of sorts today. I ought not to be here depressing other people," replied Nekhludov.

"Why are you out of sorts?"

"I must ask you to excuse me from explaining," he said, looking around for his hat.

"Why won't you say? Don't you remember how you used to tell us that we must always speak the truth, and the unpleasant truths you told us in those days? Didn't he?" said Katerina Alexeyevna, turning to Missy, who had just entered the room.

"We were playing a game," replied Nekhludov, gravely. "One may tell the truth in games. But in real life we are so wicked—I mean I am so wicked, that I should never dare to tell the truth."

"Oh, don't trouble to correct yourself; better tell us why *we* are so wicked," said Katerina Alexeyevna, still in a bantering tone, as she pretended to ignore Nekhludov's seriousness.

"There is nothing so foolish as to acknowledge that one is out of sorts," said Missy. "I never admit that even to myself, so

I am always in good spirits. Won't you come into my room? We will try to dispel your *mauvaise humeur.*"

Nekhludov understood how a horse must feel when it is being coaxed into accepting the harness and bit. Never had he felt less inclined to draw his load than today. He excused himself, declaring that he really must go home, and began to say goodby. Missy retained his hand longer than usual.

"Remember that what is of importance to you is also of importance to your friends. Are you coming tomorrow?"

"It's doubtful," he replied, blushing, hardly knowing whether he felt ashamed for himself or for her; and he left hurriedly.

"What does all this mean? *Comme cela m'intrigue,*" said Katerina Alexeyevna. "I must find out. Probably some *affaire d'amour-propre, il est très susceptible, notre cher Mitya.*"

"Plutôt une affaire d'amour sale," Missy was about to say, but she stopped and looked in front of her with a face from which all the light had gone, quite different from when she looked at Nekhludov. She could not utter the vulgar little pun even to Katerina Alexeyevna, so she contented herself with saying:

"We all have our good and bad days."

"Can it be possible that he, too, will deceive me?" she thought. "After all that has happened, it would be very cruel of him." If Missy had been asked to explain what she understood by "all that has happened," she could have told of nothing very definite, yet she felt sure that he had more than raised her hopes, and had almost given her a promise. It was not so much the words as the smiles, the hints, and the silences. She had considered him hers, and it would be hard to lose him.

❧

CHAPTER TWENTY-EIGHT

"I AM ashamed and disgusted, disgusted and ashamed," thought Nekhludov, walking home through the familiar streets. The melancholy he had experienced while talking to Missy still clung to him. While he knew that she had no formal claim on him, that he had never said anything that could be considered binding, had never made a formal proposal, yet the fact remained that he did feel himself bound to her, for he had given her a tacit if not a verbal promise. Today his whole nature rebelled against the thought of marrying her. "I am ashamed and disgusted," he kept repeating to himself, thinking not only of his relationship with Missy, but of everything else. "I am ashamed and disgusted about everything," he kept repeating as he stepped into the porch of his house.

"You may go. I shall not want any supper," he said to Korney, who had followed him into the dining room, where tea was ready for him.

"Yes, sir," said Korney, but instead of going away he began to clear the table. Nekhludov looked at him with annoyance. He longed to be alone, and it seemed as though everybody was purposely bothering him. When Korney had finally carried away the dishes, Nekhludov was about to go to the samovar to make the tea, but, hearing the footsteps of Agrafena Petrovna, he hurriedly retreated into the drawing room, closing the door after him.

In this drawing room his mother had died three months before. Now it was lighted by two tall lamps with reflectors, one standing near his father's portrait and the other near his mother's; as he looked at them his mind reverted to his relationship with his mother, which now seemed repulsive and unnatural. This, too, was shameful and disgusting. He remembered how, during her last illness, he had longed for her death. He had told himself that he wished it for her sake so that she might be free from suffering, while all he really wanted was to escape from the sight of her suffering. Anxious to recall a pleasing memory of her, he looked at her portrait, for which he had paid five thousand rubles. It was the work of a famous artist. She was painted in a low-cut gown of black velvet. Evidently the artist had taken great pains over the neck, the shadow between the breasts, and the dazzling shoulders. This seemed shameful and disgusting to him now. There was something repellent and blasphemous in that picture of his mother painted as a half-naked beauty, hanging in the very room where three months ago she had lain emaciated and dry as a mummy, filling the room and indeed the whole house with a heavy, sickening smell which nothing could overpower.

Even now he seemed to breathe it, and he remembered how the day before she died she had clasped his strong hand in her bony, discoloring fingers and, looking into his eyes, had said: "Don't condemn me, Mitya, if I have done wrong," and how the tears had come into her eyes dulled by pain. "How shocking!" he said, looking at the half-naked woman with her exquisite marble shoulders and arms and her triumphant smile. The shoulders reminded him of another young woman whom he had seen not long ago in this same half-naked state. It was Missy, who had made some excuse for calling him into her room one night just as she was ready to start for a ball in order to show herself in evening dress. The recollection of her beautiful neck and arms was disgusting to him now, and so was that coarse, vulgar father of hers with his evil past and cruelty, and that *bel-esprit,* her mother with her doubtful reputation. All this was shameful and disgusting, disgusting and shameful.

"No, no!" he thought, "I must escape from my false relationship with the Korchagins and with Maria Vassilyevna, I must give up my estate. I must get away from everything connected with them all. . . . If only I could breathe freely—go abroad, to Rome perhaps, and work at my picture." Then, as his misgivings about his talent for painting recurred to him: "Well, anyway, breathe freely. First Constantinople, then Rome." But he could do nothing until the matter of the jury and his affair with the lawyer was settled. Suddenly, with marvelous clarity, there came into his mind the image of the prisoner with her black, slightly squinting eyes. He had not forgotten the sound of her sobbing when the prisoners had been allowed to say their last words. Agitatedly stubbing out one cigarette in the ash tray and lighting another, he began to pace up and down the room; and the minutes he had spent with Katusha came back and lived with him again. He remembered their last meeting, his overmastering passion and early disillusion. He remembered the white dress with the blue sash, and the Easter service.

"I loved her really that night, with a love that was pure and good—indeed I loved her before, when I first stayed with my aunts and was writing my thesis!" And as he thought of himself as he had been then, it was like a breeze blowing from the land of youth and fullness of life, and he grew unspeakably sad.

The difference was immense between what he had been then and what he was now; as great, if not greater, than the difference between Katusha as she was in the church that night and the prostitute, condemned this very morning, who had been carousing with the merchant. Then he had been free, fearing nothing, a man with endless possibilities before him; whereas now he felt entangled in the meshes of a vapid, insignificant, and purposeless life from which he could see no way of escape—and he was not even sure that he cared to find one. He remembered how proud he had always been of his straightforwardness, how he had made it a rule always to speak the truth and had indeed been truthful; now he was living a lie, a fearful lie, and everyone who knew him accepted this lie as if it were the truth. And there was no way out of it, or if there was, he didn't know how to find it. He had been so long in the mire that he was accustomed to it and enjoyed it.

How was he to break off his connection with Maria Vassilyevna and her husband, and be once more able to look him in the eyes without a blush? How disentangle himself from Missy without a lie? How was he to reconcile two opposing duties, the responsibilities of his mother's legacy and the renunciation of that land he believed it unlawful to possess? How atone for his sin against Katusha? Something more must be done about that. He could not thus abandon a woman whom he had once loved, nor think that it was enough to pay a lawyer to rescue her from a sentence she had not deserved. To atone for his fault by a payment of money was too much like what he had done years ago.

And he vividly remembered the moment when he had overtaken her in the corridor, thrust the money into her frock, and ran away. "Ah, that money!" He remembered how disgusted he had been with himself at the time, and the same feeling came over him again. "What atrocity!" he said aloud. "Only a scoundrel and a blackguard could have done that. And I—I was the man who played the scoundrel's part. Can it be possible that I really am a scoundrel?" he said, pausing in his walk. "I, and no other? And this is not my sole offense," he continued, himself his own accuser and his own judge. "Isn't my relation to Maria Vassilyevna and her husband a base, cowardly affair? And my estate? Is it honest to use the wealth my mother left me, when I believe in my heart that it is unlawful? And what of all my idle, evil life? And the climax of all my wickedness—my conduct toward Katusha? A scoundrel and a blackguard! Men may judge me as they wish; they are easily deceived, but I cannot deceive myself."

Then suddenly it dawned upon him that the disgust he had been feeling that day for everything and everybody, but particularly for the prince, Maria Vassilyevna, Missy, and, last of all, poor Korney, was really disgust for himself. It is surprising that the recognition of one's own baseness should be accompanied by a sense of relief, and yet Nekhludov, for all his distress, felt comforted.

More than once in his life he had undertaken what he called "the cleansing of the soul." This was the name he gave to certain mental exercises to which he subjected himself at intervals on discovering the slothfulness and wickedness of his inner life:

he would work to clear away the rubbish that encumbered his soul and hindered all proper action.

After such an awakening Nekhludov would make rules, fully intending to observe them; he would keep a diary and begin a new life which, he hoped, was to go on forever. This he called (using the English phrase) "turning over a new leaf." But time after time the temptations of the world ensnared him and, before he knew it he had fallen—sometimes lower even than before.

Thus he had had several seasons of awakening and purification. He had been going through one of these periods when visiting his aunts that first time. It was his most intensely enthusiastic revival, and its effects lasted a long while. Again, when he gave up the civil service and entered the army during wartime, with the idea of sacrificing his life for his country; but there the rot set in very soon. Another awakening came when he resigned from the army and went abroad to study painting.

From that day to this there had been no period of moral renovation, and never had he felt in greater need of cleansing. He was horrified at the chasm that separated the life he was leading from the demands of his own conscience. At first it seemed hopeless. Such confusion! Such rubbish! Who could possibly set the house in order?

"Have you not already tried to be a better man, and what did it amount to?" said the voice of the tempter, speaking in his soul. "Why should you try again? You are only one of many: that is life," whispered the voice. But the spiritual nature, which alone is true, alone powerful, alone eternal, had already awakened in Nekhludov, and he could not but trust it. However vast the disparity between what he was and what he wished to be, nothing could discourage this newly awakened spiritual being.

"Cost what it may, this lie that binds me shall be broken; I shall tell the truth, the whole truth, before them all," he said aloud, with resolution. "I shall tell the truth to Missy, she shall know that I am a profligate, unfit to marry her, and have disturbed her peace for nothing. I shall tell Maria Vassilyevna— no, the better way would be to tell her husband that I am a scoundrel, that I have deceived him. I shall dispose of the estate and all the world shall know my reasons. I shall tell Katusha that I am a scoundrel, that I have sinned against her and that I shall do all in my power to make her life easier. Yes, I will see her and beg her pardon, as children do."

He stopped. "I will marry her, if I must!" He folded his hands on his breast as he used to do when he was a child, raised his eyes, and said:

"Help me, O Lord! teach me, abide in me and deliver me from all this abomination!"

He prayed, asking God to enter into him and purify him; and while he was thus praying, it came to pass. God was dwelling in his awakened conscience. He found himself one with God—and, therefore, not only the freedom, the courage, and the joy of life became his own, but all the power of righteousness. The best a man could do, he now felt himself capable of doing.

Tears came to his eyes while he was praying, good tears and evil tears: good tears of joy at the awakening of his spiritual nature, all these years buried in slumber, and evil tears of self-pity and admiration for his own virtue. He felt hot; he went and opened the window looking into the garden. It was a still, moon-lit night; the air was fresh. Something rattled past, then silence fell. Directly under the window the shadow of a tall poplar fell across the walk, the outline of its bare branches sharply defined upon the gravel. On the left, the roof of the coach house seemed white in the bright moonlight. Through the black interlacing branches of the trees he caught glimpses of the dark shadows of the garden wall. Nekhludov looked at the moonlit garden, the the roof, and the shadows of the poplar; he listened, and breathed the fresh, invigorating air.

"How beautiful, how beautiful, O Lord, how beautiful!" he said—but he was speaking of the beauty born within his own heart.

❦

CHAPTER TWENTY-NINE

IT was six o'clock in the evening when Maslova reached her cell. Unaccustomed to walking, she felt weary and footsore: she must have traveled ten miles, trudging over those stony pavements. Moreover, she was crushed by the severity of her sentence, and she was hungry.

Her mouth had watered when she saw the guards eating bread and hard-boiled eggs during the recess, but she considered it beneath her dignity to ask them for food. After three hours had gone by, hunger departed and faintness took its place. It was then she heard the unexpected sentence. At first she thought she had not heard aright; she could not believe her own ears, or think of herself as a convict. But seeing the quiet, businesslike faces of the judges and the jury, who regarded the sentence as a matter of course, she rebelled and cried aloud that she was innocent. Then, when even her exclamation was taken as a matter of course, as an incident of no account, she burst into tears, feeling that submission to injustice was all that remained to her. It surprised her above all things to be thus cruelly condemned by men—mostly young men—the very ones who had looked at her so approvingly In the waiting room before the trial and during the recesses, she had seen how these men, under the pretext of an errand, would pass the door or come into the room for nothing at all but to gaze at her. And now these very men had condemned her to hard labor, although she was innocent of the crime she was charged with. For a while she wept, then ceased and sat quietly, completely stunned, waiting to be sent back. Her only wish was to smoke. This was the state in which Bochkova and Kartinkin found her when they were also brought into the room after the sentence. Bochkova began at once to shout at her, calling her a convict.

"So you didn't get off after all, did you? You're not going to get off, you mean hussy! You've got no more than your deserts! Out in Siberia you'll have to give up your fine ways, I can tell you that!"

Maslova sat motionless, her head bowed, her hands hidden in the sleeves of the prison cloak, looking steadily at the dirty floor in front of her.

"I don't meddle with you—I wish you wouldn't meddle with me," she repeated several times, then fell back into silence. It was only after Bochkova and Kartinkin had been removed, and the guard had brought her three rubles, that she brightened up a little.

"Are you Maslova?" he inquired. "Here's something a lady sent you," he said, giving her the money.

"What lady?"

"You just take it, and make no more fuss about it."

The money had been sent by Kitaeva. When about to leave the courtroom she asked the usher if she could send Maslova some money; having received the permission, she took off her three-button glove, put her plump white hand into the pocket of her silk gown, and drew out a stylish pocketbook. She opened it and selected from a large number of new clean notes, one to the value of two rubles and fifty kopecks and, adding a few silver coins in change, handed it to the usher. A guard was called and the money entrusted to him before she left the room.

"Be sure you gif it to her," said Kitaeva. It was this implied suspicion of his honesty that had annoyed the guard and made him surly with Maslova.

Maslova was glad to have the money for the sake of what she now most craved. "If I could only buy some cigarettes," she thought; she could think of nothing else but her intense longing to smoke. So eager was she that she inhaled greedily every time a whiff of tobacco penetrated into the corridor through the doors of the lobby. But she had to wait a long time because the secretary, whose business it was to give the order for her return, forgot all about her, being engrossed in a discussion with one of the lawyers about the censored newspaper article. At last, toward five o'clock, she was allowed to leave, and the guards (the Chuvash and the man from Nizhni Novgorod) took her out through the door at the back. Before she left the corridor she gave them twenty kopecks and asked them to buy her two fancy loaves and some cigarettes. The Chuvash smiled, saying, "All right, we'll get 'em," and did in fact buy both articles, giving her back the right change. But they could not let her smoke in the street, so she returned to the prison with the craving unsatisfied.

As they approached the entrance, about a hundred convicts who had arrived by rail were being led in. She encountered them in the passage. Young and old, Russians and foreigners, bearded and clean-shaven, and some with shaven heads, these men came along, clanking their chains, and filling the passage with dust and noise and the bitter smell of sweat. All of them stared at her and some deliberately pushed against her in passing.

"Here's a good-looking lass!" said one.

"My best respects to you, miss!" said another, with a wink.

A dark man, with shaven head and a black mustache, stumbled over his rattling chains as he sprang toward her and seized hold of her.

"Don't you know a friend when you see him? Come on, none of your airs, now!" he exclaimed, grinning, and his eyes glittered when she pushed him away.

"What are you doing, you scoundrel?" cried the inspector's assistant, coming up from behind.

The fellow cringed and shrank away quickly. Then the assistant turned to Maslova.

"What are you here for?"

She was going to say that she had just been brought back

from the court, but she was so tired that she could not bring herself to speak.

"She has come from the court, sir," said the older man of the escort, stepping forward with his hand to his cap.

"Then why don't you deliver her to the chief warder and put a stop to this fooling!"

"Yes, sir!"

"Sokolov, see to her!" cried the assistant.

The chief warder went up to Maslova and gave her an angry push; then, making a sign to follow him, he escorted her into the women's ward.

In the corridor she was searched and, nothing prohibited being found on her—the box of cigarettes had been cleverly hidden in the loaf—she was taken back to the same cell she had left in the morning.

❖

CHAPTER THIRTY

MASLOVA's cell was a long room about twenty feet long and sixteen wide, with two windows, a big stove from which the plastering was peeling off, and some wooden bunks which occupied two-thirds of the floor space. In the middle of the room, opposite the door, hung a dark-colored icon with a wax taper and a dusty bunch of everlasting flowers fastened to it. Behind the door, on the dark, rotten floor to the left, stood a vile-smelling tub. The roll had just been called and the women were shut in for the night.

This cell was occupied by fifteen persons—twelve women and three children.

It was still quite light and only two of the women were lying on the bunks. One was an idiot who had been imprisoned because she had no passport; she spent most of the time sleeping, with a prison cloak drawn over her head. The other, a consumptive, was serving a sentence for theft; she was not asleep but lay with wide-open eyes, the prison cloak folded under her head, doing her best to keep from coughing as the phlegm rose in her throat and choked her. The rest of the women, bareheaded and with nothing on but coarse unbleached linen gowns, either sat on the bunks and sewed, or stood idly by the window gazing out into the yard at the passing convicts. Of the three who were sewing, one was the same old woman, Korablyova, who had seen Maslova off when she left the cell that morning. She was a tall, powerful, austere-looking woman with a flabby double chin, a hairy mole on her cheek, and gray-brown hair braided into a small, tight pigtail. She had been sentenced to penal servitude for killing her husband with an ax because she found him importuning her daughter. She was orderly of the cell and carried on a small trade in drink. She wore spectacles, and in her large sinewy hand she held a needle the way peasants do, grasping it with three fingers, the point aimed at her breast. The woman who sat next to her, making coarse linen bags, was a little creature with a pug nose, sallow skin, and small black eyes, kind and talkative. She had been employed as signal woman on the railway. One day she was not at her post, no flag was shown, an accident occurred, and she was sentenced to three months' imprisonment. The third woman who was sewing —her companions called her Fenichka, but her name was really Fedosya—was young and attractive. Her cheeks were rosy and her eyes were blue. Her thick brown hair was coiled in two plaits round her small head. She had attempted to poison her husband. It happened very soon after their marriage, when she was only sixteen. While she was on bail awaiting her trial, a reconciliation took place, and eight months afterward, when the trial was about to begin, they were living together—as tender and devoted a couple as could be found. Her husband and his parents—his mother particularly, who had become very fond of the girl—moved heaven and earth to obtain her acquittal, but it was of no use. She was sentenced to hard labor in Siberia. This good-natured, cheerful girl, her face always wreathed in smiles, had her bunk next to Maslova, of whom she had grown so fond that she did everything she could to make her comfortable. Two other women sat on the bunks doing nothing. One seemed about forty years old, probably a handsome woman in her youth, but now very pale, worn, and emaciated. She was nursing a child. One day, in the village where she lived, a young recruit was seized—illegally conscripted, so the peasants thought—and when the villagers stopped the police officer and released their comrade, this woman—an aunt of the recruit—had been the first to catch hold of the bridle of the horse on which they were taking him away. The other woman, who seemed to have nothing to do, was a small, humpbacked, gray-haired, kindly old woman. She was pretending to catch a chubby four-year-old boy with closely clipped hair who was running to and fro, laughing happily. He had nothing on but a shirt, and every time he passed her he cried out, "You didn't catch me that time!" This old woman and her son had been arrested on a charge of arson. She bore her imprisonment with the utmost patience, troubled only about her son who was in the same jail, and still more about her old husband; she was sure he was being devoured by vermin, since her daughter-in-law had gone away and there was no one to keep him clean.

Besides these seven women, there were four others who stood by one of the open windows, leaning on the grating and exchanging remarks with the passing convicts—the same gang that had encountered Maslova. One of these women, who was serving a sentence for theft, was a large, flabby, freckled creature with red hair and a double chin that hung over her unbuttoned neckband. She kept calling to the men in the yard, shouting out unseemly words in a loud, rough voice. Beside her stood an awkward, dark-skinned woman, no bigger than a child of ten, with a long body and short legs. Her face was covered with reddish blotches, her black eyes were set wide apart and, as she burst into shouts of laughter at what went on in the yard, her thick lips parted to reveal large white teeth. This prisoner, nicknamed "Horoshavka"[1] for her love of finery, was to be tried for theft and arson. Behind them, dressed in a dirty gray linen gown, stood a thin, pregnant woman, looking very wretched; she had been arrested for concealing stolen goods. She stood there without speaking, but her smile showed that she was also enjoying the goings on in the yard. The fourth woman at the window was a peasant, short and stout, with prominent eyes and a kindly face, accused of selling spirits without a license. She was the mother of the little boy who was playing with the old woman, and of a seven-year-old girl. As there was no one at home to take care of the children, she had been allowed to bring them with her. She stood near the window, knitting a stocking and glancing out from time to time; she frowned and closed her eyes, apparently in reproof of the unseemly talk. But her seven-year-old daughter, with loose flaxen hair, clothed only in a shirt, stood clutching the red-headed woman's gown with her thin little hand, and with wide-open eyes listened greedily to all the bad words, repeating them softly to herself as if she were learning them by heart. The twelfth prisoner was a subdeacon's daughter, a tall and stately girl, who had drowned her baby in a well. Her loosely braided hair hung in disorder around her face; she wore a dirty gown and her feet were bare.

[1] Formed from a Russian word meaning "to adorn oneself."—Tr.

She took no notice of anything that went on, but just paced up and down the room, her eyes fixed in a dull and glassy stare.

❖

CHAPTER THIRTY-ONE

As the lock rattled and Maslova came in, every eye was turned toward her. Even the subdeacon's daughter stopped for a moment and looked at her wonderingly, before resuming her dogged striding up and down. Korablyova jabbed the needle into her work and peered at Maslova over her spectacles with a questioning look.

"Dear me! Have you come back? I never thought they'd convict you," she said, in a hoarse, masculine voice.

She took off her spectacles and put her work down on the bunk by her side.

"Aunty and I have been talking about it, my little bird, thinking most likely you'd be let off at once," said the signal woman. "Such things have happened. I've even heard they give you money, if you're lucky. Well, we guessed wrong. God knows best, birdy," she went on, in her friendly, singsong voice.

"Have they really convicted you?" asked Fedosya, gazing at Maslova with compassionate tenderness in her large blue eyes. Her bright young face quivered as though she was going to cry.

Maslova made no reply; going silently to her bunk, the second from the door, beside that of Korablyova, she seated herself on the edge.

"I don't suppose you've had anything to eat?" said Fedosya, rising and going to Maslova.

And still Maslova said nothing. She put the loaves down at the head of the bunk and began to undress, taking off the dusty prison cloak and the kerchief from her curly hair.

The humpbacked old woman who had been playing with the boy came up also and stood in front of her. "Tck-tck-tck," she said, with a sympathetic nod, clicking her tongue.

The little boy followed her with open mouth; his eyes were fixed on the loaves. The sight of these many sympathetic faces after all she had gone through today made her want to cry, and her mouth trembled, but she controlled herself until the old woman and the little boy came up. When she heard that sympathetic clicking of the tongue, and particularly when she looked at the boy, who had transferred his earnest gaze from the loaves to her face, she could restrain herself no longer. Her face quivered and she burst out sobbing.

"I always told you to get a proper lawyer," said Korablyova. "Is it Siberia?"

Maslova could not answer but, still sobbing, she took the box of cigarettes from the loaf of bread—it had a picture of a pink-cheeked lady with a great deal of hair and a V-necked bodice painted on the lid—and handed it to Korablyova. Korablyova looked at the picture, shook her head disapprovingly at the foolish way Maslova spent her money, took out a cigarette and, lighting it by the flame of the lamp, took a whiff herself, then passed it back to Maslova. Maslova, crying all the while, began to smoke avidly.

"Penal servitude," she said at last, with a sob.

"They haven't the fear of God in their hearts, these damned bloodthirsty good-for-nothings! To condemn an innocent girl like that!" cried Korablyova.

A peal of laughter rang out from the women at the window; the little girl also giggled, her thin, childish voice chiming with the hoarse shrill laughter of the adults. A convict in the yard had done something which amused the spectators.

"You bald-headed monkey! Look what he's doing!" cried the red-haired woman, and, swaying her fat body, her face pressed close up to the grating, she shouted some silly, obscene words.

"What are you yelling for, you drum skin?" said Korablyova, shaking her head. Then turning to Maslova she asked, "How long?"

"Four years," replied Maslova, and the tears streamed down her cheeks. One of them trickled onto the cigarette. Maslova angrily crushed and flung it down, then took out another.

The signal woman, though she did not smoke, instinctively picked up the stump and tried to straighten it out as she went on talking. "It's a true saying, my little bird, 'truth has been eaten by the pigs.' They do as they please, nowadays. Some of us here thought you'd get off. Matveyevna said you'd get off. But I says, 'No,' I says, 'I feel in my heart that they'll gobble her up,' and so it turned out," she went on, evidently liking to hear herself talk.

Meanwhile the convicts had all passed through the yard, and the women who had been joking with them left the window, and also came up to Maslova. The first one to come up was the goggle-eyed woman who traded in vodka, with her little girl.

"Did you get a hard one?" she asked, seating herself beside Maslova and going on with her knitting.

"Of course she did!" Korablyova spoke up. "If there'd been money to spend on a proper lawyer who knew what was what she'd have never been condemned. That fellow what's-his-name, the one with the big nose and shaggy hair, he'd bring you out dry from the ocean! If she could only have had him!"

"Him, indeed!" said Horoshavka, with a grin, joining the circle. "He wouldn't spit for less than a thousand rubles!"

"You, too, must have been born under an unlucky star," said the old woman imprisoned for arson. "Just think of it—to entice the lad's wife away and have him locked up to feed the lice, and me in my old age . . ." And she began recounting her story for the hundredth time. "Between the prison and the beggar's pack there's small chance for you. If it isn't the one thing it's the other."

"Yes, that's the way of it," said the vodka seller; glancing at the little girl, she put away her stocking, took the child between her knees and began with practiced fingers to search her head. "A woman oughtn't to sell drink! But how is she going to feed the children?"

These words reminded Maslova of vodka.

"I wish I could have a drink!" she said to Korablyova, wiping her tears away with the sleeve of her gown; sobs still escaped her from time to time.

"All right," said Korablyova.

❖

CHAPTER THIRTY-TWO

MASLOVA took out her money, which she had also hidden in the loaf, and handed it to Korablyova, who went through the ceremony of examining it; being illiterate, she had to appeal to the superior knowledge of Horoshavka, who reported that the scrap of paper was worth two rubles and fifty kopecks; she then went to the chimney, opened the flue, and pulled out a flask filled with vodka. Seeing this, the women who were not among her neighbors in the bunks withdrew to their own places. Meanwhile, Maslova, shaking the dust from her kerchief and cloak, had got into her bunk and begun to eat the bread.

"I saved some tea for you, but I'm afraid it's cold by now," said Fedosya, taking from the shelf a mug and a tinned iron teapot wrapped in an old cloth.

The beverage was cold and tasted more of tin than of tea; but Maslova filled the mug and drank it to moisten her dry bread.

"Here, Finashka, here's a bit for you," she called out; breaking off a piece she gave it to the boy, who was staring at her.

Meanwhile Korablyova had handed her the flask of vodka and a mug. Maslova offered some to Korablyova and Horoshavka. These three prisoners, who were considered the aristocracy of the cell because they had money, shared with one another whatever they possessed.

A few minutes later Maslova had brightened up and was chatting away, describing the trial. She mimicked the prosecutor and told them how funny it had been to see the men so taken up with her. It made no difference where she was: in the courtroom they stared at her, and even when she was in the waiting room they made excuses to come and look at her.

"The guard himself said to me, 'All they come in here for is to see you.' A man would run in and ask, 'Where is such and such a paper?' or something of that sort, but I could see he didn't want any paper at all. He was just eating me up with his eyes all the while," she said, smiling, and shaking her head in wonder. "Oh, they know what they want!"

"That's so," interjected the signal woman, and on she went, pouring forth a stream of talk in her singsong voice. "They are like flies after sugar. They may not know much about other things, but where women come in, they're wide awake! They'd sooner go without bread . . ."

"And even here," interrupted Maslova, "it's the same thing. When I came in, a gang of convicts had just been brought up from the railway. If it hadn't been for the inspector I don't know how I'd have managed to get rid of them. As it was, I had all I could do to get away from one man."

"What sort of fellow was he?" asked Horoshavka.

"Dark, with a mustache."

"That must be the one."

"What one?"

"Shcheglov. The man that just went along."

"And who is he?"

"Haven't you heard about Shcheglov? He has escaped from Siberia twice. They've caught him now, but he'll get away again. Even the warders are afraid of him," said Horoshavka, who sent notes to the male convicts and knew all that was going on in the prison. "Mark my word, he'll escape again."

"If he goes, he'll not take you and me along with him," said Korablyova. "You'd better tell us what the lawyer said about your appeal," she said to Maslova. "Have you got to send it in right away?"

Maslova replied that she didn't know anything about it.

Just then the red-haired woman, with both her freckled hands plunged in her tangled hair, walked up to the "aristocracy," busily scratching her head.

"I'll tell you just what you've got to do, Katerina," she began. "In the first place you must write it down on paper that you're not satisfied with the sentence, and send that to the prosecutor."

"What business have you got around here?" cried Korablyova, in an angry voice. "You smell vodka, that's why you're so interested. We know what to do without your advice."

"What's the matter with you? I'm not talking to you!"

"It's a drink you want, isn't it? That's why you're so nice all at once."

"Well, give her some," said Maslova, who was always giving things away.

"I'll give her something she won't like—"

"Let's see you do it," began the red-haired one, advancing toward Korablyova. "D'you think I'm afraid of you?"

"You prison scum!"

"And what are you?"

"You skinful of guts!"

"A skinful of guts, am I?—You murderess!" shouted the red-haired woman.

"Now, you just keep away from me," said Korablyova, savagely.

But the red-haired woman was beyond warning; she pushed forward, and Korablyova hit her on her heavy breasts. It was as though the red-haired woman had been waiting for that signal. Out flew one hand and grabbed Korablyova by the hair, the other was aimed to strike her in the face. Korablyova warded off the blow while Maslova and Horoshavka tried to pull the red-haired woman away, but she had a firm hold of Korablyova's plait and would not let go. Only for an instant did she relax her grip, and then it was to twist the hair more tightly around her fist. Meanwhile, Korablyova, holding her head sideways, was battering the red-haired woman in the chest and trying to bite the hand tearing out her hair. All the other women crowded around the combatants, screaming and doing their best to separate them. Even the consumptive drew near and stood coughing as she watched the fight. The children huddled together, crying.

Presently, hearing the noise, the warder and the matron came in and separated them. Korablyova unbound her gray plaits and the loose hair that had been torn out fell to the floor. The red-haired woman tried to pull her ragged gown together. Both shouted loudly, complaining and trying to explain what had happened.

"It's vodka that's at the bottom of all this!" said the matron. "Tomorrow I shall report you to the inspector. He'll attend to you. I can smell it! You'd better get rid of it if you know what's good for you. We've no time to listen to your stories now. Go to your bunks and keep quiet!"

But it was a long time before they could be reduced to silence. Across the room the women kept shouting at each other about how it had all begun and whose fault it was. At last the warder and the matron went away, and the women, calming down, began to get ready for bed. The old woman stood before the icon and said her prayers.

"Aah—you convicts!" came the hoarse voice of the red-haired woman from the other end of the room; she accompanied her words with extraordinarily complicated swearing.

"You'd better look out for yourself, or you'll catch it again," retorted Korablyova, with a train of similar abuse.

Then both relapsed into silence.

"If they hadn't interfered, I'd have scratched your old eyes out!" began the red-haired one again, and again Korablyova retorted in kind.

Then came a longer interval of silence, followed by fresh abuse. However, the intervals grew longer and longer, and finally all was quiet.

Most of the women were in bed; some were snoring; the only ones still up were the old woman bowing before the icon (she always spent a long time over her prayers) and the subdeacon's daughter who, as soon as the warders had left, got up and began again to pace the room.

Maslova was not asleep. She was thinking to herself: "Now I am really a convict," for she had been called so twice: once by Bochkova and again by the red-haired woman. She could not get used to the idea.

Korablyova, who had been lying with her back toward her, now changed her position.

"I never dreamed I should come to this," said Maslova, in a low voice. "Other people do far worse things than I ever did, and they get away free while I have to suffer for a crime 1 never committed."

"Don't be so downhearted, girl! Siberia isn't death—people manage to get on there. You'll survive it," said Korablyova, trying to comfort her.

"I know I'll survive it. Still, it's hard. I didn't deserve this."

"You can't go against the will of God," said Korablyova, with a sigh. "You can't go against Him!"

"I know that, aunty, but it's hard all the same."

They were silent for a while.

"Here, listen to that wretch!" said Korablyova, calling Maslova's attention to a strange sound coming from the opposite end of the cell.

It was the suppressed sobbing of the red-haired woman. She was crying over the beating she had had and the vodka that she hadn't—vodka she wanted badly. And then she cried because her whole life had been one succession of abuse, jeers, insults, and blows. She tried to comfort herself by remembering her first sweetheart, a factory hand called Fedka Molodenkov, but when she thought of this, she also had to think of how it ended. Molodenkov had rubbed vitriol on the most sensitive spot of her body when he was drunk, and had made a joke of it with his mates while she writhed in agony. She thought of this and was full of pity for herself. Thinking that no one could hear, she began to cry aloud, as children do, sniffling and swallowing her salt tears.

"You can't help feeling sorry for her," said Maslova.

"No, of course you can't; but she's got to behave herself."

⚜

CHAPTER THIRTY-THREE

NEKHLUDOV'S first sensation when he awoke the next morning was a dim consciousness that something important and good had happened to him.

"Katusha . . . the trial!" Yes, the first thing was to stop lying and speak the entire truth. By a singular coincidence he received, that very morning, the long-expected letter from Maria Vassilyevna, the marshal's wife—a letter that was now of no especial use to him. She gave him full liberty and wished him happiness in his approaching marriage. "Marriage!" he exclaimed, sarcastically. "I am a long way from marriage."

He remembered his last night's intention of telling her husband everything, of asking forgiveness and declaring his readiness to give full satisfaction. But today this did not seem so simple a matter. After all, why make a man miserable when he might just as well be left in ignorance? "If he were to ask, then I would tell him. But what is the good of going to him voluntarily and telling him everything?" It also seemed more difficult to tell the truth to Missy, now in the new light of the morning. It really was not his place to speak: it would be insulting. The usual *convenances* called for a certain discretion, and absolute frankness was out of place. Some things must be taken for granted. He made up his mind on one problem this morning: he would visit there no more, and would speak the truth if asked the reason why. But, so far as his relations with Katusha were concerned, nothing should be left unspoken.

"I shall go to the prison and tell her everything. Then I shall beg her to forgive me and if need be—yes, if need be, I shall marry her," he said to himself.

The thought of marrying her and giving up everything for the sake of a moral principle was greatly consoling to him that morning.

He had not felt so energetic for a long time. He spoke to Agrafena Petrovna with more firmness than he had given himself credit for; he told her that he should no longer require either his present flat or her services. There had been a tacit understanding that he was keeping this spacious flat because he was going to be married. Therefore, when he said he should no longer need it, Agrafena Petrovna looked at him in surprise.

"I am much obliged to you, Agrafena Petrovna, for all your care; but I have no longer any use for this large place and so many servants. If you wish to help me, will you be kind enough to see to the furniture and have it stored for a while, as you used to do when my mother was living? And when Natasha comes, she will see to things." (Natasha was Nekhludov's sister.)

Agrafena Petrovna shook her head.

"Store away the things? Why, you'll need them again."

"No, they won't be needed, Agrafena Petrovna. That is certain," said Nekhludov, answering the thought in her mind. "Please tell Korney that I shall pay him two months' wages, and that I shall no longer require his services."

"You may be sorry, Dmitri Ivanovich," she said. "Even if you go abroad, you will still need an establishment."

"You are wrong, Agrafena Petrovna. I'm not going abroad. If I go anywhere it will be in quite another direction."

Here he suddenly blushed. "I shall have to tell her; nothing can be kept back; everyone must be told," he thought.

"A very strange and unusual thing has happened to me," he said. "I expect you remember Katusha, who used to live with Aunt Maria Ivanovna?"

"To be sure I do. I taught her to sew."

"Well, Katusha was on trial yesterday, and I was one of the jury."

"What a shame! What was she accused of?" exclaimed Agrafena Petrovna.

"Of murder, and it was all my fault."

"How can that be? That's a very strange way of talking," said Agrafena Petrovna, her old eyes sparkling as she spoke. She knew all about the affair with Katusha.

"Yes, it was entirely my fault. And that is why all my plans are changed."

"Why should you change them?" she said, repressing a smile.

"Because I am the man who started her along that path, and I must do what I can to help her."

"Of course, you may do what you please, but I must say I can't see that it's any particular fault of yours. Such things happen to everybody, and if people use their common sense affairs like that are soon overlooked and forgotten." Here her voice took a more serious tone: "You ought not to take all the blame on yourself. I heard that she had gone to the bad, but who's to blame for that?"

"I am. And that's the reason why I want to put things right."

"It's not easy to put right."

"That's my affair. But if you are thinking about yourself, then let me say that the wish which my mother expressed—"

"I am not thinking about myself. I have been so generously treated by the late princess that I have nothing more to wish for. Lizanka" (her married niece) "wants me to live with her, and I shall go there when I'm no longer wanted here. Only you ought not to take this so much to heart. Such a thing might happen to any man."

"Well, I don't think so. But I will ask you again to help me to let the flat and pack away the things. And please don't be angry with me. I'm very grateful for all you have done for me."

Strangely enough, since Nekhludov had begun to realize his own faults he no longer felt any dislike for other people. On the contrary he felt most amiably disposed toward both Agrafena

Petrovna and Korney. He was eager to confess himself to Korney also, but Korney's manner was so austerely deferential that he could not find the courage to approach him.

On the way to the courts, driving through the same streets with the same cabby, Nekhludov was surprised to find himself such a different being.

His marriage with Missy, which had seemed so probable yesterday, was quite impossible today. Yesterday he had felt that she would be only too happy to marry him; today he felt unworthy to offer her even friendship, not to speak of marriage. "If she only knew what I am, she would not receive me. And I was reproaching her for flirting with another man! Even if she consented to marry me, how could I enjoy any happiness or peace of mind knowing that Katusha was in prison, and that one of these days she would be leaving for Siberia with a party of convicts? How could I be making social calls with a young bride while the woman I had deceived was in penal servitude? Or how could I keep up my friendship with the marshal, who has been so shamefully deceived by me, how could I go on counting votes for and against proposals for inspecting schools, all the while making appointments with his wife? Horrible thought! And how could I go on with my picture? Certainly that will never be finished now. What right have I to throw my time away on painting? No," he said to himself, "that belongs to the past," and he rejoiced at the spiritual change that had come to him.

"In the first place I must see the lawyer and hear what he has decided to do, and then . . . then go and see her in prison, and tell her everything!" he thought.

And when he imagined himself in her presence, telling her everything—his repentance for his sin and his determination to atone for it by marrying her—a feeling of rapture filled his heart and brought tears into his eyes.

❖

CHAPTER THIRTY-FOUR

ON reaching the courts, Nekhludov met an usher in the corridor, the same he had seen on the previous day. He asked him where the prisoners were kept after sentence, and who could give permission to visit them.

The usher explained that the criminals were kept in different places and that, until they received their sentence in its final form, permission to visit them depended on the government prosecutor.

"I will attend to that for you after the session is over. The prosecutor isn't here yet, but after the session you can see him. Now please go into court. It will open in a few minutes."

Thanking the usher for his courtesy, Nekhludov turned toward the jury room.

As he approached, his fellow jurymen were just leaving to go into court. The merchant, having eaten and drunk well, was as merry as ever and greeted Nekhludov like an old friend. Today, even the familiarity and boisterous laughter of Piotr Gerassimovich excited no aversion in Nekhludov. He longed to tell the jurymen about his relationship with the prisoner of yesterday. "That's what I ought to have done then, while the trial was going on," he said to himself. "I ought to have made a public acknowledgment of my sin!" But when he entered the courtroom with the other jurors and heard the usual proclamation, "The judges are coming," when he saw them on the platform in their embroidered collars, saw the jurors take their seats in the high-backed chairs, saw the gendarmes and the priest, the silence of the room was so impressive that, though he still felt it his duty to speak, he had not the courage to disturb this solemn assembly.

The preparations for the trial were the same as on the day before, except that the swearing in of the jury and the address by the president were omitted.

Today the case was one of burglary. The culprit, guarded by two gendarmes with drawn swords, was a thin, narrow-shouldered, pale-faced lad of twenty, wrapped in a gray prison cloak. He sat alone in the dock, peering from under his eyebrows at the newcomers. He was accused of having broken into a shed and stolen some old mats valued at three rubles sixty-seven kopecks. According to the indictment, it seemed that the policeman had arrested him as he was walking away with one of his mates, the latter carrying the mats on his shoulder. They had both confessed at once and had been taken to jail. His mate, a locksmith, had died in prison, so the boy was to be tried alone. The old mats were lying on the table as material evidence.

The trial was conducted in exactly the same way as on the previous day, with all the ritual of evidence, oaths, questions, witnesses, experts and cross-examinations. The policeman called as a witness answered all the questions put to him by the president, public prosecutor, and counsel for the defense with equal lack of interest: "Exactly" . . . "I couldn't say" . . . "Exactly" . . . He was clearly sorry for the boy and his stereotyped replies and stolid, military manner barely concealed his reluctance to testify against him.

The other witness, an elderly, bilious man, was the owner of the mats. He identified them after some hesitation, but when the assistant prosecutor asked him for what purpose he used them and what he was going to do with them, he became excited and exclaimed: "They're of no use to me at all! I'd rather have given ten or twenty rubles than had all this fuss! If I'd known what a bother it was going to make, I would never have gone looking for them. Now I've wasted five rubles on cabbies, and I'm not in good health—I suffer from rheumatism and hernia."

So testified the witnesses. The prisoner stood like a trapped animal, casting furtive glances around the room; he confessed his guilt and in broken sentences told how it all happened.

It was quite simple. But the assistant prosecutor shrugged his shoulders as he had done the day before, and put the same kind of shrewd questions, designed to entrap a cunning culprit.

In his argument he showed that the theft had been not only committed in a dwelling place but accompanied by forcible entrance; the lad had broken the lock and must therefore be severely punished.

The lawyer appointed for the defense contended that the theft had not been committed in a dwelling place and that although the crime itself could not be denied, the criminal was not the menace to society that the assistant prosecutor had described.

As on the previous day, justice and impartiality were personified in the president; he explained to the jurors what they already knew and could not help knowing. Then came the usual recesses, which were spent in smoking, and again the usher, in his usual loud voice, proclaimed "The court is coming" and the gendarmes with their drawn swords made the same effort to keep awake.

The proceedings showed that this lad's father had apprenticed him in a tobacco factory, where he had worked for five years. This year he had been discharged by the owner after a strike. Being out of work, he hung about in public houses, spending what little he had on drink. Here he fell in with the locksmith, out of work like himself and a drinking man as well. One night, when they were both drunk, they broke the lock in question and took the first thing that came to hand. They were caught and sent to jail, where the locksmith died before the trial. The boy was now being tried as a dangerous character against whom society must be protected.

"Just as dangerous a creature as yesterday's criminal," thought Nekhludov, as he listened to the argument. "*They* are dangerous, but what about us? What are we? I am a profligate and a liar, and yet no one who knows me despises me on that account! It is easy to see that this poor fellow is just an ordinary lad—anyone could tell that. He is no villain, but simply the natural product of certain influences. If we wish to rid society of that type of boy, we must look after the influences that go to make him what he is. When hunger drove him from the village to the city, if there had been one single person to take pity on him," thought Nekhludov, looking at the boy's terrified and sickly face, "or to have lent him a helping hand—one friend to whisper in his ear, 'I wouldn't do that, Vanya, it isn't right,'—the boy, when tempted by his mates to spend his slender wages in a pothouse after twelve hours' work in the factory, would have listened to that voice; he would never have committed this offense, nor appeared where he is now. But during all those years of his apprenticeship, when the poor little fellow was living in the city like some wild creature caught in a cage, running on errands, with his hair clipped close to his head against lice—no such friend came to his rescue. He heard loud praise for men who led loose lives, for drinking and cheating, brawling and debauchery—'A man like that now, he's a fine fellow!'

"Then, when his health had been ruined by drink and overwork, as he was wandering aimlessly about the streets, he came across a shed and stole a few old mats of no use to any living soul. Now we propose to set the matter right by punishing the boy. All the causes that have contributed to make him what he is today are to be left untouched, and he is to suffer the penalty. It is terrible."

These thoughts passed through Nekhludov's mind, and he paid little heed to the proceedings. He was horrified by his discovery. He wondered why he had not been able to see it all before, and why others were blind to it now.

CHAPTER THIRTY-FIVE

DURING the recess Nekhludov went out into the corridor. He had made up his mind not to go back into the courtroom again. Let them do what they like, he would take no further part in this folly.

He inquired for the prosecutor's room, and was about to enter, but the messenger refused him admittance, saying that the prosecutor was engaged. Nekhludov, however, paid not the slightest attention, but went into the room; he asked the clerk, who came forward, to announce his name to the prosecutor and to say that he was one of the jury and wished to see him on very important business. His title and good clothes were of assistance to his cause. The clerk, after announcing his name, ushered him into the presence of the prosecutor, who had already risen to his feet, and, showing marked displeasure at the persistence with which Nekhludov had demanded this audience, asked sternly, "What is it that you wish?"

"I am on the jury; my name is Nekhludov. I must see the prisoner Maslova." He spoke forcibly and blushed as he did so, realizing that he was taking an irrevocable step which would affect his whole life.

The prosecutor was a short, swarthy man with grizzled hair and keen, sparkling eyes. A thick, closely cut beard covered his prominent chin.

"Maslova? Oh, yes, I know. That is the poisoning case," he said, quietly. "Why do you wish to see her?" Then, as though to soften the abruptness of his question, he added, "I cannot give you permission unless I know your reason for desiring an interview."

"I have a most serious reason," said Nekhludov, reddening.

"Indeed?" said the prosecutor, and, raising his eyes, gazed inquiringly at Nekhludov. "Has her case been heard yet?"

"It was heard yesterday, and she was unjustly condemned to four years' hard labor. She is innocent."

"Yes? Well, if it was only yesterday that she was sentenced," he said, paying no attention to Nekhludov's affirmation of Maslova's innocence, "she will be kept in the preliminary detention prison until the sentence is promulgated in its final form. They have certain visiting days. I advise you to inquire there."

"But I must see her as soon as possible," said Nekhludov, his chin quivering; he knew that the decisive moment was near.

"Why must you?" asked the prosecutor, uneasily, raising his eyebrows.

"Because she has been sentenced to hard labor and because she is innocent. It is I who am the guilty one," replied Nekhludov, in a voice shaking with emotion, feeling that he was uttering words which should have remained unspoken.

"How is that?" asked the prosecutor.

"Because I betrayed her and brought her to this wretched state. She could never have been subjected to such an accusation but for the harm I did her years ago."

"Still, I cannot see how this interview is going to help the matter."

"Only in this way—that I am determined to follow . . . and to marry her," said Nekhludov, and, as always when he spoke of this subject, tears came to his eyes.

"Really? Is it possible?" exclaimed the prosecutor. "This certainly is a strange case—very unusual! I believe you are a member of the Krasnopersk *Zemstvo*?" he asked, as though suddenly placing this Nekhludov who was making such unaccountable revelations.

"I beg your pardon, but I fail to see the connection with my request," replied Nekhludov, growing red and angry.

"Ah, well, of course there is none," said the prosecutor, not at all abashed, and with the shadow of a smile upon his lips. "But your intention is so unusual and extraordinary . . ."

"Then may I have the permission?"

"The permission? Certainly. I will give you an order of admittance at once. Please take a seat."

He went to his desk, sat down, and began to write.

"Please be seated," he repeated.

Nekhludov remained standing.

Having written the order and handed it to Nekhludov, he continued to look at him with an expression of curiosity.

"I must also inform you that I can no longer attend this session," said Nekhludov.

"You will be obliged to present acceptable reasons to the court."

"My only reason is that I consider every law court not only a useless but an immoral institution."

"Indeed?" said the prosecutor, with the same vague smile on his face; his tone implied that he had heard that sort of thing before and found it rather amusing. "That may be. But you will hardly expect me, in my quality of prosecutor, to agree with you. I shall advise you to state your case to the court. Then, if your reasons are valid, the court will grant your request and, if they are not, will impose a fine. All you have to do is to make your declaration to the court."

"I have made my declaration here, and I shall not go anywhere else," said Nekhludov, angrily.

"Then, good day, sir," said the prosecutor, with a bow, evidently anxious to be rid of this strange visitor.

"Who was that?" asked a member of the court entering the room just as Nekhludov was going out.

"Nekhludov. Don't you remember—the one who used to make such queer proposals in the *Zemstvo*? He is serving on the jury, and there's some woman or girl who was sentenced to penal servitude. He says he seduced her, and wants to atone for it now by marrying her."

"Good gracious!"

"Well, that's what he says. He is in a very excited state."

"There's something abnormal about all young men these days."

"He is not so very young."

"No? Oh, I must tell you, my dear fellow, how your famous Ivashenko bored us. He will be the death of us yet! He talks and talks."

"He should be stopped. Such men are nothing but obstructionists. . . ."

❖

CHAPTER THIRTY-SIX

NEKHLUDOV went directly from the prosecutor to the preliminary detention prison, but no Maslova was to be found there. The superintendent explained that she must be in the old jail.

The distance between the two prisons was such that it was nightfall before Nekhludov reached the old jail. He was going up to the entrance of the huge, gloomy building when he was stopped by the sentry, who rang the bell for him.

It was answered by a warder. When Nekhludov showed his pass, the warder said he could not admit him without the inspector's permission, and Nekhludov set off to see the inspector.

As he was going up the stairs, he heard the distant sounds of a complicated piece of bravura played on the piano. When a sulky maid with a bandage over one eye opened the door, the sounds burst out of the room. It was the well-known *Rhapsody* by Liszt, played well until a certain passage was reached; then, every time the pianist came to it, the same thing happened over and over again. Nekhludov asked the maid if the inspector was in. She replied that he was not.

"How soon will he return?"

The *Rhapsody* ceased, only to start off again loudly and brilliantly toward that one charmed note.

"I'll go and ask," said the maid, and went away.

The *Rhapsody* had just got into full swing, but it suddenly came to an abrupt pause, and a woman's voice said: "Tell him he is out and won't be in again today. He is on a visit. Why do they bother so?" The *Rhapsody* began again; but the next minute the music ceased and a chair was hastily pushed back. Evidently the irritated pianist was coming to reprimand the tiresome visitor in person.

"Papa is out," she said, crossly, coming into the anteroom. She looked pale and miserable, with puffed-out hair, and dark circles around her dull eyes. The sight of a young man in a fine overcoat mollified her. "Won't you come in? What is it you wish?"

"I should like to see one of the prisoners."

"A political prisoner, I suppose?"

"No. I have permission from the prosecutor."

"Well, I couldn't tell you, I'm sure. Papa is out. But won't you come in?" she called to him again from the little hall. "Perhaps you might speak to his assistant. He is in the office now. What name, please?"

"I thank you," said Nekhludov, and went out without answering her question.

The door had hardly closed upon him when the same gay and brilliant strain began again, utterly inappropriate to the place and to the sickly girl who was practicing with such untiring perseverance.

Out in the yard, Nekhludov met a young officer with a stiff waxed mustache; when he asked where he could find the assistant, he discovered he was addressing the assistant himself. The latter, glancing at the pass, told Nekhludov that it was made out for the preliminary detention prison, and that he would not like to take the responsibility of admitting him. "Besides, it is out of hours. You had better come tomorrow, which will be a public visiting day. The hour is ten o'clock. And the inspector will be at home. You could then see the prisoner either in the common hall, or in the office if the inspector is willing."

So Nekhludov went home without seeing Katusha after all. He walked thinking no longer of the court, but of his conversations with the prosecutor and the inspector's assistant, and of his attempts to visit Katusha in prison. The expectation of seeing her the next day agitated him to such an extent that he was unable to calm himself for a long time. When he got home he at once brought out his diary, which had long remained untouched, read over a few passages, and wrote down the following:

"It is two years since I last wrote in this diary. I thought I should never return to such childishness. Yet it was not childishness, but rather a communion with myself—with that true, divine self which dwells in every man. All this while that self has slept and I have had no one with whom to commune. It was awakened by a remarkable event which took place in the law court on the twenty-eighth of April, while I was one of the jury. I saw her standing in the prisoners' dock, wrapped in a prison cloak, the very same Katusha I had betrayed. Through a strange mistake, for which I also blame myself, she was sentenced to penal servitude. I have seen the prosecutor and been to the prison. I could not see her, but shall try again. I am determined to do all in my power to see her, and to tell her that I repent of my sin and will atone for it by marriage if need be. May God help me! I feel at peace, and joy has come into my soul."

❖

CHAPTER THIRTY-SEVEN

THAT night Maslova lay wide awake hour after hour and watched the door past which the subdeacon's daughter kept pacing to and fro.

She was thinking that she would never marry one of the convicts in Sakhalin; she was sure she could make a better match than that—perhaps one of the officers, or some clerk or warder, or warder's assistant. Men were all alike when women were about, "but I must look out and not grow thin—that would be the end of me." Then she remembered how the counsel for the defense and even the president himself had stared at her and how the other men in the court had made excuses for passing where she sat. She remembered what Bertha, who paid her a visit at the jail, had told her about the student she used to be so fond of when living at Madame Kitaeva's. He had come there after her arrest, inquired about her and said he was sorry for her. Then the fight with the red-haired woman came to her mind, and she felt sorry for the poor creature. She also thought of the baker who had sent her an extra fancy loaf. She remembered many people, but never once Nekhludov. To her childhood and youth, and to her love for Nekhludov, she never gave a thought. It was too painful. Those memories were buried deep in her heart and she never disturbed them. She never even dreamed of Nekhludov. Today, during the trial, she had not recognized him; and this was not because when she had last seen him he had been a boy in military uniform, with a slight mustache and thick curly hair, whereas now he was a bearded man approaching middle age—it was simply because she never thought of him. She had buried all her memories of him on that terrible night when he had gone through the town without visiting his aunts: that had been when he was on the way home from the war.

Until that night, so long as she had hoped to see him, the child she carried under her heart was no burden to her, indeed, she was often surprised and moved by its soft and sometimes sudden stirring inside her body. But on that night everything changed: the unborn child became nothing but a hindrance.

The aunts were expecting Nekhludov, for they had asked him to come; but he telegraphed that it would be impossible because he must reach Petersburg at a stated time. When Katusha found this out, she made up her mind to see him at the station. The train was due to pass through the station at two o'clock in the morning. After helping the ladies to prepare for the night, she put on her old shoes, tied a kerchief over her head and, taking the cook's little daughter for company, she gathered her skirts and started for the station.

It was a windy and cloudy night in autumn, with occasional showers. The path through the fields was dark enough, but in the woods it was black as pitch, so that although Katusha knew the way, she lost the path and arrived at the little station (where the train only stopped three minutes) not in good time as she had planned, but after the second bell had already rung. As she hurried up the platform she caught sight of Nekhludov

through the window of a first-class compartment. It was brilliantly lighted inside, and two officers seated on velvet chairs opposite each other were playing cards. On the small table near
the window stood two thick, dripping candles. In his close-fitting riding breeches and white shirt, Nekhludov sat on the arm
of a chair, leaning against its back; he was laughing at something. As soon as she saw him she raised her hand, benumbed
with the cold, and tapped upon the window. At that instant the
third bell was rung and the train started. Backing slowly at first
and then lurching suddenly forward, the carriages, bumping
against one another, began to move on.

One of the players stood up, cards in hand, and looked out.
She knocked again, putting her face close to the glass. At that
moment the carriage was jerked forward. She walked beside it,
gazing in at the window. The officer tried to lower the window
but failed.

Nekhludov came forward instead, pushed the officer aside,
and began to lower it himself. Meanwhile the train had increased
its speed so that now Katusha was forced to walk briskly; just
as the window was finally lowered, the guard pushed her aside
and jumped into the carriage. She was left behind, but she went
on, running along the wet boards of the platform till she reached
the end. Here she almost pitched headlong to the ground as she
hurried down the steps, running all the while; but the first-class
carriage was already far away. The second-class and third-class
carriages passed her and still she ran, so that when the last carriage with its rear lamps had gone by, she was beyond the water
tower, beyond any shelter. The wind seized her kerchief and
tore it from her head; it whirled her skirts about, twisting them
around her legs. And still she ran.

"Aunty Mikhailovna!" shouted the little girl, running after
her, "you have lost your kerchief!"

Katusha stopped, threw back her head and, clutching it with
both hands, burst into sobs.

"Gone!" she cried. And she thought: "He—sitting on a
velvet chair, joking and laughing and drinking; I—crying out
here in the dark and the mud, in the rain and the wind!" She sat
down on the ground, sobbing so loudly that the little girl was
frightened and put her arms around her, wet as she was.

"Let's go home, Aunty!"

"Oh, to end it all under the wheels of the next train!" thought
Katusha, making no reply to the little girl.

Yes, that was what she would do. But, as often happens in
the first moments of a lull after great excitement, the child—

his child—gave a push, stretched itself and again pushed with
something thin and delicate and sharp. And all at once everything that had tortured her only a moment ago so that life
seemed worthless, all her bitterness toward him and the desire
to revenge herself, even at the expense of her own life, disappeared. She grew calm, got up, arranged her dress, tied the kerchief over her head, and started for home.

She returned wet, muddy, and exhausted; and from that day
the steady moral change in her began, until she became the
woman she was now. After that dreadful night she lost her faith
in goodness and in God. Once she had believed in Him and
thought that others did too, but, since then she became convinced that no one really believed in Him, and that all that was
said of Him and His law was nothing but trickery and deception. The man she loved, and who had once loved her—of that
she was certain—had abandoned her and trampled upon her
feelings. And yet he was the best man she had ever known. The
others were even worse. Everything that happened afterward
confirmed her in this belief. The pious aunts drove her out of
the house when she could no longer serve them. All the people
with whom she had any dealings wanted to take advantage of
her in one way or another. The men, from the old police officer
to the prison warders, regarded her as an instrument of pleasure,
while the women took all the money they could get from her.
No one cared for anything else but pleasure. Her friend, the old
author whom she had known during the second year in her life
of independence, had supported her in this belief. He told her
plainly that this, which he called poetical and æsthetic enjoyment, constituted all the happiness of life.

Everyone lived for himself and his own pleasure, and all that
had ever been said about goodness and God was a fraud. People
sometimes wondered why everything was so at odds in this
world, why men must suffer and be so wicked and hurt each
other; for her part, she thought it best not to dwell on such
things. If she felt sad she would have a drink or a cigarette, or
better still, she would go with a man—and all the sadness
would vanish.

CHAPTER THIRTY-EIGHT

WHEN, on Sunday morning at five o'clock, the whistle sounded as usual through the corridor of the women's ward, Korablyova, who was already up, woke Maslova.

"I am a convict," thought Maslova, with horror, rubbing her eyes and breathing in the foul morning air. She was still sleepy, but the habit of fear and obedience was stronger than fatigue; she sat on the bunk with her feet drawn up and began to look about the room. Most of the women were up, but the children were still sleeping. The vodka seller with the goggle-eyes was pulling out a prison cloak from beneath the children very gently, so as not to awaken them. The "rebel" was drying the rags that served as swaddling clothes, while the baby was screaming desperately in the arms of blue-eyed Fedosya, who rocked him to and fro as she sang a tender lullaby. The consumptive, with a flushed face, was coughing, holding on to her chest, and gasping loudly, almost screaming, in the intervals of coughing. The woman with the red hair was lying on her back with her knees in the air, cheerfully telling her dream. The old woman accused of arson was again standing before the icon and whispering the same prayer, bowing and crossing herself. The subdeacon's daughter sat motionless on her bunk, with a dull sleepy expression in her eyes, looking in front of her. Horoshavka was curling her coarse greasy black hair round her finger.

Scuffling footsteps echoed along the corridor, the padlock rattled, and two convict-scavengers in short jackets and trousers that hardly reached their ankles, entered the room. With angry, sulky faces they lifted the foul-smelling tub onto the yoke and carried it away. The women then went out to the wash tanks in the corridor. Here again a quarrel broke out between the red-headed woman and one who came from another cell. Screams, abuse, and complaints rang through the passage.

"Is it the solitary cell you're after?" shouted the warder, giving the red-headed woman a slap on her fat back that resounded from one end of the corridor to the other. "Don't let me hear your voice again!"

"I'll be hanged if the old man isn't trying to be playful!" said the woman, taking his blow for a caress.

"Now then, hurry and get ready for Mass."

Maslova had hardly finished combing her hair when the inspector entered. "Call the roll!" he shouted.

Other prisoners came out from their cells, and they formed two ranks along the corridor, the women in the rear placing their hands on the shoulders of those in front while they were counted.

After the roll call they were led to church by a woman warder. Maslova and Fedosya were in the middle of a column made up of more than a hundred women. All wore white kerchiefs, blouses, and skirts, except for a few here and there in their own colored garments. These women were the wives of convicts, who, with their children, were following their husbands to Siberia. The entire stairway was filled with this procession. The soft patter of slippered feet mingled with voices and occasional laughter. At the turning, Maslova saw the sulky face of her enemy Bochkova, who was at the head of the column, and pointed her out to Fedosya. When they reached the foot of the stairs the women became silent; crossing themselves and bowing, they passed through the open door of the still empty church all glittering with gold, and began crowding into their places on the right. Then came the men dressed in long, loose, gray convict cloaks. Some of them were serving short terms of imprisonment, while others were to be banished in conformity with the decisions of their village communes. Coughing noisily, they took up their positions on the left and in the center, forming a solid mass. The gallery was already occupied: one side by convicts with half-shaven heads who made their presence known by the clanking of their chains, and the other by prisoners whose cases had not yet been tried. These were not shaven, and wore no chains.

The prison church was a recent structure, built and decorated by the generosity of a rich merchant who had given some tens of thousands of rubles for the purpose. It glittered with gold and bright colors.

For a time the silence in the church was broken only by coughing, by the blowing of noses, the crying of babies, and, now and then, by the clanking of chains. Presently the prisoners standing in the middle shifted and pressed against one another to make a passage for the inspector, who walked in and took his place in front of them all, in the middle of the church.

CHAPTER THIRTY-NINE

THE service began. This is the way it was conducted:

The priest, robed in a peculiar and very inconvenient garment made of cloth of gold, cut and arranged small pieces of bread on a saucer; these he put into a cup filled with wine, at the same time uttering various names and prayers. Meanwhile, the sub-deacon was steadily reading prayers and then singing them an-tiphonally with a choir composed of prisoners. These prayers were written in old Slavonic—difficult enough to understand at any time, and made still more incomprehensible by the rapid-ity of the reading and singing. They were chiefly supplications on behalf of the sovereign and his family. Their welfare was implored in prayer after prayer, either in the form of a special petition with genuflections, or included in other prayers. Then the subdeacon read several verses from the Acts of the Apostles, in such a strained tone of voice that nothing could be under-stood. Next, the priest read very distinctly that part of the Gospel according to St. Mark wherein we are told that Christ, having risen from the dead, before flying up to heaven to sit on the right hand of His Father, appeared first to Mary Magda-lene, from whom he had driven out seven devils, and then to eleven of the apostles, and ordered them to preach the gospel to all creatures, declaring that he who will not believe shall be lost, and he who believeth and is baptized shall be saved and shall, moreover, have power to cast out devils, to heal men from diseases by the laying on of hands, to speak new tongues, to handle serpents, and if he drinketh poison shall not die, but remain unharmed.

The essence of the service lay in the assumption that the small pieces of bread cut by the priest and dipped in the wine to the accompaniment of certain manipulations and prayers, became the body and blood of God. These manipulations con-sisted in the priest's raising his arms at stated intervals and, encumbered as he was with his cloth-of-gold robe, keeping them in this position, kneeling from time to time and kissing the table and all objects upon it. But the principal act came when the priest, having taken a napkin in both hands, slowly and rhythm-ically waved it over the saucer and the golden cup. This was supposed to be the moment when the bread and wine were transformed into flesh and blood, and therefore this part of the service was performed with special solemnity.

"To the holy, pure, and blessed Mother of God!" the priest cried loudly from behind the partition, and the choir solemnly chanted that it was good to glorify the Virgin Mary who had given birth to Christ, still remaining a virgin, and who was therefore worthy of greater honor than the cherubim and greater glory than the seraphim. Then the transformation was considered accomplished, and the priest, having removed the napkin from the saucer, cut the middle piece of bread into four parts and placed it first in the wine and next in his own mouth. He was supposed to have swallowed a piece of the body of God and to have drunk a portion of His blood. Then the priest drew aside a curtain, opened the middle door and, taking the golden cup in his hands, came out of the door and stood before the people, inviting those who so wished to come and partake of the body and blood of God, which were in that cup.

Only a few children responded to the invitation. Having asked them their names, the priest dipped the spoon into the cup and carefully put a piece of bread dipped in wine into the mouth of each child by turn, taking pains to push the spoon as far in as he could; meanwhile the subdeacon wiped his lips and sang in a merry tone of voice a song about the children eating the body of God and drinking His blood. After that the priest took the cup back with him behind the partition and finished all the remaining bits of God's flesh and drank all the remaining blood. Then he carefully sucked his mustaches, wiped his beard and the cup, and came briskly out from behind the partition in the most cheerful frame of mind, his calfskin boots creaking slightly as he walked.

The most important part of this Christian service was now over, but another service was added for the consolation of the prisoners. The priest stood in front of an image (with black hands and a black face, lit by a dozen wax candles, and covered with beaten gold) which was meant to represent the same God he had been eating, and in a strained falsetto voice, half singing, half speaking, he recited the following words: "Jesu, most sweet, glorified by the Apostles; Jesu, lauded by the martyrs, Almighty Lord, save me, Jesu my Saviour; Jesu most beautiful, have mercy on him who cries to Thee through the prayers of the Holy Virgin and of all Thy saints and Thy prophets; Jesu my Saviour, make me worthy of the sweetness of Heaven, Jesu, Lover of me."

Then he paused, took breath, crossed himself, and bowed to

the ground. All did likewise: the inspector, the warders, and the prisoners in the gallery with their clanking chains. He continued: "Of angels the Creator and Lord of powers, Jesu most wonderful, of angels the amazement; Jesu most powerful, of our forefathers the Redeemer; Jesu sweetest, of patriarchs the praise; Jesu most glorious, of kings the strength; Jesu most good, of prophets the fulfillment; Jesu most amazing, of martyrs the strength; Jesu most humble, of monks the joy; Jesu most merciful, of priests the sweetness; Jesu most charitable, of the fasting the continence; Jesu most sweet, of the just the joy; Jesu most pure, of celibates the chastity; Jesu before all ages, of sinners the salvation. Jesu, Son of God, have mercy upon me." Every time he repeated the word "Jesu" his voice became more and more wheezy. At last he came to a stop and, lifting his silk-lined vestment with one hand, knelt bowing to the ground, while the choir chanted the last words, "Jesu, Son of God, have mercy upon me!" The prisoners fell upon their knees and rose again, tossing back the hair from the unshaved portion of their heads and clanking the fetters that chafed their thin legs.

This continued for a very long time. First came the Gloria, ending always with the words "Have mercy upon me," followed by others ending with the word "Hallelujah." In the beginning the prisoners had crossed themselves and bowed to the ground at every pause, but, as the priest went on, their genuflections diminished in frequency, and they were all glad to have it over when at last the Gloria ended and the priest with a sigh of relief closed his prayer book and withdrew behind the partition.

One last act remained, which consisted in the priest's taking the large gold cross with enameled medallions at each end, that lay on the table, and carrying it into the middle of the church. The inspector kissed it first, then the warders, and lastly the prisoners came crowding one upon another with fiercely whispered vituperations. Talking all the while with the inspector, the priest thrust out the cross so carelessly that the prisoners were often struck upon the nose or the mouth as they tried to kiss both the cross and his hand. Thus ended that Christian service, performed for the comfort and edification of those lost sheep.

CHAPTER FORTY

NOT one among those present, from the priest and the inspector down to Maslova, seemed to be aware that this same Jesus whom the priest glorified with so many queer words and whose name was uttered by him so many times and in such wheezy tones, had expressly forbidden all that had been going on here: not only the senseless chatter and blasphemous incantations of the priest over the wine and the bread, but also, in the clearest words, had forbidden one man to call another master; had forbidden all worship in temples, commanding every man to pray in solitude; had forbidden the very temples themselves, declaring that He had come to destroy them, and that men were to pray not in temples but in the spirit and in truth; but above all the rest, He had forbidden human judgments and the imprisonment of men, and their subjection to the shame, torture or death which was visited on them in this place. He had forbidden violence in all its forms, and had proclaimed that He had come to set the captives free.

It did not occur to anyone present that all this was a sacrilegious mockery of that same Christ in whose name it was being done. No one understood that this gilded cross tipped with enamel medallions, which the priest presented to the lips of the people, was only the emblem of the gibbet on which Christ had died just because He had forbidden the same kind of worship which men were carrying on here in His name. No one suspected that the priests who imagined they were eating the flesh and drinking the blood of Christ, were indeed eating and drinking to their damnation by destroying those "little ones" with whom Christ had identified Himself, by depriving them of their natural blessings and subjecting them to terrible tortures and by concealing from them the good tidings that He had come into the world to announce.

The priest performed his functions with an easy conscience, because he had been brought up from childhood to believe that this was the only true faith. All the saints that had ever lived, the state authorities, and the clergy themselves had held that faith. Of course, the priest did not really believe that bread and wine could become flesh and blood or that it was good for the soul to say so many words or that he had indeed swallowed a piece of God—no one could believe this—but he believed that it was his duty to believe in this belief. One of the most persuasive arguments in favor of this faith of his was that for eighteen years he had received, in reward for his services, an income sufficient to support his family and educate his children in good schools.

The deacon's conviction was even firmer, since he had altogether forgotten the essence of the dogmas of this creed, and remembered only that for the warm wine, for prayers for the dead, for reading the psalms, for a plain thanksgiving service or for a choral thanksgiving service— for everything, in short —there was a fixed price, which devout Christians were ready to pay; that was why he chanted his "Have mercy, have mercy," and read what he had to read as a matter of course, just as another man sells wood or flour or potatoes.

The prison inspector and the warders (although they had never known or understood the dogmas or the significance of all the church ceremonial), all thought that a man must believe this creed because the state authorities and the tsar himself believed it. Moreover, they felt, although they could not explain why, that this creed was a justification of their cruel duties. If there had been no such creed it would have been harder for them—indeed, it would have been impossible—to spend all their energy in tormenting human beings, as they were doing now with a perfectly easy conscience. The inspector was such a kindhearted man that he could never have lived as he was now living, if he had not been sustained by his religion. So he stood motionless, or crossed himself and made devout genuflections, and tried to feel deeply moved when the Cherubim song was sung. When the priest began to administer the Sacrament to the children, he took a few steps forward and lifting a small boy held him up to the priest.

Most of the prisoners (although there were a few exceptions —men able to see the deception that was practiced on the people, and who laughed at it in the secrecy of their hearts) believed that these gilded icons, tapers, chalices, vestments, and crosses, and the repetitions of the unintelligible words, "Sweetest Jesu," "Have mercy," possessed a mysterious power which was a talisman to the goods of this life and those of the world to come. Although most of them had tried the efficacy of praying and offering *Te Deums* and candles for the goods of this life, and had been disappointed, yet they still firmly believed that their lack of success was accidental and that an institution approved by learned men and archbishops must be a thing of the greatest importance, indispensable for the next world if not for this.

This was the way in which Maslova believed. Like the rest, she felt a combination of devotion and boredom. At first she had stood in the middle of the crowd behind the partition, and could see no one except her companions; but when the communicants began to move forward she and Fedosya stepped forward too, and then she saw the inspector and the warders and, standing near them, Fedosya's husband, a peasant with a light beard and chestnut hair, who never took his eyes off his wife. Maslova, during the anthem, kept watching him and whispering to Fedosya, making a mechanical sign of the cross and genuflecting when the others did.

❖

CHAPTER FORTY-ONE

NEKHLUDOV left the house in the early morning. A peasant from the country was driving along one of the side streets crying "Milk-O" in the voice peculiar to his trade. The first warm spring rain had fallen the day before, and wherever the streets were not paved the shooting grass shone green. The birches in the gardens looked as if they were covered with green down; the wild cherries and the poplars were unfolding their long fragrant leaves, and in shops and in dwelling houses the double window frames were being removed and the windows cleaned.

As Nekhludov passed the Tolkuchi Market, a dense crowd was surging along its line of stalls. Ragged men, with boots tucked under their arms and newly pressed trousers and waistcoats hanging over their shoulders, were walking up and down. Men on holiday from their factories, in clean sleeveless coats and shining boots, women with bright silk shawls over their heads and jackets embroidered with beads, were crowding around the taverns. Policemen, with their pistols attached to yellow lanyards, were stationed here and there on the lookout for a scrimmage which might help to dispel the boredom that oppressed them. Along the paths of the boulevard and on its fresh green lawns, children and dogs were running about, while the nurses sitting on the benches were gossiping happily.

The streets, still cool and damp on the shady side, were quite dry in the middle, where heavy teams, light droshkies, and tramcars thundered and rattled and rang unceasingly. The air vibrated with the clangor of church bells calling people to a service like the one that was now going on in the prison, and the people in their Sunday clothes were on their way to their own parish churches.

The cabby drove Nekhludov, not to the prison itself, but to the turning which led to it.

Several men and women, most of them carrying bundles, were waiting at this spot, about a hundred paces from the prison. To the right were a few low wooden buildings, and to the left a one-story house with a signboard. The huge brick building of the prison proper was just in front, but visitors were not allowed to come near it. An armed sentinel paced backward and forward and shouted harshly at those who tried to pass him. On the right hand, near the small gate of the wooden buildings, a warder in gold-braided uniform was sitting on a bench. He held a notebook and, as the visitors came to him and stated the names of the persons they wished to see, he wrote them down. Nekhludov went up and named Katerina Maslova. The warder with the gold braid wrote it down.

"Why don't they admit us now?" asked Nekhludov.

"The service is still going on. When it is over you will be admitted at once."

As Nekhludov went back and joined the waiting crowd, a man in ragged clothes and a battered hat, with peasant shoes on his stockingless feet, his face covered with scars, detached himself from the crowd and started toward the prison.

"Hi, there, where are you going?" shouted the soldier with the gun.

"What are you yelling about?" the tramp replied, unabashed, and coolly turned back. "If I can't go in now, I'll wait. To hear him shout, you'd think he was a general."

The crowd laughed approvingly. Most of the visitors were poorly, even raggedly, dressed; but a few wore decent clothes. Next to Nekhludov stood a stout, clean-shaven, red-cheeked man, carrying a bundle that looked as if it might contain underclothing. Nekhludov asked him if this was his first visit. The man with the bundle replied that he came every Sunday, and so they fell to talking. He was commissionaire at a bank, and he came to see his brother, who was to be tried for forgery. The good-natured fellow told Nekhludov his whole history and was about to put some questions in his turn when their attention was attracted by the arrival of a university student and a veiled lady, who came in a rubber-tired droshky drawn by a black thoroughbred. The student carried a large bundle. He approached Nekhludov and asked if it was allowed, or if he knew what had to be done, to present this package of loaves which he had brought to be distributed among the prisoners.

"This is the wish of my fiancée, who is with me. Her parents advised us to bring this bread to the prisoners."

"I have never been here before, but I think you had better ask this man," replied Nekhludov, pointing to the warder with the notebook.

While Nekhludov was talking with the student, the large iron doors with a window in the middle were opened, and an officer in uniform accompanied by another warder came out; the warder with the notebook announced that the visitors would now be admitted. The sentry stepped aside, and the visitors hurried toward the prison door as if afraid of being too late, some walking briskly, others actually running. One of the warders stood by the door and as the people passed him counted them aloud: sixteen, seventeen, and so on. Another warder inside the building, touching each one as he came in through the second door, counted them all over again, so that the two reckonings could be checked against each other, and no visitor would be left in the prison and no prisoner allowed to get out. The warder counted the people as they passed without giving them a glance; the touch of the man's hand on his back produced in Nekhludov an immediate feeling of irritation, but remembering the reason why he had come he was ashamed of being irritable and offended.

The first room was a large vaulted hall with small barred windows. Nekhludov suddenly caught sight of a large painting of the Crucifixion hanging in an alcove.

"Why should that be here?" he thought, his mind connecting the image of Christ with liberation and not with captivity.

He walked slowly, allowing the hurrying visitors to go before him and thinking now with horror of the wretches who were imprisoned here, now with compassion of the innocent, like Katusha and the lad he had seen yesterday, now with tenderness and shyness of the meeting that awaited him. As he was leaving the first room he heard the warder say something, but, absorbed in his thoughts, he paid no attention and followed the main stream of visitors to the men's ward, instead of turning to the women's ward.

Having let those who were in a hurry pass him, he was the last to enter the visiting room. The first thing that struck him, as he opened the door, was the deafening roar of hundreds of voices. It was only when he drew nearer and saw the people like flies settled on sugar all pressing closely against some wire netting that ran the whole length of the room, that he understood what it meant. The back part of the room, where the windows were, had more wire netting stretched from the floor to the ceiling; warders passed up and down between the two; and as they were fully seven feet apart, and the prisoners were behind the farther mesh and the visitors in front of the nearer one, it was almost impossible—particularly for a nearsighted person—to distinguish a face. It was also difficult to talk: one had to shout as loudly as possible to be heard at all. Wives, husbands, fathers, mothers, and children pressed their faces close against the partitions in their efforts to see each other, and to say what they wanted. As each spoke so as to be heard by the one he was talking to, and his neighbors did the same, the result was that they did all they could to drown the voices of everyone else. This was the cause of the shouting and din that Nekhludov heard when he entered. Only by the expression on the faces could one guess at the words that were spoken or at the relations between the speakers.

An old woman with a trembling chin, wearing a kerchief on her head, stood beside him pressed to the wire, shouting something to a pale young man whose head was half shaven. The prisoner, his forehead puckered, was listening with the closest attention. Next to the woman was a young fellow in a peasant coat who listened, shaking his head, to the words of an old prisoner with a gray beard and an emaciated face very like his own. A little farther off stood a ragged man who shouted out something and waved his hand and laughed. Beside him on the floor sat a woman and a child; the woman wore a good woolen gown. She was sobbing; it seemed to be the first time she had seen the gray-haired man on the other side of the wire dressed in a prisoner's jacket, in chains and with his head shaven. Beyond her stood the commissionaire who had talked to Nekhludov. He was shouting vigorously to a bald-headed prisoner with very bright eyes.

When Nekhludov understood that he was expected to talk in these surroundings, a feeling of indignation arose within him against the men who could invent and enforce such a system. He was astounded that this terrible thing, this outrage to human feelings, should apparently offend no one. The inspector, the soldiers, the visitors, and the prisoners acted as though all this was as it should be. Nekhludov stayed in the room five minutes, very much depressed, conscious of his own weakness and of being at variance with the whole world. He was seized with a sense of moral lassitude akin to seasickness.

❖

CHAPTER FORTY-TWO

"But I must do what I can, what I came here for," he said to himself, trying to bolster up his resolution. "How should I set about it?" Looking around for some official, he perceived a short thin man with an officer's epaulettes, walking up and down behind the visitors, and went up to him.

"Can you tell me, sir," he asked, with elaborate politeness, "where the women are kept, and where I should be allowed to see one of them?"

"Do you want to go to the women's ward?"

"Yes. I should like to see one of the prisoners," he replied, with the same courtesy.

"You ought to have said so in the hall. Whom do you wish to see?"

"Katerina Maslova."

"Is she a political prisoner?" asked the officer.

"No, she is only—"

"Has she already been sentenced?"

"Yes, she was sentenced the day before yesterday," replied Nekhludov, meekly, afraid of saying something that would spoil the mood of the inspector, who seemed sympathetic.

"If you want to go to the women's ward, please come this way," said the inspector, favorably impressed with Nekhludov's appearance. "Sidorov!" he called out to a corporal with a large mustache wearing medals on his breast, "Take this gentleman to the women's ward."

"Yes, sir."

Just then a heart-rending wail was heard coming from someone near the wire.

Everything seemed strange to Nekhludov, but the strangest thing of all was that he should feel himself under an obligation to the inspector, the senior warders, and all those men who carried out the cruel deeds done in that place. The warder took Nekhludov into the corridor and thence through a door directly opposite into the women's visiting room.

Like that of the men, it was divided by wire netting into

three parts, but it was much smaller and there were fewer visitors and prisoners; yet the din was the same as in the men's room. The prison authorities were represented by a woman who walked up and down in just the same way between the wire partitions; she was in uniform with blue facings and a blue belt, and had gold stripes on her sleeves. Here also the people were clinging to the wire: on one side the visitors in all sorts of costume, on the other the prisoners, some in white prison dresses and some wearing their own clothes. The people stood packed together for the whole length of the wire. Some were poised on tiptoe so as to see over the heads of the others. Some talked sitting on the floor. The most conspicuous prisoner, shouting at the top of her voice, was a thin, disheveled gypsy woman, her scarf awry on her curly hair. She stood almost in the middle of the room near a post at the farther side of the wire and, gesticulating rapidly, shouted something to a gypsy in a blue coat tightly belted below the waist. A soldier talking to one of the prisoners sat on the floor beside the gypsy. Next, his face pressed close against the wire, was a fair-haired, bearded young peasant wearing bast shoes; his face was flushed and he was keeping back his tears with an effort. He was talking to a pretty fair-haired prisoner whose blue eyes never moved from his face. These were Fedosya and her husband. Next came a tramp talking with a slovenly, broad-faced woman; then two women, a man, and another woman—a prisoner in front of every one of them. Maslova was not among them. But, behind the prisoners on the other side, a woman was standing and Nekhludov knew at once that it was she. His heart began to beat faster and he could hardly breathe. The decisive moment was drawing near. He approached the wire and recognized Katusha. She stood behind the blue-eyed Fedosya and was listening to her with a smile. She was no longer in a prison cloak, but wore a white blouse, tightly drawn in at the waist and very full in the bosom. A few black ringlets escaped from beneath her head scarf, as on that day in court.

"It will be decided now," he thought. "How shall I call her? Or will she come herself?"

But she did not come. She was expecting Bertha, and had no idea that this visitor was for her. The matron, who was walking between the wire prisoners, went up to Nekhludov.

"Whom do you wish to see?" she asked.

"Katerina Maslova," he said, speaking with difficulty.

"Someone to see you, Maslova," cried the matron.

Maslova turned and, with head erect and bosom well forward, walked up to the wire with that expression of readiness so familiar to him, pushed in between two prisoners, and gazed at him with a surprised and questioning look. Concluding from his dress that he was a rich man, she smiled.

"Have you come to see me?" she asked, bringing her smiling face with its slightly squinting eyes nearer to the wire.

"I wished to see—" Nekhludov hesitated, wondering whether he ought to say "thee" or "you." He was speaking no louder than usual. "I wanted to see you. I—"

"Don't tell me such nonsense!" shouted the ragged fellow next to him. "Did you take it?—or didn't you take it?"

"I am telling you—she's dying, she is very weak," shouted someone on the other side.

Maslova could not hear what Nekhludov was saying, but the expression on his face suddenly reminded her of something she did not wish to recall; her smile vanished and a deep line of suffering appeared on her forehead.

"I can't hear what you say," she called out, screwing up her eyes and wrinkling her brow more and more.

"I came—"

"Yes, I am doing what I ought, I am confessing," thought Nekhludov, and at this thought he felt choked, and tears sprang to his eyes; clutching the wire tightly with his fingers he struggled to repress a sob.

"If she'd been well, I wouldn't have gone—" shouted someone at his side.

"I know nothing about it, so help me God," screamed a prisoner from another direction.

The agitation that she saw in Nekhludov communicated itself to Maslova. The color came in patches to her white plump cheeks; but her face remained stern and the squinting eyes looked fixedly beyond him.

"You look like—but, no, I don't know you," she shouted.

"I have come to ask you to forgive me," he shouted in reply, his voice loud and toneless as though he was reciting a lesson; and as he said these words shame fell upon him; he turned away. Then came the thought that if he was ashamed, so much the better, since it was his own disgrace and therefore must be borne.

So he began again in a loud voice: "Forgive me. I have sinned grievously against you."

He was unable to speak any more and turned away from the wire, trying to suppress the sobs that shook his chest.

The assistant inspector who had directed him to the women's

ward seemed to feel an interest in the affair; as he came in and noticed that Nekhludov was not at the partition, he asked him why he wasn't talking to the woman he had come to see.

Nekhludov blew his nose and made an effort to appear calm.

"I cannot speak through that wire," he said. "It's impossible to hear anything."

The inspector hesitated for a moment.

"Ah, well," he said, "she can be brought out here for a while. Maria Karlovna," he added, addressing the matron, "bring Maslova out."

❖

CHAPTER FORTY-THREE

A MOMENT later Maslova came in through the side door. Stepping softly, she came up to Nekhludov and stood in front of him, looking up from under her brows. The black ringlets were arranged over her forehead as on the day before. Her pale face, though unhealthy and puffy, was still attractive. She seemed perfectly composed, but her dark, slightly squinting eyes glittered strangely from beneath their swollen lids.

"You may talk here," said the inspector.

Nekhludov walked toward a bench by the wall. Maslova, after a glance of inquiry at the inspector, shrugged her shoulders in surprise and followed Nekhludov to the bench. She seated herself by his side and arranged her skirt.

"I know it is hard for you to forgive me," he began, and stopped as he felt the tears coming again, "but even if it is too late to atone for the past, I will do all I can for you. Tell me—"

"How did you manage to find me?" she interrupted, without looking at him.

"O God, help me! Teach me what to do!" said Nekhludov to himself, looking at her face, so different from the face he had known.

"I was on the jury the day before yesterday when you were tried. Didn't you recognize me?"

"No, I did not. I had no time for recognizing people. I didn't even look," she said.

"There was a child?" he asked, and felt himself blushing.

"He died, thank God," she answered, viciously, and turned her head away.

"Why? How did it happen?"

"I was so ill myself, I nearly died," she said, without raising her eyes.

"What made my aunts discharge you?"

"Who would keep a servant with a child? They turned me out as soon as they noticed. But what's the use of talking about it? I don't want to remember—I've forgotten it all. It is all over now."

"No, it is not all over. I cannot let matters rest as they are. I must atone for my sin."

"There's nothing to atone for. It's all past and gone," she said; then, much to his surprise, she looked at him with an enticing smile, repulsive, and yet pitiful.

Maslova had never expected to see him again, and certainly not here and not now. She was amazed when she first recognized him, and was unable to keep back memories she never wished to revive. Dimly she recalled the wonderful new world of feeling and of thought opened to her by the charming youth whom she had loved and who had loved her; then his inconceivable cruelty and the long chain of suffering and degradation which trailed after that magic joy—and she felt sick at heart. But, unable to grasp the meaning of it all, she did as she had done before: she put these memories away, flinging over them the veil of her depraved life. At first this man brought back to her the image of the lad she had loved, but she turned away from it because it hurt. Now this well-groomed, carefully dressed gentleman, with his perfumed beard, was no longer the Nekhludov she had loved, but only one of the men who used women such as herself for their own pleasure and were in turn used as a source of profit. That was why she smiled alluringly and then was silent, thinking how she could best make use of him.

"Everything's over now," she said at last. "I have been sentenced to penal servitude." Her lips trembled.

"I knew, I was certain that you were not guilty," said Nekhludov.

"Of course I am not. I am not a thief or a murderess. People say that everything depends on the lawyer," she continued. "I was told that I ought to send a petition. Only that would be expensive."

"Yes, of course. I have already engaged a lawyer," said Nekhludov.

"Don't begrudge the expense—get a good one," she said.

"I shall do everything in my power."

Neither of them spoke for a time.

"I was going to ask you for a little money, if you could spare it. Not much—ten rubles would do," she said, suddenly, and smiled again.

"Why, yes, certainly," he replied in embarrassment, and fumbled for his pocketbook.

She looked quickly at the inspector, who was walking up and down.

"Don't give it when he's looking, or they'll take it away."

Nekhludov took out the pocketbook as soon as the inspector's back was turned, but before he had time to give her the ten rubles the inspector's face was again toward them. He crumpled the note in his hand.

"This woman has died," he thought, looking at her face, once so enchanting, now defiled and bloated; he caught the evil glitter of her black, slightly squinting eyes, as they turned first to watch the movements of the inspector and then to gaze greedily at the hand that held the money. For a moment he hesitated.

Again he heard the voice of the tempter repeating the arguments of the night before and trying to turn his attention from the question of duty to the question of results and expedience.

"You can do nothing with this woman," said the voice. "You will only put a stone around your own neck that will drown you and prevent you from being of any use to the rest of the world. Would it not be better to give her some money, give her your whole fortune, and say good-by to her forever?" And all at once he felt that something of the utmost importance was taking place in his soul—that his spiritual life was being weighed in the balance and that the slightest effort would tip the scale. He made the effort. He called upon God, whose presence he had felt so intensely the day before, and God responded. Nekhludov made up his mind to tell her everything.

"Katusha, I came to ask you to forgive me and you have not answered me. Have you forgiven me? Will you ever forgive me?" he said, addressing her with the familiar "thou."

Not listening to him, she was watching his hand and the inspector. As soon as the inspector's back was turned, she reached out quickly, snatched the note, and tucked it into her belt.

"Those are queer words you're using," she said, with what seemed to him a sarcastic smile. Nekhludov felt that there was some hostile spirit within her, warding him off and preventing him from reaching her heart.

Yet, strange to say, this did not repel him but rather drew

him toward her all the more, as though by some new and un-familiar force. He felt that it was for him to awaken her spirit —no easy task, but its very difficulty attracted him. He felt now as he had never felt before, either toward her or anyone else. It was a feeling that had nothing personal in it; he wanted nothing for himself, so far as she was concerned; all he desired was that she should cease to be what she was now, that she should awaken and become like her own self again.

"Why do you speak like that, Katusha? I know you, I re-member you as you were then, in Panovo—"

"What's the good of bringing up the past?" she said, drily.

"I bring it up because I wish to make amends and to ex-piate my sin," he began to say, and was going to add that he would marry her; but he met her eyes and read in them some-thing so coarse, so revolting, so repulsive, that he could not utter the words.

At that moment the visitors began to leave. The inspector came toward Nekhludov and told him that their time was up. Maslova rose obediently and stood waiting to be dismissed.

"Good-by—I still have much to tell you, but, as you see, I cannot say any more now. I will come again," he said, and held out his hand.

"I think you've said all there is to say—"

She took his hand, but did not press it.

"No, I will try to see you again, somewhere where we can talk more freely. I have something important to tell you," said Nekhludov.

"Well, then, come if you like," she said, smiling at him as she did at men she wished to please.

"You are nearer to me than a sister," said Nekhludov.

"How queer!" she said again, shaking her head, and went behind the partition.

❧

CHAPTER FORTY-FOUR

BEFORE this interview Nekhludov was expecting that as soon as Katusha saw him and heard that he had repented and meant to do the best he could for her, she would be moved and happy, and turn at once into the Katusha he used to know. But he found to his horror that Katusha had vanished and Maslova had taken her place. He was shocked and deeply disturbed.

What surprised him most was that she showed no sign of shame, except as a prisoner: she was very much ashamed of being in jail—but of being a prostitute, not at all. On the contrary, she seemed rather pleased with herself and proud of her position. Yet, how could it be otherwise? No man can play an active part in the world unless he believes that his activity is important and good. Therefore, whatever position a man may hold, he is certain to take that view of human life in general which will make his own activity seem important and good. It is generally supposed that a thief, a murderer, a spy or a prostitute, knowing their occupation to be evil, must be ashamed of it. In point of fact, the case is precisely the reverse. Men who have been placed by fate and their own mistakes (or sins) in a certain position, however false, always adopt a view of life which makes their place in it good and appropriate. To maintain this idea, men instinctively mix only with those who accept their view of life and of their place in it. This surprises us when thieves boast of their adroitness, prostitutes flaunt their shame, murderers gloat over their cruelty. We are surprised, however, only because the circle, the sphere, of these men is limited, and principally because we are outside it; but does not the same state of things exist among the rich—who boast of their wealth, i.e., of robbery; the generals—who boast of their victories, i.e., of murder; the rulers—who boast of their power, i.e., of violence? We do not recognize their ideas of life and of good and evil as perverted, only because the circle of men holding these perverted ideas is wider and because we belong to it ourselves.

Maslova held this view of life and of her own place in it. She was a prostitute, condemned to penal servitude, yet she had formed a conception of life which allowed her to think well of herself and even to feel a pride in her position.

In her philosophy, the highest good of all men without exception—old and young, schoolboys and generals, educated and uneducated—consisted in intimate relations with attractive women; every man, although he might pretend to busy himself with other matters, in reality cared for nothing else; and she, an attractive woman, could either satisfy or disappoint their desires. The experiences of all her past and present life confirmed the correctness of this view.

During the past ten years, wherever she found herself, she saw men that needed her; they all needed her—from Nekhludov and the old police officer down to the warders in the prison. She took no notice of the men who did not need her, consequently, the whole world seemed to be made up of people driven by lust and trying to possess her by all possible means— by fraud and violence, by purchase and cunning.

This being Maslova's conception of life, it was natural that she should consider herself an extremely important person. And she prized this conception of life above all things in the world— could not fail to prize it because, if she were to change her views, she would lose the importance which this conception gave her. And in order not to lose that pre-eminence in life, she instinctively ranged herself with the class of people who shared her views. Divining that Nekhludov wanted to draw her into a different world, she opposed him, foreseeing that in that world she would lose her place in life which gave her confidence and self-respect. This was also the reason why she had banished all memories of her girlhood and her early relations with Nekhludov. These recollections did not agree with her present conception of life and were therefore entirely erased from her mind—or it might be more accurate to describe them as carefully sealed and plastered over, just as bees will sometimes plaster up a nest of wax worms to prevent the creatures from coming out and destroying their work. Therefore the present Nekhludov was no longer, in her eyes, the man she had once loved, but only a rich gentleman who could and should be made use of, and with whom she might have the same relations as with all other men.

"No, I could not say the most important thing," thought Nekhludov, as he followed the crowd to the exit. "I did not tell her I would marry her. I did not say that; but I will."

The two warders were at the door to watch the visitors as they went out and to count them again, touching each one on the shoulder, so that no extra person should either remain inside or get out. But this time the touch did not offend Nekhludov. He did not even notice it.

❖

CHAPTER FORTY-FIVE

NEKHLUDOV meant to change his outward life. He wished to let his flat, to dismiss the servants, and to move into furnished lodgings. But Agrafena Petrovna pointed out that there was no reason for changing anything before the winter: no one would think of taking a town flat in summer, and he would have to live and store his furniture somewhere. His efforts to change his outward life, which he longed to arrange in some simple student fashion, were therefore fruitless. Not only did things remain as they were, but new forms of activity began: all the woolens and all the furs were taken out to be aired and beaten; the house porter, his assistant, the cook, and even Korney himself took a share in the work; first the uniforms and various strange-looking furs, that no one ever used, were brought out and hung on the line; next came the carpets and the soft furniture; the house porter and his assistant, their shirt sleeves rolled up over their muscular arms, beat everything with vigorous rhythmical movements; the smell of mothballs filled every room. Whenever he passed through the yard or looked out of the window, Nekhludov wondered how all these things came to be his, and thought how utterly useless they all were. So far as he could see their only reason for existence was to provide exercise for Agrafena Petrovna, Korney, the house porter, and the cook.

He had made up his mind that it was not worth while changing his mode of life until Maslova's case was settled. "The change will come more naturally when she is set free, or else exiled—when I shall follow her," he said to himself.

On the appointed day Nekhludov drove up to the house of Fanarin, the lawyer. He entered the luxurious flat, decorated with huge plants and wonderful curtains—with, in fact, all the expensive furnishing which betrays easy money and is to be found in the houses of men grown suddenly rich without having had to work. A few people were sitting unhappily at several small tables in the reception room, whiling away the time as one does at the doctor's with illustrated papers supposed to distract the mind. Fanarin's assistant sat in the room at a high desk and, recognizing Nekhludov, came up and said that he would announce him at once; but the door of the study was opened before he reached it and the sound of loud, animated voices could be heard: one was the voice of a middle-aged, square-shouldered man in a brand-new suit, and the other was that of Fanarin himself. The client had a red face and a heavy mustache. Both of them looked as though they had just completed a transaction that was profitable to themselves but of doubtful honesty.

"That's your own fault, my dear fellow," said Fanarin, smiling.

"The heavenly spheres are just the place for me, but my sins won't let me in."

"Yes, yes, we know all about that," said Fanarin, and both men laughed awkwardly.

"Ah, step in, Prince," said Fanarin to Nekhludov; he bestowed a parting nod on the merchant and led Nekhludov into his study, a room furnished with rigid simplicity.

"Will you smoke?" said Fanarin, taking a seat opposite Nekhludov and repressing a smile that was evidently due to the success of the previous transaction.

"Thank you; I have come to consult you about the case of Maslova."

"Yes, yes, I know," said Fanarin. "You can't conceive what scoundrels those fellows can be, with their fat wallets! You noticed that fellow who went out? Well, he's worth twelve millions and can't even speak correctly—but he'd have a tenner off you with his teeth if he saw a chance of getting away with it."

"You say he can't speak correctly and yet you talk about a 'tenner,' " thought Nekhludov, feeling an overwhelming dislike for this man, with his free and easy air of belonging to the same class as the prince, while carefully dissociating himself from his clients as men of quite another world.

"He has given me no end of trouble, the scoundrel. I felt I must relieve my feelings," said the lawyer, as though to excuse himself for delaying the business with Nekhludov. "And now about your case. I have looked over the papers carefully and 'disapprove of the contents,' as Turgenev puts it. I mean that that confounded advocate has just missed every chance for making an appeal."

"What have you decided, then?"

"Excuse me one moment. Tell him," he said, turning to the assistant who had just entered the room, "that I shall not change my mind. If he can manage it, well and good—if he can't, I won't take the case."

"He refuses."

"Very well, then, let him go," replied the lawyer, and his cheerful, self-satisfied expression gave place to an angry frown.

"They say that we lawyers are paid for doing nothing," he said, resuming his pleasant look. "I saved a bankrupt debtor from a totally unjust accusation, and now they all besiege me. And every case calls for a tremendous amount of work. As some author once said, we also 'write with our heart's blood.' Now then, as to your case, or rather, the case in which you are interested," he went on, "it has been abominably mishandled; there are no good grounds for an appeal; still, we can have a try, and this is what I have set out."

He took up a sheet of paper covered with writing and began to read, slurring some words and emphasizing others: " 'To the Criminal Court of Appeal of the Senate, etc., etc. The Petition of so-and-so. According to the verdict, etc., Maslova has been found guilty of poisoning with intent to kill the merchant Smelkov, and, by virtue of article 1454 of the penal code, has been sentenced to penal servitude, etc.' "

He paused, and it was plain that the pleasure of hearing his own compositions never palled upon him. " 'This verdict,' " he continued, impressively, " 'was the direct result of legal omissions and mistakes sufficiently serious to enable us to ask to have it revoked. First, the president interrupted the report of the post-mortem examination of Smelkov's intestines at the very beginning of the reading.' That is point one."

"But it was the prosecutor who demanded this reading," said Nekhludov, with surprise.

"That makes no difference. The defendant might also have demanded the reading."

"But it was entirely superfluous."

"Never mind; it's a cause for appeal. To proceed: 'Secondly, when the counsel for the defense was detailing some of the moral causes that had brought about Maslova's fall, the president called him to order for wandering from the matter in hand. Now it is recognized that in criminal cases (and the Senate has repeatedly pointed this out) a delineation of the moral characteristics of the criminal is of vital importance, if only for determining the degree of his responsibility.' And here we have point number two," he said, looking at Nekhludov.

"But he spoke so wretchedly that it was impossible to understand him," replied Nekhludov, feeling more and more astonished.

"Well, as he hasn't much sense, he couldn't be expected to say anything worth hearing," replied Fanarin, with a laugh; "still, it's a cause for appeal. 'Thirdly, in the president's summing up he violated a positive condition of the criminal code (set forth in clause 1, article 801), by omitting to explain to the jurors just what is required by law for the conviction of an alleged criminal; moreover, he did not tell them that although they had agreed on the fact that Maslova had administered the poison, nevertheless, seeing that her malicious intention had not been proved, they had the right to find her innocent of actual crime, and guilty only of carelessness resulting in the merchant's death, which she did not desire.' And this is really the important point."

"Yes, but we ought to have understood that ourselves. That was our own mistake."

"And now," the lawyer went on, "we come to the fourth and last point. 'The answer of the jury to the question concerning Maslova's guilt was couched in language which contained an obvious contradiction. Maslova was accused of a deliberate intention to poison Smelkov in order to rob him—the only motive, in fact, which could be ascribed to her. But the jury in their verdict acquitted her of any intent to rob and of participation in the theft of the valuables. It is therefore evident that they intended to deny that Maslova was guilty of willful murder, and also that they would have expressed this intention in their verdict had it not been for the misunderstanding which arose from the incompleteness of the president's summing up; in consideration whereof, this verdict of the jury calls for the application of articles 816 and 808 of the criminal code—that is, the rectification of the mistake made by the president in his summing up to the jury, to be followed by another submission of the issues to them, and another hearing and verdict concerning the guilt of the accused,' " read Fanarin.

"Then why did the president do this?"

"That's what I'd like to know," replied Fanarin, with a laugh.

"Then the Senate will rectify the error?"

"That will depend on what senators are present at the time. So there you are. And furthermore, I have said: 'A verdict of this kind does not give the court a right,' " he went on reading rapidly, " 'to condemn Maslova to criminal punishment, nor to apply section 3 of article 771 of the criminal code to her case; this constitutes a direct and flagrant transgression of the fundamental laws of criminal jurisdiction. Therefore, in consideration of the causes previously described, I have the honor to petition, etc., that this verdict may be set aside in conformity with articles 909, 910, the second section of article 912, and article 928 of the criminal code, etc., etc., and that the case may be transferred to another session of the said court for revision." And now, all that can be done for the present has been done. But I will tell you frankly that there is only a very slight chance of success. Still, it all depends on what members are present in the Senate. If you have any influence, see what you can do."

"I know a few of them."

"Then don't lose any time, or else they'll all go off to cure their piles, and you may have to wait three months. Then, in case of failure, we can fall back on a petition to the tsar. But the success of that also depends on knowing how to handle your affair behind the scenes. In that case I am also at your service. I don't mean behind the scenes, but in drawing up the petition."

"Thank you. Now as to your fee—"

"When my assistant hands you the petition, he will speak to you about that."

"There is another thing I want to ask you. The prosecutor gave me a pass to see this person, but at the prison I was told that I must obtain permission of the governor if I wished for an interview at any other time than on the regular visiting days, and in any other place than usual. Is that true?"

"Yes, I think so. But the governor is not in town just now. The vice-governor is in charge, and he's such a hopeless fool that I doubt whether you can do anything with him."

"Is that Maslennikov?"

"Yes."

"I know him," said Nekhludov, and rose to go.

At this moment a horribly ugly, skinny, pug-nosed, yellow-faced woman burst suddenly into the room. It was Fanarin's wife. She did not seem in the least worried by her ugliness, and was extravagantly overdressed in bright yellow velvet and green silk; her thin hair was elaborately curled. She made a triumphant entry into the room, accompanied by a smiling, bilious person dressed in a frock coat with silk facings and a white tie. He was an author. Nekhludov had seen him before.

"Anatoli," she said, opening the door of the study, "come in here a moment. Semyon Ivanovich has promised to read us his poem, and you must come and talk about Garshin."

Nekhludov was rising to leave, but the lawyer's wife whispered a few words to her husband and turned toward him. "Since I know who you are, Prince," she said, "we may dispense with an introduction. Will you favor us with your presence at our literary matinée? It will be quite interesting. Anatoli reads charmingly."

"You see what a variety of occupations I have," said Anatoli, making a deprecatory gesture with his hands and smilingly indicating his wife, as much as to say, who could resist such a bewitching creature? With a grave and melancholy air, and with extreme politeness, Nekhludov thanked her for the honor she did him, but refused the invitation, saying that his time was much too occupied, and withdrew to the reception room.

"What affectation!" remarked Fanarin's wife after he had left the room.

In the reception room the assistant handed Nekhludov the petition and, to his question concerning the fee, replied that Anatoli Petrovich said it would be one thousand rubles, adding that he did not usually take cases of that sort, but had made an exception for Nekhludov.

"And who is to sign the petition?" asked Nekhludov.

"The petitioner herself—or Anatoli Petrovich could sign it, if he had the power of attorney."

"Then I think it would be better to get her signature," said Nekhludov, glad of an excuse for seeing Katusha before the visiting day.

❖

CHAPTER FORTY-SIX

AT the usual hour the warders blew their whistles, the grated iron doors of the cells rattled, bare feet pattered and heels clattered through the corridor, where the refuse tubs carried by the scavengers were filling the air with a disgusting stench. After they had washed and dressed, the prisoners filed out into the corridors for roll call, and then went to fetch boiling water for their tea.

The only subject talked about at breakfast was the impending punishment of two prisoners, who were going to be flogged that day. One, Vassilyev, a young man of some education, was a clerk who had killed his mistress in a fit of jealousy. His fellow prisoners liked him because he was cheerful and generous with his comrades and firm with the warders. He knew the regulations and insisted that they should be observed, and was disliked by the warders for that reason. Three weeks ago a warder had struck one of the scavengers for spilling some soup on his new uniform. Vassilyev took the man's part, declaring that it was against the law to strike a prisoner.

"I'll teach you the law!" said the warder, calling him all sorts of names. Vassilyev replied in kind. The warder was about to hit him, but Vassilyev seized him by the hand, held it fast for a few seconds, then turned him around and pushed him outside the door. The warder entered a complaint against the prisoner, and the inspector ordered him solitary confinement.

The solitary cells were small, dark closets, stone-cold, with doors bolted on the outside; they contained neither beds, chairs nor tables. The prisoner was obliged to sit or lie upon the filthy floor, where innumerable rats ran over him, so bold that it was hard to keep them from snatching the bread out of his very hands. Indeed, they often attacked the prisoners themselves when they were lying still. Vassilyev refused to go into the solitary cell, declaring steadily that he had done nothing wrong. The warders resorted to violence. A struggle ensued and two of his mates helped Vassilyev to free himself from the warders. Then all the warders, including Petrov, who was renowned for his strength, joined together; the prisoners were overpowered and pushed into the cells. The governor was immediately notified that something like a mutiny had taken place; he sent back a written order for the flogging of the two ringleaders, Vassilyev and the tramp Nepomniashchi; they were awarded thirty strokes of the rod. This punishment was due to take place in the women's visiting room.

Rumors of this had spread about the night before and caused animated discussion.

Korablyova, Horoshavka, Fedosya, and Maslova were sitting in their corner, a good deal flushed and excited by the vodka they had drunk, for Maslova, who now had a constant supply, treated her companions generously. They were chatting over their breakfast.

"He never made any disturbance," said Korablyova, biting off tiny bits of sugar with her strong teeth. "He just stood up for his mate, because it's not allowed to strike a prisoner these days."

"I heard them say he is a fine fellow," remarked Fedosya. She was sitting on a log of wood beside the teapot. She wore neither cap nor kerchief over her long plaits of hair.

"Why not tell *him* about it, Mikhailovna?" said the signal woman to Maslova; "him" meant Nekhludov.

"I will. He'll do anything for me," replied Maslova, tossing her head.

"Yes, when he comes; but they've gone to fetch the poor fellows already. It's awful!" said Fedosya, with a sigh.

"I once saw a man flogged at the police station. My father-in-law sent me to the village elder, and when I arrived, there he was, being . . ." said the signal woman, beginning on a long story.

She was interrupted by the sound of footsteps and voices in the corridor overhead.

The women stopped talking and listened.

"Those devils have got hold of him. They'll do him to death. The warders are mad with him because he tries to make them keep to the law."

When all had become still upstairs the signal woman went on with her story, telling them how frightened she was when she saw the peasant flogged at the police station, and how her insides turned at the sight. Then Horoshavka told how Shcheglov never made a sound when he was whipped. Fedosya put away the tea things, and, while the two other women took up their sewing, Maslova remained seated on the bunk, hugging her knees and feeling disconsolate and bored. She was just thinking she would lie down when the matron called her into the office to see a visitor.

"Mind you tell him all about us," said old Menshova, while Maslova stood arranging her kerchief before an old looking glass with half the silvering rubbed off. "It wasn't us who set it on fire, but that villain himself. And the laborer saw him do it. Well, he'd not damn his soul by denying it. Tell him to ask for Dmitri—he'll tell him just how it was. Here we are, locked up in prison when we never dreamt of any evil, while that fiend is carrying on in pothouses with another man's wife."

"That's against the law," declared Korablyova.

"I shall certainly tell him," said Maslova. "Suppose I take one more drop, just to keep up my courage?" she added, with a wink.

⚜

CHAPTER FORTY-SEVEN

NEKHLUDOV had been waiting in the hall for some time. When he arrived at the prison he rang at the main door and handed to the warder on duty the pass he had received from the prosecutor.

"Who do you wish to see?"

"The prisoner Maslova."

"You can't see her just now. The inspector is busy."

"Is he in his office?"

"No, he is in the visiting room," said the warder, and Nekhludov noticed that he seemed embarrassed.

"Why, is this a visiting day?"

"No, he is attending to some special business."

"When can I see him then?"

"When he comes out. You will have to wait a while."

Just then a sergeant-major, with glistening epaulettes, a smooth, shiny face, and a mustache redolent of tobacco, came out from the side door and sharply addressed the warder:

"Why did you admit anyone in here? You should have taken him to the office."

"I was told the inspector was not there," said Nekhludov, surprised at the signs of uneasiness that were evident also in the manner of the sergeant-major.

At this moment the door was opened and Petrov, hot and perspiring, came out. "He'll not forget that in a hurry!" he said to the sergeant-major who, by a swift glance, drew his attention to Nekhludov.

Petrov said no more, but turned away frowning and went through the back door. "Who will not forget what? Why are they so confused? Why did the sergeant make that sign to him?" thought Nekhludov.

"It is against the rules to wait here; will you please go into the office?" said the sergeant-major to Nekhludov; he was about to do so, when the inspector came in through the door at the back. He was sighing continually and seemed even more agitated than his subordinates.

On seeing Nekhludov he said to the warder: "Fedotov, send to women's ward number 5 and tell the matron to have Maslova brought to the office."

"Will you come with me, sir?" he added, turning to Nekhludov.

They ascended a steep staircase and entered a small room lighted by one window. It was furnished with a writing desk and a few chairs. The inspector seated himself in one of them. "Ah, my duties are too hard," he said, taking out a large cigarette and turning to Nekhludov.

"You seem to be very tired," said Nekhludov.

"Yes, I'm tired of the whole business—my duties are too hard. The easier I try to make it for the prisoners, the worse it grows. I rack my brains to discover some way of getting out of it; hard, very hard duties!"

Nekhludov did not know what made these duties so hard, but

could not help feeling sorry for the man, who seemed so upset and dejected.

"Yes, they must be," he said, "but why do you stay here?"

"I have a family, and no other means . . ."

"But if your work depresses you . . ."

"Well, still, you know—in a way I do some good. I try to make it easier for them. I do all I can. Some men in my place would not be so lenient. Just think of it, I have over two thousand persons under my charge. And such creatures! You have to know how to deal with them. After all, they are human beings. You can't help feeling sorry for them. And yet you can't be too lenient." The inspector began to describe a recent fight among the prisoners which, he said, had ended in the killing of one of the men.

His story was interrupted by the entrance of Maslova, preceded by a warder.

Nekhludov saw her in the doorway before she had noticed the presence of the inspector. Her face was flushed and she walked briskly behind the warder, smiling and tossing her head. When she caught sight of the inspector, she looked startled for a moment, but recovered quickly and went boldly up to Nekhludov.

"How do you do?" she said, in a drawling voice, smiling as she spoke. She grasped his hand firmly, quite unlike the first time.

"I have brought you a petition to sign," said Nekhludov, somewhat surprised by the pertness of her manner. "The lawyer has drawn up the petition and, after you have signed, it will be sent to Petersburg."

"That's easy enough—anything you like!" she said, winking at him and laughing.

Nekhludov took the folded paper from his pocket and went to the table.

"May she sign it here?" he asked, turning to the inspector.

"Yes, take a seat. There is pen and ink. Can you write?" said the inspector.

"Once upon a time I could," she said, and laughed again, looking back at Nekhludov; arranging her skirt and the sleeve of her blouse, she seated herself before the table and took the pen in her small energetic hand.

He showed her where to sign. She carefully dipped her pen into the ink, shook off a drop or two, and proceeded to write her name.

"Is that all you want?" she asked, looking from the inspector to Nekhludov; not knowing what to do with the pen, she put it first on the paper and then on the inkstand.

"I have something to tell you," said Nekhludov, taking the pen from her hands.

"Tell me, then," she said; and suddenly, as if remembering something or feeling sleepy, she looked quite grave.

The inspector arose and left the room, and Nekhludov remained with her face to face.

⚜

CHAPTER FORTY-EIGHT

THE warder who had brought Maslova sat down on the window seat, at some distance from the table. And now the moment had come. Nekhludov had never ceased to blame himself for not having told her the principal thing at their first interview— that he intended to marry her. He was determined to tell her now. She was sitting at one side of the table, and Nekhludov sat down directly opposite, facing her. The room was well lit, and for the first time he could see her face distinctly; he noticed her puffy eyelids and all the wrinkles around her eyes and mouth, and pitied her more than ever. Leaning across the table so as not to be heard by the warder (a man of Jewish appearance, with gray whiskers) he said:

"If this petition fails, we shall appeal to the emperor. Everything possible will be done."

"It all ought to have been done before," she interrupted. "If I'd had a decent lawyer. . . . Mine was quite silly. All he did was to pay me compliments," she said, with a laugh. "If it had been known at that time that you and I were old acquaintances, it would have been another matter for me. Now they all think I'm a thief."

"How strange she is today," thought Nekhludov, and was just about to speak when she went on:

"Oh, I wanted to tell you something. There is a nice old woman here; everyone, simply everyone, is surprised to see her here. She is a wonderful old woman, and she and her son are innocent. They were accused of arson. When she heard I was acquainted with you," she said, with a coquettish turn of her head and a glance at Nekhludov, "she said to me: 'Ask him to call for my son; he will tell him the whole story.' Menshov is their name. Will you do it? She's a wonderful old woman, and it's quite obvious that she has done nothing wrong. You'll do it, won't you?—there's a dear," she added, with an upward glance; then, letting her eyes drop, she smiled.

"Yes, I will look up the case," said Nekhludov, marveling more and more at the freedom of her manner. "But I want to speak to you about my own affairs. Do you remember what I said to you the last time?" he asked.

"You said all sorts of things. What was it?" she asked, still smiling and turning her head from side to side.

"I told you that I had come to ask your forgiveness," he said.

"Why are you always talking about forgiveness, forgiveness? It's neither here nor there—you had better—"

"I wish to atone in deeds as well as in words for the evil I have done. I have made up my mind to marry you," continued Nekhludov.

Her face suddenly took on an expression of fear. Her squinting eyes were fixed rigidly in his direction, but he could not tell whether she was looking at him or not.

"What do you mean?" she asked, frowning angrily.

"I cannot be reconciled to God until I have done this thing."

"God? What God have you found? You're talking nonsense. God, indeed! You should have remembered Him when—" she said, and paused, open-mouthed.

It was not till then that Nekhludov, smelling her breath, understood the cause of her excitement.

"Calm yourself!" he said.

"I'm calm enough. D'you think I'm drunk? Perhaps I am, but I know what I'm talking about!" Her face turned scarlet and she went on talking as fast as she could speak the words: "I am a convict and a whore, and you're a gentleman and a prince, and you've no business to mix yourself up with me. Go to your princesses. My price is a ten-ruble note."

"Say all the cruel things you choose, you can never say all that I am feeling myself," said Nekhludov, in a low voice. "You cannot imagine how deeply I feel my guilt toward you!"

" 'Feel my guilt,' " she mimicked him, angrily. "You didn't feel it then, but threw me a hundred rubles. 'Take this—it's what you're worth—' "

"I know, I know! But what is to be done now? I am determined not to forsake you, and I shall do as I have said," replied Nekhludov.

"But you shan't, I tell you," she said, and laughed loudly.

"Katusha!" he said, touching her hand.

"Go away! I'm a convict and you are a prince—you have no business to be here!" she said, her face distorted with rage, pulling away her hand. "You want to save yourself through me," she went on rapidly, as though in haste to pour out every feeling in her heart. "You had your pleasure from me, and now you want to get your salvation through me. I loathe you, and your spectacles, and your fat, disgusting face! Clear out!" she shouted, springing to her feet.

Here the warder came up.

"What are you kicking up this row for? It won't do."

"Never mind, leave her alone," said Nekhludov.

"She's got to behave herself."

"Please go back," said Nekhludov.

The warder withdrew to the window. Maslova resumed her seat, firmly clasping her little hands with interlaced fingers, and looking down.

Nekhludov remained standing. He hardly knew what to say next.

"Then you do not believe—?" he began.

"That you will marry me? That can never be! I'd rather hang myself. D'you understand?"

"But still I shall go on serving you."

"You may do as you please about that, but I want nothing from you. I'm telling you the truth," she said. "Oh, why didn't I die then!" she added, and burst out into a pitiful wail.

Nekhludov could not speak; her weeping was contagious. She raised her eyes, looked at him, and seemed surprised. Then she wiped away her tears with a corner of her head scarf.

The warder again came up to tell them that it was time to leave.

Maslova rose.

"You are excited," said Nekhludov. "If I possibly can, I shall come again tomorrow, and you must think it over in the meantime."

She did not reply, but without giving him another glance followed the warder out of the room.

"Well, lassie, you're going to have a fine time now," exclaimed Korablyova when Maslova returned to the cell. "He must be quite smitten with you. Make the most of your chances while you have him in tow. He'll get you out! A rich man can do anything!"

"That's so," said the signal woman, in her singsong voice. "A poor man must think twice before he marries, but a rich man has only to say what he wants and he gets it. There was a respectable man up our way, I must tell you, birdie, and what do you think he did? . . ."

"Did you tell him about me?" asked the old woman.

But Maslova did not say a word. She threw herself down on the bunk, and, fixing her squinting eyes on the corner of the room, she lay there till night. What Nekhludov said took her back into a world where she had suffered, which she had left without understanding but which she hated and had forgotten. Now she was wakened from her oblivion and the clear memories of what had been were a torment. That evening, therefore, she bought some more vodka and got drunk with her friends.

⚜

CHAPTER FORTY-NINE

"AND this is what it has come to!" thought Nekhludov, as he left the prison. Never until now had he realized the enormity of his crime. Had he not made an attempt to atone for it he would have never discovered how great it had been. Nor would Maslova have understood just how much she had been wronged. But now all the horror of it was made plain. Since he had seen what he had done to this woman's soul she too had come to see what had been done to her. Until this moment, Nekhludov had tended to admire his own repentance and virtuous resolutions, but this had given way to horror. He felt that he could not abandon her, and yet was unable to imagine what would come of their relationship.

As he was leaving the prison, a warder with an unpleasant, insinuating face, wearing a cross and medals on his breast, approached him with an air of mystery and said, putting a note into his hand:

"Here is a note from a certain person, Your Excellency."

"What person?"

"You will know when you have read it. She is a political prisoner, and I am in charge of her ward, so she asked me; and though it's contrary to the rules, still for humanity's sake—" said the warder, in a constrained, unnatural tone of voice.

Nekhludov was surprised. He could not understand how a warder, whose duty it was to guard political prisoners, could be delivering notes almost within sight of everyone. He did not know then that this warder was a spy. He took the note and read it as he was coming out of the prison.

It was written in a bold hand, in pencil, and ran as follows: "I have heard that you visit the prison because you take an interest in one of the convicts, and I am very anxious to see you. If you ask permission to see me, it will be granted, and I shall be able to communicate to you much that is of importance to your protégée and also to our society. Yours gratefully, Vera Bogodukhovskaya."

"Bogodukhovskaya? Who's that?" thought Nekhludov, absorbed by his interview with Maslova, and at first unable to connect the name and the handwriting with anybody he knew. "Ah!" he suddenly remembered, "the deacon's daughter at the bear hunt!"

Vera Bogodukhovskaya had been a teacher in a little village in the province of Novgorod, where Nekhludov once went bear hunting with some friends. He remembered her, a girl who had asked him to lend her money to attend a course of studies. Nekhludov did what she asked and then forgot all about her. This lady had now become a political prisoner, and, having heard of his story, was offering her services.

How simple life was then, and how complex and distressing it had since become! Nekhludov recalled those days and his acquaintance with Vera Bogodukhovskaya with genuine pleasure. It was just before carnival week, in an out-of-the-way spot some forty miles from the railway. The hunt had been successful. Two bears had been killed and the men were eating dinner before starting for home, when the owner of the cottage where they were lodging came in to say that the deacon's daughter was outside, asking to see the prince.

"Is she pretty?" inquired one of the men. "Don't be stupid!" Nekhludov had answered, rising from the table with a serious face and wondering what the deacon's daughter could want of him.

He went into the room of the owner of the cottage and saw a young girl wearing a felt hat and a short fur coat; she was sinewy and ugly, but her eyes and arching eyebrows were beautiful.

"Here, Vera Efremovna, you can speak to him now," said the old housewife. "This is the prince himself, and I will leave you with him."

"What can I do for you?" asked Nekhludov.

"I—I—You are a rich man, and squander money on all

sorts of things, you know, on hunting and—and I have only one desire in the world—I want to be useful to mankind. But I can do nothing because I am ignorant."

"How can I help you?"

"I am a schoolteacher, and I should like to take a university course, but they won't take me. That is to say, they would take me, but I have no money. If you would be willing to give me what I need, I could finish my education and then pay it back afterward."

Her eyes were so friendly and sincere and her whole attitude of determination mixed with timidity was so touching that, as often happened with him, Nekhludov put himself in her place at once, and felt sorry for her.

"I think it's wrong for the rich to kill bears and encourage the peasants to drink," she went on. "Why shouldn't you do some good? All I want is eighty rubles. But if you don't want to give it to me, I don't care," she added, crossly, interpreting unfavorably to herself Nekhludov's attentive and serious look.

"On the contrary, I am very much obliged to you for giving me the opportunity—I will get the money for you at once," said Nekhludov.

He went out into the vestibule and caught one of his friends listening at the door. Without replying to his jokes, he took out the money and gave it to her.

"Please do not thank me. It is for me to thank you."

Nekhludov recalled all this with pleasure. He was glad to remember how he had almost quarreled with the officer who wanted to turn the affair into a coarse joke, how another friend had taken his part and thereby drawn their friendship closer, and how cheerful and happy they had been as they returned by night to the railway station.

The procession of sledges gliding silently on the narrow forest road, fringed here with tall pine trees, there with stunted saplings, the snow lying heavily on them all; a red glimmer from a fragrant cigarette; Ossip, the gamekeeper, is running from sledge to sledge up to his knees in the snow, arranging fur rugs and the like, all the time talking of elks that tramp the deep snow and gnaw the aspen trees, or of bears lying asleep in their dens and sending out a stream of warm vapor through their breathing holes. All this came back to Nekhludov and, more vividly than everything else, the delicious awareness of his own health and strength: his lungs breathing in the frosty air; the snow, shaken from the trees every time the high harness frame touched them, falling upon his face; his body warm, his face refreshed, and his mind free from all care and anxiety, desire, and remorse. Ah! what a happy time it was! And now? O God, how difficult everything had become!

Evidently Vera Efremovna was a revolutionary and had been imprisoned for her activities. He was eager to see her, especially since she promised to advise him how to make things better for Maslova.

❖

CHAPTER FIFTY

AWAKENING early next morning, Nekhludov shuddered to recall what had happened the day before. Yet, in spite of his fear, he was more determined than ever to go on with what he had begun.

Conscious of this duty, he left his house and went to see Maslennikov in order to obtain permission to visit Maslova and the old woman Menshova and her son, of whom Maslova had spoken. He also wanted a pass to see Vera Bogodukhovskaya, who might be useful to Maslova.

Nekhludov had known Maslennikov when they were in the same regiment together. He was paymaster at that time, a kind-hearted and most punctilious officer without an idea in his head beyond the regiment and the imperial family. Now Nekhludov found him in an administrative office. He had married a rich and energetic woman, who induced him to exchange the army for the civil service. She laughed at him and caressed him like a pet animal. Nekhludov had spent an evening at their house the previous winter and found the couple so uninteresting that he never went there again.

Maslennikov beamed when he saw Nekhludov. His face was just as red and fat, his figure just as bulky and his dress as correct as ever. In the old days he had always worn a carefully brushed, tightly fitting military uniform, cut in the latest style; now he wore a civil-service uniform, also in the latest style, fitting his well-fed body like a glove and showing off his broad chest. Notwithstanding the difference in years—Maslennikov was about forty—they were on intimate terms.

"Hello, my boy—how good of you to come! Let's go to my wife. I have just ten minutes before the meeting. You know, the chief is away and I'm at the head of the administration," he said, with a satisfaction he could not conceal.

"I have come on business."

"Ah! What is it?" he asked, putting himself instantly on his guard and assuming an air of severity.

"There is a person in prison" (at the word "prison" Maslennikov's face became even more severe) "whom I should like to see, not in the visiting room but in the office, and not only at the hours appointed for visitors but whenever I wish. I was told that this depends on you."

"Of course, *mon cher*, I shall be glad to do all I can for you," said Maslennikov, touching Nekhludov's knees with his hands, as though to depreciate his own greatness, "but remember, I am only the caliph of an hour."

"Will you give me a pass so that I can see her?"

"Then it's a woman?"

"Yes."

"What is she there for?"

"For poisoning. But she has been condemned unjustly."

"Yes, there's your righteous court of law. *Ils n'en font point d'autres*," he said. "I know that you don't agree with me, nevertheless *c'est mon opinion bien arrêtée*," he added, voicing an opinion which he had seen expressed in different forms for the last twelve months in a retrograde conservative paper. "I know you are a liberal."

"I am sure I don't know whether I am a liberal or not," replied Nekhludov, with a smile. It always surprised him to find himself classed with a party or called a liberal, just because he believed that all men are equal before the law, that no man has a right to beat or otherwise torment his fellow men—particularly those whom the law has not yet pronounced guilty. "I don't know whether I am a liberal or not, but I do know one thing—that the present courts, faulty though they may be, are better than those of the old days."

"And what lawyer have you engaged?"

"Fanarin,"

"Dear me!" said Maslennikov, with a grimace. He had not forgotten an experience of his own the year before, when for half an hour this Fanarin had cross-examined him as a witness and, with the utmost politeness, had made him appear a fool. "I should advise you to have nothing to do with him. *Fanarin est un homme taré*."

"I have one more request to make," said Nekhludov, ignoring Maslennikov's remark. "Some time ago I knew a girl, a young schoolteacher—she is much to be pitied. She is in prison as well and wants to see me. Could you give me a pass to visit her?"

Maslennikov bent his head on one side and thought a moment.

"Is she a political prisoner?"

"Yes, I have been told so."

"Well, you see, the passes to visit the 'politicals' are only given to relatives. But I will give you a general pass. *Je sais que vous n'en abuserez pas.* What is the name of your protégée? Bogodukhovskaya? *Elle est jolie?*"

"*Hideuse.*"

Maslennikov shook his head disapprovingly. Then he went to the table and wrote on a sheet of official paper: "The bearer, Prince Dmitri Ivanovich Nekhludov, is hereby granted leave to visit in the prison office the *meshchanka* Maslova and the medical student Bogodukhovskaya." He added a final flourish to his signature.

"You will see how well-regulated the place is. And it isn't an easy thing to maintain order in a prison like that, because it is filled largely with people who are there for a short time. But I'm very vigilant, and I'm interested in the business. You'll see how well-treated and contented they are. But you must know how to manage them. We had a case of insubordination not long ago. Another man in my place might have called it mutiny and made no end of wretched victims—whereas, with us, everything passed off, quietly. It takes care and firm authority," he went on clenching the fat white fist, with a conspicuous turquoise ring adorning one finger, that emerged from the gold-linked, stiffly starched cuff on his shirt sleeve. "Yes, care and authority," he repeated.

"Well, I don't know about that," said Nekhludov. "I have been there twice and I felt very depressed."

"D'you know, you should get acquainted with Countess Passek," went on Maslennikov, growing talkative. "She has devoted herself to this work. *Elle fait beaucoup de bien.* It is due to her—and, I think I may say with false modesty, to me—that all these changes have come about. The horrors of the old days have entirely disappeared, and you'll find that the prisoners are comfortable now. You will see for yourself. Now take this Fanarin—I don't know him personally, and of course my social position keeps our ways apart—well, he is most certainly a bad character, and moreover he allows himself to say such things in court, such things that—"

"Well, I am much obliged," said Nekhludov; taking the paper and without seeming to notice that Maslennikov was still talking, he said good-by to his former comrade.

"Won't you go in and see my wife?"

"I must beg you to excuse me. I am really pressed for time just now."

"She'll never forgive me for not bringing you in," said Maslennikov, accompanying his old comrade as far as the first landing: this was his practice with people, such as Nekhludov, whom he considered of secondary importance. "Do go in for a minute."

Nekhludov was firm, however, and while the doorkeeper and the footman were fetching his coat and cane and opening the door, where a policeman stood on duty, he said again that he really could not stay.

"Well, then, come on Thursday. That's her day at home. I'll tell her you're coming," shouted Maslennikov, from the stairs.

CHAPTER FIFTY-ONE

NEKHLUDOV lost no time that day. He went directly from Maslennikov's to the prison inspector's lodging. Again he heard the familiar sound of the inferior piano; this time it was not Liszt's *Rhapsody* but Clementi's *Etudes,* played with unusual power, clearness, and rapidity. The maid with the bandaged eye, who opened the door, said that the inspector was at home, and showed Nekhludov into a small sitting room furnished with a sofa and a table. A tall lamp, with a pink shade scorched on one side, stood on a woolen crocheted mat. The inspector entered with his usual sad and weary look.

"Please take a seat. What can I do for you?"

"I have just come from the vice-governor and I have a pass from him. I should like to see Maslova."

"Markova?" asked the inspector, not hearing distinctly because of the music.

"Maslova."

"Oh, yes."

The inspector rose and went to the door through which the torrent of Clementi's *roulades* came pouring in.

"Stop a moment, Marussya! It's impossible to hear ourselves speak," he said, in a voice that showed that this music was the bane of his life.

The playing ceased; impatient footsteps were heard, and somebody came and peered through the door.

Apparently relieved now that the music had stopped, the inspector lighted a large cigarette of mild tobacco and offered one to Nekhludov, who declined.

"I should like to see Maslova."

"I doubt if you will be able to see her today," said the inspector.

"Why not?"

"Well, I'm afraid it's your own fault," he replied, with a scarcely perceptible smile. "Please don't give her any more money, Prince. If you wish to help her in that way, give it to me. I will keep it for her. You see, you probably gave her some money yesterday which she used to buy vodka—it is an evil we cannot manage to eradicate—and today she is quite drunk, even violent."

"Can it be possible?"

"Indeed it is. I was even obliged to use harsh measures: I had her removed to another cell. As a rule, she is very good-natured—but please don't give her any more money. I tell you these people are—"

Nekhludov remembered what had taken place the day before, and again a feeling of horror came over him.

"Then may I see Bogodukhovskaya, the political prisoner?" he asked, after a moment's pause.

"Certainly. Well, what do you want here?" he added, turning to a little girl, five or six years old, who had just come into the room. She ran up to her father but her eyes were fixed on Nekhludov, as if not to lose sight of him for a moment. "Mind where you're going!" cried her father, as the child tripped over a rug.

"Well, then, if I may, I will go now."

"Oh, yes," said the inspector, putting his arm around the child, who was still staring at Nekhludov. Then he rose, gently putting her aside, and went out into the hall.

Even before they left the house, while the bandaged girl was helping the inspector with his overcoat, Clementi's clear-cut *roulades* began again.

"She has studied in the Conservatoire, but everything is in such a muddle there. She is talented and hopes to play in concerts," remarked the inspector, as he descended the stairs.

As Nekhludov and the inspector walked toward the prison, the small gate flew open at their approach. The warders, raising their hands to their caps, followed the inspector with their eyes. In the corridor they met four men with half-shaven heads carrying tubs filled with something; they cringed at the sight of the inspector and one man with black eyes bent down in a peculiar way, frowning gloomily.

"Of course, a talent like that must be developed, it ought not to be buried—but, you know, in a small flat it is not always pleasant," continued the inspector who, paying no heed to the prisoners, walked wearily beside Nekhludov until they reached the visiting room.

"Who is it you wish to see?" he asked.

"Bogodukhovskaya."

"She is in the tower, I believe. You'll have to wait a little."

"Then in the meantime may I see the Menshovs, the mother and the son, who are accused of arson?"

"That's cell twenty-one. Yes, they can be called."

"But couldn't I see Menshov in his cell?"

"You will be more comfortable in the visiting room."

"Yes, but it would interest me more to see him in his cell."

"Really? I don't see what interest you can find in that."

Meanwhile, the assistant inspector, a smartly dressed young officer, came in from a side door.

"Please escort this gentleman to Menshov's cell, number twenty-one," said the inspector, addressing his assistant. "Then take him to the office and I'll summon the woman. What did you call her?"

"Vera Bogodukhovskaya," replied Nekhludov.

The inspector's assistant was a fair-haired young man with a waxed mustache and a pervasive odor of eau-de-cologne.

"This way, sir. Our institution interests you?" he asked, with a pleasant smile.

"Yes. I also take an interest in this man, who I am told is here through no fault of his."

The assistant shrugged his shoulders.

"That does happen sometimes," he said, in a quiet voice, courteously allowing the visitor to pass before him as they entered a wide, foul-smelling corridor. "Still, you can't believe all they say. This way," he added.

The doors of the cells were open and several prisoners were standing in the corridor.

With a slight nod to the warders and a rapid side glance at the prisoners, some of whom went back to their cells keeping close to the wall, while others, with hands pressed to their sides soldier-fashion, stood gazing after them, the assistant guided Nekhludov through the corridor into another on the left, barred by an iron-bound door.

This corridor was still darker and fouler than the first. On both sides were padlocked doors, each one provided with a hole about half an inch in diameter, called an "eye." There was no one in this corridor except a melancholy, wrinkled old warder.

"Which is Menshov's cell?" asked the assistant.

"The eighth on the left."

"Are all these cells occupied?" inquired Nekhludov.

"Yes, all but one."

❧

CHAPTER FIFTY-TWO

"MAY I take a look?"

"Certainly, if you wish." The assistant inspector smiled pleasantly, and turned to ask the warder a question.

Nekhludov peered through one of the holes, and saw a tall young man with a stubby black beard walking rapidly back and forth in his underclothes; hearing the noise at his door, he looked up, frowned, and went on with his walk. Nekhludov looked through the next hole. Here his eye met another— an eye so big with terror that he instinctively withdrew his own. Through the third opening he saw a small man curled up on the bed, with his prison cloak drawn up over his head. Through the fourth, he saw a pale man with broad cheeks who sat with head bowed down, leaning his elbows on his knees. At the sound of footsteps he lifted his head and looked up. His face and his large eyes bore an expression of desperate sadness. He didn't seem to care whether anyone looked at him or not. No living being could bring him any hope. It was terrible, and Nekhludov looked through no more of the holes till he reached cell number twenty-one, occupied by Menshov.

The warder unlocked and opened the door. A muscular young fellow with a long neck, a small beard, and kindly, round eyes was standing beside the bed hurriedly putting on his prison cloak. Nekhludov was particularly struck by the frightened expression of the kindly eyes that gazed inquiringly first at him and then at the warder and the inspector.

"Here is a gentleman who wishes you to tell him about your case."

"Thank you, sir."

"Yes, I have heard about your case," said Nekhludov, crossing the cell and stopping before the dirty barred window, "but I should like you to tell me about it yourself."

Menshov came up to the window and at once began his story, timidly at first and glancing continually at the inspector, then gathering courage as he proceeded. When the inspector stepped into the corridor to give some orders, he regained confidence completely. Judged by his language and manners, he was a good, ordinary peasant lad, and it seemed strange to hear his story told in a prison cell by a man wearing degrading prison clothes. While he listened, Nekhludov looked around him: he examined the low bunk with its straw mattress, the solid iron grating over the window, the damp, dirty walls, the pitiful figure of this unfortunate peasant so incongruous in his cloak and slippers, and he felt sadder and sadder. He almost wished that he did not believe that this apparently well-meaning man was telling the truth, for it was dreadful to think that people could take such a lad, without any reason except that he had suffered wrong, dress him in convict clothes, and shut him up in this horrible place. On the other hand, it was even more distressing to suspect that this seemingly true story might be a lie and this simple, honest face a deceitful mask.

This was the story: shortly after Menshov's marriage, the village innkeeper had enticed away his wife. At first he tried everywhere to get justice, but the innkeeper bribed the officials and was always acquitted. Once he brought his wife home by force, but she ran away again the next day. Then he went to the innkeeper's house and demanded his wife. He was told to clear out, that his wife was not there. But he had seen her as he came in, and refused to leave; whereupon the innkeeper and his man fell upon him and gave him a beating. The next day the innkeeper's house was burnt down. Menshov and his mother were accused of the crime, though he could prove an alibi, for at the time when the house caught fire he was visiting a friend.

"So you really did not set it on fire?"

"I never thought of such a thing, sir. My enemy did it himself, I'm sure he did. I heard he had insured it just before. And my mother and I were accused of going there and threatening him. I did give him a piece of my mind that day, my heart couldn't stand it any longer—but as to setting his house on fire, I didn't do it. I wasn't even there when the fire started. He planned it for that day because my mother and I had been seen there. He started the fire himself, to get the insurance, and then he said that we had done it."

"Can this be true?"

"It's God's truth, sir. Be a father to us," he cried. Nekhludov had difficulty in preventing him from falling at his feet. "Help me to get out, I am perishing for no reason. . . ." The muscles of his face began to twitch and he burst out sobbing. He turned up the sleeve of his cloak and wiped his eyes on his soiled shirt sleeve.

"Have you finished?" asked the assistant.

"Yes."

"Now, keep up your courage; we will do all we can," said Nekhludov, as he left the cell. Menshov stood in the doorway, so that the assistant struck him with the door when he closed it. While the warder was locking the door, Menshov looked out through the little hole.

❦

CHAPTER FIFTY-THREE

As Nekhludov retraced his steps along the wide corridor, it was dinnertime and the cells were open. He walked past the men clad in long pale yellow cloaks, short wide trousers, and prison shoes; they gazed at him with intense curiosity, and Nekhludov was divided between feelings of pity for those who were imprisoned, and of horror for those who had thrown them into prison and kept them there; besides, though he knew not why, he felt ashamed of himself for calmly examining all this.

A man hurried along the corridor, his shoes clattering as he ran, and rushed into one of the cells; presently, several men came out and stood in front of Nekhludov, barring his way, and said, bowing as they spoke:

"Your Honor, we don't know what to call you, but we beg you to get our affairs settled somehow."

"But I am not a person in authority; I know nothing about your case."

"Then tell the authorities!" said an indignant voice. "We

haven't done anything, and here we have been kept in misery for over a month."

"How is that? Why?" asked Nekhludov.

"We don't know why. This is the second month we've been sitting here, and we don't know what for."

"Yes, they are telling the truth. You see, it was a kind of accident," said the assistant inspector. "They were sent here because they had no passports; they should have been sent to their own district, but the prison there was burned down and the local authorities requested us to keep them. We have released the men from the other districts, but these are still confined."

"Is that the only reason for their detention here?" said Nekhludov, pausing at the door. Some forty men dressed in prison clothes surrounded Nekhludov and the assistant. Several began to speak at once, but the assistant stopped them.

"Let one of you be the spokesman."

A tall, good-looking peasant, some fifty years of age, stepped forward.

He explained that they had been sent to jail because they had no passports; yet they had their passports all right, only the time for which they were issued had expired about two weeks before they were arrested. This happened to people every year and no one troubled them, but this time they had been arrested and imprisoned just as if they were criminals.

"We aré all stonemasons and belong to the same *artel*.[1] We have heard that the jail in our town was burned down. But that is not our fault. Please put in a good word for us."

Nekhludov listened but did not quite grasp what the pleasant-looking old man was saying: his attention was distracted by the movements of a large, dark-gray, many-legged louse crawling along the man's cheek.

"Is all this true? Can it be possible that there is no other reason?" asked Nekhludov, turning to the inspector's assistant.

"Yes, it is true—they ought to have been sent home; there is no doubt about that."

Just then a nervous little man, also in prison dress, came out of the crowd and began to say, with strange contortions of his mouth, that they were being treated worse than dogs.

"Now, then, enough of this. Hold your tongue, or you know—"

"What do I know?" the little man cried, desperately. "We have done nothing wrong."

[1] Guild.—Tr.

"Silence!" shouted the assistant inspector, and the other's protests died away.

"What does all this mean?" Nekhludov was saying to himself as he left the cell, conscious that hundreds of eyes were following him: those of the prisoners they met on the way, and others from the holes in the doors.

"Is it really true that innocent men are kept here?" he asked, as they turned out of the corridor.

"What can we do about it? Of course they don't all speak the truth. If you were to believe their stories, not a single man of them has done anything wrong."

"But surely these men have done nothing wrong?"

"Yes, that is true. But on the whole they're an unruly lot. We have to be very strict with them—there are some dangerous types among them. One has to be on one's guard all the time. Only yesterday we had to punish two of them."

"Punish them? In what way?"

"Flog them."

"But corporal punishment has been abolished!"

"Not for those who have been deprived of civil rights. They are not exempt."

Remembering what he had seen the day before while waiting in the hall, Nekhludov understood that the flogging must have been going on during that time; such a turmoil of sadness and bewilderment arose within him that his moral nausea was on the verge of becoming actual physical sickness; he had experienced something similar before, but never as painfully as now. No longer listening to the assistant inspector, he walked as fast as he could, looking neither right nor left until he reached the office. The inspector, still in the corridor attending to some other business, had forgotten to summon Vera Bogodukhovskava. The sight of Nekhludov reminded him.

"I will send for her at once," he said. "Please sit down."

❧

CHAPTER FIFTY-FOUR

THE office consisted of two rooms; the first one was lighted by two dirty windows and contained a large, dilapidated stove. A black yard-measure for measuring the prisoners stood in one corner, while in another hung a large image of Christ—as is usual in places where people are tortured. Several warders were standing in that room.

In the next room there were about twenty men and women sitting in pairs and in groups talking quietly.

The inspector took a seat by the table near the window and offered Nekhludov a chair beside him. Nekhludov sat down and became absorbed in watching the people in the room.

The first to attract his attention was a pleasant-faced young man wearing a short jacket. He was standing in front of an elderly woman with very dark eyebrows, talking to her in an excited voice and gesticulating with his hands. Beside them an old man with blue spectacles was holding the hand of a young woman dressed in prison clothes; he was listening to something she was saying. A schoolboy with a fixed, frightened look was gazing steadily at the old man. In a corner not far from this group sat a pair of lovers. The girl was very young and pretty; she had short fair hair and an energetic expression, and was fashionably dressed. The young man's features were handsome and delicately cut; he had curly hair and wore a waterproof jacket. They were carrying on a whispered conversation in their corner and were clearly very much in love. Next to Nekhludov sat a gray-haired woman dressed in black—unmistakably a mother, for she never once turned her eyes from a young man who looked as though he were consumptive; he also wore a waterproof jacket. She kept trying to speak, but tears were choking her; over and over again she opened her lips, said a word or two, and then stopped. The young man held a slip of paper in his hand and seemed at a loss to decide what he ought to do; he looked angry as he sat there crumpling the paper. Next to them was a handsome, vigorous, rosy-cheeked girl with prominent eyes; she wore a gray dress and cape, and sat beside the weeping mother, patting her tenderly on the shoulder. Everything about this girl was beautiful: her large pale hands, her short wavy hair, her clear-cut nose and lips; but her supreme charm lay in her remarkable eyes, kind, truthful, and brown, like the eyes of a lamb. When Nekhludov entered, those beautiful eyes turned for an instant from the face of the young man's mother and met his own; but she looked away at once and began to talk to the mother. Not far from the lovers sat a ragged man with a dark, gloomy face, talking angrily to a beardless visitor who looked like a *Skopetz*.

Nekhludov, sitting beside the inspector, looked around with intense curiosity. His attention was taken by a little boy with closely cut hair who came up and cried out in a shrill voice:

"And who do *you* wish to see?"

Nekhludov was taken aback by the question but, when he glanced at the boy and saw his serious little face and bright, intelligent eyes, he replied gravely that he was waiting to see a woman he knew.

"Is she your sister?" asked the boy.

"No," replied Nekhludov, with surprise. "And whom are you with?" he asked.

"I am with Mamma. She is a political."

"Maria Pavlovna, see to Kolya," said the inspector, seeming to regard Nekhludov's conversation with the boy as an infringement of the rules.

Maria Pavlovna was the handsome girl with the lamblike eyes, who had noticed Nekhludov when he came in.

She rose to her full height and, with a firm, almost masculine step, approached Nekhludov and the boy.

"I suppose he was asking who you are?" she said, with a slight smile, gazing confidently into his eyes with the simplicity of one to whom it is natural to be on the friendliest terms with all the world.

"He wants to know everything," she said, smiling at the boy so kindly and charmingly that both the child and Nekhludov gave her an answering smile.

"Yes, he asked me whom I wanted to see."

"Maria Pavlovna, you know it is against the rules to talk to strangers," said the inspector.

"Very well, very well," she said, and, taking Kolya's little hand in her own large, white hand, she returned with him to the mother of the consumptive young man. The boy never took his eyes from her face.

"Whose child is he?" Nekhludov asked the inspector.

"He is the son of a political prisoner. He was born in prison," said the inspector, with a certain pride in displaying the curiosities of the establishment.

"Really?"

"Yes. Now he is going to Siberia with his mother."

"And that young lady?"

"I can't tell you about her," said the inspector, shrugging his shoulders. "Ah, here comes Bogodukhovskaya."

CHAPTER FIFTY-FIVE

VERA EFREMOVNA BOGODUKHOVSKAYA came in with an awkward, jerky gait; she was thin and sallow, with short hair and large, kind eyes. "Thank you so much for coming," she said, shaking hands with Nekhludov. "I'm very glad you remember me. Let us sit down."

"I didn't expect to find you in a place like this."

"Oh, I am happy, perfectly happy. I couldn't ask for anything better," said Vera Efremovna, with a startled glance of her kind, round eyes, twisting her thin, sinewy neck inside a soiled and crumpled collar.

Nekhludov asked her how she came to be in prison. She told him the story with great animation, interspersing it with many foreign words—"propaganda," "disorganization," "groups" and "sections" and "subsections"—which she seemed to assume would be familiar to everybody, but of which Nekhludov did not know the significance.

She poured it all out, fully convinced that he would be interested and delighted to hear about the mysteries of the *Narodovolstvo*,[1] while Nekhludov was looking at her miserable little neck and thin untidy hair, wondering why she did and said such astonishing things. He was sorry for her, but his sympathy was different from his feeling for Menshov, shut up in this foul prison for no fault of his own. He pitied her chiefly for the manifest confusion in her mind. She clearly considered herself a heroine and was showing off, and this made her all the more pitiable.

Nekhludov saw this element of play acting in her and also in a few other people in the room. He had attracted their attention and he felt that they behaved in a slightly different manner just because he was present. He noticed this in the young man with the waterproof jacket, in the woman wearing prison clothes, and even in the young pair of lovers. It was absent only in the consumptive young man, in the handsome girl with the lamb-like eyes, and in the disheveled man with the deepset eyes.

The case which Vera Efremovna wanted to see him about was as follows: Shustova, a friend of hers, who did not even be-

[1] "People's Freedom," a revolutionary movement.—Tr.

long to their "subgroup," as she called it, had been arrested five
months before and imprisoned in the Fortress of Peter and
Paul, merely because some books and papers, which had been
entrusted to her keeping, happened to be found in her house.
Vera Efremovna felt herself partly responsible for Shustova's
arrest, and implored Nekhludov to use all his influence to secure
her release. She had a further favor to ask also, and this was
to obtain for another of her friends, Gurevich (imprisoned in
the same fortress) permission to see his parents and to be allowed certain scientific books which he needed for research.

Nekhludov promised to do everything in his power when he
reached Petersburg.

Her own story was this: after finishing her course in mid-
wifery she had become connected with a group of *Narodovoltsi*,
and began to work with them. At first all went well, proclamations were written and propaganda was carried on in the factories; but the time came when one very prominent member
of the party was arrested. Papers were found that incriminated
others, and many arrests followed.

"I was also arrested, and now I am to be exiled," she said, as
she finished her tale. "But I don't care. I am quite well and perfectly happy," she concluded, with her pitiable smile.

Nekhludov asked her about the girl with the lamblike eyes.
Vera Efremovna told him that she was the daughter of a general
and had been a member of the revolutionary party for a long
time. She had been arrested because she had declared that she
had shot a gendarme. She was living in an apartment occupied
by conspirators, where a printing press was kept. One night,
when soldiers came to search the premises, the occupants decided to defend themselves; they put out the lights and began
to destroy the incriminating articles. But the police broke in,
and one of the conspirators fired a shot, mortally wounding a
gendarme. When questioned as to who fired the shot, Maria
Pavlovna said it was she, although she had never touched a
pistol in her life and would not kill a fly. Nevertheless, her story
was accepted and now she was sentenced to penal servitude.
"An altruistic and very noble character," said Vera Efremovna,
approvingly.

The third matter that he wanted to discuss concerned Maslova. She knew her story—nothing is ever hidden in prison
life—and advised Nekhludov to set about getting her either removed into the "political" ward, or else sent to help in the
hospital, where there were a great many patients just then and
attendants were needed.

Nekhludov thanked her for her advice and said that he would try and carry it out.

❖

CHAPTER FIFTY-SIX

THEIR conversation was interrupted by the inspector, who rose and announced that the visiting hour was over. Nekhludov said good-by to Vera Efremovna and walked to the door, where he stopped to observe what was going on.

"Time's up, time's up!" repeated the inspector, rising and then resuming his seat again. This announcement seemed to be the signal for increased animation; nobody appeared to consider it an order. A few rose to their feet, but most of them kept their seats; all went on with their conversation. Some began tearfully bidding each other good-by. The sight of the mother and her consumptive son was particularly moving. The young man was still twirling his bit of paper and his face looked fiercer than ever, so hard did he find it not to follow his mother's example; when she heard that it was time to go, she laid her head on his shoulder and cried like a child. The girl with the lamb-like eyes whom, Nekhludov could not help watching, stood in front of the sobbing mother trying to comfort her. The old man with the blue spectacles held his daughter's hand and nodded in answer to what she was saying. The young lovers were standing, clasping hands, and gazing silently into each other's eyes.

"Those two are the only happy ones here," said a young man in a short coat, pointing at the lovers. He stood beside Nekhludov, also watching.

Conscious that Nekhludov and the young man were gazing at them, the lovers stretched out their hands and, laughing merrily, began to waltz around the room. "They are to be married here this evening, and she will follow him to Siberia," remarked the young man.

"Who is he?"

"A convict, sentenced to penal servitude. Well, it's good that they have the heart to be gay. It is so distressing to hear that," he added, alluding to the sobs of the consumptive's mother.

"Please, ladies and gentlemen, please! Do not force me to use severe measures," said the inspector, repeating the same words again and again in a weak and hesitating voice. "Please go, I beg you! It's later than usual. This cannot go on! I am warning you for the last time," he kept saying wearily, now lighting, now extinguishing his cigarette. Although men use many arguments —artful, old, and stale—to justify to themselves the evil they do, yet it was evident that the inspector was distressed, feeling that he, too, was among those guilty for the sorrow which filled the room.

At last they began to depart, the visitors through the outer and the prisoners through the inner door. The man in the water-proof jacket, the consumptive, the dark man in rags and tatters, Maria Pavlovna leading the boy born in prison—all went out of the room, and the visitors left, too.

"Yes, these regulations are absurd," said the talkative young man as if continuing an interrupted conversation, as he went down the stairs with Nekhludov. "Luckily the inspector is a kindhearted chap and does not keep strictly to rules. A chat does these people good."

While they were standing on the porch, talking, the inspector came up to them with a weary step.

"If you would like to see Maslova, please come tomorrow," he said to Nekhludov, evidently trying to be friendly.

"Very well," said Nekhludov, and hurried away.

It all seemed terrible. Terrible was the suffering of Menshov —not so much his physical suffering as the bewilderment of his mind, the distrust of God and of human goodness that he must have felt when cruel men tormented him without cause. Terrible were the suffering and disgrace inflicted on those other in-nocent men, merely for an omission in some paper. Terrible were the jailers, convinced that they were performing an im-portant and useful task by tormenting their fellow men. But most terrible of all was the elderly, feeble, kindhearted in-spector, whose duty compelled him to separate mother and son, father and daughter, human beings just like himself and his children.

"And why should all this be?" Nekhludov asked himself. He felt the same moral nausea, very close to physical sickness, which he always experienced when in the prison, and he could find no answer to his question.

CHAPTER FIFTY-SEVEN

THE next day Nekhludov went to his lawyer and engaged him to conduct Menshov's case. The lawyer, after hearing the circumstances, said that he would look into it and that if the matter was really as represented, which was probably so, he would undertake the defense free of charge. Then Nekhludov told him of the hundred and thirty men imprisoned through a misunderstanding, and asked him on whom their freedom depended, and who was to blame.

The lawyer reflected in silence: he did not mean to give a hasty answer.

"Who is to blame? No one," he replied at last. "If you ask the public prosecutor, he will tell you it is the governor's fault, and the governor will say that is it the fault of the prosecutor. Oh, no, nobody is to blame!"

"I am just going to see Maslennikov. I shall tell him about it."

"That'll do no good," said the lawyer, with a smile. "He is such a—he's not a relation of yours, is he?—such a blockhead. Yet, he's a foxy fellow, too."

Recalling what Maslennikov had said of the lawyer, Nekhludov made no reply; he took his leave and went on to Maslennikov. He had two requests to make: he wanted an order for Maslova's transfer to the hospital, and redress for the hundred and thirty men without passports. He hated to ask a favor of a man he did not respect, but he had to go through with it because there seemed to be no other way.

As he drew near the house he saw a few carriages by the entrance, and remembered that this was Mme. Maslennikov's day at home, to which he had been invited. As he drove up, a carriage blocked the way; a footman wearing livery with a cockade was assisting his mistress to enter the carriage. As she lifted the train of her gown, she exposed her slippered feet and thin ankles encased in black stockings.

One of the carriages belonged to the Korchagins. The gray-haired, rosy-faced coachman saluted him respectfully and pleasantly, like an old acquaintance.

He was just about to ask the doorkeeper for Mikhail Ivanovich when Maslennikov himself appeared coming down the carpeted staircase. He was escorting a very important guest, not to the first landing only, but to the very foot of the stairs.

On his way down the important visitor was talking in French about a lottery that was to be held for the benefit of some children's homes, and expressed the opinion that it was a very suitable occupation for the ladies. "It amuses them and provides us with money. *Qu'elles s'amusent et que le bon Dieu les bénisse.* . . . Ah, Nekhludov, how are you? Where do you keep yourself nowadays?" he greeted Nekhludov. *"Allez présenter vos devoirs à Madame.* The Korchagins are there, and Nadine Bukshevden. *Toutes les jolies femmes de la ville,"* he concluded, turning his uniformed shoulders, with a slight upward movement, to his own magnificent footman, in a gold-braided livery, who stood holding his master's greatcoat.

"Au revoir, mon cher," and he pressed Maslennikov's hand.

"Now let us go upstairs. I'm so glad you came," said Maslennikov, excitedly, taking Nekhludov by the arm and, heavy man though he was, quickly running with him up the stairs.

Maslennikov's extreme good humor was the result of the attention bestowed on him by the exalted personage. Attention of that kind gave him the same sort of pleasure that a dog feels when his master strokes his back or pats him on the head or scratches him behind the ear; the dog will wag his tail, crouch on the ground, lay back his ears, and frisk wildly about the room. That was what Maslennikov would have liked to do. He did not notice the serious expression on Nekhludov's face, did not listen to what he was saying, but drew him on impetuously toward the drawing room. There was nothing for Nekhludov to do but follow him.

"We'll talk business later. I will do anything in the world for you," he said, as they were going through the dancing hall. "Announce Prince Nekhludov to Madame," he said to a footman, who ran on ahead of them. *"Vous n'avez qu'à ordonner.* But you must pay your visit to my wife; I got into trouble the other day for not bringing you in."

When they entered the drawing room, the footman had already announced him, and Anna Ignatyevna, the governor's lady ("the general-ess," as she styled herself) nodded and beamed upon him from behind the heads and bonnets that surrounded her sofa.

"Enfin! Why have you kept away so long? What have we done?" Anna Ignatyevna said to Nekhludov as he entered, implying both by word and by manner a degree of intimacy between them which in reality had never existed.

"Do you know each other? Do you know Mme. Belyavskaya?

Mikhail Ivanovich Chernov? Draw your chair nearer. Missy, *venez donc à notre table. On vous apportera votre thé.* . . . And you, too . . ." she addressed the officer who was talking to Missy, having apparently forgotten his name. "Will you have a cup of tea, Prince?"

"No, I'll never agree with you, never! She didn't love him, that's all," said a woman's voice.

"But she did love cakes."

"Oh, how silly you are!" exclaimed another laughing voice, belonging to a lady who wore a high-crowned hat and a brilliant silk dress gleaming with gold and jewels.

"*C'est excellent,* this wafer, it's so light. I'd like another."

"Are you going soon?"

"This is our last day in town. That's why we are here."

"Such a delightful spring, it must be lovely in the country."

Missy was beautiful in a dark striped gown that fitted her like a glove. She blushed when she saw Nekhludov.

"I thought you were gone," she said.

"I should have gone," he replied, "but business detained me. I have come here today on business, too."

"I wish you would go and see Mamma. She would be so pleased." Her color deepened as she spoke, for she knew she was telling a falsehood and that he could not fail to see through it.

"I shall hardly have time," said Nekhludov, sullenly, pretending not to notice that she was blushing.

Missy frowned angrily, shrugging her shoulders, and turned to an officer wearing a brilliant uniform, who took her empty cup and manfully carried it across the room to a tea table, hitting his saber against every chair on the way.

"You really must give something for the orphanage."

"I don't mean to refuse. I only wish to keep my largesse for the lottery. There I shall let it appear in all its glory."

"Well, see that you do!" exclaimed a voice, followed by a noticeably artificial laugh. Anna Ignatyevna was beaming: her at-home was a great success.

"Mika tells me that you are interested in prison work," she said to Nekhludov. (Mika was her fat husband, Maslennikov.) "I sympathize with you deeply. Mika may have his faults, but he has the kindest heart in the world. All these unfortunate prisoners are just like his own children. That is the way he feels about them. *Il est d'une bonté* . . ."

She broke off, finding no words to do justice to the "kindness" of her husband, by whose orders men were flogged, and turned with a smile to welcome a wrinkled old lady with purple ribbons who was just coming in.

Having said as much as was absolutely necessary and with as little meaning as the conventions required, Nekhludov rose and went up to Maslennikov.

"Can you give me a few minutes now?"

"Yes, of course. Let's go in here."

They entered a small room furnished in Japanese style, and sat down near the window.

❧

CHAPTER FIFTY-EIGHT

"AND now *je suis à vous*. Will you smoke? Wait a moment, we must take care not to make a mess here," he said, bringing out an ash tray. "Now then!"

"There are two things I want to speak to you about!"

"Dear me!"

Maslennikov's face grew listless and dejected; every trace of his doglike excitement vanished. Voices were coming from the drawing room: a woman's voice saying, "*Jamais, jamais je ne le croirai—*" and a man's voice from another direction relating some incident and repeating the names *la Comtesse* Vorontzova and Victor Apraksine over and over again. This was succeeded by laughter and a hum of voices. Maslennikov was endeavoring to listen to what was going on in the drawing room and to Nekhludov at the same time.

"I have come to speak to you again about that woman," said Nekhludov.

"The one who was unjustly convicted? Yes, I remember."

"I should like you to give me an order for her transfer to the hospital; there is work for her there. They tell me it can be done."

Maslennikov compressed his lips together as though he were pondering.

"I should hardly think so," he said. "But I will inquire and send you a telegram tomorrow."

"They tell me that there is a great number of patients and that more assistants are needed."

"Well, it may be so. Anyway, I'll let you know."

"Please do," said Nekhludov.

A general burst of laughter came from the drawing room, this time sounding sincere.

"That's Victor," said Maslennikov, smiling. "He's very brilliant when he chooses."

"And one thing more," said Nekhludov. "There are a hundred and thirty men in the prison being kept there simply because their passports had run out. They have been there a month." And he related the details of the affair.

"How did you find that out?" asked Maslennikov; a shadow of annoyance and uneasiness crossed his face.

"I went to see one of the prisoners, and while I was in the corridor these men surrounded me and pleaded—"

"Which prisoner did you visit?"

"A peasant who is unjustly accused. I have put his case into the hands of a solicitor. But that's another story. Can it be possible that all those innocent men are imprisoned just because their passports had run out and—"

"That's the prosecutor's business," interrupted Maslennikov, impatiently. "You were telling me a little while ago that the new courts are so much better and more just than the old ones! Now it is the duty of the assistant prosecutor to visit the prisons and find out whether the prisoners are detained lawfully. But these gentlemen are too much interested in their whist to attend to their duties."

"Then there is nothing you can do?" said Nekhludov, drily, remembering that the solicitor had foretold that the governor would lay the blame on the prosecutor.

"Oh, yes, I can inquire into the case."

"So much the worse for her. *C'est un souffre-douleur*," said a woman's voice, evidently quite indifferent to what she was saying.

Then came the voice of a man, who seemed to be wheedling for something that was refused him: "All right, then. I shall take this instead."

There was a good deal of jesting and laughter.

"No, no, I shan't let you have it," said a woman's voice.

"Very well, then, I'll do all I can for you," repeated Maslennikov, putting out his cigarette with a white hand adorned with a turquoise ring. "Now let us go to the ladies."

"One thing more," said Nekhludov, pausing in the doorway. "I was told that some men were given corporal punishment in the prison yesterday. Is that true?"

Maslennikov blushed.

"Good Heavens! My dear fellow, what will you ask next?

You're not the man to let loose in a prison—you're too in-quisitive. Come, Annette is calling us," he said, taking Nekh-ludov by the arm. He was beginning to be as excited as he had been over the honor which the important personage had paid him, but it was not a joyful excitement this time. He seemed a good deal ruffled.

Nekhludov snatched away his arm and, without a word of salutation to anyone, strode through the drawing room and the hall, past the footmen, who jumped up, and went out into the street.

"Why, what's the matter with him? What did you do to him?" Annette asked her husband.

"That's à la française," said someone.

"I should call it à la Zulu."

"He's always been like that."

Guests were coming and going and the twittering went on. The Nekhludov incident furnished the company with a topic of conversation for the rest of the afternoon.

The next day Nekhludov received a letter from Maslennikov. It was written in a clear, bold handwriting on heavy cream-laid paper decorated with an official crest and seal. This letter stated that he had written to the doctor about transferring Maslova, and that in all probability his request would be granted. He signed it, "Your affectionate elder comrade Maslennikov," end-ing with a large, firm, elaborate flourish.

"Idiot," Nekhludov could not help saying. "Elder com-rade" savored too much of condescension. Maslennikov seemed to think that the holding of an office, whose duties from a moral point of view were as base and contemptible as could be, gave him a right to regard himself as a man of importance; and he wished if not exactly to flatter Nekhludov, at least to show him that he was not too proud to call himself a comrade.

❧

CHAPTER FIFTY-NINE

It is one of the most common and generally accepted super-stitions to attribute some particular leading quality to every man—to say of him that he is kind, wicked, wise, foolish, energetic, or dull. This is wrong. We may say of a man that he is more frequently kind than cruel, wise than foolish, en-

ergetic than apathetic, or vice versa—but it could never be true
to say of one man that he is kind or wise, and of another that
he is wicked or foolish. Yet this is our method of classifying
mankind, and a very false method it is. Men are like rivers.
The water is alike in all of them; but every river is narrow
in some places and wide in others; here swift and there slug-
gish, here clear and there turbid; cold in winter and warm in
summer. The same may be said of men. Every man bears within
himself the germs of every human quality, displaying all in
turn; and a man can often seem unlike himself—yet he still
remains the same man.

In some people—Nekhludov was an example of this class
—these changes are very abrupt, and he was just then passing
through one of these transitions, which are often due as much
to physical as to spiritual causes; fear and even aversion after
his last interview with Katusha were succeeding the triumphant
and joyful regeneration which he had experienced after the
trial and their first meeting. He was still determined not to
leave her, nor to abandon his intention of marriage, if she
would consent, but it seemed grievously hard.

The day after his visit to Maslennikov he went again to
the prison to see her.

The inspector consented to the interview, but said it could
not take place in the office nor in the lawyer's room; Nekhludov
would have to see her in the women's visiting room. The inspector was more distant in his manner than previously. One
of the results of Nekhludov's conversation with Maslennikov
had apparently been an order for greater reticence toward this
visitor.

"You may see her," he said, "but please do as I asked you
about the money. As to her transfer to the hospital, His Excellency has written about it and the physician has given his
consent—but Maslova does not wish to go. She says she doesn't
care to empty slops for those dirty creatures. You don't know
these people yet, Prince," he added.

Nekhludov made no reply, but asked to see her. A warder
was dispatched and Nekhludov followed him into the visiting
room, where there was no one but Maslova waiting.

She came from behind the rail timidly and quietly and said,
keeping her eyes averted:

"Forgive me, Dmitri Ivanovich—I said wicked things the
day before yesterday."

"It isn't for me to forgive you," began Nekhludov.

"But you must leave me alone all the same," she interrupted, and in the squinting eyes she turned upon him Nekhludov could read the old strained and evil expression.

"Why must I leave you alone?"

"Because—"

"Because?"

Again he seemed to see that evil glance.

"All I can say is, let me alone," she said. "I couldn't bear it. Don't think about it any more." Her lips trembled, and after a moment's silence she said:

"I'd rather hang myself."

Nekhludov recognized in the voice hatred and bitter resentment for an unforgiven offense. But there was also something else in it—something important and good. Uttered in a calm and self-controlled state of mind, this repetition of her former refusal relieved all his uncertainty and brought back his previous solemn and tender feelings for her.

"I can only repeat what I have said before, Katusha," he said, earnestly. "I ask you to be my wife. If you don't want to marry me, I shall not urge you, but I shall remain near you and follow you wherever you may be sent."

"That's your own affair—I've nothing more to say," she replied, and her lips began to tremble again.

He was silent for a moment, unable to speak; but soon, recovering himself, he continued:

"I am going into the country now, and afterward to Petersburg. I shall do all I can about your—about our—case, and, God willing, the verdict may be set aside."

"Never mind if it isn't. If I don't deserve it for this, I deserve it for other things," she said, and he saw now that she was struggling to keep back her tears. Suddenly, to cover her emotion, she asked:

"Well, did you see Menshov? It's true that they are not guilty, isn't it?"

"Yes, I think it is."

"She is such a wonderful old woman," she said.

He repeated what Menshov had told him, and then asked her whether she needed anything for herself. She replied that she did not.

Again they were silent.

"And as to the hospital," she said, suddenly, glancing at him with her squinting eyes, "I will go if you wish it, and I won't touch a drop of drink, either. . . ."

Nekhludov gazed silently into her eyes. They were smiling.

"That's good," was all he said, and then bade her good-by.

"Yes, she is a different being," he thought, experiencing after all his former doubts a feeling he had never known before—the certainty that love is invincible.

When Maslova returned to her cell, she took off her prison cloak and sat down on the bunk, letting her hands fall on her knees. The only other prisoners in the cell were the consumptive girl, the woman from Vladimir with her baby, old Menshova, and the signal woman with her two children. The subdeacon's daughter had been pronounced insane the day before and sent to the hospital. The old woman was asleep in her bunk. The rest were out washing. The cell door stood open and the children were playing in the corridor. The woman from Vladimir, with her baby in her arms, and the signal woman, who was knitting a stocking, came up to Maslova.

"Well, did you see him?" she asked.

Maslova sat dangling her feet over the edge of the high bunk; she made no reply.

"What's the use of sniveling?" said the signal woman. "You've got to keep up your spirits. Ah, Katusha, come now!" she said, her fingers moving like lightning.

But Maslova still would not open her lips.

"Our folks are all out washing. You can't think how many people were giving alms today!" said the Vladimir woman.

"Finashka!" cried the signal woman. "What's become of the little rascal?"

She stuck a knitting needle through both the ball and the stocking and went out into the corridor.

Just then the sound of footsteps and women's voices was heard from the corridor, and presently the other occupants of the cell came in. They were all wearing prison shoes but no stockings, and were carrying loaves in their hands; some had two.

Fedosya went straight to Maslova.

"Has anything gone wrong?" she asked, with a tender glance at her friend from her clear blue eyes. "Those are for our tea," she added, as she put two fancy loaves on the shelf.

"Has he changed his mind about marrying you?" asked Korablyova.

"No, but I don't want it," said Maslova.

"The more fool you!" said Korablyova, in her deep voice.

"What's the use of marrying if you can't live together?" said Fedosya.

"But *your* husband is going with you," retorted the signal woman.

"Yes, but we're already married. I don't see why he should tie himself up if he can't live with her afterward."

"Why should he? Don't be such a fool! You know if he marries her she'll be rolling in money."

"He said, 'No matter where you are, I'll follow you,'" said Maslova. "But I don't care whether he does or not. I'm not going to ask him to. He's going to Petersburg now, to look after my case. He is related to all the ministers there. But I've no use for him all the same."

"No, of course you haven't," Korablyova unexpectedly agreed. She was rummaging in her bag, and was evidently thinking of something else. "Let's have a drink."

"You have some. I won't," said Maslova.

END OF BOOK I

BOOK II

CHAPTER ONE

MASLOVA'S case was due to come before the Senate in about a fortnight, and Nekhludov intended to be in Petersburg by that time, so that if matters went wrong he would be able to petition the emperor; such was the advice of the lawyer who had already drawn up the petition. If this were dismissed (and according to the lawyer it was best to be prepared for that, as the grounds for appeal were by no means indisputable), Maslova was to start off early in June with her party of convicts. Therefore, in order to be ready to follow her to Siberia, as he was determined to do, it was necessary for Nekhludov to visit his estates and settle matters there.

He went first to the nearest, Kuzminskoe, a large estate in the black soil belt, from which he derived the chief part of his income. He had lived there in his childhood and youth and had since visited it twice. On one occasion, at his mother's request, he had taken a German bailiff with him and made an inventory of the property, so that he was familiar with its condition and the relations of the peasants to the "office" (that is, to the landlord). These relations were such that the peasants were entirely dependent. Nekhludov had appreciated this when as a university student he accepted and professed the doctrines of Henry George and, under the influence of these doctrines, had given to the peasants the estate left him by his father. It is true that when he left the army and acquired the habit of spending some twenty thousand rubles a year, he ceased to regard his former views as binding; he did not care to inquire very deeply about the origin of the money he received from his mother, and preferred to dismiss all thought of it from his mind. But his mother's death, his own subsequent inheritance, and the necessity of managing his estate brought up again the question of his attitude to the private ownership of land. A month before, Nekhludov would have told himself that he could never change the existing order of things and that he was not the bailiff; and he would, one way or another, have eased his conscience, continuing to live at a distance from his estates and having the money sent to him. But now he decided that he could not leave matters as they stood, even though he had the journey to Siberia before him, as well as a difficult and complicated relationship with the prison world, which would require influence and money. He had to make a change, even though he himself would be the loser by it.

In the first place, he decided not to cultivate the land himself any longer but to let it at reasonable rents to the peasants, thus giving them a chance to become partly independent of the land-owner. Many a time, comparing the present position of landed proprietors with that of serf-owners, he would draw a parallel between renting the land to the peasants (instead of cultivating the same land with hired labor) and the old system of making the serfs pay quitrent in the place of their labor. Clearly, renting the land was not a complete solution of the problem, but it was a step in the right direction, a change from a harsh to a mild form of tyranny. And this was what he determined to do.

Nekhludov arrived at Kuzminskoe about noon. Trying to simplify his life in every respect, he did not telegraph, but hired a two-horse carriage at the station. The driver was a young fellow wearing a peasant's coat of nankeen, belted below the waist. He sat sideways on the seat, as country drivers usually do, and was all the more talkative since the conversation gave him an excuse for driving at a foot pace, to the satisfaction of the lame white horse inside the shafts and the gaunt, broken-winded one outside.

The driver gossiped about the bailiff at Kuzminskoe. He did not know that it was the master he was driving, for Nekhludov had purposely concealed his name.

"That German fellow is a swell," said the driver, who, having lived in the town and read novels, was rather proud of his education. He sat partly facing Nekhludov, grasping his whip now by the handle and now by the lash. "He's bought himself a troika of light bays, and when he drives out with his lady, everybody else is put properly in the shade," he went on. "At Christmas time he had a tree up at the big house; I drove some of the company. It was lighted by electric lights. There was nothing like it in the whole district. With all the money he's raked in, he can have anything he wants. I've heard people say he has bought a fine estate."

Nekhludov had thought that he was perfectly indifferent to the way the German managed his estate or whether he made much or little out of it, but the story of the driver made unpleasant hearing. He enjoyed the beautiful day and looked happily at the heavy dark clouds that every now and again obscured the sun, the brown fields where the peasants were ploughing for oats, the larks soaring above the green fields, the forests which except for the tardy oaks were already covered with fresh verdure, the meadows dotted with grazing cattle and horses—and suddenly he was reminded that something unpleasant had happened; when he asked himself what it was, he remembered the driver's story about the way the German bailiff was managing Kuzminskoe. But after he reached Kuzminskoe and set to work, this unpleasant feeling was forgotten.

The inspection of the books and the talk with the bailiff, who artlessly demonstrated to him the advantages arising from the fact that the peasants had very little land of their own and that what they had lay in the midst of the landlord's fields, confirmed Nekhludov in his intention to give up farming and let all the land to the peasants.

From the office books and the talk with the bailiff he learned that now, exactly as before, two-thirds of the finest arable land was being cultivated with the best modern implements by laborers, while the other third was tilled by peasants who were paid five rubles a *dessyatina*[1]: that is to say, for five rubles a peasant agreed to plough each *dessyatina* three times, harrow it three times, sow and reap the corn, make it into sheaves, and deliver it to the threshing yard; all this meant an amount of labor which cost at least ten rubles when hired workmen did it. Moreover, the peasants paid with their labor—and dearly, too—for all they got from the farm management; they paid with their labor when they rented meadow land or bought wood and potato tops, and most of them were in debt to the office. Consequently the peasants paid four times as much for the land they rented to raise their crops as the owner could have derived from the sale of the land and the investment of the money at 5 per cent.

Nekhludov had known all this before, but now it seemed to strike him afresh, and he only wondered how he or any other landowner could help seeing the wickedness of such a

---

[1] About two and three-quarter acres.—Tr.

state of affairs. He listened to all the arguments of the bailiff, who told him what a loss there would be on the agricultural implements which could not be sold for a quarter of their cost, how bad it would be for the land in every way, and how much of his income he would lose if the peasants were allowed to rent the land—but all these arguments served only to confirm him in the conviction that he was doing right in giving the land to the peasants and depriving himself of the larger part of his income. He decided to settle the business then and there before he left the place. The harvesting, the sale of the crops and cattle and of the useless outbuildings, he would leave to the care of the bailiff after his departure. But he asked the bailiff to lose no time in calling a meeting of the peasants from the three villages lying in the middle of his estate, so that he could tell them what he meant to do, and make an agreement with them about the rent they were going to pay.

Pleased with himself for resisting the arguments of the bailiff and elated with the idea of the sacrifice he was going to make, Nekhludov left the office and strolled around the house, thinking over the business before him. Walking across the flower beds, which had been neglected this year—except for the one in front of the bailiff's house—he crossed the tennis court, now overgrown with chicory, and entered an avenue of lime trees where he used to go to smoke his cigar and where three years ago he had carried on a flirtation with pretty Kirimova, a visitor of his mother's. After he had planned his speech to the peasants, he went in to the bailiff, and again discussed over the tea table the winding up of his affairs. Then he withdrew, calm and contented, to the bedroom in the large mansion which had always been used for guests.

It was a neat little room, with views of Venice on the walls, a mirror between the two windows, and a clean bed with a spring mattress. By the bedside stood a table holding a decanter of water, some matches, and a candle snuffer. On the large table under the looking glass his suitcase stood open, revealing his dressing case and some books that he had brought to read on the journey: one in Russian, *Studies in Criminality*, another in German, and a third in English on the same subject. He had intended to read them during his leisure moments while travelling to and fro between his estates, but, when he saw them now, he felt himself remote from these matters. He was preoccupied with something quite different.

An ancient inlaid mahogany armchair stood in one corner and at the sight of this chair, which he remembered in his mother's bedroom, an emotion suddenly sprang up in his heart for which he was totally unprepared. He began to feel sorry for the house that would tumble to ruin, the garden that would be overgrown with weeds, the forests that would be destroyed, and all the barns, sheds, stables, and toolhouses, the machinery, the horses and the cows—the whole establishment which he had not created, to be sure, but which had been acquired by his family and kept up with such infinite pains. He had thought that it would be easy enough to give it all up, but now a sense of loss came over him. How could he give up the land and half his income, when he was so likely to need them?

Plausible arguments against the wisdom of letting out the land to the peasants and abandoning the responsibility of the estate came crowding into his mind.

"I have no right to own that land," said one voice. "And if I do not own it, I shall not be able to keep up the house and the farm. Besides, I shall very soon be going to Siberia, and then I shall have no use for either house or land." "That may be true," answered a second voice, "but you are not going to live in Siberia all your life. If you marry, you may have children and, as you have inherited the estate in good order, it is your duty to transmit it to them in as good a condition as when you received it. You owe a duty to the land. It is an easy matter to give it all up or to destroy it, but it was not so easy to acquire. You ought to take time for reflection and then, having decided upon your future course of life, dispose of your property accordingly. First of all, are you sure of yourself? Then you should also ask yourself: am I acting as my conscience bids me, or only posing for effect, to win the applause of others, and to take pride in what I have done?"

Nekhludov asked himself these questions and was forced to admit that public opinion did influence his decision to a certain extent. And the longer he thought, the more questions presented themselves and the more insoluble they became. To escape from his thoughts he went to bed and tried to go to sleep and refresh himself against the morning, when all these puzzling questions would have to be decided.

But he could not sleep. Together with the fresh night breezes and the moonlight, the croaking of the frogs came in through the window; now he heard the nightingales trilling in the park —some far away, and one just under his window in a bush of lilac in bloom. As he lay there listening to the nightingales and the frogs, something made him think of the inspector's daughter, and the inspector himself; that brought Maslova to his mind, and the tremulous croaking of the frogs reminded him of her quivering lips when she said, "Don't think about it any more." Then the German bailiff began going down to the frogs. He should have been held back, but he went down and turned into Maslova, saying with reproach, "I am a convict and you are a prince."

"No, I must not give in," thought Nekhludov, waking up; and then he asked himself: "Am I doing right or wrong? I cannot tell, but it makes no difference, no difference at all. The thing is to sleep." And he slipped slowly down toward where he had seen Maslova and the bailiff, and there it all ended.

❧

CHAPTER TWO

WHEN Nekhludov woke the next morning, he found that it was nine o'clock. The young clerk who waited on him heard him stir and brought his shoes, shining as they had never shone before, and some cold clear spring water. He announced that the peasants were beginning to assemble. Nekhludov jumped out of bed and collected his thoughts. His regrets of the previous evening, about disposing of the land and winding up the estate, had vanished. He was surprised that he had ever felt them. Now he rejoiced at the thought of the task before him, and felt proud of it.

From the window he could see the tennis court, now overgrown with chicory, where the peasants were assembling in obedience to the orders of the bailiff. No wonder the frogs had been croaking the night before: it was a cloudy morning; earlier in the day a warm and gentle rain had been falling and the drops still clung to the branches of the trees, to the leaves, to every blade of grass. Sweet scents came in at the window—a fragrance of fresh vegetation and the peculiar smell of moist soil that has been crying out for rain and is not yet satisfied.

While dressing, Nekhludov several times put his head out of the window and watched the peasants gathering on the tennis court. They came up one by one, taking off their hats and bowing to one another; placing themselves in a circle, they stood resting on their sticks. Dressed in a short loose coat with big buttons and a high green collar, the bailiff—a stout, muscular, robust man—came in to tell Nekhludov that the peasants were all assembled, but that they might as well wait until he had drunk his tea or coffee, both of which were prepared.

"No, I would rather go and see them at once," said Nekhludov, and at the thought of the talk he was going to have with the peasants an unexpected feeling of timidity and shame took possession of him.

He was about to grant one of their dearest wishes—a wish which they had never hoped to be fulfilled: to rent the land at a low price; and yet he felt ashamed of something. When he approached them, and the brown heads and gray heads, curly heads and bald heads appeared as hats were doffed before him, he was so confused that he could say nothing. A fine rain was falling, and the drops clung to the hair, the beards, and the coarse woolen coats of the peasants. They stood gazing at their landlord and waited for him to speak, while he was too embarrassed to open his lips. This awkward silence was interrupted by the self-possessed German, who flattered himself that what he didn't know about the Russian peasant was not worth knowing, and who could speak the language like a native. Nekhludov and this strong, overfed man presented a striking contrast to the peasants with their thin, shriveled faces and prominent shoulder blades only half concealed by their coarse coats.

"The prince wishes to help you; he is thinking of letting you rent the land; it's a pity you're not more worthy of his kindness," said the bailiff.

"Why aren't we worthy of it, Vassili Karlovich? Haven't we worked well for you? We are much indebted to the deceased lady—may God grant her the Kingdom of Heaven—and to the young prince, who looks after us," said a red-bearded peasant, who was reckoned a fine talker.

"We have nothing against our master," said a broad-faced peasant with a long beard. "All we complain of is that we're so cramped. Not enough land to live on."

"That is precisely why I have asked you to come here this morning. I want to let you have all the land if you wish it," said Nekhludov.

The peasants made no reply; either they did not understand him, or they could not believe their ears.

"What do you mean, 'let us have it'?" a middle-aged peasant asked at last.

"I mean to let you have it to use, and charge you a very small rent."

"That's good," said an old man.

"If only the price isn't more than we can pay," said another.

"Well, why should we refuse? We know how to farm the land—that's what we're used to. It'll be better for you, too, you'll only have to take the money and be saved from all sin!" cried voices from the crowd.

"The sin is on your side," said the bailiff. "If you'd only attend to the work and keep the peace."

"That's easier said than done, Vassili Karlovich," said an old peasant, with a sharp nose. "You say, 'Why did you let the horse get into the oats?' but let me ask you, who let it get in? All the day long—and sometimes a day is as long as a year—I may have swung a scythe, or I may have dropped to sleep, and before I know it the horse is in your oats. Then you skin me."

"You ought to be more careful."

"It's all very well to say 'careful,' we simply can't do it," said a tall, black-haired, middle-aged peasant.

"I told you to build a fence."

"Then why don't you give us the wood?" asked a nondescript little man, who stood behind the others. "I was going to build one this summer and began to cut down a sapling, but you had me in the lockup feeding lice for three months. How could I build a fence, I'd like to know?"

"What does he mean?" Nekhludov asked the bailiff.

"Der erste Dieb im Dorfe,"[1] replied the bailiff, in German. "He's been caught in the wood every year. You'd better learn to respect your neighbors' property," he said.

"Don't we show you enough respect?" asked the old man. "We don't dare to show you anything else, because we're in your power. You could twist us into rope."

"Oh, we don't expect to get the better of you, my fine fellows; all we ask is that you shouldn't get the better of us."

"You don't get the better of us? And how about your smashing my jaw last summer? Did I get any damages for that? You know yourself that a rich man can't be taken to court."

"Then why do you keep breaking the law?"

And so this tournament of words went on, though neither party clearly understood what they were arguing about. But it was not difficult to discern repressed anger on one side and a consciousness of superiority and power on the other. It distressed Nekhludov to listen to all this, and he made an effort to bring them back to the matter in hand, in order to come to an agreement about rents and dates of payment.

[1] The greatest thief in the village.

"Now, how about the land? Do you want it? And if you do, what rent will you pay?"

"You have the land to let; it is for you to say how much you want for it."

Nekhludov named a price, but although it was much lower than rents locally, the peasants as usual began to find fault and tried to beat him down, saying that it was more than they could pay. He had expected that his proposal would be welcomed with delight but, if they were delighted, they took great care not to show it. The only sign which betrayed their satisfaction was an immediate discussion of the way the land should be divided, whether it should be held by the whole commune, or apportioned in lots to each village. Disputes raged hot and fierce between those who wanted to keep out the shirkers as being unlikely to pay the rent, and those whom they proposed to exclude. The bailiff finally took the affair into his own hands, and so the prices and dates of payment were settled. When an arrangement had been reached, the peasants, still talking noisily, started off for home down the hill, while Nekhludov went back to the office with the bailiff to draw up the contract.

Everything had been arranged according to his wishes. His peasants were going to get their land for about 30 per cent less than other peasants in the district; his own income from the estate was diminished almost by half; but it would still be sufficient for him, especially as the proceeds from the sale of a wood as well as from his livestock and farm machinery would also be coming in. So everything seemed to have been settled satisfactorily—and yet Nekhludov felt depressed and sad and ashamed of something. A few of the peasants had expressed their gratitude, but most of them seemed rather disgruntled and he felt that more had been expected of him. So it turned out that he had made a serious sacrifice, and yet fallen short of their expectations.

The next day the agreement was signed, and Nekhludov, escorted by a deputation of old peasants who had come to see him off, got into the bailiff's "swell" equipage (as the driver from the station had called it). He bade the peasants good-by and drove to the station, leaving them shaking their heads dubiously. The peasants were dissatisfied, Nekhludov was dissatisfied with himself. He could not have told the reason for this dissatisfaction—he simply felt sad and ashamed of something.

CHAPTER THREE

From Kuzminskoe he drove to the estate he had inherited from his aunts, where he had first met Katusha.

He wanted to make the same arrangement here as in Kuzminskoe and, moreover, to find out all he could concerning Katusha and their child—if it really was dead and, if so, how it had died. He reached Panovo early in the morning, and the first thing that struck him as he drove up was the air of decay and neglect that hung over everything, particularly over the old house itself. The iron roof, once green, was now reddened with rust; several layers of its iron sheathing were bent back—evidently the work of a storm; some of the weather boarding had been wrenched off the house; he could see where the rusty nails had been pulled out and the boards stripped off wherever they could be easily reached; both the porches—the back porch, which he had particular reason to remember, and the front one—had rotted away and broken down. Nothing was left of the steps except the supports on which they had rested.

Some of the windows were boarded up where the glass had been broken, and the building occupied by the bailiff, as well as the kitchen and the stables, was gray and dilapidated. The garden alone had escaped the universal blight; it was wilder and more luxuriant than ever. Everything was in full bloom. The cherry, apple, and plum trees beyond the garden fence looked like so many white clouds. The lilac hedge was in bloom, too, just as it had been twelve years ago when Nekhludov played *gorelki* with sixteen-year-old Katusha and fell among the nettles. The larch which Sophia Ivanovna had planted near the house—he remembered it as a slender sapling—had grown into a tall tree with a trunk fit for a good solid beam; its yellow-green needles, soft and fluffy, were pricking out all over it. The river, now within its banks, was rushing noisily over the mill dam. Herds of cattle of all sorts and kinds, belonging to the peasants, were grazing in the meadow beyond. The bailiff (a former seminary student who had never finished his course) met Nekhludov in the yard with a fixed smile that was peculiar to him, and invited him into the office, still smiling as if he had something pleasant to tell. He withdrew behind the partition; mysterious whispering was heard and then there was silence. Nekhludov heard his cabby drive away (he had been waiting for a tip); the tiny bell jingled for an instant, and again there was silence. A barefooted peasant girl ran past the window; she was wearing an embroidered blouse and strange silk tassels for earrings. Then a peasant clattered along the well-trodden path; he was running, too, as fast as he could in his heavy hobnailed boots.

Nekhludov sat beside the window, looking into the garden and listening. A fresh spring breeze wafted the scent of newly turned soil across the window sill, all scarred with marks of a knife. It lifted the hair from his moist forehead and rustled the papers that lay on the sill. He heard the swift regular patter of the wooden paddles which the women used to beat the clothes they were washing, as it echoed over the glittering sun-lit surface of the mill stream, the rhythmical sound of the water rushing over the wheel, and the loud buzzing of a startled fly.

And suddenly he remembered hearing these very sounds many years ago, when he was young and innocent, and how the spring breeze had blown the hair back from his moist forehead and stirred the papers on the scarred window sill, just as now, and how a startled fly had buzzed loudly past his ear; it was not exactly that he remembered himself as a boy of eighteen, but he seemed to feel himself the same as he was then; he felt the freshness, the purity, the great possibilities, and all the aspirations of his youth; and yet, like one in a dream, he knew that all this could be no more, and he felt very sad.

"When do you wish to have your meal served?" asked the bailiff, with a smile.

"Oh, any time. I am not hungry. I am going to the village now."

"Wouldn't you like to go over the house? I keep everything in good order inside, even though outside it certainly looks . . . Please come in!"

"Not now. I wonder if you know of a woman here called Matryona Kharina?" (This was Katusha's aunt.)

"Oh, yes, I know her. There's nothing I can do with her. She sells spirits without a license. I know it perfectly well, and I've told her so over and over again, and threatened her, but I haven't the heart to take her up; she's an old woman, you know; she has grandchildren, and I'm sorry for her," said the bailiff, with his conventional smile, which seemed to say: "I should like to please you because you're the master, but you know yourself how it is."

"Where does she live? I should like to see her."

"At the end of the street, the last cottage but one. There is one made of brick on the left, and hers is just behind that. Let me show you the way," said the bailiff, smiling good-humoredly.

"No, thank you; I can easily find it. And, while I'm gone, will you please call a meeting of the peasants? I want to speak to them about the land," said Nekhludov, meaning to make the same sort of contract with them as with the peasants of Kuzminskoe and, if possible, to accomplish the business that very evening.

❖

CHAPTER FOUR

NEKHLUDOV passed through the gate and followed the hard-trodden path across the pasture overgrown with dock and plantain; he met the same stout-limbed, barefooted girl with the checked apron and large earrings. She was walking very fast, evidently on her way home, swinging her left arm vigorously backward and forward; with her right arm she held a red cockerel pressed tightly against her stomach. The cock seemed not much disturbed, though his red comb quivered and his eyes rolled from side to side, and occasionally he thrust out a black clawed foot and made a futile grab at the girl's apron. As she drew near the master her pace slackened, changing from a run to a walk.

When she was abreast of him, she paused to greet him with a funny little jerk of the head, and then walked on. As Nekhludov went down toward the well he met an old woman in a dirty unbleached linen blouse, carrying two heavy pails of water slung across her bowed shoulders. The old woman carefully set the pails on the ground, and then she, too, bowed to him with just the same backward jerk of the head.

Just beyond the well was the beginning of the village. It was a bright, hot day. Rising clouds now and then obscured the sun, but even at ten o'clock the heat was excessive. A pungent and unpleasant smell of dung was carried along the street. It came partly from the carts which were rumbling over the smooth and shining hillside road, but principally from the dung-heaps lately forked over in the yards, whose open gates Nekhludov was passing as he came along. The peasants walking barefooted beside the carts, their shirts and breeches smeared with dung, turned back to stare at the tall, stout master with the gray hat and silken hatband shining in the sun, as he walked up the village street, touching the ground at every other step with a gleaming silver-headed cane. The peasants returning from the fields, jogging along on their empty carts, took off their hats and gazed with astonishment at this extraordinary person walking up their street. Women came out of their gates or stood on their porches, making signs to one another to look at him and following him with their eyes as he passed by.

When Nekhludov reached the fourth gate he had to wait for a cart just driving out of the yard. Its wheels creaked under the weight of a heavy load of dung piled high. A mat lying on the top of it served for a seat. A barefooted six-year-old boy followed the cart. A young peasant striding along in bast shoes was leading the horse out of the yard. A long-legged colt of a blue-gray color jumped out of the gate; startled at the sight of Nekhludov, he pressed close to the cart and, scraping his legs against the wheels, slipped through ahead of the mare, who showed her uneasiness by a gentle whinny as she drew the heavy load through the gate.

A barefooted old man led the next horse. Thin and wiry, with protruding shoulder blades, he wore striped breeches and a long dirty shirt. When the horses reached the hard-beaten road, strewn with bits of dry, ash-colored dung, the old man went back and saluted Nekhludov.

"You're the mistresses' nephew, aren't you?"

"Yes, I am."

"You're very welcome. And you've come to see how we're getting along?" asked the talkative old man.

"Precisely. . . . And how *are* you getting along?" asked Nekhludov, not knowing what else to say.

"How are we getting along? Badly as can be," drawled the old man, as though it gave him pleasure to say so.

"Why so badly?" asked Nekhludov, entering the gate.

"What is our life? It's the very worst there is," said the old man, following Nekhludov into the part of the yard which was roofed over.

Nekhludov stopped under the roof.

"I have twelve mouths to feed," continued the old man, pointing toward a couple of women who stood sweating over the last dunghill. Their kerchiefs were awry, their skirts tucked up, their bare legs soiled with dung, and they stood with forks in their hands, resting a moment. "Every month I have to buy seven stone of rye—and how am I to pay for it?"

"Doesn't your own see you through the year?"

"My own?" said the old man, with a scornful smile. "I've only land enough for three, and last autumn we gathered but eight stacks that didn't last till Christmas."

"What do you do, then?"

"What do we do? Well, I hired one son out as a laborer, and then I borowed a little money from Your Honor. We spent it all before Lent, and the taxes aren't paid yet."

"How much do you have to pay?"

"Seventeen rubles for my household. I tell you, it's a hard life. Sometimes I wonder myself how we manage at all."

"May I come into your cottage?" asked Nekhludov, stepping across the yard over the ill-smelling, saffron-colored heaps of dung that had been raked up here and there.

"Why not? Come in," said the old man. Going on ahead of Nekhludov with a brisk and active step, treading on the soft manure that oozed between his toes, he opened the door of the cottage. The women straightened their kerchiefs and let down their skirts, looking with curiosity and awe at the well-washed master with the gold cuff links who was entering their house.

Two little girls, with nothing on but shirts, rushed past him. Taking off his hat and stooping low, he managed to make his way into the passage and thence into a dirty little room where most of the space was taken up by two hand looms; the air smelled of sour food. An old woman was standing by the stove, her sleeves rolled up over her thin sunburnt, sinewy arms.

"Here's our master come to see us," said the old man.

"He's very welcome, I'm sure," replied the old woman kindly, pulling down her sleeves.

"I wanted to see how you live," said Nekhludov.

"Well, we live just as you see. The cottage is nearly falling down; I suppose it will kill us someday; but the old man says it's good enough, so here we live and enjoy ourselves," said the lively old woman, jerking her head nervously. "I'm getting the dinner ready now to feed our men."

"And what will you have for dinner?"

"What shall we have? Fine food! First course: bread and kvass.[1] Second course: kvass and bread," said the old woman with a laugh that revealed her partly decayed teeth.

"No, I am serious—please show me what you are going to eat."

[1] A drink made of rye and malt.

"It won't take long to show you that," said the old man laughing. "Let him have a look, old woman!"

She shook her head.

"So you want to see our peasant fare? Well, you are looking into things, I must say! You want to know all that's to be known. Is that the sort you are? I told you we have bread and kvass, and then some soup; a woman brought us some fish last night, that's what the soup is made of; and then we have potatoes."

"Is that all?"

"What else could we have? We'll finish off with milk," said the old woman, glancing toward the door with a shrewd wink.

It stood open. The passage was crowded with people—boys, girls, women nursing babies in their arms—all staring at this queer man who was investigating the peasants' diet. The old woman was evidently proud of herself for knowing so well how to talk to a gentleman.

"Yes sir, it's a miserable life, no doubt about it. . . . Here, you get out of here!" shouted the old man to the women and children by the door.

"Well, good-by," said Nekhludov, with a feeling of embarrassment and unaccountable shame.

"It was good of you to come and see us, and we thank you kindly," said the old man.

The peasants, still crowding in the passageway, hugged the wall to let Nekhludov pass. As he walked along the street, two barefooted boys followed him. The older of the two wore a shirt that once upon a time had been white; the younger boy's was pink, quite faded and frayed.

Nekhludov caught sight of them when he turned around.

"Where are you going now?" asked the boy in the white shirt.

"To Matryona Kharina's. Do you know her?"

The little boy in the pink shirt began to laugh, but the elder boy asked in a serious tone:

"Which Matryona do you mean? Is she an old woman?"

"Yes."

"Aha!" he drawled. "He means Semyonikha. That's at the end of the village. We'll show you the way. Won't we, Fedka?"

"But what'll we do about the horses?"

"Never mind about them. They'll be all right, I dare say."

Fedka agreed, and the three walked up the village street together.

NEKHLUDOV felt more at ease with the boys than with the older folk, and talked to them as they went along. The younger, in the pink shirt, stopped laughing and talked as intelligently and sensibly as the elder one.

"Which are the poorest families in your village?" Nekhludov inquired.

"The poorest families? Mikhail is poor, and so is Simon Makarov. Marfa, she's very poor, too."

"Anissya is poorer than any of them. She hasn't even got a cow. They have to beg for their living," said little Fedka.

"She hasn't got a cow, but she has only three to feed, and Marfa has five, counting herself," objected the elder boy.

"Yes, but the other one's a widow," said Anissya's small advocate.

"But Marfa is just the same as a widow. She hasn't got any husband," said the older boy.

"Where is her husband?" asked Nekhludov.

"Oh, feeding the lice in prison," said the older boy, using the expression common among the peasants.

"He cut down a couple of birch trees in the forest, so they shut him up—because the forest belongs to the gentry, you know," the little boy in the pink shirt hastened to explain. "He's been there six months now, and his wife has to go out begging; they've got three children and an old grandmother."

"Where do they live?" asked Nekhludov.

"Over there—that's their home," said the boy, pointing to a cottage in front of which stood a tiny child, on the very path that Nekhludov was following; his hair was the color of tow, and his little legs were so bowed that he could hardly balance himself on his feet.

"Vaska, what's become of you, you little scamp?" A woman in a dirty blouse that looked as if it had been rolled in ashes rushed out in front of Nekhludov, seized the boy, and ran back into the hut with him. She looked as frightened as if she expected Nekhludov to do the child some bodily harm. It was the woman whose husband was in jail for cutting down Nekhludov's birches.

"And this Matryona—is she poor?" asked Nekhludov, as they approached her cottage.

"Oh, no, she isn't poor—she sells vodka," the slender boy in the pink shirt replied emphatically.

When they came to Matryona's cottage, Nekhludov left the boys outside and, stepping into the entry, went through into the cottage. It was only fourteen feet long, and the bed which stood behind the stove would have been too short for a tall man to stretch out in. "That's the very bed in which Katusha's baby was born, and where she was so ill afterward," he thought to himself. A loom took up most of the room. The old woman and her eldest granddaughter were about to begin their weaving when Nekhludov, hitting his head against the lintel, came in through the low doorway. The other grandchildren followed Nekhludov into the room and stopped at the door, clinging to the doorpost.

"Whom do you want to see?" asked the old woman; she was as cross as she could be, for her loom had been going wrong. Besides, the arrival of a stranger is always disquieting to someone who sells spirits illegally.

"I am the landlord. I should like to speak to you."

The old woman, looking at him intently, made no reply; then all at once her manner changed.

"Why, is that you, my dear! Well, what an old fool I am! I thought it was some stranger," she said in a sweet voice that was obviously artificial. "My blessed lamb!" she exclaimed.

"I should like to see you alone," said Nekhludov, glancing at the open door where the children were standing, and, beyond them, an emaciated woman with a baby in her arms. The child was smiling in a sickly way; on his little head was a cap made of odd bits of cloth.

"What do you want here? I'll give it you! Just hand me my crutch, will you!" the old woman shouted at them. "Go on, shut that door!"

The children ran off, and the woman with the baby closed the door.

"Thinks I to myself, now who the devil can that be? And it turns out to be the master himself, my precious, my beauty, my darling! That he should ever condescend to come here! My jewel!" said the old woman. "Sit here, Your Excellency, here," she said, dusting the seat with her apron. "And thinks I to myself, who in the world is coming in here? And it's His Excellency, the master, our benefactor, our breadwinner! Forgive me for an old fool! I must be going blind."

Nekhludov sat down, but the old woman continued to stand in front of him. Leaning her cheek on her right hand and supporting her elbow with the other, she went on talking in a sing-song voice:

"How Your Excellency has aged! Why, you used to be as pretty as a pink! Nothing like what you are now. It must be all the worry you have."

"I have come to ask you if you remember Katusha Maslova?"

"Katerina? Of course I remember Katerina. She's my own niece. No, indeed I'm not likely to forget her, after all the tears I've shed for her. Why, I knew all about it at the time. But where'll you find the man that hasn't sinned before God, that hasn't offended the tsar? You were both young in those days, you used to come together for a drink of tea or coffee, and then the devil got the upper hand. He's a strong one, I tell you! Then came the sin. How could you help it? But you did your part honest and fair, you gave her a hundred rubles. It wasn't as if you'd neglected her. But what did she do? She wouldn't be reasonable. If she'd listened to me she'd have been all right. I must say the truth, even though she is my niece: the girl's no good. I got a fine place for her but she wouldn't submit, she was high and mighty with the master. Is it for the likes of us to put on airs? Of course she lost that place. Then she might have lived with the forester; but no, you couldn't do a thing with the girl. Such notions!"

"I wanted to ask you about the child," said Nekhludov. "She was confined here, was she not? Can you tell me where the child is?"

"Oh, my dear, I had to fix up everything at that time. She was very ill; I hardly expected she'd get up from her bed again. So I had the baby christened and taken to the foundling hospital. Why should a little angel be left to suffer because the mother is dying? I know plenty of them that just leave a baby alone, and never think of feeding it, and so it just dies. But I thought it was better to take a little care, and I sent it to the hospital. We had the money, so we could send it away."

"Did you get the registration number?"

"Oh, yes, we got the number right enough, but the baby died straight away. She said she'd hardly got to the hospital before it died."

"Who is *she*?"

"The woman who used to live in Skorodnoe. She carried on that sort of business. Her name was Malanya—she's dead now. She was a clever woman, and this was how she used to work it:

whenever a baby was brought to her, she'd keep it for a while and feed it; and after she'd collected three or four of the little things, my dear, she'd take them off to the foundling hospital. She had a big cradle, like a small double bed, broad enough to put the babies in three or four together. There was a handle to it. She'd put them feet to feet and heads apart, so that they couldn't knock against each other, and that way she'd carry four at a time. She'd give them some pap in a rag to keep them quiet, the pets."

"Well? Go on."

"Well, she took Katerina's baby, too, and I believe she kept it 'a fortnight. It was taken ill at her house."

"Was it a healthy child?" asked Nekhludov.

"A splendid baby! I don't know where you'd find a better. The image of its father," she said with a wink.

"Then why did it fall ill? I suppose the food was bad."

"Eh, what food could it be? A makeshift—just what you might expect; the child was none of hers. All these women care for is to get the babies to the hospital before they are dead. She said it died just as they reached Moscow. She brought back the death certificate all right. Oh, she was a bright one!"

This was all that Nekhludov could find out about his child.

⚜

CHAPTER SIX

NEKHLUDOV, banging his head against the lintel once again before he reached the street, found the pink and white boys waiting for him. Several recruits had joined the group. A few women standing about were nursing babies in their arms and among them he recognized the emaciated woman, holding her blood-less infant with his patchwork cap as if he were no more than a feather's weight. There was a strange fixed smile on his little wizened face, but Nekhludov knew that it was caused by pain. His crooked toes were continually moving about. Nekhludov asked who the woman was.

"Why, that's Anissya, the one we told you about," said the older boy.

"How are you getting on? How do you manage for money?" he asked her.

"How do I manage? I go begging," said Anissya, and began to cry.

The ancient baby kept smiling all over his face and wriggling his skinny, wormlike legs.

Nekhludov took out his pocketbook and gave the woman ten rubles. Before he had gone two steps another woman with a baby overtook him, and then an old woman with still another behind her. All spoke of their poverty and asked him to help. He divided sixty rubles among them—all he had with him—and hurried back to the bailiff's house, feeling sick at heart.

The bailiff met him with a smile and told him that the peasants would assemble that evening. Nekhludov thanked him; he turned away from the house and went into the garden.

As he paced up and down the neglected paths, now carpeted with the petals of falling apple blossom, he pondered upon all that he had seen. At first the silence was unbroken, but presently the sound of voices reached Nekhludov's ear.

It came from the bailiff's house: the angry voices of two women talking simultaneously or interrupting each other, with the calm voice of the ever-smiling bailiff breaking in from time to time. Nekhludov listened.

"I am sick of it all! You'd steal the very cross from around my neck!" cried a woman's voice in accents of fury.

"Why, she barely got inside," said another voice. "Do give her back. It's only tormenting the poor beast and making the children go without their milk!"

"Take your choice, then. Pay the money or work out the fine," replied the calm voice of the bailiff.

Nekhludov left the garden and walked up to the porch, where he saw two disheveled women, one of whom was pregnant and near her time. On the steps of the porch, his hands in the pockets of his linen coat, stood the bailiff. When the women recognized the landlord, they stopped talking and began to rearrange their kerchiefs, while the bailiff drew his hands out of his pockets and smiled.

It was the old story, he explained: the peasants always turned their calves and even their cows into the master's meadow to graze. Two cows belonging to these women had been caught there, and were now shut up. The bailiff demanded thirty kopecks from each woman, or two days' work. The women, however, maintained that the cows had strayed into the meadow by accident and that anyway they hadn't a kopeck in the world; they asked that the cows, which had stood without food in the blazing sun ever since morning and were lowing piteously, should be returned to them straight away, even if it had to be on the understanding that they would work out the fine later on.

"How often have I begged of you, 'If you drive your cattle home during your dinner hour, keep an eye on them'? I've said it to them over and over again," said the smiling bailiff, turning to Nekhludov as if calling on him to be a witness.

"I left them just for a moment to see to the baby, and they strayed away."

"But you shouldn't go off, when it's your business to watch them."

"And who's going to feed the child? Tell me that. Will *you* suckle him?"

"If they'd really done any damage we'd understand," said the other woman, "but they just strayed in for a minute."

"They are ruining the meadows, and if they are not fined there won't be any hay," said the bailiff to Nekhludov.

"How can you tell such wicked lies! My cows have never been caught there before!" shouted the pregnant woman.

"Well, they've been caught now, and you've either got to pay the fine or work it off."

"All right, I'll work it off then, but don't keep the cow there starving! Let her go!" she exclaimed angrily. "I've no peace by day or night. My mother-in-law is sick, my husband is always drunk. I have to do everything myself, and where to get the strength from I don't know! I hope the work you screw out of me chokes you!"

Nekhludov asked the bailiff to release the cows, and went back to the garden to be alone with his thoughts; but there was nothing left to think about.

Everything seemed so clear to him now that he could not help wondering how it was that others couldn't see it, and how there could have been a time when he himself had been unable even dimly to discern what he now saw so vividly.

The people are dying out; they are accustomed to dying out, they have formed habits of life adapted to dying out—the untimely deaths of the children, the overworking of the women, and the insufficient nourishment, particularly of the old people. And this state of affairs has been of a growth so gradual that the peasants themselves have not understood the full horror of it, nor raised their voices in protest; and, for the same reasons, we too have looked upon the situation as normal. But now he saw it clear as day. It was just as the people always said: the landowners are responsible for their poverty—the landowners who deprive them of the land which is their only means of support.

No one could deny that infants and old people die for want of milk: the reason they have no milk is because they have no pasture for their cattle, no land for growing corn, no hayfields. It was perfectly plain that all the people's misery—or, anyway, the greater part of it—arose from the fact that they do not own the land which should support them, this land being in the hands of men who take advantage of their ownership to live by the work of the people. The peasants, reduced to the depths of poverty, actually dying for want of enough land to support them, go on toiling so that the landowners may have crops to sell in foreign countries and thus buy all the hats and walking sticks, carriages, and bronze statues that their hearts desire.

This was as evident to him now as it is evident that a horse shut up in an enclosure until he has eaten every blade of grass under his feet will, sooner or later, starve to death unless he is removed to another pasture. A terrible state of affairs, and one that must not be allowed to continue. Some means could surely be found to remedy the evil; he at all events would have nothing more to do with it. "And I shall certainly find a way out," he thought as he walked to and fro in the birch walk near the house.

"In scientific societies, in government institutions and in the newspapers, we are always discussing the causes of poverty and ways of betterment, but we neglect the only method of uplifting the people—which is to return the land that has been taken from them and which they need so much." Here he vividly recalled the fundamental principles of Henry George and his own former enthusiasm for them, and wondered how he could ever have forgotten. "Land ought not to be subject to private ownership any more than water, sun or air. Every man has a right to land and to all the benefit that can be derived from it."

Now he understood why he had felt ashamed of the transaction he had made at Kuzminskoe. He had unconsciously deceived himself, for he knew that he had no right to the land; yet the implication was that he had such a right, when he gave to the peasants a part of something which, at the bottom of his heart, he knew did not belong to him. He would act differently now, and also alter the arrangement in Kuzminskoe; in his mind he sketched a plan for letting the land to the peasants and, from the money he received, establishing a fund to be used for their own benefit—with the condition that they should draw on it for their own taxes and common needs. It was not the "single-tax system," but the nearest approach to it that would be practicable in existing circumstances. The main thing was to renounce his right to hold land for personal profit.

When he returned to the house, the bailiff with an especially joyful smile announced that dinner was ready for serving, but he was afraid that the food, prepared by his wife with the help of the girl with the earrings, might be overdone.

The table was covered with an unbleached cloth. An embroidered towel served for a napkin and on the table stood an old saxon-ware tureen with a broken handle, filled with potato soup in which floated fragments of the very same cockerel whose struggles he had lately watched, chopped into small bits still covered with feathers. The cockerel in person, with his feathers thoroughly roasted, appeared during the second course, which was followed by cream cheese fried in butter and generously sprinkled with sugar.

This unpalatable fare made no impression upon Nekhludov. He was completely absorbed in the thoughts which had already dispelled the melancholy created by his visit to the village. The bailiff's wife now and then looked in at the door and watched the frightened maid with the tassels in her ears as she carried in the dishes, while the bailiff himself grinned from ear to ear with pride at his wife's skill.

After dinner, insisting that the bailiff should take a seat, Nekhludov began to unfold his plans for the peasants. This he did partly to arrange his own thoughts and partly to discover what impression his scheme would make on another mind. The bailiff smiled as though the very same ideas had occurred to him and as though he were delighted to hear them expressed, but the truth of the matter was that he had not the vaguest notion what Nekhludov was talking about. This was not because the language was obscure, but because the idea of any man giving up his personal gain for the good of others was inconceivable to one whose maxim had always been to benefit himself at the expense of other people. Therefore he imagined that there was something he had misunderstood when Nekhludov said that all the income from the estate would go to form the communal capital of the peasants.

"I see," he said, brightening up. "So the income from this capital will belong to you?"

"No, of course not. Don't you understand that I am giving up the land altogether?"

"Then you will have no income at all?"

"No, I am renouncing it."

The bailiff heaved a sigh, then, recollecting himself, began to smile again. Now he understood: Nekhludov's mind was affected. And at once he began to consider how he himself could make use of this land which was to be given away; but when he saw that no such scheme was practicable he felt aggrieved, lost interest in the affair, and only continued to smile vaguely to please his master. When Nekhludov perceived that the bailiff did not understand his plan, he sent him away. Taking a seat before the scarred and ink-stained table, he began to sketch his project on paper.

The sun had barely gone down behind the newly budded lime trees, and the mosquitoes swarmed into the room and stung him. When he finished writing, he could hear the lowing of cattle, the creaking of opening gates, and the voices of the peasants as they gathered together for the meeting. He had told the bailiff not to call them to the office, preferring to meet them in the village. He hurriedly swallowed a tumbler of tea offered him by the bailiff, and set off for the village.

※

CHAPTER SEVEN

As Nekhludov drew near the house of the village elder, in front of which the peasants had assembled, the noisy talk died down and one man after another took off his cap. These people looked far more wretched than the peasants in Kuzminskoe. Most of the men wore bast shoes and homespun coats; some were barefooted and in their shirts, straight from the fields. Nekhludov overcame his embarrassment with an effort and began to speak, declaring that he meant to give them the land. The peasants were silent and their faces unmoved.

"I am doing this," said Nekhludov, and his cheeks flushed as he spoke, "because I believe that everyone has a right to the use of the land."

"That's so! That's right!" said several voices from the crowd.

Nekhludov went on to tell them that the income from the land ought to be divided among all; he proposed that the peasants should pay a certain rent—which they were to agree upon among themselves—into a common fund which they were to control. In spite of occasional exclamations of approval, however, the faces of the peasants grew more and more stern; eyes which had been fixed on the master were now averted, as if to spare him the knowledge that his double-dealing had been discovered. Nobody could be taken in by such talk as that.

Nekhludov spoke plainly enough, and his listeners were intelligent men; but they did not and could not understand him, for the same reason that the bailiff had been unable to understand him: they were firmly convinced that it is natural for every man to seek his own advantage. Had they not for many generations seen the landowners seeking their own profit at the expense of the peasants? Therefore, if a landlord calls them together to make this surprising offer, it can only be for the purpose of getting the better of them in some new way. When Nekhludov asked, "What rent would you fix?" a voice from the crowd called out: "How can *we* fix rents? The land is yours, and you're the master."

"But you will use the money yourself for communal purposes."

"We cannot do that. The commune is one thing, and this is another."

"Now listen," said the bailiff with a smile, in an attempt to throw more light on the matter; "the prince is giving you the land in return for payments of money, and that money will then be given back to form capital for the commune. Don't you understand?"

"We understand quite well," a toothless old man said crossly, without raising his eyes. "It's like putting money in a bank. We should have to pay at a fixed time. Well, we don't want that, because we are poor enough as things are, and that would ruin us altogether."

"It won't do!" "Leave things alone!" cried several voices from the crowd, some discontented, some even hostile.

When Nekhludov went on to speak of the contract which he would sign and would expect them to sign also, the opposition grew more and more determined.

"What's the use of signing anything? We've always worked and we'll go on working. What's the good of all this? We're ignorant peasants. We don't agree to this business, it's all so strange. Leave things alone!"

"But it would be a good thing if we didn't have to find the seed," suggested a voice.

Grain for seed had always been provided by the peasants, and this was a request to the landowner to provide it.

"Then you refuse to take the land. Is that what you mean?" said Nekhludov, turning to a middle-aged, barefooted peasant in a torn coat, who was holding his ragged cap stiffly in his left hand, like a soldier ordered to uncover.

"Yes, sir," replied the peasant, who had evidently not yet rid himself of the hypnotic influence of a soldier's training.

"Then you have all the land you want?"

"Oh, no, sir," said the ex-soldier with an artificially cheerful air, still holding the torn cap in front of him, as if offering it to any passer-by who would like to make use of it.

Nekhludov, surprised, again repeated his offer and added: "Would it not be better to think the matter over?"

"There's nothing to think over. We hold by what we've said," said the toothless old man in his angry voice.

"Very well," replied Nekhludov. "Let me know if you change your mind. I shall be here all day tomorrow."

To this the peasants made no reply, and Nekhludov went back to the office.

"If you will permit me to say so, Prince," said the bailiff, "you'll never come to terms with your peasants. They're an obstinate lot, and at a meeting they jib and there's no moving them. That's because they mistrust everybody. And yet there are some clever ones among them. Take that gray-haired man, for example, or the dark one who raised objections to everything—they're both intelligent men. Whenever they come to my office, I ask them to sit down and offer them a cup of tea," continued the bailiff with a smile, "we talk about things in general and you'd be surprised to hear them, they're so wise, they can discuss anything like politicians. But let the same men come to a meeting and they just keep repeating the same things over and over again."

"Then why not ask a few of the more intelligent ones to come to the office?" said Nekhludov. "I could easily explain the details to them more fully."

"Yes, that can be done," answered the smiling bailiff.

"Then please ask them to come tomorrow."

"Very well," said the bailiff, and smiled even more cheerfully. "I will do so. I'll send them word to come here tomorrow."

"There's an artful man for you!" exclaimed a black-haired, swarthy peasant with an unkempt beard, as he sat jolting from side to side on a well-fed mare, addressing a lean old man in a torn coat who was riding by his side. Both men were on their way to pasture their horses for the night by the roadside, or, if they got a chance, in their landlord's fields.

" 'I'll let you have all the land for nothing if you'll only sign!'

They've made fools of us long enough. In these days we know a thing or two ourselves," the black-haired peasant added and began to call the colt that had strayed away from the mare. He stopped and looked around, but no colt was to be seen. It had evidently gone into the landlord's meadow.

"Damn the beast; he's taken to getting into the master's fields," said the peasant as he heard a loud neighing from the damp, sweet-smelling meadow.

"Just look at the meadow," said the thin peasant in the torn coat. "It needs a good weeding. We'll have to send the women out some holiday, else we'd be blunting our scythes."

"He says, 'Sign!' " the black-haired peasant went on, criticizing his master's address. "But if you were to sign, he'd swallow you alive."

"That's certain," replied the old man.

They said no more, and the only sound to be heard was the clopping of the horses' feet on the hard road.

❖

CHAPTER EIGHT

When Nekhludov entered the house, he found that the office had been arranged as a bedroom for him. A high bedstead with a feather bed and two pillows had been placed in the room, covered with a crimson-silk quilt, a marvel of needlework, borrowed no doubt from the trousseau of the bailiff's wife. The bailiff offered him what was left of the dinner and, when Nekhludov declined, apologized for the poor food and the uncomfortable quarters, and went away, leaving Nekhludov to himself.

The peasants' refusal had not disturbed him. On the contrary, although the offer that had been gratefully accepted at Kuzminskoe had here met with suspicion and even with hostility, he felt happy and calm.

The office was dirty and smelled badly. Nekhludov went into the yard and was going into the garden when he was stopped by memories of another night, of a window in the maids' room, and the porch at the back of the house.

He hesitated to go past a place polluted by guilty memories. He went to the seat on the porch and sat there for a long time, breathing the warm air heavy with the sharp fragrance of young birch leaves, looking into the dark garden and listening to the mill wheel and the singing of the nightingales; another strange bird was whistling monotonously in a bush close by.

The lights of the bailiff's quarters went out. The first glow of the rising moon appeared beyond the barn, toward the east; from time to time, distant sheet lightning lit up the deserted garden and the dilapidated house; far away, the thunder rolled and a black cloud covered a full third of the sky within his view. The nightingales fell silent. The cackling of geese sounded above the noise of the water mill, and the village cocks began to call to their fellows in the bailiff's yard. Cocks always begin to crow early on hot, thundery nights.

There is an old saying that the night will be gay when the cocks crow early. For Nekhludov, this night was better than gay: it was peaceful and joyous. He thought of the happy summer he had spent in this place, and suddenly felt himself to be as he was then—innocent and young—and as he had been at all the best moments of his life. He felt like the boy of fourteen praying to God to reveal His truth, like the child who at parting with his mother had cried at her knees and promised to be good and never to grieve her; he felt as he had felt in the days when he and Nikolenka Irtenev made resolutions to live good lives and make everybody happy.

The moment at Kuzminskoe came back to him, when he had been tempted to regret the estate, the land, the house, and the forest, and he asked himself if he still regretted them—but it seemed strange now that he could ever have felt regret. He recalled everything he had seen on that day: the woman with the children, whose husband had been sent to prison for cutting down trees in his forest, and that horrible creature, Matryona, who thought (or at least talked as if she thought) that the best thing for a woman of her kind was to become the mistress of a gentleman; he recollected the way the children were hurried off to the foundling hospital, and particularly the miserable little smiling child in the skullcap, dying for want of food. He remembered the pregnant, tired woman who had to work for him because, overburdened with all her cares, she had let her cow stray into his meadows. And then the prison rose before his eyes—the shaven heads, the chains, the cells, the disgusting smell—and beside these horrors, the mad luxury of his own life and the lives of other people of his class. All this was now clear and unambiguous.

The bright moon, now nearly full, rose from behind the barn; dark shadows fell across the yard, and the iron roof of the crumbling house glistened brightly. The nightingale, as though reluctant to waste this light, began singing and trilling in the garden.

Recalling all the questions which had occupied him at Kuzminskoe and his perplexity in finding satisfactory answers, Nekhludov was surprised to find how simple the same questions had become. They seemed simple now because he had stopped thinking of himself and his future in terms of personal gain or loss—and strangely enough, although he had never succeeded in finding out what he needed for himself, he now saw plainly what he must do for others. He knew beyond all doubt that he must give the land to the peasants, because to keep it would be wrong. He knew that he must never leave Katusha but must help her as best he could to expiate his own guilt. He knew that he must begin to study, investigate, and try to understand all this system of trial and punishment, which, he felt, he saw differently from other men. He did not know what the result would be, but he knew exactly what he himself must do, and this clear knowledge filled his heart with joy.

The black cloud had grown till the whole sky was overspread and the forked lightning that followed the sheet lightning now lit up the yard and outlined the dilapidated house with its crumbling porches; the thunder rolled overhead. The birds were silent, but the leaves began to rustle and a breeze stirred Nekhludov's hair as he sat on the porch. Presently drops of rain began to fall, drumming on the dock leaves and the iron roof. There was a brilliant flash and all was still; before he could count three, a tremendous roar sounded directly overhead and went rolling along the sky. He rose and went into the house.

"No, no," he thought to himself, "the work accomplished in our lives, all this work and its meaning, is not and never will be clear to me. What were my aunts for? Why did Nikolenka Irtenev have to die, while I go on living? Why should there be a Katusha? Or my own madness? Why should there have been this war? And my reckless life afterward? To comprehend these things and the purpose of the Master is beyond me, but to do His will, inscribed in my own conscience—I have no doubts about that. While I obey His commands, my soul is at peace."

Now the rain was coming down in streams; it rushed gurgling from the roof into a tub on the ground; the flashes of lightning had become less frequent. Nekhludov went back to his room, undressed, and crept into the bed, not without a dread of bugs, whose presence was betrayed by dirty ragged strips of paper hanging from the wall.

"Yes—to understand that one is not a master, but a servant!" he said to himself, and rejoiced at the thought.

No sooner had he put out the candle than his fears were realized: the bugs began to crawl over him and bite.

"To give up the land, to go to Siberia, to endure the fleas, the bugs, and the filth. . . . Well, does that matter? If it must be, I will bear it." But in spite of his exalted mood he could not bear it: he got up and sat by the window, where he watched the clouds withdraw and the moon reappear.

❖

CHAPTER NINE

NEKHLUDOV did not fall asleep till daybreak, and woke up late.

At noon, the seven peasants who had been chosen and summoned by the bailiff assembled in the orchard under the apple trees, where the bailiff had arranged a table and some benches with posts driven into the ground and boards fixed on top of them. It was a long time before the peasants could be persuaded to put on their caps and sit down. The ex-soldier in particular, wearing bast shoes and strips of cloth bound around his legs, insisted on holding his ragged cap in front of him, in the way laid down in army regulations for funerals. One of the peasants, however, a portly old man with an iron-gray beard reminiscent of Michelangelo's *Moses* and thick gray hair curling around his sunburnt forehead, at last put on his cap, wrapped his homemade coat around him, pushed along the bench, and sat down. The others followed his example. When the last man was in his place, Nekhludov sat down facing them. Leaning on his elbows and bending over his paper, he began to explain the substance of what he had written.

It may have been because his listeners were few, or because he was absorbed in the business at hand and had forgotten himself, that Nekhludov felt so perfectly at ease. Involuntarily he turned toward the dignified old patriarch with the curly gray beard, as if depending on him for approval or disapproval; but he mistook his man. True, he nodded his handsome head encouragingly, or shook it and frowned at the interruptions, but it soon became clear that he found it extremely difficult to follow what Nekhludov was talking about, even after the other peasants in turn had explained it in their own words. More intelligent was a small beardless man with one eye, sitting next to the patriarch; he wore a patched cotton waistcoat and old boots worn down on one side. Nekhludov afterward learned that he was a stove builder. The effort to take in every word kept his eyebrows in perpetual motion; he repeated to the others, in his own words, all that Nekhludov had said. A short, thickset old man with a white beard and bright intelligent eyes also understood quite well. He lost no chance to fling sarcastic remarks at the speaker, evidently rather proud of his wit. The ex-soldier would have been clever enough to understand if his military life had not stupefied him. But the man who was really most earnest was a tall peasant with a long nose and a small beard, wearing a suit of neat homemade clothes and new bast shoes; he took in everything, and spoke only when it was necessary. Two more men, one of whom was the toothless man who had yesterday shouted a flat refusal to every offer made by Nekhludov, and the other a crippled old man with a kindly face, tall and pale, his thin legs tightly bound in wrappers, listened attentively but said little.

First of all, Nekhludov explained his ideas about the private ownership of land. "I maintain that land should be neither bought nor sold because, if it is sold, it will be bought by men who have money and they will demand whatever they wish for the use of it. They will take money for the right to stand on the earth," said Nekhludov, using a phrase of Spencer's.

"The only thing to do would be to fix up a pair of wings and fly about," said the old man with the white beard and laughing eyes.

"That's true enough," said the long-nosed man in a deep bass voice.

"Quite right, sir!" said the ex-soldier.

"A woman just gathers a few shoots for her cow, and she is caught and taken off to jail," remarked the lame old man with the good-natured face.

"Our land is three miles from here, but none of us can afford to rent anything nearer. They've raised the price so high that we couldn't make it pay," said the toothless old man. "They twist us around their fingers. It's worse than serfdom."

"That is what I think myself," said Nekhludov. "I consider it a sin to own land. I want to give it away."

"Well, that would be a good thing," said the patriarchal old man with the curly beard, evidently thinking that Nekhludov meant to let the land.

"That is why I have come here. I do not wish to own land

any longer. But, of course, we must talk the matter over and decide on the best way to do it."

"Why, just give it to the peasants, that's all," said the toothless old man.

Nekhludov hesitated for a moment. He felt that those words implied a suspicion of his sincerity. But he quickly recovered and took advantage of the remark to express what he wished to say.

"I should be glad to do that," he said, "but to whom shall I give it and how? Why should I give it to you rather than to the peasants at Deminskoe?" (a neighboring village with very little land).

No one spoke, except the ex-soldier who exclaimed, "Quite right, sir!"

"Now tell me," Nekhludov went on, "if you were going to distribute the land among the peasants, how would you set about it?"

"Why, we'd divide it equally, of course," said the stove builder, raising and lowering his eyebrows.

"What else could we do? We must share equally, so much for every person, I should say," said the good-natured man in the white leg wrappers.

Everybody agreed that this arrangement would be the most satisfactory one.

"But what do you mean by an equal share? Would that include the house servants?" asked Nekhludov.

"Oh, no, sir!" said the ex-soldier, trying to look amused. But the tall, serious peasant did not agree with him.

"Everybody must have a share," he said in his deep bass voice.

"No," replied Nekhludov, who had prepared his reply in advance. "That can never be done. If we divide the land in equal parts, those who have never used a plough will sell their shares to the rich, and the rich will again have the land while those who live by working their own holdings will multiply, and there will be no land left for them—so the rich will again control those who need land."

"Quite right, sir!" said the ex-soldier, hastily supporting this statement.

"Selling land ought to be forbidden. The only ones to have it should be those who plough it themselves," cried the stove builder, angrily interrupting the ex-soldier.

To this Nekhludov replied by asking how anyone could be

sure that the ploughman was the owner of the land he was ploughing.

Here the tall, thoughtful peasant suggested a partnership arrangement, the land to be divided among the men who did the ploughing. "Then unless a man ploughs, he gets no land," he said in his imperative bass voice.

Nekhludov was prepared for this sort of communistic project. He said that for such an arrangement it would be necessary that every man should have a plough, that every horse and every farming tool should be of equal value, so that no one should be left behind—and to make a scheme of that kind a real success, all must be of one mind.

"You'll never make our people agree among themselves," said the cross old man.

"They'd never stop fighting," said the old man with the white beard and laughing eyes. "The women would scratch each other's eyes out."

"Then there's another thing," said Nekhludov, "the division of the land according to its quality. Why should one man have rich soil and his neighbor have sandy soil?"

"It ought to be divided so that every man will get some poor soil and some good soil," said the stove builder.

To this Nekhludov answered that the problem was not confined to one community but concerned the different provinces of Russia, among which an equitable division of land must be made. If land were to be given away free, why should some peasants have good holdings and others bad ones? Every man would naturally want good soil.

"Quite right, sir!" said the ex-soldier.

The others said nothing.

"So you see, this is not so simple as it may seem," Nekhludov went on. "Many a man puzzled over this problem before now. There is an American, Henry George, who proposed a plan that seems satisfactory to me. It agrees with my own ideas."

"But you are the master! What do you care what other people say? All you have to do is to give us the land, nobody can stop you," said the cross old man.

Nekhludov was annoyed by the interruption, and it pleased him to see that others among his listeners shared his annoyance.

"Wait a moment, Uncle Simon, let him tell us about it," said the serious peasant in his deep voice.

Thus encouraged, Nekhludov went on to expound Henry George's single-tax theory.

"The land belongs to God," he began.

"That's so! That's true," said several voices.

"The land is common property. One man has as good a right to it as another. But since there is good soil and bad, and every man wants the good soil, how is it to be shared equally? Shall the man who owns the good land pay to those who own none at all as much money as his land brings in?" Nekhludov went on to answer his own question: "As it is not easy to tell who should pay and who should be paid, and as some money must be collected for public expenses, it ought to be so arranged that every man pays into the public fund as much money as his land is worth. Then every one would share equally. If you wish to own good land, you must pay more for it than the man who owns poor land. But if you do not care to own land, you will have nothing to pay. Those who own land will pay the taxes and other communal expenses for you."

"That's right," said the stove builder, twitching his eyebrows. "The man who has the better land must pay more."

"He has brains, that George," said the portly old man with the curly beard.

"If we can only afford to pay the price," said the tall man with the bass voice, who evidently saw what it all led to.

"The payments must be neither too high nor too low, for if they are too high they may not be paid, and if they are too low, everybody will want to buy his neighbor's land, and it will end with trading in land again," said Nekhludov. "Well, now you understand what it is that I wish to do here."

"That's right, that is just. Yes, that would do," said the peasants, approvingly.

"That George was a mighty clever man," the portly old man with the curly beard said again. "Hear what he's invented!"

"How will it be if I want to have some land?" asked the bailiff with a smile.

"If there is a holding to spare, you may take it and cultivate it," said Nekhludov.

"What do *you* want with land? You're well fed as things are now," said the old man with the laughing eyes.

With this the conference came to an end. Nekhludov again repeated his offer, but he had ceased to expect an immediate answer. He advised them to talk things over with the other villagers and then come back and give him their answer. The peasants said that they would do so, and left in a state of great excitement. Their loud talk could be heard as they went down the road, and late into the night the wind carried up the echoes of their voices from the riverbanks.

The following day was spent by the peasants in discussing Nekhludov's offer. The village was divided into two parties: one of them thought that the offer was advantageous and could surely do them no harm; the other party could not understand it and therefore suspected a trick. The consultation lasted two days and, on the third day, they all agreed to accept the proposal, and came to Nekhludov to announce their decision. It seemed that the village had been much impressed by the opinion of an aged woman who suggested that the master had begun to be anxious about his soul and was doing this in order to save it—therefore he could not be trying to cheat the peasants. This explanation was further confirmed by the generous alms which Nekhludov had distributed while he stayed at Panovo. These alms were the result of his finding himself for the first time face to face with the extreme poverty of the peasants: he was appalled and, though he saw that it was unwise, he could not resist giving them money. Just then he chanced to have a large sum at hand—the receipts from the sale of a forest—and certain smaller sums as well, which had been paid in for farming implements.

No sooner was it known that the master was giving money to anyone who asked for it, than crowds of peasants, chiefly women, began to come in from all the neighboring villages, begging for help. Nekhludov was utterly at a loss to know how to deal with them. What was there to guide him in the distribution of alms? To whom ought he to give, and how much? Their misery was plain to be seen, and he had not the heart to refuse them when his own purse was full. At the same time there was no sense in giving indiscriminately to all who asked. The only way out seemed to leave the village—and this he hurried to do.

During his last day at Panovo he went into the house and spent some time rummaging in the cupboards and drawers; among other things he found a large number of letters in an old mahogany chiffonier with a bow front and brass lion's-head handles that had belonged to his aunts. Among the letters there was a photograph: it showed a group consisting of Sophia Ivanovna, Maria Ivanovna, himself as a student, and Katusha looking very innocent and happy and pretty. From all the objects in the house, Nekhludov selected these letters and the photograph. Everything else he left to the miller, who

had, on the recommendation of the smiling bailiff, bought the
house and furniture for a sum far below its real value. Recalling his sense of regret at the loss of his estate at Kuzminskoe, Nekhludov could not imagine how he could have
felt it. All he experienced now was a feeling of liberation and
novelty, as though he were a traveler discovering new lands.

❖

CHAPTER TEN

NEKHLUDOV reached the city after nightfall and the lighted
streets impressed him strangely, as he drove from the station
to his house. The rooms there smelled of naphthaline; Agrafena
Petrovna and Korney, tired and bad-tempered, were quarreling
over things that were never used but only brought out, aired,
and then put away again; his own room was not ready, and
was, indeed, so cluttered with piles of boxes and trunks that
it was difficult to get inside. It was evident that his unexpected
arrival interfered with the life of the house which seemed to
go on with a queer momentum of its own. The contrast between
the abject poverty in the village and this stupid waste in which
he himself had once taken part was so unpleasant that he decided to move to a hotel the next day, leaving Agrafena
Petrovna to manage matters in her own way until his sister
should arrive and finally dispose of everything in the house.

Nekhludov went out early the next morning. He took two
furnished rooms in one of the modest and rather dirty lodging-
houses in the vicinity of the prison; then, giving orders for a
few things to be fetched from his house, he went to see his
lawyer.

It was cold out of doors. After the spring rains and the
thunderstorm, a cold spell had set in. It was so chilly, and
the wind so piercing, that Nekhludov shivered in his thin
overcoat and walked as fast as he could, trying to get warm.
He thought of the village folk, women and children and old
people, whose misery he had seen as if for the first time, particularly of the wizened, smiling baby and his writhing little
legs, and he could not refrain from comparing them with the
townsfolk. As he passed the butchers', the fish shops, and the
ready-made clothes shops, he was struck by the prosperous
look of so many well-fed, neatly dressed tradesmen. Nothing

like this could be found in the countryside. All these men seemed satisfied that their efforts to cheat others who knew nothing about the quality of their wares was an important and useful occupation.

The coachmen in padded coats with buttons down their backs looked equally well-fed, and so did the house porters with gold braid on their caps, and the chambermaids with their curled fringes and their aprons, and especially the cab drivers, with the nape of their necks clean-shaven, as they dashed about the streets, lolling back in their seats and staring insolently at pedestrians. Nekhludov could not help seeing in all these people just the same peasants driven from their homes to the city by land hunger. Some had adapted themselves to city life, had made the most of their opportunities, had become something like their masters, and were well pleased with their situation; others had fallen into a condition worse than they had known in the country, and had become even more pitiable. The shoemakers whom he saw working at basement windows belonged to the second sort, and also the pale, disheveled washerwomen with thin, bare arms, ironing in front of open windows where the soapy steam poured out in clouds. He noticed two house painters, their bare legs and long aprons bespattered from top to bottom with paint. Their sleeves were rolled up on their lean brown arms and showed their swollen veins. Each man carried a pail of paint. Their faces looked haggard and ill tempered, and they quarreled without stopping. The same expression was to be seen on the faces of the carters as they jolted along. The ragged men and women who stood begging at the street corners with children clinging to them, and the few faces Nekhludov caught sight of as he passed the open windows of an eating house—all had the same look. Sweating, red-faced, dull-eyed men sat singing and shouting at dirty tables littered with bottles and crockery, white-coated waiters rushing about among them; by the window sat a man with uplifted eyebrows, pouting lips, and a fixed stare; he seemed to be struggling to remember something.

"I wonder why they have all gathered here," thought Nekhludov, breathing in the dust driven into his face by the cold wind, mixed with a smell of rancid oil and fresh paint.

In one of the streets he came across a procession of carts loaded with iron, making such a terrific din on the uneven pavement that his head and eyes began to ache. He was hurrying along to overtake the carts when suddenly he heard a voice calling him. He stopped and saw, a few steps ahead of him, an officer with a pointed waxed mustache and smooth shining face, waving his hand from the smart droshky in which he sat, with a friendly smile revealing a row of remarkably white teeth.

"Nekhludov! Can it be you?"

At first Nekhludov felt delighted. "Why—Schoenbock!" he exclaimed; but the next moment he knew that this was no occasion for delight. This was the same Schoenbock who had been to stay with his aunts. Nekhludov had not met him for some time. Rumors had reached him, however, that though heavily in debt he was still in his cavalry regiment and managed somehow to keep his place in the society of the wealthy. His gay, contented appearance seemed to corroborate this report.

"So glad I saw you! There isn't a soul in town," he said, getting out of his droshky and straightening his shoulders. "But you've grown old, my dear fellow! I only recognized you by your walk. Can't we dine together? Is there anywhere we can find a decent meal?"

"I am afraid I cannot spare the time," said Nekhludov, trying to think of some way of escape that would not offend his former comrade. "What are you doing here?" he asked.

"Business, my dear fellow, business; a matter of a trusteeship. I'm managing Samanov's affairs for him. Do you know him? He is tremendously rich, but his brain has gone soft. Imagine owning 130,000 acres!" he exclaimed with pride, as if he himself had made all that land. "His affairs were in a very bad way. The entire estate was in the hands of the peasants. They cultivated the place and paid nothing in rent. They owed him eighty thousand rubles—just think of it!—but in one year I made a big change and increased the revenue by 70 per cent. What do you say to that?"

Nekhludov now remembered having heard that Schoenbock, who had spent all his own fortune, had through private influence been appointed trustee for the property of a rich old man who was squandering his estate. There could be no doubt that the trustee was getting on famously. "How can I get away without offending him?" he kept wondering, as he looked at the plump face and pomaded mustache, and listened to the friendly chatter and bragging.

"Now, then, let's talk about our dinner. Where shall we go?"

Nekhludov took out his watch. "Really, I have no time," he said.

"Well, then, you must come to the races with me this evening."

"No, I can't do that either."

"Oh, please do! I haven't any horses of my own these days, but I always back Grishin's. Do you remember him? He has a first-rate stable. Do come, and we'll have supper together."

"No, I can't have supper with you either," said Nekhludov with a smile.

"Oh, that's too bad! Where are you going now? Let me give you a lift."

"I'm only going to see a lawyer who lives around the corner," said Nekhludov.

"Oh, yes, of course! You've become interested in prisons. Have you taken to defending prisoners? The Korchagins told me something about it," said Schoenbock, laughing. "They've already left town, by the way. What does it all mean? Do tell me about it."

"Yes, everything you have heard is true, but I can't tell you about it in the streets," replied Nekhludov.

"No, of course, of course. . . . Well, you always were a crank. Once more, won't you come to the races?"

"No, I won't," said Nekhludov, "but please don't be annoyed."

"Why should I be annoyed? But where are you living?" asked Schoenbock and, all at once, his face grew serious. He raised his eyebrows and his eyes became fixed, as if he were struggling to remember something. Nekhludov recognized the same expression he had seen on the face of the man with pouting lips at the restaurant window.

"Good heavens, isn't it cold?"

"Yes, indeed it is."

Schoenbock turned to the driver. "You have the parcels safe?" he asked. "Well, then, I'll say good-by. I'm awfully glad to have met you, old man," he said and, shaking Nekhludov by the hand, he jumped into his seat. He turned, waved his glove, and smiled his conventional smile with a flash of gleaming teeth.

"Is it possible that I could ever have been a man like that?" thought Nekhludov. "Perhaps not quite like that, but I wanted to be like him, and intended to spend my life in the same sort of way."

THE lawyer admitted Nekhludov before his turn, and at once began to discuss the Menshov case, which he had just been reading over. He was indignant about the baselessness of the accusation brought against them.

"It's a crying shame," he said. "It is extremely probable that the owner started the fire himself to get the insurance money. There is no sound evidence against the Menshovs—in fact, there's no evidence at all. It was all due to the carelessness of the examining magistrate and the overzealousness of the assistant prosecutor. If the case is heard here and not in a provincial court, I will guarantee an acquittal and I won't take a fee. Now, about this other matter: the petition of Fedosya Birukova to the emperor is ready. If you are going to Petersburg you must take it with you and present it personally. Otherwise, they will simply hold an inquiry and nothing will come of it. You must try to get in touch with people who are influential in the Court of Appeal. Well, is there anything more?"

"Yes, I received a letter—"

"Oh, I see: you've become a sort of spout—a funnel for the complaints of the whole prison," said the lawyer with a smile. "It's too much—you won't be able to cope with it."

"But this is a really astounding case," said Nekhludov. He briefly summarized the main points of the case. A peasant who could read and write had been explaining the Gospel to his friends in the village. The priests regarded this as a crime, and informed the authorities. The man was examined by the magistrate, the public prosecutor drew up an indictment, and the court committed him for trial. "I call that a terrible state of affairs," said Nekhludov. "Do you think it can be true?"

"What is it that surprises you?"

"Everything. I can understand how a country policeman might do it under orders—but the prosecutor who made out the indictment is an educated man—"

"But that is just where we are mistaken," said the lawyer. "We are in the habit of thinking that our prosecutors and judges are men of liberal views. Once upon a time that was so, but it is quite different in these days. They are simply officials whose chief interest is the twentieth day of every month, when their salaries become due—and which they'd like to see increased—and there their principles stop. They are prepared to accuse, try, and sentence anyone you like."

"But are there really laws now in existence that permit them to exile a man for reading the Gospel to other people?"

"Yes, he can be exiled and even condemned to hard labor, if it is proved that he has been interpreting the Gospel not according to the orders of the Church but according to his own ideas. To asperse the Orthodox Church in the presence of the people means exile to Siberia, according to Article 196."

"Impossible! I can't believe it."

"But it is the truth I am telling you. I always say to the gentlemen of the law courts that I never look at them without a sense of gratitude: we should all be in prison if it weren't for their kindness. It is such an easy matter to take away a man's lawful rights and send him to 'parts not too remote.' "

"But if everything depends on the arbitrary will of a prosecutor, what's the use of having trials at all?"

The lawyer laughed heartily. "What questions you do ask! That is philosophy, my dear friend. But there is no reason why we shouldn't discuss philosophy. You must come to our Saturdays. I think you've met my wife? You will always find scientists, literary men, and artists at our house, and we all discuss these 'abstract problems' together," said the lawyer, emphasizing ironically the word "abstract." "Do come if you can."

"Thank you, I will try," said Nekhludov, conscious that he was lying and that if he did try to do anything it would be to keep away from Fanarin's literary evenings and his circle of artists, scientists, and literary men. His laugh in reply to Nekhludov's remark that trials are meaningless if the judges can apply the laws at pleasure, as well as his tone when he spoke of "philosophy" and "abstract questions," showed Nekhludov how differently he and the lawyer, and probably the lawyer's friends, looked at such matters, and that in spite of his alienation from his own friends—Schoenbock, for example—he had even less affinity with the lawyer and his set.

CHAPTER TWELVE

It was growing late and the prison was a long way off, so Nekhludov hired a cab. As they drove along, the driver, a middle-aged man with a kindly, intelligent face, turned to Nekhludov, and called his attention to an enormous house that was just going up.

"Isn't that a huge affair?" he asked, as though he had helped to build it himself and was proud of his work.

It really was an enormous structure, planned in an extraordinarily complicated style. A solid scaffolding of heavy timbers, joined together by iron clamps, surrounded the building, which was separated from the street by a hoarding. Workmen bespattered with plaster were scurrying to and fro like so many ants. Some were laying bricks, some were dressing the stonework, others carried up heavily laden pails and hods, and brought down empty ones. A stout, well-dressed man, probably the architect, was standing by the scaffolding, pointing upward as he talked to the contractor, who listened to him with an air of respectful attention. All the while empty and loaded carts were rolling in and out of a gate near by.

"How sure they are, all of them—those who do the work and those who compel them to do it, that it is right for laborers to be building a stupid palace for some stupid man who is of no use to the world—probably one of the very same men who ruin and rob them—while their weary, pregnant wives are slaving at home beyond their strength and the children are crying for food —poor starved little babies in skullcaps, grinning like toothless old men," thought Nekhludov.

"Yes, that is a stupid house," he said aloud.

"Why stupid?" retorted the driver in an offended tone. "It gives people work. I don't call that stupid."

"But it is such useless work."

"That can't be so. They wouldn't be building it if it wasn't any use. It means food for the people," said the driver.

Nekhludov said no more. The wheels made such a noise on the cobblestones that it was difficult to hear or to make oneself heard. As they drew near the prison, the driver turned into a macadam road where it was easier to talk, and went on: "And such crowds of people are coming into town nowadays." He turned around on his seat and pointed at a group of country laborers with saws and hatchets, sheepskin coats, and sacks slung across their backs.

"More than in other years?" asked Nekhludov.

"I should say so! It's terrible this year. Every place is crowded. The employers fling workmen about like wood shavings. It is crowded everywhere."

"What's the reason for it?"

"They've multiplied so fast, there's no room for them."

"But what of that? Why don't they stay where they belong, in the villages?"

"There's no work for them in the villages. They've got no land."

Nekhludov felt like a man with a bruise which seems to get all the knocks that are going—yet it is only because the bruise is the spot that most feels the pain.

"I wonder if it is the same everywhere," he thought to himself, and began to question the driver about the land in his village, how much land he had himself, and why he was living in the city. The driver seemed eager to tell him all about it.

"There are three of us," he said, "and not more than two and a half acres apiece. I have a father and a brother at home and another brother in the army. They manage—but there's so little to manage on that my brother wanted to go to Moscow."

"Can't you rent land?"

"Where can you find it? The masters have squandered theirs. The merchants have got hold of it all—and you can't buy it from them, they want to work it themselves. In our parts it's a Frenchman who owns it. He bought it from our old mistress and he won't rent any of it, and that's all there is to say."

"Who is this Frenchman?"

"His name is Dufar. Perhaps you've heard of him? He makes wigs for the actors in a big theater. It's a good business, and he's made money. He bought the whole estate that used to belong to our mistress, and he rides us as he pleases. It's lucky for us he's a good man. But his wife, she's a Russian, and a real bitch. She just robs the people. It's dreadful! . . . But here is the jail. Where shall I drive in? I don't think they'll let you in at the main entrance."

CHAPTER THIRTEEN

OPPRESSED by the thought of the state he might find Maslova in, and by the mystery which he felt surrounding her and the other people collected in the prison, Nekhludov rang the bell at the main gate. When the warder came to the door, he asked where he would find Maslova. The warder went to inquire and came back saying that Maslova was in the hospital. The watchman of the hospital, a kindly old man, on being told whom Nekhludov wished to see, showed him the way to the children's ward. A young doctor, smelling of carbolic, came out into the passage and asked him sternly what he wanted.

This doctor was friendly to the patients and tried to make things easier for them, which resulted in frequent conflicts with the prison authorities and even with the senior doctor. Now, fearing that Nekhludov would ask him to break some rule, and anxious to show that he made no exceptions for anybody, he pretended to be annoyed.

"This is the children's ward; we have no women here," he said.

"Yes, I know," said Nekhludov, "but there is an attendant here who was transferred from the prison."

"Yes, there are two," said the doctor. "Which one do you want?"

"I am a friend of the one named Maslova," said Nekhludov. "She is the woman I want to see. I am going to Petersburg to enter an appeal on her behalf, and I wanted to give her this," he continued, taking an envelope from his pocket. "It contains only a photograph."

"Oh, yes, we can allow that," replied the doctor, mollified; he turned to an old woman wearing a white apron and told her to call the prisoner Maslova.

"Please take a seat; or perhaps you would prefer to go to the reception room."

"Thank you," said Nekhludov; taking advantage of the favorable change in the doctor's manner, he asked him how they liked Maslova in the hospital.

"Quite well. She works fairly well, considering her past life," answered the doctor. "But here she comes."

The old woman entered, followed by Maslova wearing a

striped dress and a white apron. Her hair was completely hidden under a three-cornered kerchief. At the sight of Nekhludov she turned scarlet and paused irresolutely; then, with downcast eyes and frowning brows, she walked quickly along the passage toward him. When she came up to him she did not at once shake hands, but after a pause held out her hand, blushing more than ever. Nekhludov had not seen her since the conversation when she had apologized for her outburst, and he was expecting to find her in the same frame of mind. But she was very different now. Her face showed self-restraint; she seemed shy and yet, as it appeared to Nekhludov, hostile. He repeated to her what he had told the doctor about his intended visit to Petersburg and gave her the envelope with the photograph.

"I found this at Panovo," he said; "it is an old photograph. I thought you might like it. Won't you take it?"

Lifting her black eyebrows, she gazed at him in surprise with an expression in her squinting eyes that seemed to say, "What is this for?" She took the envelope in silence and tucked it into her apron.

"I saw your aunt while I was there," said Nekhludov.

"Did you?" she said indifferently.

"Are you comfortable here?"

"Yes, quite."

"You are not finding it too hard?"

"No, but I'm not quite used to it yet."

"I am very glad for you. It is better here than there."

"What do you mean by 'there'?" she said, blushing.

"There, in the prison," Nekhludov said hastily.

"In what way?" she asked.

"The people here must be better."

"There are plenty of good people there," she said.

"I have been looking into that affair of the Menshovs, and I hope they will be set free," said Nekhludov.

"Thank God!" she exclaimed. "She is such a wonderful old woman," she said, repeating her former description of old Menshova and smiling slightly.

"I am going to Petersburg today," said Nekhludov. "Your case is coming up shortly, and I hope that the sentence will be quashed."

"Whether or not, it's all the same to me now," she answered.

"Why do you say 'now'?"

"Oh, because—" she began, looking up into his face with a questioning glance.

Nekhludov understood the words and the glance to mean

that she wanted to know whether he still kept firm to his decision, or had accepted her refusal.

"I do not know why *you* are indifferent," he said, "but so far as I am concerned it will not alter things at all whether you are found guilty or innocent. In either case I am ready to keep my promise," he concluded firmly.

She lifted her head, and her black squinting eyes rested for a moment on his face and then looked beyond him, while her face beamed with happiness; but what she said was something different from what her eyes were saying. "It's no use speaking like that," she exclaimed.

"I say it so that you should know."

"We've talked it all over, and there's no more to be said," she replied, repressing a smile with difficulty.

A sudden noise and the voice of a child crying came from the ward.

"I think they're calling me," she said, looking around anxiously.

"Well, then, I'll say good-by," said Nekhludov.

She pretended not to see his outstretched hand and, turning away in an attempt to hide her triumph, walked back along the passage.

"I wonder what is going on in her mind now?" thought Nekhludov. "What is she thinking about and what does she really feel? Is she testing me, or can she really not forgive me? Perhaps she doesn't know how to express her feelings, or perhaps she doesn't care. Has she softened toward me, or does she still feel hostile?" He found no answer to these questions, and yet he knew for certain that the girl had changed, and that the change was an important one. It united her not only to himself but also to Him in Whose name it had been accomplished. And this union lifted him into a state of joyous exaltation and humility.

When Maslova entered the ward, which held eight children, the nurse told her to make one of the beds. Bending over with the sheet, she slipped and nearly fell; then, when a convalescent boy with a bandage around his neck, who had been watching her, began to laugh, she could no longer restrain herself. She sat down on the edge of the bed and burst into a peal of laughter so infectious that several of the children joined in, too, and the nurse shouted at her:

"What are you guffawing at? Do you think you are still in the place you came from? Go and fetch the dinners."

Maslova stopped laughing and went with the dishes as she

was bidden; but when on her way she exchanged a glance with the bandaged boy who had been forbidden to laugh, she could not suppress a giggle.

Several times when she happened to be alone during the day, Maslova took the photograph out of the envelope and looked at it admiringly. But it was not until the evening, when her duties were over and she was alone in the room she shared with a nurse, that she sat down to enjoy it. For a long time she sat still and looked, caressing every detail of the faces and the dresses, the balcony steps, the shrubbery which served as a background for the aunts, Nekhludov, and herself. As she gazed at the faded yellow photograph she could not help admiring the beauty of her young face, with the hair waving around the forehead. She was so absorbed that she did not notice the other woman enter the room.

"What's that? Did he give it to you?" asked the plump, good-natured nurse, stopping over the picture. "Is that you?"

"Who else could it be?" asked Maslova, lifting her head and smiling.

"And who is that? Is that him? And is that his mother?"

"No, that's his aunt. Would you have known me?"

"Never in my life! Your face is entirely changed. This must have been taken ten years ago at least."

"Not ten years, but a lifetime," said Maslova; all her animation died away, her face grew stern, and a deep wrinkle came between her eyebrows.

"But it was an easy life, wasn't it?" asked the nurse.

"Yes, an easy life . . ." repeated Maslova, closing her eyes and shaking her head. "Worse than hard labor."

"What do you mean?"

"I mean that from eight o'clock in the evening till four o'clock in the morning, every night of our life—"

"Then why don't women give it up?"

"They want to give it up, goodness knows, but how can they? Oh, what's the use of talking about it?" cried Maslova, springing to her feet and flinging the picture into the table drawer. Unable to restrain her tears of rage, she ran out of the room and banged the door behind her. While she had been looking at the picture she had felt as she used to feel then, and dreamed of her past happiness and of how happy she would be with him even now. The nurse's words reminded her of what she had become and of the horror of her past life, which even at the time she had recognized but had not admitted.

Now memories of hideous nights came back to her—of one

particularly, during Carnival week, when she was waiting for a student who had promised to buy her out. She was wearing a low-necked red gown spotted with wine stains, and in her ruffled hair was a red bow. In an interval between dances she saw her guests away. It was about two o'clock in the morning and she felt weak, exhausted, and a little drunk. She took a seat behind the thin, pimpled bony woman who accompanied the violinist, and began to complain that life was so hard. She remembered the pianist saying how tired she was of her life, too. Presently her friend Bertha joined them, and all three decided to give up that kind of life. They were just about to separate when the drunken voices of new guests were heard in the hall. The violinist played a *ritournelle* and the pianist pounded out the first figure of a quadrille, introducing the accompaniment to a cheerful Russian song. A little man in evening clothes and a white tie, hiccuping and smelling of drink, caught her in his embrace; another man, fat and bearded, also in evening dress —they had come from a ball—seized Bertha and together they whirled and danced and shouted and drank. . . . And so it went on for a year, and another year, and another. How could any-one have helped changing? And it was he who had been the cause of it all. Again the old furious rage was let loose in her heart and she longed to give it words. She was sorry she had missed the opportunity of telling him that she knew the sort of man he was and would not give in to him again, that she would not let him use her spiritually as he had used her physically, nor give him the satisfaction of showing magnanimity toward her. Pity for herself and rage against Nekhludov had thrown her into such a state of excitement that she longed for drink. Had she been in prison instead of the hospital she would not have hesitated to break her promise and drink some vodka; but the only way to obtain it here would be through the doctor's assistant, and she was afraid to approach him because he had already annoyed her with his attentions. She had come to hate the sight of a man. She sat for a while on a bench in the passage, then went back to her room; making no response to the other woman's talk, she wept for a long time over her ruined life.

NEKHLUDOV had four matters to see to in Petersburg: Maslova's appeal to the Senate; the case of Fedosya Birukova in the Committee of Petitions, another case which he had taken up at the request of Vera Bogodukhovskaya in the Department of Gendarmes, or in the Third Department,[1] for the liberation of Shustova; and a petition from a woman who had begged him to visit her son confined in the Fortress. These two cases he considered as one. The fourth concerned the Sectarians who were to be sent to the Caucasus for reading and interpreting the Gospel. He had promised, not so much to them as to himself, to look into the matter.

Since his last visit to Maslennikov and his stay in the country he had conceived a loathing for the society in which he lived: a society where millions struggled to provide an easy life for a few, and where sufferings were so carefully hidden that the very ones who benefited by them did not and could not see them, nor the wickedness and cruelty of their own lives. In their company he felt guilty and ill at ease, yet his former habits (and, naturally, his family and friends) contributed to keep him from making a clean break. Moreover, he knew that for the sake of Maslova and the other unfortunates whom he was anxious to help, he would have to call on the assistance of these people, for whom he had no esteem and who even aroused his contempt and indignation.

On reaching Petersburg, he went to stay with his maternal aunt, the Countess Charskaya, the wife of a former minister of state, and thus found himself in the center of just that aristocratic society which had become repugnant to him. But what else could he do? If he had gone to a hotel it would have vexed his aunt, and she was too influential to be overlooked. He needed her assistance in the affairs he was so eager to promote.

"What are all the marvelous tales we hear about you?" asked Countess Ekaterina Ivanovna as she offered him coffee after his arrival. *"Vous posez pour un Howard,* helping criminals, visiting prisons, putting things right."

"Oh, no, not at all. . . ."

[1] Secret police.—Tr.

243

"Why not? It's a good thing. But haven't I heard that there is some romance connected with all this? Do tell me all about it."

Nekhludov described his relations with Maslova exactly as they were.

"Oh, yes, of course, I remember now! Poor Hélène told me something about that, when you were staying with the old ladies. They tried to marry you to a ward of theirs, I believe." (Countess Ekaterina Ivanovna had always looked down on the kinsfolk of Nekhludov's father.) "So that's the girl, is it? *Elle est encore jolie?*"

Ekaterina Ivanovna was a woman of sixty, tall and stout, with a black mustache on her upper lip. She was jolly, robust, energetic, and talkative. Nekhludov was fond of her, and even as a child had found her high spirits and energy infectious.

"No, *ma tante,* all that is over. I only want to help her. It is I who am to blame for the life she has led. Now she has been unjustly sentenced, I must do all I can for her."

"But somebody told me you wanted to marry her."

"So I did, but she refused me."

Ekaterina Ivanovna, eyebrows raised and eyes lowered, listened to her nephew in silent amazement. Suddenly her expression changed and, with a look of pleasure, she exclaimed:

"Well, she is wiser than you! What a fool you are. . . . And you really would have married her?"

"Of course I would."

"After the life she has led?"

"All the more reason why I should marry her, since it was *my* fault."

"No, you're simply a goose, that's all!" said the aunt, repressing a smile. "A terrible goose. And that is the very reason why I love you—because you're a goose." She fondly repeated the word "goose," apparently regarding it as specially apt for the mental and moral state of her nephew. "I will tell you how this affair can be settled. Aline is in charge of a wonderful asylum for fallen Magdalenes. I went to visit them once. They are disgusting. After that visit I couldn't stop washing myself. But Aline is in it, *corps et âme.* That's the very place for that girl of yours. If anybody can reform her, it is Aline."

"But she has already been condemned to hard labor," said Nekhludov, "and I have come here to get the sentence quashed. This is the chief thing I've come to see you about."

"I see! Well, how far has the case gone?"

"To the Senate."

"The Senate? Why, that's where my dear cousin Levushka is. But he's in the Herald's office. I don't know any of the senators themselves. Heaven only knows who they are. Some are Germans, I fancy, Geh, Feh, Deh, *tout l'alphabet*, and every variety of Ivanovs, Semyonovs, Nikitins, or Ivanenkos, Simonenkos, Nikitenkos *pour varier. Des gens de l'autre monde.* But I'll speak to my husband. He knows them. He knows all sorts of people. But you'd better explain everything to him yourself. He never understands what I tell him. No matter how hard I try to make things clear, he says he doesn't understand. *C'est un parti pris.* Everybody else understands me, but he never does."

Just then a footman in knee breeches brought in a letter on a silver tray.

"Why, it's from Aline herself! You'll have a chance of hearing Kiesewetter."

"Who is Kiesewetter?"

"Come tonight and find out for yourself. He speaks with such eloquence that the most hardened criminals fall on their knees and weep and repent."

Countess Ekaterina Ivanovna, however inconsistent it may appear with her temperament and character, was a devout adherent of the doctrine which teaches that redemption is the essence of Christianity; she went to all the meetings where this doctrine, fashionable at the time, was expounded, and she also held meetings at her own house. But although the doctrine excluded all ritual, icons, and even sacraments, the countess had an icon in every room and even one above her bed, continued to observe all the ceremonial of the church, and saw no inconsistency in it.

"I wish your Magdalene could hear him; he would convert her. Now don't forget to be at home tonight. He is a very remarkable man."

"But, *ma tante,* I'm not interested."

"But I assure you it *is* interesting. And you must come. Now what else can I do for you? *Videz votre sac.*"

"I have another case in the Fortress."

"The Fortress! Well, I can give you a note to Baron Kriegsmuth. *C'est un très brave homme.* You know him, don't you? He was a comrade of your father. *Il donne dans le spiritisme,* but never mind, he's a very kind man. What is it you want there?"

"I want permission for a woman to visit her son who is imprisoned there. But I was told that it depended on Chervyanski, not on Kriegsmuth."

"I don't like Chervyanski, but he is Mariette's husband. We can ask her. She will do it for me. *Elle est très gentille.*"

"Then I want to present a petition on behalf of a woman who has been in prison several months and has no idea why."

"Oh, I daresay she knows well enough—they usually do. I think those short-haired women get just what they deserve."

"I don't know whether they deserve it or not, but I do know how they suffer," said Nekhludov. "You are a Christian, you believe in the Gospel, and yet you have no pity."

"That has nothing to do with it. The Gospel is one thing and what we despise is another. It would be disgraceful if I pretended to love Nihilists—particularly those short-haired women of theirs—when the truth is that I can't bear them."

"Why can't you bear them?"

"Do you ask me *why,* after the first of March?"[1]

"But they are not all responsible for that."

"All the same, they ought to keep away from what does not concern them. A woman ought not to go in for public affairs."

"Yet you seem to think that your Mariette can attend to public affairs."

"Mariette? Mariette is Mariette, but these girls come from goodness knows where and yet they want to go teaching everybody."

"Not at all. All they want is to help the people."

"We don't need them to do that. We know very well who needs help and who doesn't."

"But the people are suffering. I have just come from the country. Do you call it right that the peasants should work to the limits of their strength and never get enough to eat, while we are living in a terrible luxury?" said Nekhludov, beguiled by his aunt's good nature into confiding his thoughts to her.

"Well," she said, "would you like it if I worked hard and did not eat?"

"No, I shouldn't like you not to eat," replied Nekhludov, smiling. "What I should like is that we should all work and all eat."

His aunt again fixed her eyes on him with an expression of curiosity. *"Mon cher, vous finirez mal,"* she said.

"But why?"

---

[1] The Tsar Alexander II was assassinated on the 1st of March 1881.—Tr.

Just then a tall, broad-shouldered man entered the room. It was the countess's husband, General Charski, former minister of state.

"Ah, how are you, Dmitri?" he said, presenting a clean-shaven cheek for his nephew to kiss. "When did you arrive?"

He kissed his wife's forehead without a word.

"Non, il est impayable," said the countess to her husband. "He wants me to be a washerwoman and live on potatoes. He is a terrible fool—a terrible goose," she corrected herself, "but I want you to help him all the same. Have you heard about Madame Kamenskaya?" she went on. "They are afraid for her life. You must call."

"Yes, it is dreadful," said her husband.

"Now," she said, turning to Nekhludov, "you'd better go and tell him all about your cases while I write my letters."

Nekhludov was just going out of the room when she called after him:

"Shall I write to Mariette, then?"

"Please do, *ma tante.*"

"I'll leave a blank space for you to tell her about your short-haired woman, and she will tell her husband what to do. He'll do it. You mustn't think me unkind. Your protégées are nasty creatures, *mais je ne leur veux pas de mal.* You may go now, but be sure to be back this evening to hear Kiesewetter. We will all pray together, *ça vous fera beaucoup de bien.* I know Hélène and the rest of you were very lacking in those things. *Au revoir.*"

❖

CHAPTER FIFTEEN

COUNT IVAN MIKHAILOVICH was a former minister of state and a man of strong convictions. These convictions consisted in the belief that just as it was natural for a bird to feed on worms and be covered with down and feathers and fly about in the air, so it was for him to eat delicate food prepared by first-class cooks, to wear expensive clothes, to drive fast horses; and he expected all these things to be laid before him. Moreover, he believed that the more money he got out of the Treasury, the more decorations he received (including, if possible, the diamond-mounted insignia of something or other), and the oftener he spoke to highly placed persons of both sexes, so much the better it was. Measured by these standards, everything else in the world was uninteresting and insignificant. Everything else might be as it was or just the reverse, for all he cared. And after having lived by this creed for forty years, Count Ivan Mikhailovich reached the position of a minister of state.

The chief qualities which contributed to his success were these: first, he was able to understand legal documents already written, and to write them himself intelligibly and without spelling mistakes; secondly, he had a commanding presence and could impress people with his dignity and aloofness, while at the same time, if need arose, he was capable of abject servility; and thirdly, having no real guiding principles, he could agree or disagree with anybody just as best suited his immediate purpose. When acting thus, his one endeavor was to keep up appearances and avoid being too obviously inconsistent. Whether his actions were moral or immoral, whether great good or great evil would result from them for the Russian Empire and the rest of the world—these were matters of supreme indifference to him.

When he became minister of state not only his dependents—and there was a great number of them—but many strangers, as well as he himself, were convinced of his political wisdom. But as time went on and he accomplished nothing, showed no ability in any direction, and finally, in obedience to the law which governs the struggle for existence, lost his place to other men exactly like himself—handsome and unscrupulous officials who had learned to write and understand documents—and had to resign, then it became clear to everybody that, far from being exceptionally clever, he was a shallow, ignorant, though very conceited man, whose ideas scarcely reached the level of the leading articles in the conservative newspapers. It became evident that there was nothing to distinguish him from any other half-educated, self-confident official, from the very men who had elbowed him out. This he understood himself, but was not shaken in his conviction that he deserved a large income and new decorations every year. This conviction was so firmly rooted that no one dared dispute it, and every year he received, partly in salary and partly in pensions, tens of thousands of rubles for being a member of important government institutions, and chairman of various committees and commissions; furthermore, he was continually adding new braid to his epaulettes and trousers, ribbons to go over his evening shirts, and enameled stars for his evening coats. As a result of all this, Count Ivan Mikhailovich was highly connected.

The count now listened to Nekhludov as he used to listen to his secretary. Having heard all he had to say, he said he would give him two letters. One was to Senator Wolf in the Department of Appeals. ("They say all sorts of things about him, but at all events *il est un homme très comme il faut*. He owes me a great deal and he will do what he can.") The other letter was to an influential person in the Committee of Petitions. The case of Fedosya Birukova seemed to interest him very much and, when Nekhludov proposed writing to the empress, he said that it was indeed a touching story and that he himself would mention it at court if an occasion arose. However, he could not promise anything. The petition had better be sent in. But if he were invited to the *petit comité* on Thursday, he would probably refer to it.

Taking both these letters and his aunt's note to Mariette, Nekhludov set out on his errands.

He went first to Mariette. He remembered her as a girl in her teens, the daughter of a poor but aristocratic family, and he knew that she had married a man who had made a career for himself but who did not enjoy a good reputation. Indeed, very bad things had been said of him, and Nekhludov always strongly disliked asking a favor of a man he did not respect. He would in the circumstances put off making his request for some time and, although usually coming around to it in the end, he would do so with a feeling of dissatisfaction with himself. To ask favors of men of a class he had ceased to regard as his own embarrassed him all the more since they still looked upon him as one of themselves; for his part, he felt himself caught in the old rut and in spite of himself influenced by the frivolous, immoral tone reigning in that circle. He felt this that very morning, at the house of his aunt Ekaterina Ivanovna, when he found himself involuntarily imitating her light and bantering ways of speech.

Petersburg, where he had not been for a long time, was always bracing for him physically, but spiritually relaxing. Everything was so clean and comfortable, so well arranged and the people so tolerant, that life seemed perfectly easy. A fine, clean, civil cabby drove him past fine, clean, civil policemen along well-watered pavements and clean, beautiful houses, till he came to the house of Mariette.

At the entrance stood a pair of English horses with blinkers in the English style; a bewhiskered, English-looking coachman in livery sat on the box on the carriage, holding his whip proudly. Inside the vestibule stood the doorkeeper in a wonderfully clean uniform, a footman with carefully combed side whiskers and a still cleaner and more elaborately braided uniform, and an orderly on duty, also in a new, clean uniform.

"The general is not receiving. Her Excellency is not receiving either. She is going out directly."

Nekhludov gave Ekaterina Ivanovna's note to the doorkeeper and, taking out a visiting card, approached the table where the visitors' book lay; he was beginning to write a few words of regret, when the footman went to the staircase, the doorkeeper went out and shouted to the coachman, and the orderly stood to attention, holding his hands motionless by his sides and looking toward a small, slender lady who was hurrying down the stairs at a pace that could hardly be considered dignified in a person of her social rank.

Mariette was wearing a large hat with a plume, a black gown, black mantle, and black gloves. Her face was hidden by a veil. At the sight of Nekhludov she threw back the veil, showing a very pretty face with brilliant eyes. She looked at him inquiringly, then in a gay, pleasant voice exclaimed:

"Why, it is Prince Dmitri Ivanovich! I ought to have recognized—"

"You even remember my name?"

"Of course I do! My sister and I were in love with you," she said in French. "But how you have changed! I wish I weren't going out—" she added and paused irresolutely, looking at the clock on the wall. "No—I can't stay. There is a Requiem at Madame Kamenskaya's. She is in a terrible state."

"What has happened to her?"

"Why, haven't you heard? Her son was killed in a duel. He fought with Pozen. He was an only son. It is terrible. The mother is prostrated."

"Oh, yes, I have heard about it."

"I wish you could come tomorrow—or perhaps tonight?" she said, as she walked lightly toward the door.

"I cannot come tonight," he replied, escorting her to the carriage. "But I have a request to make to you," he went on, looking at the pair of bays, now drawing up at the door.

"What is it?"

"Here's a note from my aunt, with a full explanation, you'll find it all there," said Nekhludov, handing her a narrow, crested envelope.

"Yes, I know Countess Ekaterina Ivanovna thinks that I can influence my husband. She's quite mistaken. I can do nothing of the sort and I hate to interfere. But, of course, for you or the countess, I will break my rules. What is it about?" she went on, vainly struggling to find her pocket with her small, tightly gloved hand.

"There is a girl imprisoned in the Fortress who is innocent and ill."

"What is her name?"

"Lydia Shustova. You'll find it all in the letter."

"Very well, I'll do everything I can," she said; stepping lightly into the softly upholstered carriage with its lustrous splash-guards glistening in the sun, she opened her parasol. The footman climbed in the box and signaled to the coachman. But the carriage had barely started when she touched the coachman's back with her parasol and the beautiful slim-legged mares stopped, quivering and stamping and arching their handsome necks.

"But remember you are coming to see me and—*disinter-estedly*," she said with that smile of hers whose power she well knew; then, the play being ended, the curtain fell—that is, she drew down her veil. "You may go on now," she said, touching the coachman again with her parasol.

Nekhludov lifted his hat. The thoroughbred mares, snorting, struck their hoofs on the pavement, and the carriage rolled swiftly away, its rubber tires bounding over the cobblestones.

❖

CHAPTER SIXTEEN

RECALLING the smiles he had exchanged with Mariette, Nekhludov shook his head at himself. "I shall be drawn in with these people before I know what I'm doing," he thought, affected by the inner disharmony which was usual with him when he was seeking favors from people he could not respect.

In order to waste no time, he considered his route carefully and decided to go first to the Senate. He was shown into the office, a magnificent apartment where there were several neatly dressed and very polite clerks. Nekhludov was informed that Maslova's petition had been received and was already in the hands of Senator Wolf, the man to whom his uncle had given him a letter. Although the Senate was to sit that week, Maslova's case was unlikely to come before it. One of the clerks suggested, however, that if a special request were made it might possibly come up on Wednesday.

While Nekhludov stood waiting in the office he overheard more about the duel which was the talk of Petersburg and learned just how young Kamenski had been killed. It seemed that a group of officers were eating oysters in a shop and, as usual, drinking freely. One man made some deprecatory remarks about Kamenski's regiment. Kamenski called him a liar, whereupon the other struck him. The next day they fought with pistols and his opponent's bullet entered Kamenski's stomach. In two hours he was dead. The murderer and the seconds were arrested and sent to the guardhouse, but it was said that they would probably be set free in a couple of weeks.

Nekhludov drove from the Senate directly to the Committee of Petitions to meet Baron Vorobyov, an influential official who occupied magnificent apartments in a house belonging to the Crown. Here the doorkeeper and the footman told him in a severe tone of voice that the baron could be seen only on reception days; at present he was with His Majesty, and would again have to deliver a report on the following day.

Nekhludov left his letter and went to Senator Wolf. Wolf had just finished luncheon, and was helping his digestion by pacing up and down the room and smoking a cigar. Vladimir Vassilyevich Wolf was indeed *un homme très comme il faut,* and was prouder of that attribute than of any other. From this sublime altitude he looked down upon the rest of the world. Indeed, he could not but esteem the quality which had given him the brilliant career he coveted—namely, to have obtained an income of 18,000 rubles a year by marriage, and acquired the appointment of Senator by his own exertions. However, he considered himself not only *un homme très comme il faut* but also a man of honor. For him, honor consisted in refusing secret bribes offered him by private individuals. It never occurred to him that there was anything dishonest in extorting traveling expenses or postage money and other allowances from the Crown, since in return he performed many servile tasks which the government required of him. To lay waste, to destroy, to take a leading part in the banishment or imprisonment of hundreds of innocent people for their patriotism and devotion to the faith of their fathers—crimes which as governor of a Polish province he had constantly committed—he regarded not as dishonorable but as evidence of noble courage and patriotism. Nor did he consider it dishonest to fleece his wife, who was in love with him, and his sister-in-law: on the contrary, it seemed to him a clever way of arranging his domestic life. His household consisted of his nonentity of a wife; her sister, whose fortune he had appropriated by selling her estate and investing the proceeds in his own name; and a meek daughter, a plain, gentle, terrorized creature who had lived a lonely life till she became interested in the evangelical lectures at Aline's and the Countess Ekaterina Ivanovna's. Vladimir Vassilyevich's son, a goodhearted sort of fellow whose beard had developed at the age of fifteen (when he also began drinking and leading a dissolute life), had in his twentieth year been turned out of the house partly because he had failed to graduate, partly for frequenting low company and compromising his father by running into debt. Having paid debts, one of two hundred rubles and one of six hundred, his father finally told him that this was the last time and that, unless he reformed, he would be turned out. Far from reforming, he soon ran into debt for a thousand rubles and moreover told his father that it was a perfect torment to go on living in his house. Vladimir Vassilyevich then told him to go where he pleased, being no longer a son of his. After that he pretended not to have a son, and no one ventured to mention his name. And Vladimir Vassilyevich was quite sure that domestic life could not have been more satisfactorily arranged.

Wolf stopped short in the middle of his stroll up and down the room; greeting Nekhludov with a smile at once gracious and ironical, which was intended to reveal to the world in general the superiority of a personage *comme il faut*, he opened the letter and read it.

"Please take a seat—but, if you will excuse me, I will go on walking," he said. He put both hands in his pockets and continued to pace delicately up and down his large, severely furnished study.

"I am very glad to make your acquaintance. Naturally I should like to do all in my power to please Count Ivan Vassilyevich," he added, blowing a puff of aromatic blue smoke out of his mouth, and holding his cigar carefully in order not to drop any ash.

"I should be glad to have the case considered as soon as possible, since—if the prisoner is sent to Siberia—the earlier she starts the better," said Nekhludov.

"Yes, yes, I understand, by the first steamer from Nizhni," said Wolf, with his condescending smile. He always knew in advance what anybody was going to say. "What is the prisoner's name?"

"Maslova—"

Wolf walked to the table and glanced at a paper that was lying among other documents.

"Yes, Maslova, to be sure. . . . Very well, I will speak to my fellow members and we will take up the case next Wednesday."

"May I telegraph to my lawyer about it?"

"You have a lawyer? But what for? Still, of course, you can send him a telegram if you like."

"The grounds of the appeal may not be sufficient," said Nekhludov, "but no one can doubt that the verdict was the result of a misunderstanding."

"Yes, yes, that might be so, but it is not the Senate's business to consider the affair on its intrinsic merits," said Vladimir Vassilyevich sternly, gazing at the ash of his cigar. "The Senate is only concerned with the correct interpretation and application of the law."

"But this seems to me an exceptional case," said Nekhludov.

"I know—every case is exceptional. We shall do our duty and that is all that can be expected." The ash still held on, but had cracked and was in imminent danger of falling. "Do you often come to Petersburg?" he asked, holding his cigar in such a way that the ash could not fall; but it was so near falling that he finally carried it to an ash tray and there allowed it to drop.

"What a shocking thing that was about Kamenski," he said. "Such a fine young man, and an only son. Just picture the poor mother," he went on, repeating word for word the talk of the day in Petersburg. After a few words more about Ekaterina Ivanovna and her enthusiasm for the new religious movement (which he neither approved nor disapproved, but which, as one so *comme il faut,* he had no use for whatsoever) he rang the bell, and Nekhludov took his departure.

"If you find it convenient, come to dinner on Wednesday," said Wolf, extending his hand, "and I will give you a definite answer."

❖

CHAPTER SEVENTEEN

EKATERINA IVANOVNA dined at half past seven, and the dinner was served in a way that was new to Nekhludov. The servants placed the dishes on the table and at once withdrew, so that the diners waited on themselves. The men would not let the ladies undergo any exertion, but manfully took upon themselves the burden of serving the food and pouring out the wine. As soon as one course was finished, the countess pressed an electric button under the table; the waiters returned in silence, quickly removed the dishes, changed the plates, and served the next course. The dinner was *recherché*, and so were the wines. A French chef, with two helpers dressed in white, was at work in the large, airy kitchen. There were six persons at the table: the count and the countess, their son (a surly officer in the Guards, who put his elbows on the table), Nekhludov, a French lady's companion, and the count's bailiff who had come up from the country.

Here also the conversation turned on the duel. It was known that the emperor was deeply grieved for the afflicted mother, and all were grieved for her, but it was also known that the emperor did not mean to be very severe with the murderer, who had defended the honor of his uniform; and in this, too, everybody agreed with His Majesty. Countess Ekaterina Ivanovna, with her free and easy ideas, was the only one to condemn the murderer.

"Getting drunk, killing a decent young man. . . . No, I would never forgive that!"

"I cannot understand you," said the count.

"I know, you never understand what I say," said the countess, and added, turning to Nekhludov: "Everybody understands me except my husband. All I say is that I am sorry for the mother and I do not wish the murderer to be pleased with himself for having killed a man."

Hereupon her son, who had so far listened in silence, took the murderer's part and rudely attacked his mother, telling her that an officer would be turned out of his regiment were he to act otherwise. Nekhludov listened and played no part in the conversation. Having served in the army himself he understood the validity of young Charski's argument, but could not refrain from comparing the officer who had killed Kamenski with the fine-looking fellow he had seen in the prison, sentenced to hard labor for killing a man in a brawl. Both had become murderers because they had been drinking. Yet the peasant, who had killed a man in a moment of passion, was taken away from wife and family, thrown into prison, and now, in chains and with shaven head, was on his way to Siberia, while the officer was living in a pleasant room in the guardhouse, eating good dinners, drinking good wine, and reading books. In a few days, he would be set free to pursue his career, having only become more interesting by this affair.

He said what he was thinking and at first his aunt agreed with him but, after a while, lapsed into silence with the others, and Nekhludov felt almost as if he had committed a social impropriety.

In the evening, soon after dinner, rows of high-backed carved chairs were arranged as for a meeting, with an easy chair and a table carrying a tumbler and a decanter of water for the preacher, and the company assembled for a sermon by the distinguished Kiesewetter. Expensive carriages drove up before the entrance. Women, dressed in velvet and silk and lace, with false hair and padded busts, came in and sat down. There were men, too, both officers and civilians, as well as five or six of the common sort of people: house porters, a shopkeeper, a footman, and a coachman.

Kiesewetter was a robust man with hair just turning gray. He spoke English, which was readily and smoothly translated by a thin girl wearing pince-nez. So great were our sins, he said, so severe and unrelenting the punishment they deserved that no one could go on living under such a threat.

"If we pause, my dear brothers and sisters, to reflect on the sins we commit every day of our lives, on the way in which we offend our Heavenly Father and our dear Lord, His Son, then we may come to understand how vast is our sin, and that we are doomed to eternal damnation. Dreadful doom, everlasting torment await us!" he cried in a trembling voice, the tears about to fall. "Oh, how can we be saved from this unquenchable fire? The house is already in flames and there is no escape."

He paused, and tears were running down his cheeks. He had been giving the same address for eight years and, whenever he came to this passage (which he especially liked), he always felt a tickling in the nose, a choking in the throat, and the tears always began to flow.

These tears increased his emotion. Sobs were heard throughout the room. Countess Ekaterina Ivanovna was sitting beside an inlaid table, leaning her head on her folded arms while her broad shoulders heaved convulsively. The coachman gazed at the foreign gentleman with fear and amazement, looking as though he were about to run someone down who refused to get out of the way. Most of the company sat in attitudes not unlike that of the countess. Wolf's daughter, a thin, fashionably dressed girl very like her father, was kneeling with her face in her hands.

Suddenly the speaker raised his head and, assuming the smile that actors use to express joy, began in a sweet and gentle voice:

"But lo, salvation lies before us: so simple, so blissful! Our salvation is the blood of the only-begotten Son of God, who gave Himself up to be tortured for our sakes. His agonies, His martyrdom will be our salvation. Oh, my brothers and sisters!" he cried in his tearful voice, "let us praise the Lord who gave His only Son for the redemption of mankind. His precious blood . . ."

Nekhludov felt so deeply disgusted that he rose, frowning, and keeping back a groan of shame, left on tiptoe and went to his room.

❦

CHAPTER EIGHTEEN

THE next morning, just as Nekhludov had dressed and was about to go downstairs, the footman brought him a card from Fanarin, who had come to Petersburg on business of his own and partly (if it were to come up soon) to be present at the hearing of Maslova's case in the Senate. Nekhludov's telegram had missed him. When he heard which senators were to be present he smiled.

"Exactly—all three types: Wolf, the Petersburg official; Skovorodnikov, the learned jurist; and Beh, the practical lawyer; therefore the most wide-awake of them all. He is likely to do most for us. But what about the Committee of Petitions?"

"I am going to call on Baron Vorobyov today. I couldn't see him yesterday," said Nekhludov.

"Do you know how Vorobyov comes to be a baron?" asked the lawyer, observing the slightly ironical stress Nekhludov placed on this foreign title preceding so very Russian a name. "His grandfather was a footman at the court, I think, and managed to please the Emperor Paul in some way, so he made him a baron. 'This is my wish—don't argue about it!' And behold, there is a 'Baron Vorobyov,' and very proud of the title. He's a sly creature."

"I'm on my way to see him now," said Nekhludov.

"Excellent! We can go out together. Let me give you a lift."

As they were setting out, a footman came up to Nekhludov and gave him a note from Mariette.

Pour vous faire plaisir, j'ai agi tout-à-fait contre mes principes, et j'ai intercédé auprès de mon mari pour votre protégée. Il se trouve que cette personne peut être relachée immédiatement. Mon mari a écrit au commandant. Venez donc disinterestedly. *Je vous attends.*

"What do you say to that?" exclaimed Nekhludov. "It is simply outrageous. This woman, who has been kept in solitary confinement for several months, proves to be innocent, and only a word is needed to have her released."

"That's the way it always is," said the lawyer. "But you've got what you wanted."

"Yes, but this very success distressed me. Just think what must be going on there. Why were they keeping her?"

"Well, if I were you, I wouldn't go too deeply into the matter. Will you let me give you a lift?"

By this time they had left the house, and a fine carriage hired by the lawyer drove up to the entrance.

"So you're going to Baron Vorobyov's?"

The lawyer gave the address to the coachman, and the swift horses quickly took Nekhludov to the baron's house.

In the first room were two ladies, and a young official in uniform, who had a long, thin neck with a conspicuous Adam's apple, and a remarkably light way of walking.

"Your name, please?" he said, stepping lightly and gracefully toward Nekhludov. Nekhludov gave his name.

"The baron has spoken about you. One moment, please!"

The aide-de-camp left the room and returned, escorting a lady with a tear-stained face, dressed in black. Her bony fingers were fumbling to pull her crumpled veil over her face and so hide her tears.

"This way, please," said the young man to Nekhludov, walking lightly toward the door and opening it.

When Nekhludov entered the study he found himself in the presence of a stout man of medium height, wearing a frock coat; he was sitting in an easy chair at a large desk and looking very cheerful. His hair was cut short; his good-natured face, pink, and framed by a white beard, lighted with a friendly smile at the sight of Nekhludov.

"I am very glad to see you. Your mother and I were old friends. I remember you as a boy, and later when you became an officer. Please sit down and tell me how I can be of use to you. . . . Yes, yes," he kept saying, shaking his cropped white head, while Nekhludov was relating Fedosya's story. "Go on—I understand—yes, indeed—it is certainly very touching. Well—have you sent in the petition?"

"I have prepared it," said Nekhludov, taking it out of his pocket. "But I wanted to speak to you first. I hoped that this case might receive special attention."

"You have been very sensible. I shall certainly present the report myself," said the baron, vainly trying to put a sorrowful expression on his cheerful face. "It is indeed a very moving story. She seems to have been no more than a child, and her husband was too rough with her and this repelled her. Then, later on, they fell in love with each other. . . . Yes, I will report it."

"Count Ivan Mikhailovich said he would ask you—"

Hardly had Nekhludov said these words than the baron's expression changed.

"Perhaps, after all, you had better send in the petition yourself, and I will do what I can for my part," he said.

At this moment the young man who seemed so vain of his light walk came into the room.

"That lady wished to have another word with you, sir."

"Very well, let her come in. Ah, *mon cher,* if you but knew what floods of tears we see! If only we could hope to dry them! We do what we can."

The lady entered.

"I had intended to ask you not to let him give up his daughter; he's capable of . . ."

"I told you I would do that."

"Thank God, Baron—you will save a mother!" She seized his hand and began to kiss it.

"Everything shall be done."

When the lady had gone, Nekhludov also rose to take leave.

"We will do the best we can," said the baron. "We will first write to the Ministry of Justice and, when their answer comes, we will do all we can."

Nekhludov left and went into the office. Again, as in the Senate, he found superb officials in a superb apartment—officials who were neat, polite, scrupulous in their dress and in their speech, precise and rigid in their manner.

"How many there are of them! How terribly many and how well fed! And what clean shirts and hands! How well their shoes are polished! And who looks after all this? How comfortable they are, compared with the prisoners—and even compared with the peasants!" Nekhludov could not keep such thoughts from his mind.

CHAPTER NINETEEN

THE man who had the power to relieve the hardships of the prisoners in Petersburg was a very old general descended from a family of German barons. He had received enough decorations to cover himself with, although he never wore anything except a white cross in his buttonhole. He had seen many years of active service, but people said that he was now in his dotage. The white cross, which he valued so highly, he had received in the Caucasus for commanding close-cropped Russian peasants, dressed in uniforms and armed with guns and bayonets, who had killed more than a thousand men bent on defending their homes and their families. Afterward he had served in Poland, where he also compelled Russian peasants to commit all sorts of crimes, and for this he received more orders and decorations. Then he served somewhere else; finally, grown old and feeble, he was appointed to this post, which provided him with a good house, a good salary, and public respect. He was rigid in his obedience to "orders from above," and very proud of his rigor. He believed that everything in this world could be changed except those "orders from above." His duty consisted in keeping political prisoners of both sexes confined in such conditions that in the course of ten years half of them died or became insane. Some died of consumption, others committed suicide by starving themselves, cutting their arteries with bits of glass, hanging themselves, or burning themselves to death. The old general knew about these things very well (for they had all happened under his eyes), but looked upon them as accidents of nature, such as might arise from storms or floods. They did not weigh on his conscience in the least, even though they were the direct result of "orders from above" issued in the name of His Majesty the emperor. Such orders were to be scrupulously obeyed, and it was not his affair to consider the consequences. He believed that it was his duty as a soldier and a patriot not to reason, since this might make him falter in executing these immensely important orders. Once a week the old general went the rounds of the cells (this being a duty) and asked every prisoner if he or she had any requests to make. The requests were made. He heard them calmly, in silence, but never granted them because they were all contrary to the provisions of the law.

As Nekhludov was drawing near the old general's home, the treble bells of a belfry clock played *Praise Ye The Lord* and then struck two. As he listened to the chimes, Nekhludov remembered having read in the memoirs of one of the Decembrists[1] how heavily this sweet music, repeated hour after hour, had fallen on the hearts of prisoners confined for life.

Meanwhile, the old general was sitting in his dimly lighted drawing room at an inlaid table, occupied with a young artist, the brother of one of his subordinates, in moving a saucer around a piece of paper. The frail, moist fingers of the artist were interlaced with the hard, stiff-jointed, wrinkled fingers of the general; their clasped hands placed on the saucer were jerking to and fro over the sheet of paper, which had all the letters of the alphabet written upon it. The saucer was answering a question put by the general: "How do the souls of the departed recognize one another after death?"

The spirit of Joan of Arc was communicating with them through the saucer when an orderly came in with Nekhludov's card. The spirit had already spelled out, "They will know each other by—" and they had written this down. When the orderly came in, the saucer paused near the letter *c*, passed to *l* and then to *e*; after moving to *a*, it began to jerk about. The general thought that Joan of Arc was going to say that souls would know each other because they had been "cleansed" of earthly impurities (or words to this effect) and he therefore argued to himself that the next letter should be *n*; but the artist was sure that the next letter ought to be *r* and that the spirit of Joan of Arc meant to say that souls would know each other by the "clear light" emanating from their ethereal substance.

The general wrinkled his bushy gray eyebrows and stared morosely at the saucer. He kept pulling it toward the letter *n*, all the while imagining that it moved of its own accord. The pale young artist, with thin hair brushed smoothly behind his ears, had his dull blue eyes fixed on a dark corner of the room; his lips twitched nervously as he urged the saucer toward the letter *r*.

The general frowned at the interruption, put on his pince-nez, and looked at Nekhludov's card, rubbing his numbed fingers. A pain in his broad back made him groan as he drew himself upright and said, "Show him into the study."

[1] A group who attempted to overthrow absolutism in Russia by means of a military revolt in December 1825.—Tr.

"If Your Excellency will permit me," said the artist, rising, "I will finish this alone. I feel the presence."

"Just as you like. I have no objection," said the general severely, and went into the study with a quick, firm, even step.

"Glad to see you," he said to Nekhludov, uttering the friendly words in a gruff tone and pointing to an easy chair beside the writing desk. "How long have you been in Petersburg?"

Nekhludov replied that he had only just arrived.

"I trust your mother the Princess is well?"

"My mother is dead."

"Oh, I beg your pardon. I am very sorry to hear that. My son told me about meeting you."

The general's son was pursuing a career not unlike his father's. After leaving the Military Academy he had been appointed to the Intelligence Department and was very proud of the work given to him: it was the supervision of government spies.

"Yes, I served with your father. We were comrades and friends. Are you in the government service?"

"No, I am not."

The general shook his head disapprovingly.

"I have come to make a request of you, General."

"Indeed? I shall be pleased to do what I can for you."

"If what I am going to ask is improper, I hope you will pardon me; but I must tell you what it is."

"Well?"

"There is a certain man, Gurkevich by name, who is confined in the Fortress. His mother asks for permission to visit him, or at least to send him books."

The general showed neither pleasure nor displeasure at Nekhludov's request. He bowed his head as if in thought, but the truth was, he was not thinking about anything, and was not even interested, knowing beforehand that his answer would be given in accordance with the law; he was simply taking a mental rest and his mind was a perfect blank.

"Matters of this kind, you see," he began at last, "do not depend on me. There is a regulation concerning interviews, confirmed by His Majesty, and whatever has been decreed is carried out. As to books—we have a library, and books proper for them to read are to be found in it."

"But he needs scientific books; he wants to study."

"Don't you believe it." The general again relapsed into a short silence. "It is not study that he wants," he went on; "he's just restless."

"But don't you think," said Nekhludov, "that, considering their unfortunate condition, it is better to keep these men occupied?"

"They are forever grumbling," objected the general. "We know them." He spoke of them as though they belonged to a different and inferior sort of being. "They have comforts here that are seldom found in prisons. I assure you—" and he began, as though in self-justification, a detailed description of all the conveniences provided for the prisoners, as though the chief aim of the institution was to make a pleasant home for them. "It was not like that in the old days, I must admit. It used to be very hard. But nowadays they are well cared for. They have three courses to their meals, and one is always meat, either mince or *rissoles*. On Sunday they get a fourth course, a sweet. I would thank God if every Russian were as well fed."

Like all old people, the general, having once got on to something he knew by heart, said all the things he had so often said before to show the unreasonableness of the prisoners' demands, and their ingratitude.

"They get old periodicals and books on spiritual subjects. We have a whole library of suitable books. But they don't read much. When they first arrive they seem interested, but very soon new books are returned with the leaves half cut, while the pages of the old ones are not even turned. We used to try them by putting in bits of paper," said the general with a dim likeness of a smile, "but we always found them at exactly the same place. Neither do we hinder them from writing. Slates and slate pencils are provided. They can occupy themselves in writing, rub out what they have written and write over and over again. But they don't do it. No, they very soon quiet down. It's only at first that they are restless. As time goes on, they even begin to grow fat and become very quiet," said the general, never suspecting the terrible meaning of his words.

Nekhludov listened to the hoarse old voice, looked at the stiffened limbs and the dull eyes half hidden under gray eyebrows, at the carefully shaven, flabby jowl supported by a military collar, at the white cross of which the old man was so proud and which commemorated his cruel slaughter of thousands of men—all the while seeing the utter folly of contradicting him or even trying to explain the meaning of the request he had just made. However, he made an effort and inquired about another case, that of Shustova. He had heard that morning that orders had been given for her release.

"Shustova? Shustova? I cannot possibly recall all their names

—there are so many of them," said the general, as if they were to blame for being so many. He rang the bell and sent for his clerk, in the meantime trying to persuade Nekhludov to enter the service. "Every honest and high-minded man"—he included himself in the number—"is needed by the Tsar . . . and the country," he added to round off the sentence. "I am an old man, he went on, "but so far as my strength permits, I go on serving."

The clerk, a thin, withered man with restless, intelligent eyes, came in and reported that Shustova was still imprisoned in some fortified place and that no formal order had been received concerning her release.

"We shall certainly discharge her as soon as we get the papers. We don't keep them any longer than we can help. We are not particularly anxious for their company," said the general, with another attempt at a playful smile which only distorted his aged face.

Nekhludov rose, trying to conceal the mingled feelings of disgust and pity which that sinister old man excited in his heart. And the general, on his side, thought he must not be too hard on the thoughtless and erring son of an old comrade. He also felt that he ought to give him some good advice before he left.

"Good-by, my dear fellow! Now don't be vexed with me for what I am going to say, because my motives are friendly. Don't have anything to do with our prisoners. There are no innocent ones here. All these people are most immoral. We know them," he concluded, and the tone of his voice admitted of no possible doubt. His reasons for not doubting their guilt were not disinterested: if they were not guilty, he would be forced to see himself as a villain who had sold (and in his old age went on selling) his conscience, rather than a venerable hero who was honorably using the last years of a good life.

"There is nothing finer for us than service. The Tsar needs honest men . . . and so does the country," he added. "What do you suppose would happen if we all behaved like you and refused to serve? We are ready to condemn the government, and yet we are not willing to help it."

Nekhludov, sighing deeply, made a low bow as he pressed the big bony hand held out to him with condescension, and left the room.

The general shook his head in displeasure and, rubbing his back, returned to the drawing room where the artist, who had already written down Joan of Arc's reply, was waiting for him. "They will recognize each other by the clear light emanating from the astral body."

"Ah!" said the general with approval and closed his eyes. "But if everybody emits the same light, how are we to know one from another?" Interlacing his fingers with the artist's, he again took his seat at the table.

Nekhludov's cabby drove out of the gate.

"That's a dreary place, sir. I had half a mind to drive off without waiting for you."

"Yes, it is a dreary place," said Nekhludov; he drew a deep breath and gazed with relief at the smoke-colored clouds flitting across the sky and at the shimmering ripples in the wake of the boats and steamers on the Neva.

❖

CHAPTER TWENTY

MASLOVA'S case was brought up on the following day, and Nekhludov drove to the Senate. He met Fanarin at the impressive entrance, where several carriages were already drawn up. They ascended a magnificent staircase to the second story, where the lawyer, who knew all the ins and outs of the place, went to a door on the left which was carved with the date of the introduction of the judicial code. As he took off his overcoat he learned from the doorkeeper that the senators were all assembled, the last one having just gone in. Fanarin, wearing a tail coat and white tie, walked jauntily into the next room. On the right-hand side there was a large cupboard, then a table, and on the left a winding staircase. Just at that moment an elegant official was coming down the stairs with a portfolio under his arm. The attention of everybody was drawn toward an old man in a short coat and gray trousers, whose long white hair gave him a patriarchal appearance. Two attendants stood beside him in respectful attitudes. The white-haired old man opened the cupboard and vanished. Fanarin, who had met a colleague with whom he was on friendly terms, dressed in a tail coat and white tie like himself, at once began a lively conversation, while Nekhludov watched the people in the room.

In all there were about fifteen, two of them ladies. One of these was young and wore pince-nez, the other had gray hair. The case to be heard that day was a newspaper libel, and therefore the audience was larger than usual; it consisted chiefly of journalists.

The usher, a florid, handsome man in a gorgeous uniform, holding a slip of paper in his hand approached Fanarin to ask him which case he was interested in; on learning that it was Maslova's, he made a note and departed. At this moment the cupboard door swung open and the patriarchal old man came out. He had exchanged his short coat for a uniform furnished with metal plates across the chest and trimmed with gold, in which he resembled a bird. This queer costume seemed to embarrass the old gentleman himself, for he walked much more rapidly than usual and left the room by the opposite door.

"That's Beh, a most estimable man," said Fanarin to Nekhludov, and then having introduced him to his colleague, explained the case which was coming up, and which he considered to be of unusual interest.

After a short time the hearing began; Nekhludov, going to the left with Fanarin and the rest of the audience, entered the Senate chamber. They all took their places in the enclosure railed off for the public. Only the Petersburg lawyer went up to a desk in front of the rail.

The Senate chamber was smaller and more plainly furnished than the criminal court. The chief difference was that the cover of the table where the senators sat was made of crimson velvet instead of green cloth, and had a gold fringe. Otherwise, all the usual trappings were there just the same: the mirror of justice, the icon—emblem of hypocrisy—and the portrait of the emperor—emblem of servility. The usher announced in the usual solemn tones, "The Court is coming," and everybody rose in the usual way. The senators, in uniform, entered and sat down in their high-backed chairs, leaning on their elbows and trying to look natural. There were four senators. The presiding senator, Nikitin, a clean-shaven man with a narrow face and eyes like steel; Wolf, with significantly compressed lips and small white hands, fingering the papers of the case; Skovorodnikov, the learned jurist, stout and untidy, with a pockmarked face; the fourth was Beh, the patriarchal old man who had been the last to arrive. The chief secretary and assistant prosecutor, a slender young man of medium height with a smooth face, dark skin, and sad black eyes, also entered with the senators. In spite of the unfamiliar uniform Nekhludov recognized him at once, though it was six years since they had met: he had been one of Nekhludov's closest friends in their student days.

"Is that Selenin?" he asked his lawyer.

"Yes, why?"

"I know him very well; he is a fine man."

"And an admirably competent prosecutor; we should have had him acting for us," said Fanarin.

"Well, I am sure he will be guided by his conscience," said Nekhludov, remembering his former friendship with Selenin and his attractive qualities of purity and honesty.

"But it's too late now, anyway," whispered Fanarin, who was listening to the report of the case just beginning.

The case was an appeal to the superior court to reverse the verdict of a district court.

Nekhludov listened attentively, trying to understand what was going on; but just as in the criminal court, so here the biggest difficulty was the persistent emphasis on side issues and the shelving of the main issue. The case concerned a company director who in a newspaper article had been accused of fraud. The important problem could only be to decide whether or not the company director had been robbing the shareholders, and how he could be prevented from continuing to do so. But this problem was never raised. What was discussed instead was whether the editor had a right to publish the article, whether it was to be considered as libel or defamation, and whether libel includes defamation or defamation includes libel—not to mention other matters even less comprehensible to laymen, concerning the various statutes and decisions drawn up by some general department.

The only thing that Nekhludov saw quite clearly was that Wolf, who was now making the report and who had only yesterday insisted that the Senate could not judge a case on its merits, was at this moment arguing with obvious partiality for the reversal of the judgment of a district court, while in a manner quite unlike his customary self-control Selenin stated the opposite opinion with unexpected violence. Selenin was excited because he knew the company director to be a scoundrel and had by chance heard that Wolf, the evening before, had been this man's guest at a magnificent dinner party. After Wolf had made a report couched in terms which, while guarded, showed a distinct bias in favor of the director, Selenin grew agitated and expressed himself more strongly than seemed warranted in such an everyday affair. Clearly the words gave offense to Wolf, for he blushed, moved about in his chair, made gestures of surprise, and withdrew with the other senators to the conference room with an air of injured dignity.

"Which case are you interested in?" the usher asked again, approaching Fanarin.

"We've told you once already—the Maslova case," replied Fanarin.

"Oh, I remember now! It was to be heard today, but—"

"Well?" asked the lawyer.

"We were not expecting a defense, you see, and the senators are not likely to come back after reaching their decision in this case. Still, I will call their attention to it—"

"What do you mean by that?"

"I will certainly call their attention," said the usher, and began to write something on a slip of paper.

The senators actually had intended after the decision in the libel suit to dispose of all the other cases, Maslova's included, while they sat comfortably smoking and taking their tea in the conference room.

❧

CHAPTER TWENTY-ONE

As soon as the senators had taken their seats at the table in the conference room, Wolf began very excitedly to show the reasons why the judgment ought to be reversed. The president, an ill-natured man at best, was in a particularly bad humor today. He had arrived at a definite opinion while listening to the report, and now, intent upon his own thoughts, he heard not a word that Wolf said. He was trying to recall what he had written in his memoirs about the appointment of Velyanov to an important position he had wanted for himself. President Nikitin honestly believed that his opinions about the officials in the two higher grades with whom he was connected would furnish precious material for future historians. He had on the previous night finished a chapter full of shrewd criticisms of certain officials who had hindered his plans to save Russia from the destruction into which her rulers were dragging her (this was his way of describing it, but the truth of the matter was that he was angry because they had prevented him from getting a higher salary), and he was thinking just then that owing to his revelations posterity would see these matters in an entirely new light. "Yes, of course," he replied to Wolf, without hearing what had been said.

Beh listened to Wolf with a melancholy expression, drawing garlands all the while on the sheet of paper lying before him. Beh was a liberal of the very first water. He religiously treasured the traditions of the sixties, and if he ever departed from his strictly neutral attitude it was always in favor of liberalism. In this case, for instance, apart from the fact that the company director complaining of the libel was himself an unscrupulous man, Beh was in favour of rejecting the suit because it was in itself a restraint on the freedom of the press.

When Wolf had completed his argument, Beh stopped drawing his garland and with a note of regret—for it grieved him to be compelled to demonstrate such truisms—proceeded in a low and gentle voice to prove concisely, simply, and convincingly the utter groundlessness of the suit for libel; when he had finished, he bent his white head and went on drawing his garlands.

Skovorodnikov, who sat opposite Wolf and kept stuffing his mustache and beard with his fat fingers into his mouth and chewing them, suddenly dropped this occupation when Beh paused, and said in a loud, croaking voice that although he knew the company director to be a great rascal, he would have advocated putting the judgment aside if any legal grounds had existed for doing so; but as there were no such grounds he agreed with Ivan Vassilyevich Beh, he said—pleased at the opportunity of getting in a hit at Wolf. The president supported Skovorodnikov, and the case was decided in the negative.

Wolf was particularly annoyed because he seemed to have been caught showing dishonest partiality. Assuming an air of indifference, however, he opened the next case on the agenda, that of Maslova, and became absorbed in it. Meanwhile the senators rang the bell, called for tea, and began discussing an event which together with the Kamenski duel was the talk of Petersburg. It concerned the chief of a government department who had committed the crime covered by article 995.

"How revolting!" said Beh in disgust.

"Where's the harm? I can show you a book where a German writer openly puts forward the view that such acts ought not to be considered criminal, and says that marriage between men should be allowed," said Skovorodnikov, noisily and greedily inhaling the smoke from a squashed cigarette which he held close in the palm of his hand, and laughing loudly.

"Impossible!" said Beh.

"I will show it you," Skovorodnikov replied, quoting the full title, the year, and place of publication.

"I heard that he was to be appointed governor of some place in Siberia," remarked Nikitin.

"That's fine. The bishop will meet him with a crucifix. They ought to appoint a bishop of the same kind. I could recommend them a suitable one," said Skovorodnikov and, flicking the stump of the cigarette into his saucer, he took into his mouth as much of his beard and mustache as possible and began to chew them.

Just then the usher appeared and reported the request of Nekhludov and his counsel to be present during the hearing of Maslova's case.

"This case," said Wolf, "is quite romantic," and he related what he knew of Nekhludov's relationship with Maslova.

They discussed it for a while and, finishing their cigarettes and their tea, returned to the Senate chamber. The decision in the previous case was announced and Maslova's case began.

In his thin voice Wolf made a full report of Maslova's appeal, again with a personal bias, evidently wishing to have the sentence reversed.

"Have you anything to add?" said the president to Fanarin.

Fanarin rose, and throwing out his broad white chest began with remarkable persuasiveness and precision to prove the misinterpretation of the law by the court on six counts. He went further, and touched briefly on the facts of the case and the evident injustice of the sentence. The tone of his short but forceful address seemed to beg the pardon of the Senate for insisting on matters which they, with their wisdom and knowledge of the law, should know far better than he. He said that only his obligation to his client made it his duty to speak.

After Fanarin's speech there seemed little reason to doubt that the Senate would set aside the decision of the court. As he finished his pleading, Fanarin smiled triumphantly. When Nekhludov looked at him he left sure that the case was won; but when he turned toward the senators, he realized that Fanarin alone was triumphant and smiling. The senators and the assistant prosecutor were neither smiling nor triumphant. They looked profoundly bored and seemed to say to themselves and to each other: "We have heard that kind of talk before, but what does it all amount to?" They were apparently much relieved when the lawyer finished, and stopped wasting their time. The president then turned to the assistant prosecutor. In a few brief and clear words Selenin declared that he had heard nothing in the lawyer's appeal that would warrant reversing the judgment. The senators then rose and went into the conference room. Here the votes were divided. Wolf favored reversal. Beh, who understood the issue, was on the same side, vividly painting for the senators the scene in the court and what he rightly interpreted as the misunderstanding of the jury. Nikitin, a believer in strict formality and never inclined to be lenient, was opposed to reversal. The matter therefore depended on the vote of Skovorodnikov, and his vote was cast for rejection of the appeal, chiefly because he was outraged by Nekhludov's determination to marry the girl for moral reasons. Skovorodnikov was a materialist and a Darwinian: he looked upon all manifestations of abstract morality or religious belief not only as despicable folly but as a personal affront to himself. All the fuss in the Senate about a prostitute, the presence of Nekhludov and a famous lawyer to defend her, were extremely distasteful to him. And he began to stuff his beard into his mouth again and to make grimaces, pretending that he knew nothing whatever about the case except that the reasons for an appeal were inadequate; he therefore agreed with the president in rejecting it.

The appeal was rejected.

CHAPTER TWENTY-TWO

"Terrible!" said Nekhludov as he went out into the waiting room with Fanarin, who was putting his papers into his portfolio. "Whatever the justice of your case, they discover flaws in the form and refuse it. It's terrible."

"The case was mismanaged at the trial," replied the lawyer.

"Selenin, too, was in favor of rejection. Terrible. Terrible," repeated Nekhludov. "What is to be done now?"

"We will petition His Imperial Majesty. Present the petition yourself while you are in Petersburg. I will write it out for you."

Meanwhile Wolf, a small figure in his uniform, had come out into the waiting room; he went up to Nekhludov.

"It's too bad, my dear Prince. Your grounds weren't good enough," he said, shrugging his shoulders and closing his eyes as he passed by. After Wolf came Selenin, who had just heard that an old friend of his was there.

"I certainly had not expected to meet *you*," he said, walking up to Nekhludov with a smile on his lips, though his eyes remained sad. "I had no idea you were in Petersburg."

"And I did not know that you were a public prosecutor," said Nekhludov.

"Assistant," Selenin corrected him. "But how did you happen to come to the Senate?" he went on, looking at his friend with a sad and melancholy air. "I *had* heard that you were in Petersburg, by the way, but how do you come to be here?"

"Here? I hoped to find justice and to save an innocent woman."

"What woman?"

"The one in the case that has just been decided."

"Ah, Maslova's case," said Selenin, remembering. "There was no ground for an appeal."

"The question is not of the appeal, but of an innocent woman being punished."

Selenin sighed.

"Perhaps, but—"

"There's no perhaps about it. It is beyond any doubt."

"How do you know?"

"Because I was one of the jurors. I know how the mistake was made."

Selenin reflected.

"You should have spoken out at the time," he said.

"I did."

"Your statement should have been added to the documents of the case. If it had been joined to the petition for appeal—"

Always absorbed in work and rarely going into society, Selenin evidently had not heard of Nekhludov's romance. Taking this into account, Nekhludov decided that no good would be served by speaking of his relationship with Maslova.

"But it was perfectly plain that the verdict was absurd," he said.

"The Senate has no legal right to declare such a thing. If the Senate ventured on setting aside judgments given in the courts because it thought them unjust, trial by jury would lose all meaning—besides, no legal basis could be found for the Senate's doing so, and there would be a very great risk of hindering justice instead of upholding it," said Selenin, referring in his mind to the preceding case.

"All I know is that this woman is completely innocent, and that the last hope has gone of saving her from a punishment she hasn't deserved. The very highest court has confirmed an illegal action."

"No, it has not—it could not have made, nor can it make, a factual judgment," said Selenin, screwing up his eyes. "I suppose you are staying with your aunt," he went on, evidently wishing to change the subject. "I heard last night that you had arrived. Countess Ekaterina Ivanovna sent me an invitation to meet you at a gathering where a foreign preacher was to speak," he added, smiling with his lips only, while his eyes remained sad.

"Yes, I was there, but left in disgust," said Nekhludov irritably, annoyed that Selenin wanted to change the conversation.

"Why in disgust? After all, it's a manifestation of religious feeling, even though it may be one-sided and sectarian," said Selenin.

"It's all so wildly absurd," said Nekhludov.

"Not at all. The really strange thing is that we know so little of the dogma of our church that we learn of our own doctrines as though they were a new revelation," said Selenin, apparently eager to inform his former friend of his new views.

Nekhludov looked at him in surprise. Selenin lowered his eyes, which now expressed a certain hostility as well as sadness.

"Do you believe in the dogmas of the church?" asked Nekhludov.

"I certainly do," replied Selenin, looking straight at Nekhludov with lifeless eyes.

Nekhludov sighed. "I am surprised," he said.

"But we can discuss this later," said Selenin. "Yes, I am coming," he said to the usher who had respectfully approached him. "We must certainly see each other again," he added with a sigh. "But when shall I find you in? I always have dinner at home at seven o'clock. Nadezhdenskaya Street—" and he gave his number. "Many things have changed since the old days," he added, as he turned to go, smiling with his lips only.

"I will come, if I have time," said Nekhludov, feeling that this man, once so near and dear to him, had after this brief talk become suddenly strange, remote, and incomprehensible, almost antagonistic.

CHAPTER TWENTY-THREE

THE Selenin whom Nekhludov had known as an undergraduate was a good son, a faithful friend, and for his years a well-educated man of the world with a great deal of tact, good-looking, well groomed, and at the same time exceptionally truthful and honest. He learned easily and was a gold medalist, though free from all pedantry. As a young man, he aimed at nothing less than the service of mankind, in deeds as well as in words, and could see no better way than service under the state; on leaving the university, therefore, he thought over all the various possible fields of activity open to him, and decided that he would be most useful in the Second Department of the Imperial Chancellery (where the laws are drafted) and here he entered himself; but though he carried out precisely and conscientiously every duty that fell to him, he never convinced himself that he was being useful to mankind nor that he was doing "the right thing." Friction with a vain and small-minded superior increased his dissatisfaction so much that he resigned and then entered the Senate, where he felt more contented. Even so, his feeling of dissatisfaction persisted. He felt all along that it was not what he had expected or what he sought to be doing. While he was in the Senate his relatives succeeded in obtaining for him the appointment of *Kammer Junker*,[1] and he was obliged to drive in a closed carriage, to wear an embroidered uniform and white linen apron, and to thank all sorts of people for having got him a lackey's place. However much he tried, he could find no reasonable justification for such a post, and more than ever he felt that it was not "the right thing." Still, he could not refuse the appointment for fear of offending those who were so certain they were giving him great satisfaction; and to say the truth, he was also a little flattered by it and was pleased when he saw himself in the mirror wearing a gold-embroidered coat, and when he was deferred to by a certain type of person.

The same sort of thing happened over his marriage. A very brilliant marriage from a worldly point of view had been arranged for him, and again, his chief reason for marrying was that a refusal would have hurt both the young lady who desired the marriage and the people who had arranged it; it also pleased him and gratified his ambition to marry a young, pretty girl of good family. But it was not long before married life proved still less satisfactory than government service and the place at court. After the birth of their first child his wife refused to have any more children and plunged into society, where he also felt obliged to play a part. Although she was poisoning her husband's existence and deriving nothing but excessive weariness from the life she was leading, she still persevered. All his efforts to make a change were broken, as against a stone wall, by her conviction (in which she was supported by her family and friends) that this was the proper life to lead.

The child, a girl with long golden curls and bare legs, was

[1] Gentleman of the Bed Chamber.—Tr.

like a stranger to her father, the more so as she was not brought up as he wished. There sprang up between husband and wife the usual mutual misunderstandings, even an absence of desire to understand one another, and a silent struggle, concealed from outsiders and tempered by the wish to preserve appearances, made his home life very difficult. His married life thus proved still less "the right thing" than his government position or the place at court.

But above all it was his attitude toward religion which was not "the right thing." Like all men of his circle and his time he had during the progress of his intellectual growth easily shaken off the fetters of the religious superstitions in which he had been reared, without actually noticing just when the change took place. In the earnest, honorable years of his youth, when he and Nekhludov were friends, he had not concealed his freedom from the superstitions of official religion. As the years went by, bringing promotion with them—and particularly during the conservative reaction which set in about that time—this spiritual freedom began to be a disability: it was so not only in his private life, when, for example, a requiem was held after his father's death and his mother (supported by public opinion) wished him to fast and prepare himself to receive the sacrament; but also in his government service which required him to be present at festivals, consecrations, thanksgivings, and the like. Hardly a day passed without his taking part in some outward form of religion that was impossible for him to escape. He had to choose between two courses: either to pretend that he believed what he did not believe, which his natural truthfulnss forbade—or else to declare that all these outward forms were false, and arrange his life in some way by which he could avoid the necessity of taking part in what he believed to be false. But this apparently trifling matter could be accomplished only at a heavy cost: not only would he always be coming into opposition with the people about him, but he would have to change his whole life and give up his government position, thereby sacrificing his work for the good of mankind which he thought he had already begun and hoped to be able to continue with greater efficacy in the future.

To make this sacrifice required a firm belief that he was in the right. And he did firmly believe that he was in the right, as no educated man of our day can help being convinced of the soundness of his own common sense, especially if he has studied history and knows the origin of religions in general, and the origin of and divisions in the Christian church. He could not help knowing that he was right in rejecting the church's doctrines. Yet, under the stress of daily life, he—an honest and upright man—allowed a trifling falsehood to creep in. He told himself that before proclaiming an unreasonable thing to be unreasonable, one should study that unreasonable thing. It was this trifling falsehood which drew him into the swamp of greater falsehoods in which he now found himself caught.

When he put to himself the question whether the Orthodox religion was true—the religion in which he was born and bred, outside which he would not be able to continue his work, and which people expected him to profess—he had already decided on the answer. To find further light on the subject he did not go to Voltaire, Schopenhauer, Spencer, or Comte; instead, he read Hegel and the religious works of Vinet and Khomyakov, naturally finding there what he sought—a semblance of peace and a vindication of the doctrines in which he had been brought up, which his reason had long since rejected, but the lack of which filled his life with unpleasantnesses that would vanish forthwith if he but accepted them. So he adopted the usual sophisms, such as the incapacity of the individual intellect to grasp the truth which can be revealed only to an association of men, or that the only way of knowing it is by revelation, which is preserved in the church, and so on. Since then he could calmly and without being conscious of hypocrisy assist at festivals, requiems, masses; he could fast and go to confession and cross himself before the icons and continue his government service, which assured him of his personal usefulness and brought consolation into his joyless married life. He thought that he believed, and yet he knew at the bottom of his heart that this faith of his was further than anything else from being "the real thing." This is why his eyes were always sad. Seeing Nekhludov, whom he had known before these lies had taken root, recalled to him what he had been; and particularly after hurrying to hint at his present religious views, he felt more acutely than ever that they were not "the real thing" and became sad and distressed. Nekhludov also felt this, after his first moment of joy at seeing an old friend had passed.

These were the reasons why, after having promised to meet, neither of them felt anxious for the reunion; and so they did not see each other again during Nekhludov's stay in Petersburg.

ON leaving the Senate, Nekhludov walked on with the barrister, who gave orders for his carriage to follow, and began to tell Nekhludov the history of the director of the government department whom the senators had been discussing—how he had been found out and how, instead of being sentenced to hard labor (which according to law he deserved), he was to be appointed a governor in Siberia. He told the story in all its nastiness, and then with evident relish began another about some highly placed men who had stolen money destined for the never finished monument they had passed that morning; and how the mistress of So-and-So had made millions on the stock exchange; and how this man had sold his wife and that man had bought one, and so on and so forth. Then he began another story about the frauds and crimes of high officials, who were not put into prison but went on presiding over various institutions. These stories, of which the lawyer seemed to have an unlimited supply, gave him much pleasure, for they served to show that the means he used to earn money were innocent compared with those used for the same purpose by the high officials of Petersburg. He was therefore very much surprised when Nekhludov, without listening to the end of his last story, said good-by, hired a cab and drove home.

Nekhludov felt very sad. He was sad chiefly because the rejection of Maslova's appeal confirmed the senseless torture she was enduring, and because this rejection made his unalterable decision to unite his fate with hers still more difficult; moreover, this sadness was deepened by the terrible tales of existing evils which the barrister had related with such gusto; nor could he forget the cold, hostile look given him by the once sweet-natured, frank, and noble Selenin.

On his return, the doorkeeper handed him two notes, one of which, he said contemptuously, had been written in the hall "by some person or other." It was a note from Lydia Shustova's mother. She had come to thank the benefactor of her daughter and also to implore him to call at their house on Vassilievski Island, 5th Line, house No. —. This was very important for Vera Bogodukhovskaya, she wrote. He need not fear to be burdened with expressions of gratitude—that subject would not be mentioned—they would simply be glad to see him. Could he come tomorrow morning?

The other note was from an old friend, Bogatyrev, an aide-de-camp of the emperor, whom Nekhludov had asked to hand to the emperor personally the petition prepared on behalf of the sectarians. In a large, firm hand Bogatyrev wrote that he would present the petition to the emperor but that it occurred to him that it would perhaps be better for Nekhludov himself to call on the person on whom this matter depended, and petition him in the first place.

After the impressions of the last few days in Petersburg, Nekhludov felt utterly hopeless about all his projects. The plans he had made in Moscow now appeared to him mere youthful dreams of the sort that are inevitably disappointed when life has to be faced. Still, he considered it his duty to do what lay in his power and decided that, after seeing Bogatyrev tomorrow, he would follow his advice and call on the person on whom the case of the sectarians depended.

He took the petition from his pocket and was reading it over when there was a knock on the door; one of Countess Ekaterina Ivanovna's footmen came in with an invitation to go upstairs and take a cup of tea. Nekhludov put away his papers in his portfolio and went upstairs to his aunt. From a window in the hall he caught a glimpse of Mariette's pair of boys; all at once his spirits rose and he wanted to smile again.

Mariette, no longer in black but wearing a gay hat and a light, many-colored gown, was sitting beside the countess's easy chair, holding a cup of tea in her hand and chattering happily while her beautiful eyes glistened with laughter. Nekhludov entered the room just as Mariette had finished telling a funny story—funny and improper, Nekhludov guessed from the way they were laughing. The good-natured countess with the dark shadow of down upon her upper lip, was laughing helplessly; Mariette was watching her in silence out of the corner of her eye, a particularly mischievous expression on her shrewd, amused face, and her mouth drawn a little to one side. From the few words that reached his ears, Nekhludov could tell that they had been talking of the second topic in Petersburg, namely the episode of the Siberian governor, when Mariette had said something so funny that for some time the countess could not control herself.

"You will be the death of me," she said, gasping.

Nekhludov greeted them and took a seat. It was in his mind to rebuke her for her flippancy when she, noticing the serious and somewhat disapproving expression of his face, suddenly to please him—and this was what she had wanted to do ever since she had met him—changed not only the expression of her face, but her actual feelings. In a twinkling of an eye she became serious, dissatisfied with her own life, seeking something, striving after something. She was not pretending, but really seemed to have absorbed Nekhludov's state of mind, even though it would have been impossible for her to express in words what Nekhludov's state of mind actually was.

She inquired about the success of his affairs, and he told her of the disappointment in the Senate and his meeting with Selenin.

"Ah, there's a pure soul! Indeed he is a *chevalier sans peur et sans reproche*. A pure soul," both ladies repeated, using the epithet commonly given to Selenin in society.

"How about his wife?" asked Nekhludov.

"His wife? Well, I don't want to criticize her, but she does not understand him. But is it possible that he, too, was in favor of dismissing the appeal?" Mariette asked with genuine sympathy. "That's terrible! How I pity her!" she added with a sigh.

He frowned, and wishing to change the subject began to speak about Shustova, who had been kept in the Fortress and had now been set free at Mariette's request. Thanking her for influencing her husband, he was going to say how dreadful it was that this woman and all her family were suffering just because no one had thought of them, when she interrupted him to give utterance to her own indignation.

"Don't say another word," she said. "As soon as my husband told me that she was to be released, that very thought came into my mind—why has she been kept there if she is innocent? It's shocking, shocking!"

Countess Ekaterina Ivanovna saw that Mariette was flirting with her nephew and was amused.

"Now that I think of it," she said to Nekhludov, "do come to Aline's tomorrow evening. Kiesewetter will be there. You must come, too," she added, addressing Mariette. *"Il vous a remarqué,"* she said to her nephew. "He told me—for I repeated to him all you said—that what you say is a good sign and that you will surely come to Christ. Be sure and come tomorrow. Tell him to come, Mariette, and come yourself."

"In the first place I have no right to advise the prince about anything whatever," said Mariette, looking at Nekhludov, and by that glance establishing between them a full agreement concerning the words of the countess and Evangelism in general, "and secondly, you know, I'm not particularly fond of—"

"Yes, I know, you must always have your own ideas about everything."

"My own ideas? But I hold the same faith as any common peasant woman," Mariette said, smiling. "And in the third place, I am going to the French Theater."

"Ah! And have you seen that—what's her name?" said Ekaterina Ivanovna to Nekhludov. Mariette mentioned the name of a famous French actress.

"Be sure and go. She's wonderful," said Ekaterina Ivanovna.

"Well, who shall I go to see first, *ma tante*—the actress or the preacher?" asked Nekhludov, smiling.

"Don't you take me up on my own words!"

"I think I had better hear the preacher first and see the French actress afterward—otherwise I might lose all interest in sermons," said Nekhludov.

"I advise you to begin with the French Theater and do penance afterward," said Mariette.

"Stop making fun of me. The preacher is all right in one way and the theater in another. There is no need to pull a long face and weep all the time to be saved. You must have faith, and then you will feel gay."

"You preach better than all the preachers, *ma tante*."

"Now let me think," said Mariette. "Couldn't you come to my box tomorrow?"

"I'm afraid I shan't be able to."

Here the conversation was interrupted by the footman, announcing a visitor. It was the secretary of a benevolent society of which the countess was president.

"Oh, he's a dreadful bore! I'd better receive him in the other room. I'll join you later. Give him some tea, Mariette," she added, and waddled briskly out of the room.

Mariette took off a glove, baring her firm, rather flat hand, the fourth finger of which was laden with rings.

"Will you have some tea?" she said, taking the silver teapot from the spirit stand and holding her little finger stiffly away from the others. Her face was sad and grave.

"It always makes me feel very, very sad when people whose good opinion I value fail to see me apart from the position I'm placed in."

She seemed ready to cry as she said these words, and though, had they been analyzed, they would not have been found to contain any definite meaning, they seemed to Nekhludov to be profound, sincere, and generous, so appealing was the look in the shining eyes of this young, beautiful, well-dressed woman.

Nekhludov watched her in silence, unable to take his eyes from her face.

"You think I don't understand you and what is going on within you? What you have done is known to all. *C'est le secret de polichinelle.* I think it is good and I admire it."

"There's nothing to admire. I have accomplished very little."

"That makes no difference. I understand your feelings and I understand her— Very well, I will say no more." She broke off, noticing a shadow of displeasure on his face. "But I can also understand that seeing all this misery, all these horrors in the prisons . . ." Mariette went on, desiring only one thing— to attract him—and guessing with her woman's instinct what he prized and treasured. "You want to help those who are made to suffer at the hands of other men, through indifference or cruelty. . . . I understand how one can give up one's life to this, and I would give up mine. But to each his own fate. . . ."

"Are you dissatisfied with yours?"

"I?" she said, as though struck with surprise that such a question could be asked. "I ought to be contented, and I am. But there is a worm that sometimes wakes up—"

"—And should not be allowed to fall asleep again. It is a voice that must be obeyed," said Nekhludov, won over by her deceit.

Later, Nekhludov often remembered this conversation with shame. He recalled her words, which were perhaps an unconscious imitation of his own rather than deliberate falsehoods, and the expression of eager attention with which she listened when he told her of the horrors of the jail and of his experiences in the countryside.

When the countess returned, they were conversing not only like old friends but like two people who alone understand each other among an uncomprehending crowd.

They spoke of the injustice of power, of the sufferings of the unfortunate, of the poverty of the people, but the reality was that their eyes, gazing at each other as they talked, kept asking "Could you love me?" and answering "I could." Physical drawing them together.
desire, assuming the most unexpected and radiant forms, was

As she was leaving she said that she was always anxious to be useful, and asked him to be sure and come to her box the following night, if only for a moment, since she had something important to tell him.

"For when shall I see you again?" she added with a sigh, pulling a glove carefully over her jeweled hand. "Please say you will come."

Nekhludov promised.

That night, when he had gone to bed and put out his candle, he could not sleep for a long time. While he was thinking of Maslova, of the decision of the Senate, of his resolve to follow her and to give up his estates, Mariette appeared before him with her sigh, and the glance as she said, "When shall I see you again?" and her smile—all so distinctly that he smiled back as though she were before him. "Am I doing right in going to Siberia? Have I done right in giving up my wealth?" he thought.

The clear, northern light streamed through the closed window blinds, but the answers to these questions were vague and confused. He tried to feel and think as formerly, but the thoughts were uncertain. "What if all this should prove an empty vision evoked by my imagination, and I should find myself unable to live in that way? What if I were to regret having done the right thing?" he asked himself and, unable to answer these questions, he felt more pained and grieved than he had ever felt before, and dropped into a deep sleep, such as he had known sometimes after losing heavily at cards.

❧

CHAPTER TWENTY-FIVE

NEKHLUDOV's first impression on awakening the next morning was that he had on the previous day done something nasty. He tried to remember. No, there had been nothing nasty, he had done nothing wrong, but his thoughts had been wrong—about his marriage with Katusha and about giving up his land to the peasants. He had endeavored to persuade himself that such vague dreams would be impossible to carry out, that it was all too artificial and unnatural, that it was his duty to go on living as before. No, he had committed no evil act but he had done worse: he had indulged in evil thoughts, the generators of evil acts. An evil act need not be repeated and one may repent of it, but evil thoughts engender evil acts. An evil act only smooths the path for other evil acts, whereas an evil thought irresistibly drags one along.

In recalling his thoughts of the previous night he wondered how he could have believed them even for a moment. However difficult and unfamiliar might be the things he intended to do, he knew that it was the only life now possible for him, and however easy it might seem to return to his former life, he knew it would mean death to him. Yesterday's temptation made him think of a man who indulges in lying in bed in the morning. He lies snugly cuddled up, though he is wide awake and knows that it is time to rise and start the important and joyful work that awaits him.

That morning, which was to be his last in Petersburg, Nekhludov went to the Vassilyevski Island to see Lydia Shustova. She lived on the second floor. The house porter directed him to the back entrance, and climbing a steep staircase he walked into a stuffy kitchen where the smell of cooking almost suffocated him.

An elderly woman with her sleeves rolled up, wearing spectacles and an apron, stood beside the stove. She was stirring something in a steaming saucepan. "Who do you want?" she asked severely, peering at the newcomer over her spectacles.

Nekhludov had hardly uttered his name when an expression of alarm mingled with joy came over her face.

"Oh, Prince!" she cried, drying her hands on her apron. "But why did you come up the back way? Our benefactor! You have saved us!" she exclaimed, seizing Nekhludov's hand and trying to kiss it. "I went to see you yesterday. My sister was wanting to see you so much—she's here with us now. Please come this way, after me," she said, showing him through the narrow door and along the passage, all the while pulling at her skirt, which was tucked up, and smoothing her hair. "My sister's name is Kornilova. You may have heard of her," she added in a whisper, as she paused at the door. "She has been mixed up in politics. A very clever woman—"

Opening the door that led from the passage, she showed Nekhludov into a small room, where a short, rather stout young girl in a striped cotton blouse was seated on a sofa in front of a table. Her round, pale face, very like her mother's, was framed with fair, wavy hair. A young man with a small black beard and mustache, dressed in a Russian shirt with an embroidered collar, sat in an armchair opposite, leaning forward bent almost double. Their talk was so absorbing that they did not turn around till Nekhludov was inside the room.

"Lydia, this is Prince Nekhludov, the same, you know—"

The girl sprang nervously to her feet, pushing back an unruly strand of hair, and looked at the newcomer with large, gray, frightened eyes.

"So *you* are the dangerous woman that Vera Efremovna interceded for," said Nekhludov with a smile, extending his hand.

"Yes, I am that woman," replied Lydia, with a broad, child-like smile which displayed a row of beautiful teeth. "It's my aunt who was particularly anxious to see you. Aunty!" she called through the door in a sweet, gentle voice.

"Vera Efremovna was very upset by your arrest," said Nekhludov.

"Will you take a seat? No, you had better sit here," said Lydia, pointing to the dilapidated armchair from which the young man had just risen.

"My cousin, Zakharov," she said, noticing that Nekhludov was scrutinizing the young man.

The young man smiled as good-naturedly as Lydia herself. He greeted the guest and, when Nekhludov had sat down, he took a chair from near the window, placed it beside Nekhludov and sat down himself. A fair-haired schoolboy, about sixteen years of age, came in through another door and silently took a seat on the window sill.

"Vera Efremovna is a great friend of my aunt, but I hardly know her," said Lydia.

Just then a woman with a pleasant, intelligent face, wearing a white blouse with a tight leather belt, came in from the next room.

"Good morning. Thank you for having come," she said, sitting down on the sofa near Lydia. "Do tell us about Vera. How is she? Have you seen her? How does she find the conditions she is in now?"

"She does not complain," said Nekhludov. "She says she feels perfectly contented."

"Ah, that sounds just like Verochka!" said the aunt, nodding her head and smiling. "One has to get to know her. She is a wonderful character. She always thinks of others, never of herself."

"It's quite true—she didn't ask anything for herself. She was only anxious about your niece. She was particularly distressed, she said, because there was no cause for her arrest."

"Yes, yes, it's all terrible. The truth of the matter is, she was really a scapegoat for me."

"Not at all!" said Lydia. "I should have taken care of the papers anyway."

"Allow me to know better," said the aunt. "You see," she said, turning to Nekhludov, "it all happened because a certain person asked me to take care of the papers for a while and, as I had no apartment of my own, I brought them to Lydia. The same night she was searched, the papers were found, and she was arrested and kept in prison until now, because they wanted her to say who it was gave them to her."

"And I didn't," said Lydia quickly, nervously pulling back her hair from force of habit, for it was really not in the way.

"I didn't say you did."

"If they got hold of Mitin, it was through no fault of mine," said Lydia, blushing and glancing about uneasily.

"Don't talk about it, Lydia," said her mother.

"Why not? I should like to," said Lydia, no longer smiling or pulling her hair, but twisting a strand of it over her finger and still looking around the room.

"You know what happened yesterday when you began talking about it."

"That's all right . . . just leave me alone, Mamma . . . I said nothing, I only kept silent. When he questioned me about Mitin and about Aunty I said nothing, except that I would not answer. Then he—that man, Petrov. . . ."

"Petrov is a blackguard, a gendarme—a spy," interrupted the aunt, explaining her niece's words.

"Then," continued Lydia, excitedly and hurriedly, "he tried to persuade me, 'Whatever you tell me will harm no one. On the contrary, if you tell me everything you will set the innocent free. We may be uselessly tormenting the wrong person.' But still I kept saying that I would not tell. Then he said: 'All right, don't say anything—just don't deny what I'm going to say.' Then he began going through names, and among them the name of Mitin."

"Don't talk about it," said the aunt.

"Please, Aunty, don't interfere." She went on pulling at the strand of hair and looking around. "So you can imagine how I felt when I was informed the next day—we communicated with each other by tapping on the wall—that Mitin had been arrested. I was sure that I had given him away, and this tormented me so that I nearly went mad."

"And you see, it turned out that it wasn't through you at all that he was arrested," said the aunt.

"Yes, but how could I know? I thought I had given him

away, that's what I thought. I walked and walked, from wall to wall, and couldn't stop thinking. I thought I had given him away. I would lie down and cover my head and a voice would keep whispering: 'You have given Mitin away, you have given Mitin away.' I knew it was nothing but an hallucination, but I couldn't help listening. I used to try and go to sleep and couldn't, and I tried to stop thinking and couldn't. It was terrible!" said Lydia, growing more and more excited and still winding and unwinding the strand of hair over her finger and looking round.

"Calm yourself, Lydochka," said her mother, touching her on the shoulder, but Lydia had gone too far.

"It's all the more terrible . . ." she began again, but broke off with a sob. She jumped up from the sofa and ran out of the room, tripping over a chair. Her mother went after her.

"Those scoundrels ought to be hanged," said the schoolboy sitting on the window sill.

"What's that?" asked his aunt.

"Oh, nothing. . . . I was simply . . ." and he picked up a cigarette from the table and lighted it.

CHAPTER TWENTY-SIX

"YES, solitary confinement is a terrible thing for these young people," said the aunt, shaking her head and lighting a cigarette also.

"I should think it would be terrible for anybody," replied Nekhludov.

"No, not for anybody. I've been told it's actually a relief— a rest—for the real revolutionaries. An outlaw lives in constant anxiety, enduring all sorts of hardships, and in a constant state of fear for himself and others, and for the cause as well. But, when he's finally arrested and everything is over, the whole responsibility is at an end. Then, he can rest in peace. In fact, I've been told that some people are glad to be arrested. But for the young and innocent—and they always pick on innocent creatures like Lydia first—the shock is terrible. The loss of freedom, the rough treatment, the bad food and bad air—all that would not matter. The hardship could be three times as great and could all be endured easily, if only it weren't for the nervous shock you receive when you're arrested for the first time."

"Have you been through it?"

"Yes, I have been in prison twice," replied the aunt, with a sad smile. "When I was arrested the first time, I was only twenty-two. I had one child and was expecting another. And however hard it was to lose my freedom and to be separated from my child and husband—it was nothing compared with seeing that I wasn't a human being any longer. I was just a thing. I wanted to say good-by to my little daughter, but they told me to get into the cab. I asked where I was going and was told I would find out when I arrived. I asked what I was accused of and got no reply. After the examination I was put into prison clothes marked with a number and taken to a vaulted passage; the door was opened, I was pushed in, and then the door was locked. There remained only a guard with a rifle who walked up and down the passage past the cell, and peered in occasionally through a crack in the door. I felt terribly depressed. What affected me most was that the gendarme officer offered me a cigarette while he was examining me. So he must have known that people are fond of smoking, that they love light and liberty, too. He must have know that mothers love their children, and children love their mothers. So why did they tear me pitilessly from all that was dear to me and lock me up like a wild beast? Nobody can submit to this and not protest. If one has believed in God and in humanity, or believed that human beings love each other, one loses all faith after such treatment. Since then I have ceased to believe in men and I have become bitter," she said, and smiled.

Lydia's mother came into the room and said that Lydochka was very much upset and would not come back.

"What has this young life been ruined for? I feel it all the more bitterly since I was unwittingly responsible," said the aunt.

"God willing, she will get better in the country air. We'll send her to her father," said the mother.

"Yes," said the aunt, "if it hadn't been for you, she would have perished altogether. We are grateful to you indeed. I also wanted to see you because I want you to deliver a letter to Vera Efremovna," she added, taking a letter from her pocket. "It isn't sealed—you may read it, and tear it up or hand it to her; let your own conscience be your guide. There is nothing compromising in the letter," she concluded.

Nekhludov took it and promised to deliver it. Then he rose,

said good-by and went out. He sealed the letter without reading it, meaning to deliver it as he had been asked.

❖

CHAPTER TWENTY-SEVEN

THE last matter to keep Nekhludov in Petersburg was the case of the sectarians, whose petition to the tsar he meant to hand to an officer of his old regiment, Bogatyrev, now aide-de-camp to the tsar. He called on him in the morning and found that he was still at home having his luncheon, but nearly ready to leave the house. Bogatrev was a short, thickset man of unusual strength—he could bend a horseshoe. He was honest, kindly, straightforward and even liberal; yet, in spite of these qualities, he was an intimate at the court, devoted to the tsar and to his family; some strange freak permitted him, while moving in these exalted circles, to see only what was good there and remain untouched by evildoing and corruption. He criticized neither persons nor their acts, but was either silent or said what he was thinking in a loud, clear voice, almost like a shout, and frequently accompanied by equally loud laughter. He behaved like this not for any interested purpose, but simply because it was his nature.

"Ah, I'm so glad you called! Won't you have lunch? Do sit down. This is excellent steak. I always begin and end with something substantial. Ha! ha! ha! Have some wine, anyway!" he shouted, pointing to a decanter of red wine. "I was thinking about you. Yes, I will hand in the petition. I will give it into His Majesty's own hands. You can count on that. But it occurred to me—hadn't you better first call on Toporov?"

Nekhludov frowned at the mention of Toporov.

"But everything depends on him. He would be consulted in any event. He might even meet your wishes himself."

"Very well, I will call on him if you advise it."

"Good! Well, how does Petersburg strike you, eh?" shouted Bogatyrev.

"I feel as if I were being hypnotized," said Nekhludov.

"Hypnotized?" repeated Bogatyrev and laughed boisterously. "You're sure you won't have anything? Well, just as you please!" He wiped his mustache with a napkin. "So you will call? Eh? If he refuses, then let me have it and I will hand it in tomorrow," he shouted, and leaving the table crossed himself energetically, evidently as unconsciously as he had wiped his mouth. While he was buckling his saber, he said: "Now I must say good-by and leave you."

"Let us go out together," said Nekhludov, and shaking Bogatyrev's strong hand he left him at the door with the pleasant impression one always feels on coming in contact with anything so unself-consciously fresh and healthy.

Although he expected no good results from his visit, Nekhludov followed Bogatyrev's advice and went to see Toporov, on whom the case of the sectarians depended.

The position occupied by Toporov contained an inner contradiction which only someone very dull, or lacking in moral sense, could fail to notice. The contradiction lay in this, that it was his duty to support and defend by secular means, extending to violence, a church that claimed to be founded by God and secure against both the jaws of hell and the attacks of man. This divine and unchangeable institution had come to need the support and defense of a human institution, with Toporov and his officials at the head of it. Toporov himself did not see (or did not wish to see) this contradiction, and was therefore very seriously concerned lest some Roman Catholic priest, Protestant clergyman or other sectarian should destroy this church against which hell itself could not prevail. Like all men who lack the fundamental religious sense of human equality and brotherhood, he was certain that the common people were vastly different from himself and needed something that he could very well do without. At the bottom of his heart he really believed in nothing, and found this attitude very convenient and pleasant; but fearing that the people themselves might someday attain this state of mind, he considered it his sacred duty (as he called it) to guard them from it.

Just as the cookery book tells us that crayfish like to be boiled alive, he was fully convinced—not figuratively, as in the cookery book, but literally—that the people like to be kept in a state of superstition. His ideas about the religion he upheld were like those of a poultry keeper about the garbage he uses to feed his fowls: garbage is very loathsome, but fowls like it and eat it, therefore they must be fed on garbage.

Of course, all that worship of the icons of Iberia, Kazan, and Smolensk is gross idolatry, but the people enjoy it and believe in it: therefore these superstitions should be encouraged. This was how Toporov thought, not seeing that if the people are superstitious, it is only because at present, as in the old days, cruel men like himself are always to be found, who, being enlightened themselves, use their enlightenment not to help others to struggle out of their dark ignorance, but to plunge them into it deeper.

As Nekhludov entered the reception room, Toporov was in his study conversing with an abbess, a lively aristocrat who spread and supported Orthodoxy in western Russia among the Uniates who had been forcibly converted to the Orthodox church.

A secretary in the reception room inquired about the business that had brought Nekhludov there and, on finding that he had taken upon himself to hand the petition of the sectarians to the emperor, asked if he might see it. Nekhludov gave it to him and he took it into the study. The abbess in her wimple, flowing veil, and trailing black dress, left the study and went out clasping a rosary of topaz in her pale, well-cared-for hands. Nekhludov was still not asked to go in. Toporov was reading the petition and shaking his head. He was unpleasantly surprised by its clear and forcible wording.

"If this should come into His Majesty's hands it might raise unpleasant questions and misunderstanding," he thought as he finished reading. And, laying it on the table, he rang and ordered Nekhludov to be shown in.

He recalled the case of these sectarians, for he had had a petition from them before. The substance of the case was that they were Christians who had fallen away from Orthodoxy and had been first exhorted, then prosecuted, but finally acquitted. Next, the bishop and the governor had decided, because of the illegality of their marriages, to separate husbands, wives, and children, and send them into exile. What these fathers and wives asked was that they should not be separated. Toporov remembered the case when the first petition had come into his hands. Even then he had hesitated and had half a mind to quash the sentence—but while it could do no harm to confirm the decree to separate and exile these people—to allow them to remain together might have a bad effect on the rest of the population and might lead them also to fall away from Orthodoxy. Moreover, the case was evidence of the bishop's zeal, and therefore Toporov finally decided to let it proceed.

Now, with such a defender as Nekhludov, who had influential connections in Petersburg, the case might be presented to the emperor as an act of cruelty, or might find its way into the foreign newspapers. He therefore made a quick and unexpected decision.

"How do you do?" he said, with the air of a very busy man,

continuing to stand after greeting Nekhludov, and beginning at once on the business in hand. "I am familiar with this case. As soon as I saw the names, I remembered the whole unfortunate business," he went on, taking up the petition and showing it to Nekhludov. "And I am very grateful to you for having reminded me of it. The provincial authorities have been over-zealous."

Nekhludov was silent, gazing with distaste at the pale, immobile mask of a face before him.

"I will give orders to have this measure revoked and the families returned to their former homes."

"So that there willl be no need to present this petition?"

"Most assuredly not. I give you my word," he said with a stress on the "I," evidently convinced that *his* word, his honesty, were the best of guarantees. "I will write at once. Take a seat, please."

He went up to the table and began to write. But Nekhludov, without taking a seat, looked down at the narrow, bald skull, at the hand with its thick blue veins rapidly moving the pen, and wondered why he was doing it, why a man who seemed so indifferent to everything should apparently be so eager about this matter. What was the reason?

"There you are," said Toporov, sealing the envelope. "You may announce this to your 'clients,' " he added, pursing his lips in imitation of a smile.

"Why, then, were these people made to suffer?" asked Nekhludov, taking the envelope.

Toporov raised his head and smiled, as though gratified by Nekhludov's question.

"That I cannot tell you. I can only say that the interests of the people over which we stand guard are of such great importance that too much zeal in matters of religion is not so dangerous or harmful as the present widespread indifference."

"But why should the fundamental conditions of morality be violated in the name of religion, families broken up. . . ."

Toporov still smiled condescendingly, evidently finding Nekhludov's words quite amusing. From the heights of the broad plateau of statesmanship on which he imagined himself standing, anything Nekhludov might have said would have seemed amusing and one-sided.

"That, in the eyes of a private person, may seem to be the position," he said, "but in the eyes of the state it is quite a different matter. However, I must now bid you good-by," he added, bowing and holding out his hand.

Nekhludov pressed it in silence and quickly left the room, regretting that he had taken that hand.

"The interests of the people! Your own interests, you mean —yours, yours!" he thought as he went out.

In his mind he counted the people he knew who were suffering under these institutions for the re-establishment of justice, the support of religion, and the education of the people—the peasant woman punished for selling vodka without a license, the young fellow for stealing, the tramp for vagrancy, the incendiary for arson, the banker for misappropriation of funds, and that unfortunate Lydia for withholding information, and the sectarians for violating Orthodoxy, and Gurkevich for desiring a constitution—and he saw with remarkable clarity that all these people had been arrested, locked up, and exiled not because they had committed lawless acts, but only because they hindered the officials and the rich from using the wealth which they took from the people.

They were all hindrances—the woman who sold vodka, the thief wandering about the town, Lydia with her proclamations, Gurkevich with his constitution, and the sectarians attacking superstition. All these officials, therefore, from his uncle and the senators and Toporov, down to the petty, neat, conventional gentlemen sitting at desks in various departments, were not in the least troubled that such a state of things should cause suffering to the innocent, but concerned themselves only with putting down all dangerous movements. And so it came about: the commandment to forgive ten guilty men rather than let one innocent man suffer was not merely disregarded, but on the contrary, ten who were not dangerous were punished for the sake of getting rid of one dangerous person; just as, when a piece of decay is cut out, parts' that are sound have to be cut out also.

This explanation of what was taking place seemed very clear and simple to Nekhludov, and yet its very clearness and simplicity made him hesitate. Could so complex a system possibly have an explanation so simple and so terrible? Could all this talk about justice, law, religion, and God possibly be just so many words to conceal the most brutal cruelty and greed?

NEKHLUDOV would have left the city that evening, but he had promised Mariette to call on her at the theater and, although he knew he ought not, he went, justifying himself with the thought that a promise must be kept. There was his desire to see Mariette, but he also wanted, he told himself, to take for the last time the measure of the world which had once been so close to him and was now so alien.

"Can I withstand all these temptations?" he thought, somewhat insincerely. "I will try for the last time."

He put on evening dress and arrived in time for the second act of the perennial *Dame aux Camélias* in which a foreign actress was demonstrating anew how consumptive women die.

The house was crowded, and Nekhludov was at once shown respectfully to Mariette's box. A footman in livery, as he opened the door for him, bowed as to a friend of the family.

The people sitting in the boxes opposite, those standing behind, the backs of those nearby, the gray, grizzled, bald, pomaded, or curly heads of those in the orchestra stalls—the entire audience was absorbed in watching the contortions of a thin, angular actress dressed in silks and lace, who was speaking her monologue in an unnatural voice. Someone said "Hush!" as the door opened, and two currents of warm and cold air swept over Nekhludov's face. Mariette and another lady in a red cloak and elaborate coiffure, and two men occupied the box. One was Mariette's husband, the general—tall and handsome, with an aquiline nose and an inscrutable expression. He wore a uniform padded across the chest. The other was a fair, baldheaded man with a cleft chin appearing between his pompous side whiskers. Mariette, slim and graceful in a low-necked gown that exposed her strong, firm, sloping shoulders and a tiny black mole at the base of her neck, turned to look around the moment Nekhludov entered, and with her fan motioned to a chair behind her, giving him a grateful and (as he thought) meaningful smile. The husband in his usual quiet manner looked at Nekhludov and bowed. The glance he exchanged with Mariette showed that he was master and owner of his handsome wife.

When the monologue ended the theater echoed with applause.

Mariette rose and, holding up her rustling silk gown, stepped to the rear of the box and introduced Nekhludov to her husband. Smiling with his eyes alone, the general said that he was "delighted," and fell back into impenetrable silence.

"I ought to have gone today, but I promised you I would come here," said Nekhludov to Mariette.

"If you should be bored with me, you will at least see a wonderful actress," said Mariette, answering the implication of his words. "Don't you think she was wonderful in that last scene?" she said, addressing her husband.

He bowed.

"This sort of thing leaves me unmoved," said Nekhludov. "I have seen so much real misery today—"

"Do sit down and tell us about it."

The husband listened, and the smile of his eyes seemed to grow more and more ironical.

"I went to see the woman who was kept in prison for such a long time. She broke down completely."

"She is the one I spoke to you about," said Mariette to her husband.

"I am very glad she could be released," he said quietly, with a nod and, as Nekhludov thought, with a smile of unconcealed irony. "I am going out for a smoke."

Nekhludov remained, expecting that Mariette would now speak of that "something" which she had said she wanted to tell him, but she made no allusion to it, and went on joking and talking about the play, which she thought should have a special appeal for Nekhludov.

He saw that she had nothing to say, but only wished to show herself in all the splendor of her evening gown, and to display her shoulders and the mole; and he felt at once pleased and disgusted.

The veil of enchantment was now transparent to Nekhludov, if not yet withdrawn, and he could see what was behind it. Looking at Mariette, he admired her beauty, but he knew that she was a liar, who lived with a husband making his way in the world through the tears and the lives of hundreds and hundreds of men, and who remained completely indifferent to it; he knew that all she had said yesterday had been untrue, but that she was anxious—though neither he nor she knew why—for him to fall in love with her. He was at once attracted and repelled. Several times he meant to go and took up his hat, but still lingered.

When the husband returned, a strong smell of tobacco about his mustache, he looked patronizingly and contemptuously at

Nekhludov, who got up and went out while the door of the box was still open. He found his overcoat and walked out of the theater.

On his way home, in the Nevski Prospect, he noticed a well-built, provocatively well-dressed woman walking slowly along the wide pavement just ahead. Her face and figure expressed the consciousness of evil power. All the passers-by were turning to look at her. Nekhludov quickened his step to overtake her and he, too, involuntarily looked into her face, which was handsome and appeared to be painted. The woman gave Nekhludov a brilliant smile; strangely enough, Nekhludov immediately thought of Mariette and was again attracted and repelled as he had been in the theater. Quickly passing her by, he turned into the Morskaya and thence to the quay, where a policeman was surprised to see him stroll up and down.

"It is the same smile the other one gave me when I entered the theater box," he thought; "the same meaning was in both. The only difference is that one of them says plainly and openly, 'If you want me, take me; if not, go your way,' while the other pretends that she has no such thoughts in her mind but lives in a world of subtle, lofty aspirations. This one at least is truthful, while the other is lying. Moreover, this woman has been driven to these straits by necessity, while the other amuses herself playing with that enchanting, revolting, and terrible passion. This streetwalker is like filthy, putrid water offered to those whose thirst overcomes their aversion. The woman in the theater is a poison that imperceptibly destroys all who touch it." He recalled his liaison with the wife of the marshal of the nobility, and shameful memories flooded his mind. "The brutishness of men is disgusting," he thought, "but as long as it remains undisguised a man may look down from the heights of his spiritual life and despise it and, whether he falls or resists, he still remains himself. But when this brutishness is hidden under a pseudo-æsthetic veil of poetry and demands to be adored, a man loses all sense of fitness and, when he worships brutishness, can no longer distinguish good from evil. Then it becomes terrible!"

Nekhludov saw this now as clearly as he saw the palaces, the sentries, the Fortress, the river, the boats, and the stock exchange. And just as, that night, no soothing, restful darkness hung over the land, but only a dismal, dreary, unnatural light of which the source was not apparent, so the comfortable darkness of ignorance vanished from Nekhludov's mind. Now everything was clear. It was clear that all the things which are commonly considered good and important are actually repulsive or insignificant, and that all this glitter, all this luxury, serve but to cover old familiar crimes which not only go unpunished, but rise triumphant, adorned with all the charms which human imagination is able to conceive.

Nekhludov endeavored to forget all this, to close his eyes to it, but he had lost the power. Although he could not see the source of the light which revealed it all to him, just as he could not see the source of the light which lay that night over Petersburg, and although the light itself seemed dim, obscure and unnatural, he now could not help seeing what that light revealed, and he felt both happy and disturbed.

❧

CHAPTER TWENTY-NINE

ON his arrival in Moscow, Nekhludov went at once to the prison hospital to tell Maslova the sad news that the Senate had confirmed the decision of the court and that she must make preparations for the journey to Siberia. He had but little hope that the petition to the emperor which he was now taking to be signed by her would amount to anything, and, strangely enough, he was no longer anxious for success. He had grown accustomed to the thought of going to Siberia and living among exiles and convicts, and he could not imagine what arrangements he should make for Maslova and himself if she were to be acquitted. He remembered the words of the American writer Thoreau, who said that "under a government which imprisons anyone unjustly, the true place for a just man is also a prison." After his visit to Petersburg and all he had discovered there, Nekhludov thought the same.

"Yes, the only place for an honest man in Russia at the present time is in prison," he thought, and felt this even more strongly as he drove up to the jail and entered within its walls.

The doorkeeper at the hospital recognized him and informed him at once that Maslova was no longer there.

"Where is she, then?"

"She's gone back to prison."

"Why was she removed?"

"Ah, Your Excellency, what can you expect from such people?" said the doorkeeper, with a contemptuous smile.

"She was running after the doctor's assistant and the doctor sent her away."

Nekhludov would never have believed that Maslova and her spiritual life could be so near to him. He was stunned, as though some unforeseen calamity had befallen him. His first sensation was one of mortification. It made him ridiculous in his own eyes to remember how happy he had felt for the supposed spiritual revival of Maslova's soul—while all that talk, he thought, of her unwillingness to accept his sacrifice, her tears, and her reproaches, had been a ruse of a depraved woman who was using him for her own advantage. It seemed to him now that at the time of his last visit he had already noticed signs of the incorrigibility which had now come to light. All this passed through his mind while mechanically he put on his hat and left the hospital.

"But what am I to do now?" he thought. "Am I still bound to her? Does not her present behavior set me free?" But no sooner had he asked this question than he understood that to consider himself free to abandon her to her fate would be to punish not her but himself, and he was seized with fear. "No, what has happened cannot alter my decision, it can only strengthen it. Let her do as she pleases. Her intrigue with the doctor's assistant is her own affair and no concern of mine. All that concerns me is to do what my own conscience tells me, and my conscience demands that I should sacrifice my freedom to redeem my sin. I am determined to marry her, even it be not a real marriage, and to follow her wherever she goes," he said to himself with bitter obstinacy, as he left the hospital and turned resolutely toward the big gates of the jail.

He asked the warder on duty to tell the inspector that he wished to see Maslova. The warder, who knew him, told him at once an important piece of prison news, namely, that the captain formerly in charge had been dismissed, and that a new and very severe inspector had been appointed in his place.

"They have become so strict, it's terrible," he said. "The inspector is here just now—I'll call him."

Indeed, the inspector was in the prison and came out almost immediately. He was a tall, angular man, with projecting cheekbones, morose, and very slow in his movements.

"Interviews are only allowed on stated days in the visiting room," he said, without looking at Nekhludov.

"But I have a petition to the emperor for her to sign."

"You may leave it with me."

"I must see the prisoner myself. I always have had leave before."

"Yes, that was before," said the inspector, with a quick glance at Nekhludov.

"I have the governor's permission," insisted Nekhludov, taking out his pocketbook.

"Allow me to see it," said the inspector, still not looking him in the eyes, and with his dry, long white fingers—a gold ring on the index—he took the paper that Nekhludov gave him and read it slowly.

"Will you come into the office?" he said.

The office was empty. The inspector sat down at a table and began to turn over the pages of some documents lying on it, evidently intending to be present at the interview.

Nekhludov inquired whether he might also see the political prisoner Bogodukhovskaya, but was told curtly that he could not. "Interviews with political prisoners are not allowed," said the inspector and again became engrossed in his papers. With the letter for Vera Bogodukhovskaya in his pocket, Nekhludov felt as if he had been trying to commit some offense and his plans were discovered and frustrated.

When Maslova entered the office, the inspector raised his head and said, "You may talk." Then, without looking at Nekhludov or Maslova, he continued to busy himself with the papers.

Maslova was wearing the same clothes as before: a white blouse, a skirt, and kerchief on her head. When she went up to Nekhludov and saw his cold, stern face, she blushed scarlet and, fingering the hem of her blouse, averted her eyes. Her confusion seemed to confirm the hospital doorkeeper's story. Nekhludov would have liked to treat her as before and meant to shake hands with her, but she had grown so repulsive to him that he could not bring himself to do it.

"I have brought you bad news," he said in a flat voice, without looking at her or extending his hand.

"I knew they would," she said with difficulty, as though gasping for breath.

Before Nekhludov would have asked her what reason she had for saying this, but now he only looked up at her. Her eyes filled with tears. But instead of softening him, the sight of her tears irritated him even more.

The inspector rose and began to walk up and down the room.

In spite of the aversion which Nekhludov now felt for

Maslova, he still attempted to express his regret at the refusal of the Senate.

"Don't despair. The petition to the emperor may yet be granted and I hope—"

"I don't care about that," she said, giving him a pitiable glance from her squinting, tearful eyes.

"What is the matter, then?"

"You have been to the hospital, and they probably told you that I—"

"Well, that's your own affair," said Nekhludov coldly with a frown. The cruel feeling of wounded pride rose once more with renewed force when she mentioned the hospital. He, a man of the world, whom any girl of good family would have been happy to marry, had offered himself to this woman as a husband, and she could not even wait but began to amuse herself with a doctor's assistant. He looked at her with hatred.

"You will have to sign this petition," he said, taking the large envelope from his pocket and laying it on the table. She wiped away her tears with a corner of her kerchief and asked where and what she should write. He told her, and she sat down, arranging the cuff of her right sleeve with her left hand. He stood silently behind her and looked down at her as she bent over the table, shaken again and again with suppressed sobs. Two conflicting emotions of good and evil were struggling in his heart, his own offended pride and pity for the suffering girl—and it was pity that won.

He did not know which came first, pity for her or the thought of himself and his sins and his contemptible life— exactly what he condemned in her. All of a sudden he was aware that he was guilty, and that he pitied her.

When she had signed the petition and had wiped some ink off her finger on to her skirt, she rose and looked at Nekhludov.

"No matter what happens, nothing will alter my decision," said Nekhludov. His pity and tenderness were increased by the very thought that he had forgiven her, and he longed to comfort her. "I shall do as I have always intended. Wherever you may be sent, I shall go with you."

"What's the use?" she interrupted quickly, but her face lit up.

"You had better think about what you may need for the journey."

"Thank you, but I can't think of anything in particular."

The inspector walked up to them and Nekhludov, anticipating what he was going to say, bade her good-by and went out, his heart filled with tranquil joy and love for all mankind.

The certainty that his love for Maslova could never be changed by anything she might do lifted him to a level he had never reached before. Let her flirt with the doctor's assistant—that was her affair. He loved her not selfishly but for her own sake and for God's.

As for the flirtation with the doctor's assistant for which Maslova was turned out of the hospital, and which Nekhludov believed to be true, it amounted to this: ordered by the ward sister to fetch some herb tea from the dispensary at the end of the corridor, Maslova found there Ustinov, the doctor's assistant—a tall man with pimples on his face, who had been pestering her for some time; trying to get away from him, she gave him such a violent push that he was thrown against a shelf, and two bottles fell off and were broken. The senior doctor, who happened to be near by, hearing the crash of broken glass and seeing Maslova run out of the room, her face all red, shouted angrily:

"Look here, my good woman, unless you can behave yourself, I shall have to send you away!"

"What's the trouble in here?" he said to the assistant, looking at him over his spectacles. The assistant smilingly began to apologize; the doctor lifted his head so that he was now looking through his spectacles and went on his way without waiting to hear the end. The same day he told the inspector to send him a more sedate person to take Maslova's place.

This was Maslova's intrigue. Dismissal from the hospital on an accusation of flirting was all the more painful to her as relations with men, which had long been disgusting to her, became especially revolting since she had met Nekhludov again. What hurt her most deeply and made her pity herself even to the point of weeping, was that everybody, including the pimpled assistant, knowing what her past life had been, felt that they had a right to insult her and seemed surprised when she resented it. When she went out to Nekhludov, she intended to clear herself of the false accusation which she knew he would hear about sooner or later, but as soon as she began to speak, she felt that he did not believe her and that her excuses would only serve to confirm his suspicion. Tears choked her and she broke off.

Maslova was still trying to persuade herself that she had not forgiven Nekhludov and that she hated him, as she had told him at their second interview, but the truth was that she loved him again and was only too glad to do all she could to please him. She had given up drinking and smoking, she

no longer flirted, and she went to work in the hospital. All
this she had done because she knew it would please him. And
if every time he referred to it, she refused so determinedly
to accept his sacrifice and marry him, this was partly because
she enjoyed repeating the angry phrases she had used at first,
but above all because she saw that such a marriage would
be a misfortune for him. She had made up her mind not to
accept his sacrifice, yet it hurt her deeply to think that he
despised her and believed that she still was what she had been,
and that he had not noticed the change that had taken place
within her. That he might still be thinking she had done wrong
tormented her more than the news that her sentence was
confirmed.

CHAPTER THIRTY

Maslova was likely to be sent off with the first gang of
prisoners, and Nekhludov began to prepare for his own departure; but there was so much to do that he felt no amount
of time would enable him to finish. It had been very different
in the old days, when he was interested exclusively in Dmitri
Ivanovich Nekhludov, and found everything else a bore. Now
all this attention centered on the affairs of other people, and
they were all interesting and absorbing, and there was no end
to them. In the old days, he had often become very much
tired and annoyed over his own affairs, whereas now the affairs
of others never ceased to entertain him.

The occupations that absorbed Nekhludov at that time could
be divided under three heads. This he did, in his usual systematic way, and accordingly grouped his papers in three
portfolios.

The first referred to Maslova and consisted at that stage in
following up the petition addressed to the emperor, and in
making preparations for the probable journey to Siberia.

The second concerned the organization of affairs on his
estates. In Panovo, the land had been given to the peasants
on the condition that they paid rent, which was to be used
for their communal needs; but to make this transaction valid,
he had to sign his deed of gift and alter his will in accordance
with it. In Kuzminskoe everything was still as he had first
arranged it, that is, he was to receive the money for the land;

but he still had to fix the dates of payment, the amount of money to be reserved for himself, and the amount to be set aside for the benefit of the peasants. Not knowing what his expenses would be on the journey to Siberia, he hesitated to forgo this income altogether, although he had reduced it by half.

The third of his responsibilities was to help the prisoners, who sought his assistance more and more.

At the beginning, when he first came in contact with people who asked his help, he began to intercede for each separately, trying to assist everyone individually; but there were soon so many appeals that he felt the impossibility of attending to all of them, and this led him to take up a new kind of work which seemed to him more interesting than all his other tasks.

This new business consisted in the solution of the following questions: What was that astonishing institution called "criminal law," whose end was the jail that he had come to know, and all the other places of confinement where hundreds and thousands of victims were wasting, from the Fortess of Peter and Paul to the Island of Sakhalin? Why did this astonishing criminal law exist? Where did it come from?

From his personal relations with the prisoners, from the lists of those imprisoned, and from questioning his lawyer, the prison chaplain and the inspector, Nekhludov came to the conclusion that the so-called criminals could be divided into five classes.

The first class was composed of innocent people, victims of judicial errors, like the alleged incendiary Menshov, like Maslova and others. This class was not numerous—about 7 per cent according to the observations of the prison chaplain—but the fate of these people excited particular interest.

The second class was made up of men sentenced for crimes committed in peculiar circumstances, while drunk, for example, or in a fit of passion or jealousy—crimes that in similar circumstances would very likely have been committed by those who judged and punished them. This class, according to Nekhludov's observations accounted for more than half the criminals.

The third class consisted of people punished because they had done what was good and natural according to their own lights, but what, according to the ideas of the men who made the laws and who were utter strangers to them, was considered criminal. To this class belonged those who secretly traded in spirits, smugglers, trespassers on fields and forests owned by the government; to this class might also be added the robbers from the Caucasus mountains and the unbelievers who robbed churches.

The fourth class was made up of men who were looked upon as criminals only because they stood morally above the common level of society. Such were the sectarians; such were the Poles and the Cherkess who rebelled in order to gain their independence; such were the political criminals, the Socialists, the strikers condemned for opposition to authorities. According to Nekhludov's observations, the percentage of such people, who were among the best elements of society, was very large.

Finally, the fifth category consisted of men who in their relations with society were far more sinned against than sinning. They were the outcasts, stupefied by unceasing oppression and temptation—like the boy who stole the mats, and hundreds whom Nekhludov had seen in jail and elsewhere, whose conditions of life seemed to lead automatically to those actions which are called "crimes." To this class, according to Nekhludov's estimate, belonged most of the thieves and murderers with whom he had come in contact at that time. Into this class he also put the depraved and demoralized men whom the new school of criminology classifies as the criminal type and whose existence in society is considered the chief argument for the necessity of criminal law and of punishment. These so-called depraved, criminal, abnormal types were, by Nekhludov's ideas, just like the other people against whom society had sinned—but in these instances society had sinned not directly against them but against their parents and forbears.

Among this class of people, Nekhludov was struck particularly with the thief Okhotin; he was a habitual criminal, the illegitimate son of a prostitute, brought up in a doss house; when he was still a child he had joined a band of thieves, and it appeared that up to the age of thirty he had never met men of any higher moral status than that of a policeman. He was gifted with an extraordinary sense of humor which made him very popular. He asked Nekhludov to intercede for him, all the while making fun of himself and the judges, the jail, and laws both human and divine. Another was a handsome peasant called Fedorov, who, together with the band of which he was the leader, had robbed and murdered an old man. Fedorov's father had had his house unlawfully taken from him. While a soldier he had been punished for falling in love with an officer's mistress. He had a lovable, passionate nature and longed to enjoy life at any cost. He had never met any people

who would deny themselves anything for the sake of their
own enjoyment, or even heard a word said about any aim in
life higher than pleasure. Nekhludov could clearly see that both
these men had been richly gifted by nature, but had been
neglected and mutilated, like uncared-for plants. He also met
a tramp and a woman who both repelled him by their mental
dullness and apparent cruelty, but he failed to discover in
either of them the criminal type which is described in the
Italian school of criminology; all he could see were individuals
personally repellent to him, just like many he had met outside
the prison, dressed in tail coat, epaulettes, or lace.

Thus, studying the reasons why all these totally different
persons were imprisoned, while others just like them were at
large—and even sitting in judgment upon them—formed the
fourth of the tasks that occupied Nekhludov.

At first he had hoped to find the answer in books, and
bought everything he could find on the subject. He bought
the works of Lombroso and Girofalo, Ferry and List, Mauds-
ley and Tarde, and read them carefully. But as he went on
he became more and more disappointed. It was with him as
with all who turn to science, not because they intend to write
or discuss or teach, but because they want to find a solution
to the simple, straightforward problems of everyday life.
Science answered thousands of intricate, ingenious questions
touching criminal law—but not the only question whose answer
he was seeking.

He asked a very simple question: Why and by what right
do some men imprison, torture, exile, flog, and kill other
men, while they themselves are just like those they torture,
flog, and kill? And he was answered by debates: Has man
free will or not? Can a man be proved a criminal by the dimen-
sions of his skull? What part does heredity play in crime? Is
there such a thing as congenital depravity? What is morality?
What is insanity? What is degeneracy? What is temperament?
How does climate, food, ignorance, initiativeness, hypnotism,
or passion affect crime? What is society? What are its duties?

These investigations reminded Nekhludov of a small boy
he had once met returning from school. Nekhludov asked
him if he had learned how to spell. "Yes, I have." "Well, then,
how do you spell 'paw'?" "What sort of paw—a dog's paw?"
asked the little boy, with an artful expression on his face.
Nekhludov found just such answers in the form of questions
in the scientific books. These books contained much that was
clever, learned, and interesting, but they gave no answer to his

fundamental question: What right have some people to punish others? Not only was there no answer, but all the investigations were intended solely to explain and justify punishment, the necessity for which was accepted beforehand.

Nekhludov read a great deal, but only in snatches, and putting down his failure to this superficial way of reading, hoped to find an answer later on. He would not yet believe in the justice of the answer that came more and more frequently to his mind.

❖

CHAPTER THIRTY-ONE

THE party that Maslova was to join was due to set off on the fifth day of July, and Nekhludov arranged to start the same day. His sister and her husband came to town to see him on the day before he left.

Natalya Ivanovna Ragozhinskaya was ten years older than her brother, who had grown up partly under her influence. She was very fond of him as a boy, and later, before her marriage, they became as intimate as though they were equals—she a woman of twenty-five, he a boy of fifteen. At that time she had been in love with his friend Nikolenka Irtenev, who later died. They had both loved Nikolenka, and they loved in him and in themselves that which was good and which unites all men.

Since then both had deteriorated—he through his military service and dissolute life, she through marriage to a man who, though she loved him sensually, cared not at all for what she and Dmitri had once held sacred and precious, who never understood her and put down her aspirations for moral perfection and longing to serve mankind to the only motive comprehensible to him—ambition and the desire for display.

Ragozhinski was not rich, nor did he come of good family, but he was very adroit and had made a fairly good career for himself in the law by maneuvering artfully between liberalism and conservatism, using each alternately for his own ends and, moreover, exploiting to the utmost his success with women. He was already middle-aged when he met Natasha abroad—herself no longer young—and made her fall in love with him. She married him against the wishes of her mother, who considered the marriage to be a misalliance.

Though he would not admit it even to himself, and tried hard to suppress this feeling, Nekhludov hated his brother-in-law. He loathed him for his vulgarity, his conceit, and his mediocrity—but above all, because his sister could bring herself to love this stunted creature so passionately, so egotistically, so sensually, and for his stake stamp down her own noble aspirations.

It hurt him to think of Natasha as the wife of this hairy, self-satisfied man with a shiny bald patch on his head. He could not even conceal his dislike of the children and, each time she was pregnant, felt that she had been infected with something evil by this man whose nature was so foreign to theirs.

The Ragozhinskis came without the children (they had two, a boy and a girl) and occupied the best room in the best hotel. Natalya Ivanovna at once drove to her mother's old flat. She did not find her brother, but Agrafena Petrovna told her that he was now living in furnished rooms, and she drove on there. An untidy servant met her in the dark, smelly passage, which required artificial light even in the daytime, and told her that the prince was out. When Natalya Ivanovna expressed the wish to go into his rooms to write a note, the man showed her in.

She carefully examined the two small rooms and saw everywhere familiar signs of neatness and order—but she was struck by the simplicity of the surroundings, quite unusual for him. She noticed on the writing table a paperweight decorated with a bronze dog, the neatly arranged folios, papers, and writing materials, and some volumes on criminal law, a book in English by Henry George, and a French book by Tarde, with a familiar crooked ivory knife to mark the place.

Seating herself at the table she wrote a note to ask him to be sure and call on her that day; then, shaking her head in surprise at what she saw, she went back to her hotel.

Two things about her brother interested her just then: his proposed marriage to Katusha, which she had heard about in the town where she lived, and his gift of land to his peasants —which was also known to everybody and looked upon by many as an act of a dangerous political character. In one way his proposal to Katusha pleased her; she admired his courage and recognized in it her brother and herself as they had been in the happy days before her own marriage; but at the same time she was appalled at the thought that her brother was going to marry such a horrible woman. This was the stronger feeling, and she decided to use all her influence to dissuade him from taking this step, although she realized how difficult it would be.

The other matter—the gift of land to the peasants—did not concern her so much, but her husband was very indignant about it and insisted that she should use her influence with her brother. Ignati Nikiforovich said that an act of that sort was the height of inconsistency, thoughtlessness, and arrogance; that the only explanation for it—if any could be found —was the desire to attract attention and be talked about. What sort of gift is it, he asked, when the peasants will pay rent to themselves? If Nekhludov was determined to do such a thing, why did he not sell the land to them through the Peasants' Bank? There might have been some sense in that. "But what he has done shows that he is on the verge of insanity," said Ragozhinski, already beginning to think of a possible trusteeship; and he insisted that his wife should have a serious talk with her brother about his eccentric plans.

❖

CHAPTER THIRTY-TWO

As soon as Nekhludov came home that evening and saw his sister's note on the table he set off to her hotel. He found Natalya Ivanovna alone; her husband was resting in the next room. She was wearing a tightly fitting black silk gown with a red bow at the waist, and her black hair was puffed and arranged in the latest fashion. She tried to look young for the sake of her husband, who was the same age as herself. When her brother came in she jumped up from the sofa to greet him, her silk gown rustling with every movement she made. They kissed and gazed at each other smilingly. Between them passed a secret, indescribable exchange of looks charged with import and truth; but their exchange of words was not truthful. They had not met since their mother's death.

"You have grown stouter and you look younger," he said, and her lips puckered up with pleasure.

"And you have grown thinner," she said.

"Well, and how is your husband?" asked Nekhludov.

"He is having a rest. He did not sleep all night."

Much ought to have been said, but their words meant nothing. Their eyes spoke of what had been left unsaid.

"I called on you at your old home."

"Yes, I know. It was too big for me there, and lonely. I have no use for all that stuff. You had better take it yourself—the furniture, I mean, and the rest of the things."

"Yes, Agrafena Petrovna told me about that. I saw her. . . . It's very nice of you, but . . ."

The hotel waiter entered at that moment, bringing in a silver tea service; while he was arranging it they did not speak. Natalya Ivanovna sat at the small table and silently made the tea. Nekhludov also was silent.

At last Natalya Ivanovna began resolutely:

"Dmitri, I know all about it." She looked straight into his eyes.

"I'm glad you do."

"Can you possibly hope to reform her after the life she has led?"

He sat erect on a low chair, listening closely and trying to grasp her meaning so that he would be able to answer it rightly. The experience of his last interview with Maslova had left him full of tranquil joy and good will.

"She is not the one I want to reform," he replied. "It is myself."

Natalya Ivanovna sighed. "There are other ways besides marriage."

"I believe it is the best way; what is more, it will introduce me into a world where I can be useful."

"I hardly think that you will be happy."

"It is not a question of my own happiness."

"Of course not. But if she has a heart, she cannot be happy either; she cannot even wish it."

"She does not wish it."

"Yes, I understand, but life—"

"Life?"

"Life requires other things from us."

"Life only requires us to do what is right," said Nekhludov, looking at her face, which though still handsome was beginning to be wrinkled about the eyes and mouth.

"I cannot understand it," she said with a sigh.

"Poor darling! How could she have changed like this?" thought Nekhludov, remembering her as she had been before her marriage with a tenderness in which were woven the countless memories of childhood. At that moment Ragozhinski entered the room, nose in the air as usual and chest out, walking lightly and softly—his spectacles, his black beard, and his bald patch all gleaming.

"How are you—how are you?" he exclaimed, in his artificial and self-conscious way. Although after his marriage both men had tried to use the familiar "thou," they addressed each other still with the formal "you."

They shook hands, and Ragozhinski sank gently into an armchair.

"I hope I'm not interrupting your conversation?"

"Not at all. There is nothing I want to hide from anyone."

As soon as Nekhludov saw that face, those hairy hands, and heard the patronizing, self-assertive tone, his meekness left him in a moment.

"We were talking about his plans," said Natalya Ivanovna. "Shall I pour you a cup of tea?" she added, taking the teapot.

"Yes, please. What plans do you mean?"

"Going to Siberia with a gang of convicts, among them the woman I have sinned against," said Nekhludov.

"I have been told that you meant to do more than escort her to Siberia."

"Yes, I shall marry her, if she will agree."

"Indeed? But would you mind explaining your reasons to me? I do not understand."

"My reasons are that this woman. . . . That the first downward step on the road to a dissolute life. . . ." Nekhludov was angry with himself for not being able to find the right words. "I mean that I am guilty, and that she has been punished."

"If she has been punished, then she must have been guilty, too."

"She is absolutely innocent." And with extreme agitation he related the story.

"Yes, it was carelessness on the part of the president of the court that was responsible for the inexact verdict of the jury," said Ragozhinski. "It's a case for the Senate."

"The Senate has disallowed the petition."

"If the Senate disallowed it, then there can have been no adequate grounds for the appeal," said Ragozhinski, evidently sharing the view that truth is a product of judicial argument. "The Senate cannot review the case on its merits. If there really was an error by the court, you should address a petition to His Majesty."

"That has been done, but there is no chance whatever of success. An inquiry will be made in the Ministry, and the Ministry will make an inquiry in the Senate; the Senate will repeat its decision, and as usual the innocent will be punished."

"In the first place, the Ministry will not address an inquiry to the Senate," said Ragozhinski, with a condescending smile; "it will have the original papers sent up from the court and, if there is an error, will give an opinion on it. Secondly, the innocent—with rare exceptions—are never punished," said Ragozhinski deliberately, with a self-satisfied smile.

"And I have become fully convinced of the contrary," retorted Nekhludov with a feeling of irritation against his brother-in-law. "I have come to the conclusion that more than half the people sentenced by the courts are innocent."

"What do you mean?"

"I mean it in the literal sense. They are as innocent as that woman is innocent of poisoning, as a peasant I have just come to know is innocent of the murder he is accused of, as an old woman and her son are innocent of the crime of arson committed by the owner himself—but they came very near to be sentenced."

"Certainly, judicial errors have always occurred and will continue to occur. Human institutions can never be perfect," interrupted Ragozhinski.

"And then very many are morally innocent, because they were brought up in such surroundings that they do not consider their acts as crimes."

"Pardon me, but that is not correct. Every thief knows that stealing is wrong and that he ought not to steal: that theft is immoral," said Ragozhinski, with a calm, self-contented, somewhat supercilious smile specially irritating to Nekhludov.

"No, he does not. He has been told not to steal—but he knows that owners of factories steal his labor and keep back his wages, that the government and all its officials rob him continually through taxation."

"This sounds like anarchism," said Ragozhinski calmly.

"I do not know what it sounds like. I only know it is true," said Nekhludov. "He knows that the government robs him; he knows that we, the landowners, robbed him long ago when we took away his land, which should be common property. And now, when he gathers a few dry twigs to light his fire, we imprison him and tell him he is a thief. He knows that not he but the man who robbed him is a thief, and that to take back what has been stolen from him is a duty he owes to his family."

"I do not understand, or if I do I cannot agree. Land must have an owner. If you were to divide it today," began Ragozhinski, fully convinced that Nekhludov was a Socialist and that the theory of Socialism demands that land should be divided equally—foolish as such a division would be, as he could easily prove—"if it were to be equally divided today, tomorrow it would again pass into the hands of the most industrious and the most capable."

"No one thinks of dividing the land equally. Land should be no man's property. It should not be bought, or sold, or rented."

"But the right of property is natural to men. Without ownership there would be no incentive to cultivate land. Destroy the right of property, and we shall return to the primitive state," said Ragozhinski with authority, repeating the usual argument for the ownership of land which is considered to be unanswerable and is founded on the assumption that people's desire to own land is a proof of their right to own it.

"On the contrary, it is only when landowners stop their dog-in-the-manger behavior, stop preventing other men from cultivating the land they cannot use themselves—it is only then that the land will cease to be idle and become useful."

"Just one moment, Dmitri Ivanovich! Why, this is sheer madness! Is it possible to abolish the ownership of land in these days? I know it's a favorite notion of yours, but let me tell you frankly—" Ragozhinski's voice shook, and he turned pale; evidently the question touched him very closely. "I advise you to think this problem over carefully before you attempt to solve it in practice."

"Are you speaking of my own personal affairs?"

"Yes. I take it that we are all placed in a certain position, that we are expected to bear the burden of its duties, to maintain its traditions and to hand on to our heirs what we have ourselves inherited from our ancestors."

"But I consider it my duty to—"

"Allow me to continue," said Ragozhinski, refusing to be interrupted. "I am not thinking of myself or my children. Their future is safe. I earn enough to live in comfort, and I hope that my children will also live in comfort; therefore my protest against your intentions—which, if you will allow me to say so, are not well considered—does not come from any selfish, personal motives. I cannot agree with you on this as a matter of principle. I advise you to think it over and to read—"

"Perhaps you will allow me to order my own affairs and to use my own judgment in the selection of books that I shall read," said Nekhludov, turning pale. He found that his hands were growing cold, and feeling that he was losing his self-control, he broke off and began to drink his tea in silence.

CHAPTER THIRTY-THREE

"WELL, and how are the children?" Nekhludov asked his sister, when he had become a little more composed.

She told him that they were with their grandmother, her husband's mother; and, relieved that the dispute with her husband had come to an end, she went on to describe how they pretended to be going on voyages, just as he used to do with his two dolls—the little Negro and the one which he called the French lady.

"D'you really remember that?" asked Nekhludov, smiling.

"Yes; and isn't it odd that they should play the very same game?"

The disagreeable conversation ended, Natasha felt more at ease, but she did not like to talk before her husband about things which her brother alone could understand, so, in order to make the conversation general, she raised the subject of Mme. Kamenskaya, whose only son had been killed in a duel (for the news had lately reached here from Petersburg). Ragozhinski stated his disapproval of a system which excluded murder committed in a duel from the list of common criminal offenses.

Nekhludov disagreed, and a dispute began again, in which neither antagonist fully expressed what was in his mind and each stood fast on his own ground. Ragozhinski felt that Nekhludov despised him and was anxious to prove the injustice of his opinion. Nekhludov, on the other hand, was annoyed at his brother-in-law's interference in his plans for the estates (though at the bottom of his heart he felt his sister and brother-in-law and their children had a certain right to protest, being his heirs), and was indignant because this narrow-minded man so calmly and dogmatically persisted in regarding as lawful and right what Nekhludov now considered mad and criminal.

"What could a court have done?" he asked.

"It would have sentenced one of the duelists like an ordinary murderer to hard labor."

Again Nekhludov felt his hands grow cold and said excitedly:

"And what would have been the result?"

"It would have been just."

"As if justice were the aim of courts of justice!" said Nekhludov.

"What else, then?"

"Their aim is to uphold class interests. The courts are only an instrument for upholding the existing order of things in the interest of our class."

"Well, this is really a novel point of view," said Ragozhinski, with a quiet smile. "The courts are commonly supposed to have a different aim."

"In theory they have, but not in practice, as I have had occasion to discover. The courts are only meant to keep things as they are, and that is why they persecute and pass sentences on people who stand above the general level and want to raise it—the so-called political criminals—and those who are below it, the so-called criminal types."

"I cannot agree with you. In the first place because I do not believe that the political criminals are sentenced because they are above the average. They are, generally speaking, the refuse of society—as depraved, though perhaps in a different way, as the criminal types whom you consider below the average."

"But I know people who are immensely superior to their judges. The sectarians, for example, are all good, courageous men determined—"

But Ragozhinski, being a man unaccustomed to interruptions, paid no heed to Nekhludov and went on talking.

"I cannot agree that the courts aim to uphold things as they are. The court has its own aims; either to reform—"

"It's a fine way of reforming a man, to put him in jail!" interrupted Nekhludov.

"Or to remove the brutal and the depraved, who are undermining the existence of society," continued Ragozhinski, persistently.

"That's just what they don't do: neither the one nor the other. Society has no means for doing it."

"What do you mean? I don't understand," said Ragozhinski with a forced smile.

"I mean there are only two reasonable forms of punishment, that were applied in olden days—corporal punishment and capital punishment—and these, as time went on and customs relaxed, have been almost wholly set aside."

"This is a little strange, coming from you."

"Yes, I believe it is reasonable to cause a man bodily pain, in order to restrain him from committing a second time the crime he is being punished for; it is reasonable even to behead a member of the community who is injurious to it, or dangerous. Both punishments are reasonable. But what sense is there in locking up a man already depraved by idleness or evil influences and continuing to support him in idleness along with other men even more depraved? Or for some inscrutable reason to transport him at the public expense—and the cost is five hundred rubles—from Tula to Irkutsk, or from Kursk—"

"But people dread those journeys at the public expense, and if these journeys and jails did not exist, you and I would not be sitting here so peacefully as we are now."

"But jails are powerless to assure our safety—just the reverse, in fact, since in these places men are forced into greater and greater depravity and the danger is therefore increased, for men are not kept there forever, but eventually set free."

"You mean that the penal system ought to be improved?"

"It cannot be improved. An improved prison system would cost far more than is spent on education in this country, and would lay a still heavier burden on the people."

Ragozhinski again resumed his speech without listening to his brother-in-law. "However, the defects of the penal system do not in the least invalidate the law itself."

"Those defects cannot be made good," said Nekhludov, raising his voice.

"Well, what then? Are we to kill them off? Or, as a certain statesman suggested, put their eyes out?" said Ragozhinski, smiling triumphantly.

"That might be cruel, but it would be consistent. What is going on at present is not only cruel and inconsistent, but so stupid that it is impossible to understand how normal people can take part in such an inhuman institution as the Criminal Court."

"I take part in it," said Ragozhinski, turning pale.

"That is your affair. But I fail to understand it."

"It seems to me that you fail to understand most things," said Ragozhinski in a trembling voice.

"I have seen the assistant prosecutor, in court, trying his best to convict a poor lad whose condition could have roused nothing but pity in any normal man. I heard another prosecutor cross-examine a sectarian and make the reading of the Gospel a criminal offense—the whole business of the courts is made up of such stupid and cruel actions as these."

"I should not serve in them if I thought so," said Ragozhinski, and rose.

Nekhludov saw a queer glitter under his brother-in-law's spectacles. "Can it be tears?" he thought, and indeed they were tears of injured pride. Ignati Nikiforovich went up to the window, took out his handkerchief, coughed, and rubbed his spectacles; then he removed them and wiped his eyes. When he returned to the sofa, he lighted a cigar and did not say another word. Nekhludov felt pained and ashamed to have so greatly offended his brother-in-law and his sister, all the more since he was going away the next day and would probably never see them again. He took his leave in confusion and drove home.

"All I have said may be true—in any case he had no answer to it," he thought. "But that was not the way I should have spoken. How little I have changed if I can be so carried away by hard feelings as to offend him and hurt poor Natasha."

CHAPTER THIRTY-FOUR

THE party of convicts to which Maslova belonged was to set off from the railway station at three o'clock in the afternoon, so that in order to see them start from the jail Nekhludov had to be there before noon.

While he was packing his clothes and papers he stopped to read some passages in his diary. The last thing he had written in it before leaving Petersburg was this: "Katusha will not accept my sacrifice, but is willing to sacrifice herself. She has conquered, and so have I. I rejoice in her change of heart. I dare hardly believe it, but I cannot help feeling that she is coming back to life." Then, further on he had written: "I have experienced feelings both painful and joyful. When I was told that she had misbehaved in prison I felt greatly hurt. The pain was more than I could have expected. I spoke to her in tones of disgust and hatred, but then I thought of myself, of how often I had committed, though only in my mind, the very sin I condemned and despised in her—and at once I became disgusting to myself, and I pitied her. Then I felt happy again. If only we could see the beam in our own eye soon enough, how much more charitable we should be!" Then he wrote: "I called on Natasha, and just because I felt satisfied with myself, I was unkind and angry and now my heart is heavy. What is to be done? Tomorrow I begin a new life. Good-by forever to my old life! I have had many experiences, but I cannot piece them together yet."

When he woke up the next morning, Nekhludov's first feeling was of repentance for what had passed between him and his brother-in-law. "I can't leave it that way, I must go and make it up with them," he thought; but glancing at his watch he saw that there was no time and that he must hurry so as not to miss the party as it set out. He made ready in haste, sent off the door-keeper and Tarass, Fedosya's husband, who was to travel with him, directly to the station with the luggage, then took the first cab he could find and drove to the prison.

The mail train by which he was going started only two hours after the prisoners' train, and he paid for his rooms, not intending to return.

It was hot July weather. The pavements, the houses, and the iron roofs were throwing their heat into the still air. There was no breeze—or, when there was one, it came like a sultry wave full of dust and the smell of paint. The streets were almost empty and the few people who were out tried to keep in the shade of the houses; only some sunburnt peasants in bast shoes sat working in the sun, hammering at the stones they were setting in the burning sand; doleful policemen in unbleached tunics with revolvers fastened to orange-colored lanyards, stood sullenly in the middle of the road shifting from one foot to another; tramcars clattered along with blinds drawn down on the sunny side, and the horses had white hoods on their heads with slits for the ears.

When Nekhludov drove up to the prison, the party had not yet left and the strenuous business of handing over the prisoners (which had begun at four o'clock in the morning) was still going on. There were six hundred and twenty-three men and sixty-four women in the party. Every one was checked against a list, the sick and the feeble were segregated, and the party put under a guard. The new inspector, his two assistants, the doctor and his assistant, the officer of the escort and the clerk, all sat at a table in the shade of a wall, with papers and writing materials before them; they called the names one by one, questioned, inspected, and made notes about the prisoners as they came up in turn.

The rays of sun gradually reached the table; it was growing very hot and oppressive from the stillness of the air and the breathing of the prisoners crowded around the table.

"It seems as if this business will never end," said the officer of the escort. He was a tall, stout, red-faced man with high shoulders and short arms, who never stopped drawing in and blowing out the smoke of a cigarette through his thick drooping mustache. "I'm dead beat! Where did you get them all? How many more are there?"

The clerk consulted the list.

"Twenty-four more men, and the rest are women."

"Well, what are you hanging about for? Come on!" shouted the officer to the prisoners who had not yet been checked. For more than three hours they had been standing in the sun awaiting their turn.

While this was going on inside the prison yard, an armed sentry stood as usual outside the gate, where about twenty carts were drawn up to carry the belongings of the prisoners, with a group of relatives and friends waiting to see them as they came out and, if possible, to say a few words or give them something. Nekhludov joined the group.

He had been standing there about an hour, when a clanking of chains, a sound of footsteps, the orders of officers, a great deal of coughing, and the low murmur of a large crowd were heard from behind the gates. This lasted about five minutes, while the warders came to and fro through the wicket gate. At last the order was given. The gates opened with a thundering noise, the clanking of chains became louder; the escort of soldiers in white tunics, armed with muskets, came out into the street and performed the customary evolution, posting themselves in a wide half-circle around the gate. When they were in their places, another command was given and the prisoners came out in pairs, wearing flat pancake-shaped hats on their half-shaven heads, carrying sacks slung over their shoulders, dragging their chained legs and swinging one hand, while with the other they supported the sacks on their backs. First came the men condemned to hard labor, in gray trousers and loose coats with black marks like aces on the back. All—young, old, thin, fat, pale, florid, dark, bearded, mustached, smooth-faced, Russians, Tartars, Jews—came clanking their chains and briskly swinging their arms, as though preparing to walk a long way; but after taking a few steps they halted and meekly arranged themselves four abreast, one behind the other. They were followed by others dressed like the first lot, and with half-shaven heads also; they had no chains on their legs but were manacled together. These were the exiles. They came out as briskly, halted as suddenly, and also placed themselves four abreast. Then came those exiled by their village communes. Then the women, also in order; those condemned to hard labor in gray coats with kerchiefs on their heads, followed by the exiles and those who were going voluntarily; some were dressed like peasants and some like townspeople; some carried babies tucked into the front of their coats.

The children came with the women, and crowded among the prisoners like young colts in a herd. The men stood in silence, sometimes coughing or exchanging a few words, but the women talked incessantly. Nekhludov thought he recognized Maslova as she came out, but she was soon lost among the others, and he saw only a crowd of gray creatures that had no mark of womanliness or even of humanity, carrying sacks and children and taking up their places among the men.

Although the prisoners had all been counted inside the prison walls, the escort counted them over again and made a check against the first list. This took a long time—all the longer because some of the prisoners would move about and so muddled the counting. The soldiers of the escort shouted and pushed the prisoners, who gave way obediently and sullenly, and began the count all over again. When all had been counted at last, the officer of the escort gave an order which caused some confusion in the crowd. The invalid men, the women, and the children jostled their way into the carts and began to arrange their sacks and to climb up themselves. Women with crying babies, children gaily fighting for seats, and sullen, dejected men—all climbed up and sat down in the carts.

Several prisoners, taking off their hats, approached the officer of the convoy. Nekhludov found out later that they were asking for places in the carts. The officer took a long pull at his cigarette and then, without looking up at the inquiring faces, suddenly lifted his podgy arm in front of one of the prisoners, who jerked up his shaven head and sprang back, as though to avoid a blow.

"I'll give you the sort of lift you don't expect!" shouted the officer. "You'll get there on foot right enough!"

Only an old and tottering man with fetters on his legs was allowed a seat in one of the carts, and Nekhludov saw him take off his pancake-shaped hat and cross himself; for some time he was unable to climb up, for his chains prevented him from raising his old legs; then a woman already sitting in the cart gave him a helping hand.

When the carts had been loaded with the sacks, and those with permission to ride had climbed on, the officer of the escort took off his cap; he wiped his forehead, his bald head and thick red neck, and made the sign of the cross.

"Forward—march!" he commanded. The soldiers' rifles rattled, the prisoners took off their caps, some of them at the same time crossing themselves with their left hand; the people who were seeing them off shouted something and the prisoners shouted in reply, the women began to wail, and the party moved off, surrounded by soldiers in white tunics, raising the dust with their feet. The soldiers marched at the head; next, four abreast, clanking their chains, came those sentenced to hard labor; then the exiles and those exiled by their village communes, manacled in twos; and then the women. Last of all came the carts with the sacks and the ailing prisoners. On one of the carts, sitting high up among the baggage, a woman kept sobbing and shrieking.

CHAPTER THIRTY-FIVE

THE procession was so long that by the time the carts with the feeble-bodied and the sacks had started, the men in the front ranks were no longer in sight. Nekhludov jumped into the droshky which was waiting for him and told the driver to catch up with the prisoners in front, thinking he might see some men he knew among the prisoners, and ask Maslova, if he could find her among the women, whether she had received the things he had sent her.

It had grown very hot. There was no wind, and the cloud of dust raised by thousands of feet hung over the prisoners as they marched along the middle of the street. They were marching quickly, and the slow-moving horse belonging to Nekhludov's cab took a long time to pass them. Row after row they marched, strange fearful creatures dressed alike, thousands of feet shod alike, all in step, swinging their arms as though to keep up their spirits. There were so many of them, they looked so much alike, and their condition was so extraordinarily strange, that to Nekhludov they no longer seemed to be men but some uncanny, supernatural order of beings. This impression, however, was dispelled when he recognized Fedorov, the murderer, among the criminals, and, among the exiles, Okhotin, the wag, and a tramp who had also appealed to him for assistance. Most of the prisoners turned to take a quick glance at the gentleman in the droshky. Fedorov jerked back his head as a sign that he had recognized Nekhludov, and Okhotin gave him a wink; neither of them bowed, thinking it was not allowed.

When he came abreast of the women, Nekhludov saw Maslova at once. She was walking in the second rank. On the ouside was a hideous, dark, short-limbed woman, her cloak tucked into her girdle; then came a pregnant woman hardly able to drag her feet; Maslova was the third. She carried a sack on her shoulder and was looking straight in front of her. Her face was calm and resolute. The fourth in the row was a good-looking young woman in a prisoner's short coat, a kerchief on her head worn peasant-fashion. This was Fedosya. Nekhludov got off and went up to the women, wanting to ask Maslova if she had received the things he had sent her and also to know how she was feeling. But the sergeant who was marching along-side noticed him at once and came running up.

"You are not allowed to go near the gang, sir," he shouted as he ran. When he reached Nekhludov he recognized him (everyone in the prison knew him by sight) and giving a mili-tary salute stopped beside him and said:

"You musn't do that, sir. Wait till we reach the station. It's against the regulations to do it here. Now, then, don't lag be-hind, there! Keep up!" he shouted to the prisoners and, briskly in spite of the heat and his smart new boots, he ran back to his place.

Nekhludov returned to the pavement; telling his driver to follow, he walked after the gang. As the prisoners proceeded through the streets, they roused a mingled feeling of pity and horror. People passing in their carriages looked out of the windows and followed the prisoners with their eyes. People on foot stopped and gazed in surprise and alarm at the terrible sight. Some went up and offered alms, which were accepted for the prisoners by the escort. Some joined on behind, as though hypnotized, but finally broke off and stood shaking their heads, following only with their eyes. People ran out of gates and doors calling to each other, others leaned out of windows, silently watching the fearful procession. At one crossing a fine open carriage was held up by the gang. A coachman with a shiny face, wearing a padded coat with rows of buttons down the back, sat on the box. The rear seats were occupied by a man and his wife. The wife, pale and slender, in a light-colored bonnet, carrying a bright sunshade, the husband in a top hat and light, well-cut coat. The children sat on the front seats—a carefully dressed little girl as fresh as a flower, also holding a bright sunshade, and an eight-year-old boy with a long, thin neck and prominent collarbones, wearing a sailor hat trimmed with a long ribbon. The father was upbraiding the coachman for not crossing in time, while the mother pursed her mouth in disgust and almost covered her face with her silk sunshade to keep out the sun and dust. The padded coachman frowned angrily at the unjust reprimand, for he had been ordered by the master himself to drive along this street, and was now having some difficulty in restraining the shining black stallions flecked with foam under their collars and impatient to go on. The policeman at the corner would have gladly obliged the owner of such a fine equipage by stopping the column of convicts and allowing him to pass, but he felt that there was a certain somber solemnity which could not be disturbed even to please such a wealthy gentleman as this. Therefore he only raised his fingers to the peak of his cap to show his regard for wealth and position, and looked at the convicts severely, as though promising in any case to protect the occupants of the carriage from them.

The carriage had to wait until the column had passed and the last cart with the sacks and the prisoners seated on top of them had rattled by. The hysterical woman, who had quieted down, began to sob and shriek again when she saw this luxurious turnout. It was only then that the high-stepping black horses, at a twitch of the reins from the coachman, with a clatter of hoofs against the cobbles whirled off the carriage on its resilient rubber tires to the country house where the husband, his wife, the little girl, and the boy with the thin neck and projecting collarbones were going to amuse themselves.

Neither the father nor the mother made any comment, so that the children had to find for themselves some meaning in what they had seen.

The girl, watching the expressions on the faces of her father and mother, decided that the people she had seen were of a different kind from her parents and their friends, that they were bad people who had to be treated in that way; so she only felt frightened, and was glad when the prisoners were out of sight.

But the long-necked boy, who had watched the procession intently, decided the question differently. He knew without any doubt, for he had the knowledge from God, that these men and women were like himself and like other people, and that something wicked was happening, something that ought not to be done to them; he was sorry for them and was frightened not only of them, for being shaven and chained, but of those who had shaved and chained them. That was why the boy's lips pouted more and more, and he made ever greater efforts to keep back his tears, ashamed of crying at such a time.

❖

CHAPTER THIRTY-SIX

NEKHLUDOV kept up with the quick pace of the convicts, but dressed even as lightly as he was in a thin overcoat, he found the dust and the close hot air of the streets extremely oppressive. After walking for half a mile he took his seat in the droshky and drove ahead; but in the middle of the street, in the sun, he felt the heat still more. He tried to recall last night's conversation with his brother-in-law, but it no longer agitated him as it had done that morning. The impressions made by the start of the prisoners and their march had overshadowed the memories of the day before. Above all, he was overcome by the heat. Two schoolboys were standing in front of an ice-cream seller squatting in the shade of a fence. One of the boys was already enjoying his ice, licking a little horn spoon; the other was waiting for a tumbler which was being filled with something yellow.

"Where can I get a drink?" Nekhludov asked his cab driver, feeling an overwhelming desire for some refreshment.

"We're just coming to a nice place," said the cabby turning the corner and driving Nekhludov up to a door with a large sign above it. A plump man in a Russian shirt stood behind the counter; the waiters, in clothes that had once been white, were sitting at the tables, for there were hardly any customers; they stared inquisitively at this unusual visitor and offered their services. Nekhludov asked for seltzer water and sat down at a little table far away from the window, covered with a dirty cloth. Two men were sitting at another table, a tea tray and a frosted glass bottle in front of them, mopping their brows and assisting each other over some calculation. One was dark and bald, with a line of black hair at the back of his head, like Ragozhinski's. This reminded Nekhludov again of last night's conversation and of his intention to see his sister and her husband once more before going away. "I shall hardly have time to do it now," he said to himself, "I suppose it would be wiser to write." Asking for a sheet of paper, an envelope and a stamp, he began to consider what he should say as he sat sipping the fresh sparkling water. But his thoughts were so vague and distraught that he found it impossible to finish the letter.

"My dear Natasha," he began, "I cannot bear to go away remembering my conversation last night with your husband, without—" "What next?" he thought. "Am I going to apologize? But I only said what I thought, and it would give him the impression that I am eating my words. And then there was his meddling in my affairs, too. . . . No, I can't do it." Again there arose his hatred for that unpleasant, conceited man, that stranger who had never understood him. He put the unfinished letter into his pocket and, paying for the glass of seltzer, went out and drove on to catch up with the party.

The heat had grown worse. The walls and the stones seemed to give off hot air. When he touched the lacquered wing of the droshky it scorched his hand. The horse jogged wearily along the dusty, uneven road, clanking its hoofs monotonously while the driver dozed on his box. Nekhludov sat indifferently gazing ahead, thinking of nothing in particular. At the end of a street, before the gate of a large house, stood a soldier of the escort with his rifle. A little crowd was gathered around him.

Nekhludov told the driver to stop.

"What's going on here?" he asked a horse porter.

"Something's the matter with one of the convicts."

Nekhludov left the droshky and approached the group. A thickset, elderly convict with a ginger beard, red face and snub nose, dressed in a gray coat and gray trousers, was lying on the uneven cobblestones curving down to the gutter, his head resting lower than his feet. He was on his back with the palms of his freckled hands downward; at long intervals his deep broad chest heaved convulsively and he gasped and sobbed, gazing at the sky with fixed, bloodshot eyes. A frowning policeman was looking down at him, surrounded by a small crowd: a peddler, a postman, a clerk, an old woman with a sunshade, and a boy with clipped hair holding an empty basket.

"They're weak. They get weak in jail, and then they're brought out into a regular furnace like this," said the clerk, addressing Nekhludov, who had joined the group.

"He'll most likely die," said the woman with the sunshade, in a tearful voice.

"You ought to loosen his shirt," said the postman.

The policeman bent down; with thick, trembling, clumsy fingers he began to undo the fastening around the muscular red neck. He was evidently agitated and confused, but still felt that his duty required him to speak to the crowd.

"Come along, don't stand around here gaping—it's quite hot enough as it is without all of you to keep off the breeze."

"The doctor should have seen to it that the weak ones stayed behind in the prison, and not allowed a man like this to be led out half alive," remarked the clerk, evidently proud of his knowledge of the regulations.

The policeman, having untied the fastening of the shirt, straightened himself and looked around.

"I've told you to move along there! This is nothing to do with you. What is there to stare at, I'd like to know?" he asked, turning toward Nekhludov for sympathy; not finding it there, he glanced at the soldier; the soldier, however, was absorbed in examining the heel of his boot where it was worn away, and was not interested in the policeman's problems.

"They just don't care, those who ought to be looking after things. Is it right to do a man to death like this? He may be a convict, but he's a human being all the same," people were heard to murmur.

"Prop his head up higher and give him water," said Nekhludov.

"They've gone to fetch some," replied the policeman and, taking the convict under the arms, with difficulty pulled the body a little higher.

"Now, then, what's this crowd here for?" suddenly came a firm, commanding voice; a police officer walked up briskly to the group gathered around the prisoner; he was very smart in a spotlessly clean white uniform and highly polished top boots.

"Move along! Nobody has any business here!" he shouted to the crowd, without waiting to learn why they had gathered. As he came near and saw the dying convict, he nodded his head as though it was only what might have been expected.

"What happened?" he asked the policeman. The policeman reported that while a gang of convicts was passing, this man had collapsed and the officer of the escort had ordered him to be left behind.

"Well, what about it? Why didn't you take him to the police station? Call a cab!"

"The house porter has gone to get one," said the policeman, raising his hand to his cap.

The clerk began to make a remark about the heat.

"Is that your business, eh? Move on!" said the police officer and gave the clerk such a severe look that he said no more.

"He should have water to drink," said Nekhludov. The police officer frowned at him but said nothing. When the house porter brought a jug of water he told the policeman to offer some to the convict. The policeman raised the prisoner's head, which had fallen backward, and tried to pour the water into his mouth, but he could not swallow. The water ran down his beard, wetting the front of his jacket and his coarse, dusty shirt.

"Pour it over his head," ordered the officer, and the policeman, taking off the pancake-shaped cap, poured the water over the red, curly hair and the bald, shaved patch. The convict's eyes seemed to open a little wider as though in surprise, but he did not move. Streams of dirty water trickled down his dusty face; from his mouth came the same regular gasping and sobbing, and his whole body was contorted.

"What about the cab here? Take this one," the officer said to the policeman, and added pointing at Nekhludov's driver, "Drive up this way."

"Engaged," said the man surlily, without raising his eyes.

"This is my driver," said Nekhludov, "but you can take him. I will pay you now," he said, turning to the cabby.

"Well, why don't you make a move? There, take hold!" cried the police officer.

The policeman, the house porter, and the soldier from the escort lifted up the dying man and carried him to the droshky, where they tried to make him sit up. But he could not support himself. His head fell back and his body slipped off the seat.

"Lay him down!" ordered the police officer.

"That's all right, your honor, I'll manage to get him there," said the policeman, seating himself firmly beside the dying man and passing his strong right arm under the arms of the prisoner.

The soldier from the escort lifted the feet, bare inside prison shoes, and stretched them out in the droshky.

The police officer looked back; noticing the convict's flat cap lying on the pavement, he picked it up and put it on the wet, drooping head. "Go on!" he shouted.

The cabby looked around angrily and, accompanied by the soldier, started to walk his horse slowly toward the police station. The policeman sitting beside the convict kept dragging up the limp body with its swaying head. The soldier walked beside the droshky and kept tucking in the feet. Nekhludov followed them.

PASSING the fireman on duty at the gate of the police station[1] the droshky drove into the yard and stopped at one of the doors.

Some firemen in the yard, their sleeves rolled up, were laughing and talking loudly over a cart they were busy washing. As soon as the droshky stopped, it was surrounded by several policemen; taking hold of the lifeless body by the arms and legs they lifted it out of the droshky, which creaked under their weight. The policeman got out and began to swing his numbed arm about; then he took off his cap and crossed himself. Nekhludov followed as the body was carried up the stairs into a small, dirty room with four bunks. Two sick men in hospital dressing gowns were sitting on their bunks; one had a twisted mouth and bandaged neck, the other was a consumptive.

The two remaining bunks were unoccupied; the body of the convict was laid on one of them. A small man with glittering eyes and quivering eyebrows, dressed in underclothes and stockings, came up swiftly and silently, looked first at the convict and then at Nekhludov and burst into loud laughter. It was a madman who was being kept in the police hospital.

"They're trying to scare me, but they won't succeed," he said.

A medical assistant and a police officer came in. The medical assistant went up to the body, touched the cold, yellow, freckled hand which, although not quite stiff, already had the pallor of death; he held it awhile and then dropped it; it fell lifeless on the dead man's stomach.

"It's all over with him," said the medical assistant; but evidently intending to keep all the rules, he undid the coarse, wet shirt and, tossing aside his curly hair, put his ear against the yellow, unstirring chest. Everyone was silent.

The medical assistant straightened himself and nodded; then, pressing a finger first on one and then on the other lid, he closed the staring blue eyes.

"You're not going to scare me, you're not going to scare me," the madman kept saying, spitting in the direction of the medical assistant.

---

[1] The fire brigades and the police generally shared the same quarters in Moscow.

"Well?" said the police officer.

"Well?" repeated the medical assistant. "He'll have to be carried into the mortuary."

"Are you sure?" asked the police officer.

"I ought to be," replied the medical assistant, closing, for some reason, the shirt over the dead man's chest. "But I can send for Matvey Ivanovich and let him have a look. Petrov, call him," he said and stepped aside.

"Take him to the mortuary," said the police officer. "Then come to the office and sign," he added, addressing the soldier of the escort, who all this time had not left the convict for a moment.

"Very good, sir," replied the soldier.

The policeman lifted the dead body and carried it again downstairs. Nekhludov wanted to follow them, but the madman detained him.

"You can give me a cigarette, as you're not one of the conspirators," he said.

Nekhludov took out his cigarette case and gave him one. The madman began to talk rapidly, his eyebrows twitching, and told how he was being tormented by means of thought suggestion.

"They are all against me, every one of them. They torment me, they torture me through their mediums—"

"Excuse me," said Nekhludov and, without stopping to listen, went out into the yard, wanting to see where the dead man would be taken.

The policemen with their load had crossed the yard and were just about to enter the door of the basement. Nekhludov made to follow them, but the police officer stopped him:

"What do you want?"

"Nothing," replied Nekhludov.

"If it's nothing you want, you'd better keep away."

Nekhludov obeyed and returned to his cabby, who was dozing. Nekhludov roused him and they started once more toward the railway station. But they had hardly driven a hundred feet when they met a cart also accompanied by a soldier of the escort with a rifle on his shoulder. Another dead convict was stretched out on it. He lay on his back. His shaven head and black beard, and the pancake-shaped hat which had slipped down to his nose, swayed and jerked up and down at every jolt. The driver, in thick boots, walked beside the cart, holding the reins in his hands. A policeman was walking behind him. Nekhludov touched the cabby on the shoulder.

"Look what they're up to!" exclaimed the cabby, stopping his horse.

Nekhludov jumped off the droshky, followed the driver of the cart, and went into the yard of the police station again. The firemen had finished cleaning the cart; a tall, rawboned man, the captain of the fire brigade, a band around his cap and his hands in his pockets, was standing in their place. He was inspecting a thick-necked bay stallion, which a fireman was leading up and down before him. The stallion was slightly lame in his foreleg and the captain was angrily remonstrating with the veterinary.

The police officer was also there. Seeing another corpse, he went up to the cart.

"Where did you pick him up?" he asked, shaking his head disapprovingly.

"On Old Gorbatovski Street," replied the policeman.

"A prisoner?" asked the captain of the fire brigade.

"Yes, sir. It's the second today."

"Well, their way of going about things seems a bit queer," said the captain and, turning toward the fireman who was leading away the lame stallion, he shouted, "Put him in the corner stall! I'll teach you, you son of a bitch, to maim a horse worth more than yourself!"

The second corpse was also lifted from the cart by the policeman and carried into hospital. Nekhludov followed as though hypnotized.

"What do you want?" a policeman asked him; he went in without replying, and followed the body to the room where it was being carried.

The madman, seated on a bunk, was greedily smoking the cigarette that Nekhludov had given him.

"So you've come back," he cried and burst out laughing. On seeing the corpse he made a face. "Another one! I'm tired of them. I'm not a child, am I?" he added, turning to Nekhludov with a questioning smile.

Nekhludov was looking at the dead man. The face formerly hidden by the cap was in full view. As the other convict had been uncommonly hideous, so this one was remarkably handsome in face and in body. He was still in the full strength of manhood. The low, straight forehead over the now lifeless black eyes was beautiful, and so was the finely curved Roman nose above a small black mustache. A smile still hovered on his lips, now turning blue. A small beard followed the line of the lower part of the face. The shaven side of the skull revealed a delicately shaped ear. The expression of the face was calm, severe, and kind. Besides the spiritual and intellectual possibilities revealed in this face, no one could fail to perceive from the slender bones of the fettered hands and feet, and the strong muscles of the well-proportioned limbs, what a fine, vigorous, agile human animal he had been—more perfect even than the young stallion whose injury had stirred the captain of the fire brigade to such fury. And yet there was no one to pity him as a human being; more, no one was even sorry that such a beautiful and useful animal had been done to death. The only feeling evoked by his death was annoyance at the trouble of having to get this body out of the way before it began to putrefy.

A doctor, accompanied by his assistant and a police inspector, entered the room. The doctor was a thickset man in a tussore coat and narrow trousers that clung to his muscular thighs. The inspector was short and fat, with a round red face that looked still rounder from his habit of puffing out his cheeks. The doctor sat down on the bunk by the side of the dead man, lifted the hands and put his ear to the heart as his assistant had done. Then he rose and straightened his trousers.

"Couldn't be more dead," he said.

The inspector filled his cheeks with air and slowly let it out again.

"From what prison?" he asked the escort.

The escort told him and reminded him of the chains which were still on the dead man's feet.

"I will have them removed. We'll send for a blacksmith," said the inspector and went toward the door, again puffing out his cheeks and slowly allowing the air to escape.

"Why did this happen?" Nekhludov asked the doctor.

"What do you mean? How do men die of sunstroke? This is one of the ways; you keep them without light and exercise all through the winter, then suddenly bring them out into the sunshine on such a day as this and make them march in a crowd, so that they don't get the slightest breeze to cool them. Then they get sunstroke."

"Then why are they sent out?"

"My dear sir, you must find that out from those who send them. But may I ask who you are?"

"A stranger."

"Ah! . . . Well, good afternoon, I'm busy," said the doctor, seeming to be annoyed; he began to pull his trousers into shape and crossed over to the other bunks.

"Well, how are you feeling?" he asked the pale man with the crooked mouth and bandaged neck.

Meanwhile the madman, sitting on his bunk, had finished smoking and was now spitting toward the doctor.

❖

CHAPTER THIRTY-EIGHT

WHEN Nekhludov reached the station he found the convicts already seated in the railway carriages behind barred windows. Several people who had come to see them off were standing on the platform; they were not allowed to approach the train. The escorts were worried. On the way from the prison to the station three other men, besides the two whom Nekhludov had seen, had fallen and died of sunstroke. One had been removed, like the first two, to the nearest police station, and two had died in the railway station.[1] The escorts were not troubled because five men who might have been still living had died while in their charge. That did not worry them. All they worried about was to do what the law required of them on such occasions, which meant delivering the dead, their documents, and their possessions and removing their names from the list of those to be sent to Nizhni. All this was very troublesome, particularly in such weather.

It was this that worried the escort. Until all the details of the business had been settled, therefore, neither Nekhludov nor anyone else could get permission to approach the train; but Nekhludov by bribing the sergeant was allowed to slip in, on condition that he made his leave-taking brief, so as to elude the observation of the officers. There were eighteen carriages; all, with the exception of the carriage for the officials, were packed tight with prisoners. As Nekhludov passed by the windows of the train he could hear what was going on inside—the incessant clank of chains, the bustle and the talk and the senseless bad language; nowhere did he hear what he had expected—some mention of the men who had died on the way. The talk was

---

[1] At the beginning of the eighties, five convicts died of sunstroke in one day while being transported from the Butirski Prison in Moscow to the Nizhni railway station.—L.T.

chiefly about sacks, drinking water, and the distribution of seats.

Looking into the window of one of the carriages, Nekhludov saw two of the escorts taking off the prisoners' manacles in the corridor. The prisoners held out their hands while one of the soldiers unlocked and removed the cuffs and the other collected them.

Passing carriage after carriage, he came to those occupied by the women. In the second of these he heard a voice groaning monotonously: "Oh, my God! Oh, oh, my God . . ."

Nekhludov walked on; directed by one of the escorts, he stopped beside a window of the third carriage occupied by women. As he looked in he could breathe the hot air heavy with the smell of human sweat and hear the shrill sound of women's voices. All the benches were occupied by red-faced, sweating women dressed in prison cloaks or blouses, all talking in high-pitched voices. Nekhludov's face at the window attracted their attention. Those nearest ceased talking. Maslova in a blouse, her head uncovered, was sitting by the opposite window. On her nearer side was the white-skinned, smiling Fedosya.

Recognizing Nekhludov, she nudged Maslova and pointed to the window.

Maslova rose hastily and threw her kerchief over her black hair; with a flushed, animated, sweating face she approached the window and took hold of the bars.

"Isn't it hot?" she said, smiling joyfully.

"Did you get the things?"

"I did, thank you."

"Do you want anything else?" asked Nekhludov, while the hot air came out from the carriage as from a glowing furnace.

"Nothing, thank you."

"It would be nice to have a drink of water," said Fedosya.

"Yes, a drink would be nice," repeated Maslova.

"Isn't there any water?"

"We had some, but it's all gone."

"One moment," said Nekhludov, "I'll ask the escort. We shall not see each other again till we reach Nizhni."

"Why, are you coming?" said Maslova as if she had not known, and looked joyfully at Nekhludov.

"I am leaving on the next train."

Maslova said no more, and only sighed deeply.

"Is it true, sir, that twelve convicts have been done to

death?" asked a stern-looking woman, in a gruff, mannish voice. It was Korablyova.

"I did not hear that there were twelve. I saw two," said Nekhludov.

"They told us there were twelve. Won't they be punished for that, the devils?"

"Were any of the women ill?" asked Nekhludov.

"Women are tougher," a short woman replied laughingly. "But one girl here took it into her head to have a baby. Hark at her now," she said pointing to the next car, from which the groans were coming.

"You asked just now if I needed anything?" said Maslova, her lips on the verge of a glad smile. "Could that woman be left behind? She is in such pain. Couldn't you speak to the officer?"

"Yes, I will."

"And couldn't *she* see her husband, Tarass?" she added, indicating with her eyes the smiling Fedosya. "He's coming with you, isn't he?"

"No talking allowed, sir," said the voice of a sergeant. It was not the one who had let Nekhludov pass. Nekhludov drew back and went in search of the commanding officer to ask him about Tarass and the woman in labor, but could not get any answer from the soldiers of the escort. They seemed very busy: some were taking a convict from one place to another, some were running about buying food for themselves and arranging their own belongings in the carriages; others, waiting upon a lady who was accompanying an officer of the escort.

Nekhludov did not find the officer until the second bell had been rung.

This officer, wiping his drooping mustache with his hand, was reprimanding a corporal for something or other.

"What is it you want?" he asked Nekhludov.

"A woman on the train has begun her labor pains. I thought it would be . . ."

"Let her get on with it. We'll see to that later," said the officer; he climbed into the carriage with brisk movements of his short arms.

At that moment the guard went by with a whistle in his hand. The last bell rang; sobs and wails came from the women's carriages and from the people on the platform. Nekhludov stood beside Tarass and watched the carriages pass one by one. He could see the shaven heads of the men through the barred windows. Then, the first of the women's carriages went by, and women's heads could be seen at the windows, some bare and some covered; from the second carriage moans could still be heard; then came the carriage with Maslova in it. She was standing with some other women at the window and she looked at Nekhludov with a pitiful smile.

❧

CHAPTER THIRTY-NINE

NEKHLUDOV had two hours to wait for the next passenger train. At first he thought of going to see his sister, but the morning's experiences had so agitated and saddened him that finding himself on a sofa in the first-class waiting room he felt suddenly drowsy; he turned on his side and at once fell asleep with his cheek resting on the palm of one hand. A waiter in a tail coat, carrying a napkin on his arm, woke him up.

"Sir, sir, are you not Prince Nekhludov? There is a lady looking for you."

Nekhludov started up and rubbed his eyes, recalling where he was and all that had happened that morning.

The column of convicts, the corpses, the women behind the barred windows of the railway carriages and the woman suffering the torture of labor pains, the other woman who had smiled at him sadly—he saw them again with his mind's eye, though the scene before him was very different: nimble waiters moving around a large table covered with bottles, vases, candelabra, and plates; in the background, behind bottles and vases with fruit, the bartender standing in front of a buffet and passengers crowding around it.

Nekhludov sat up and gradually collected his thoughts; he noticed that the people in the room were glancing inquisitively at something going on at the door. He looked that way and saw a procession of men carrying a lady in a sedan chair. Her head was wrapped up in a light veil. The man in front, a footman, seemed familiar to Nekhludov. He also remembered to have seen somewhere the man in the rear—a doorkeeper with braid on his cap. A stylish maid with a curled fringe and an apron was carrying sun shades, a bundle, and something in a round leather case. Farther behind came Prince Korchagin with his imposing chest and apoplectic neck, wearing a traveling cap, and after him—Missy, her cousin Misha, and the long-necked Osten, with his prominent Adam's apple and ever cheerful expression—a diplomat whom Nekhludov knew slightly; he was speaking emphatically, though jokingly, to Missy, who was smiling. The doctor, angrily puffing at a cigarette, brought up the rear of the procession.

The Korchagins were going from their own estate near the city to the estate of the prince's sister, which was on the Nizhni railway.

The procession with the chairmen, the maid, and the doctor, vanished into the ladies' waiting room, exciting the respect and curiosity of all beholders; but the old prince stayed behind; seating himself at a table he immediately called a waiter and ordered something to eat and drink. Missy and Osten also stopped in the dining room and were about to sit down when they saw a friend entering the room, and at once walked up to her. It was Nekhludov's sister, Natalya Ivanovna, accompanied by Agrafena Petrovna. She looked around and saw Missy and Nekhludov almost simultaneously. She greeted Missy first, merely nodding to her brother; then, having kissed Missy, she addressed him.

"So I have found you at last!"

Nekhludov rose, greeted Missy, Misha, and Osten, and stood for a few minutes chatting with them. Missy told him that they had had a fire at their country house and were obliged to go to their aunt's. Osten seized the opportunity to tell a funny story about a fire. Without heeding him, Nekhludov spoke to his sister.

"How glad I am that you came," he said.

"I have been here for some time," she replied. "I came with Agrafena Petrovna." She pointed at Agrafena Petrovna who, in a waterproof cloak and a bonnet, bowed to him with some constraint and remained standing at a distance, not wishing to intrude. "I have been looking for you everywhere."

"I fell asleep on this sofa. I'm so glad you came," repeated Nekhludov. "I began a letter to you."

"Really? What about?" she asked with a startled look.

Missy, noticing that a private conversation was taking place between brother and sister, withdrew surrounded by her cavaliers, while Nekhludov and his sister sat down on a velvet sofa by the window near some luggage—a box and a traveling rug.

"When I left you last night I wanted to come back and say how sorry I was—but I didn't know how your husband would take it. I shouldn't have spoken to him as I did, and it worried me," said Nekhludov.

"I was certain that you did not mean it," said his sister. "You know how it is . . ." and the tears came to her eyes as she touched his hand. Her words were not clear but he understood them and was touched by what she was trying to express: that apart from the love for her husband which filled her heart, her love for her brother also meant a great deal to her, and that every misunderstanding between them caused her much suffering.

"Thank you, thank you. . . . But—what things I have seen today!" he exclaimed, suddenly recalling the second of the dead convicts. "Two convicts have been murdered."

"Murdered? How?"

"Murdered. They were made to march in this heat and two of them died of sunstroke."

"Impossible! When did it happen? Today?"

"Yes, just now. I saw their corpses."

"But why—murdered? Who murdered them?" asked Natasha.

"Whoever it was that compelled them to march," said Nekhludov, annoyed by the feeling that she was looking at the matter through her husband's eyes.

"Ah, dear God!" exclaimed Agrafena Petrovna, who had now approached them.

"We haven't the slightest idea of the things that are done to these unfortunate beings, and yet we ought to know," said Nekhludov, glancing at the old prince, who, with a napkin under his chin, was sitting at a table with a bottle before him and had just looked around at Nekhludov.

"Nekhludov!" he cried, "won't you take something before you start? There's nothing better on a journey!"

Nekhludov refused and turned away.

"But what can you do about it?" continued Natalya Ivanovna.

"I shall do what I can. I don't know what, but I feel that I must do something, and what I can do I shall."

"Yes, yes, I quite understand. But tell me," she said, glancing at the Korchagins, "is it all over between you and . . ."

"Yes. And I believe we parted without regret on either side."

"It is a pity. I'm sorry. I like her. But never mind. But even if this is so, why do you want to bind yourself? Why are you going?" she asked timidly.

"Because I must," he replied gravely and drily, by way of

putting an end to the conversation. But, in the same moment, he felt ashamed of showing coldness toward his sister. "Why shouldn't I tell her about everything?" he said to himself; "Agrafena Petrovna might as well hear it, too," he thought, glancing at the old servant. Her presence made him even more determined to speak of his decision to his sister again.

"Are you thinking of my offer to marry Katusha? I must tell you that she has firmly refused," he said, and his voice shook, as it did always when he spoke of this. "She will not accept my sacrifice, but chooses to make the sacrifice herself —and, in her present position, that means a great deal. I cannot allow this sacrifice if it is only a passing impulse. I am going to follow her wherever she may be, and I'm going to make things as easy for her as I can."

Natalya Ivanovna made no reply. Agrafena Petrovna, shaking her head, looked at her questioningly. At that moment the procession reappeared from the ladies' waiting room. The same handsome footman, Philip, and the doorkeeper, were carrying the princess. She told them to stop and called Nekhludov to her side, extending her white, jeweled hand with a languishing air, fearing he should grasp it too firmly.

"*Epouvantable!*" (She meant the heat.) "I cannot endure it! *Ce climat me tue.*" After some remarks about the horrors of the Russian climate she invited Nekhludov to visit them, and gave the men a signal to go on.

"Be sure and come," she added, turning her long face toward Nekhludov as they were bearing her away.

Nekhludov went out onto the platform. The procession with the princess turned to the right toward the first-class waiting rooms. Then Nekhludov with the porter who was carrying his things, and Tarass with his sack, turned to the left.

"We are traveling together," said Nekhludov to his sister, indicating Tarass, whose story he had already told her.

"Are you really going to travel third-class?" said Natasha, as Nekhludov paused before a third-class carriage which Tarass and the porter with the luggage had already entered.

"Yes, I prefer to be with Tarass," he said. "Now—one thing more: I have not yet given the land in Kuzminskoe to the peasants, so that in the event of my death it will come to your children."

"Don't, Dmitri," said Natalya Ivanovna.

"But even if I should give the land away," he continued, "all I want to say is, the remainder of the property will be theirs. It is unlikely that I shall marry, and, even if I do, there won't be any children, so . . ."

"Please don't say that, Dmitri," said Natasha, but Nekhludov perceived that she was pleased.

At the front of the train a small group of people was gathered outside a first-class carriage, staring at the compartment into which Princess Korchagina had been carried. Most of the passengers were already in their seats. The late ones hurried clattering along the wooden station platform; the porters slammed the doors, telling the passengers to get in and the friends who had come to see them off to get out.

Nekhludov entered the hot, evil-smelling carriage, but at once went out onto the small platform at the back.

Natalya Ivanovna, in her fashionable bonnet and wrap, stood with Agrafena Petrovna outside the carriage and appeared to be trying, unsuccessfully, to think of something to say. She could not say *"Ecrivez,"* because she and her brother had often laughed over this word, so frequently repeated to people starting on a journey. The brief talk about money matters and the legacy had immediately put an end to the old warm feeling between them of being brother and sister, and now they were estranged. So that Natalya Ivanovna was glad when the train started and she could only nod her head and say again in a sad and tender voice, "Good-by, Dmitri, good-by."

But no sooner was the car out of sight than she began thinking out the best way of reporting to her husband the conversation with her brother, and her face became anxious and grave.

Nekhludov also, though he had the kindest feelings for his sister and had never hidden anything from her, now felt uncomfortable in her presence and was thankful to escape. He could not help feeling that the Natasha who once had been so dear to him no longer existed; that the woman in front of him was the slave of her husband, an unpleasant, dark, and hairy stranger. He perceived it clearly as soon as he had begun speaking of things that concerned her husband—of the land question and the inheritance—for her face had lit up with special animation, and this made him very sad.

The sun beating down all day had made the large, overcrowded third-class carriage so oppressively hot that Nekhludov did not go inside but remained on the platform. Even there, however, there seemed to be no current of air and Nekhludov breathed easily only when the train had left the houses behind and he began to feel the breeze. *Yes, they were murdered.* He repeated to himself the words he had used to his sister, and the handsome face of the dead convict arose in his imagination with extraordinary sharpness—the smiling mouth, the stern forehead, and the delicate small ear on the blue, shaven skull.

"Most terrible of all," he thought, "was that the man has been murdered—but no one knows by whom. Yet it *is* murder —there is no doubt of that. He was led out with the others, on Maslennikov's instructions. Maslennikov probably made out the usual order, putting his stupid, florid signature on some formal document with a printed heading, and naturally he won't consider himself responsible. The prison doctor is even less to blame. He did his duty carefully, he picked out the ones who were not strong, and couldn't have been expected to foresee the terrific heat or that the gang was going to be taken out so late in the day, or that they were going to be so closely packed together. What about the inspector?—but he was only obeying orders to send off a certain number of exiles and convicts of both sexes on a given day. Nor can the officer commanding the escort be blamed, for his duty lay in accepting a certain number and dispatching a certain number. He led them off according to instructions, and he couldn't have known that those two robust-looking men were going to fall and die. Nobody is to blame, and yet the men are dead— killed by the very people who cannot be held to blame for their deaths.

"And all this," said Nekhludov to himself, "is because all these governors, inspectors, police officers, and policemen consider that there are circumstances when man owes no humanity to man. Every one of them—Maslennikov, the inspector, the officer of the escort—if he had not been a governor, an inspector, an officer, would have thought twenty times before sending people off in such a press and in such heat; they would have stopped twenty times on the way if they had noticed a man getting faint and gasping for breath; they would have led him apart from the others, allowed him to rest in the shade, given him water, and then, if anything had happened, they would have shown some pity. But they—they did nothing like that, they even prevented others from helping: and this was only because their eyes were set not on human beings and their duty toward them but on the duties and responsibilities of their office, which they placed above their duty to men. That is the whole truth of the matter.

"If a man has admitted, be it for a single hour or in a single instance, that there can be something more important than the love he owes his fellow men, he may commit every conceivable crime and yet consider himself innocent."

Nekhludov was so absorbed in his thoughts that he had not noticed the change in the weather. The sun had gone behind a low, ragged cloud, and from the west another cloud, dense and pearly gray in color, was coming up fast. He could see the rain far away in the distance, across the fields and across the forest, falling in slanting, driving streamers. The air was humid. From time to time flashes of lightning tore across the cloud and claps of thunder mingled more and more frequently with the noise of the train. The cloud came steadily nearer and the wind drove the slanting rain onto the platform of the carriage and onto Nekhludov's coat. He crossed to the other side and breathed in the refreshing moisture and the fragrant smell of growing wheat standing in the earth now wet after waiting long for rain; he watched the gardens go spinning past, the thickets and fields of ripening yellow rye, the lines of green oats and the black furrows between the dark green rows of potatoes in flower. Everything looked as if it had been varnished: the green was greener, the yellow yellower, and the black blacker.

"More, more!" said Nekhludov, rejoicing at the sight of the reviving fields and gardens.

But the rain, though violent, did not last long. The cloud partly spent itself and partly passed over, and soon the last fine drops were falling gently on the damp ground. The sun came out again, everything glistened, and the low arch, broken at one end, of a brilliant rainbow, the band of violet particularly bright, glowed in the eastern sky.

"What was I thinking about?" Nekhludov asked himself, these changes on the face of nature lost to view as the train rushed into a deep cutting with high, sloping sides. "Ah, yes, I remember—I was thinking that the inspector, the officer of the escort, and all the others are for the greater part gentle and kind: it is their calling that makes them cruel."

He remembered the indifference of Maslennikov when he was told what was going on in the prison, the severity of the inspector, the harshness of the officer of the escort when he was refusing places on the carts to the people who asked for them, and would pay no heed to the woman on the train who was in child labor. Evidently the reason why all these people were so invulnerable, so immune from pity, was simply that they were officials. "As officials, they can no more be filled with pity than this paved ground can absorb the rain from heaven," he thought, as he looked at the sides of the cutting paved with stones of many colors, down which the rainwater was streaming, instead of soaking into the earth. "It may be necessary to pave the cutting, but it is sad to think that so much soil must be made barren when it might yield grain, grass, shrubs, and trees. And it is the same among men," he thought; "it is possible that governors, inspectors, and policemen may be useful, but it is terrible to see men lose the quality that distinguishes them from beasts—pity and love for one another.

"This is what it comes to," he went on. "These men accept as a law something that is not a law, and they do not accept the eternal, immutable law that God Himself has written in man's heart. That is why I am so unhappy in their presence," he thought. "They frighten me, and they are indeed terrible. More terrible than brigands. After all, a brigand may be open to pity, but these men are not. They are as safe from pity as these stones are from vegetation. That is what makes them so terrible. Pugachev and Razin[1] are considered terrible—but these men are a thousand times worse. Suppose a problem in psychology was set: What can be done to persuade the men of our time—Christians, humanitarians or, simply, kindhearted people—into committing the most abominable crimes with no feeling of guilt? There could be only one way: to do precisely what is being done now, namely, to make them governors, inspectors, officers, policemen, and so forth; which means, first, that they must be convinced of the existence of a kind of organization called 'government service,' allowing men to be treated like inanimate objects and banning thereby all human brotherly relations with them; and secondly, that the people entering this 'government service' must be so unified that the responsibility

[1] Leaders of the rebellion in Russia: Razin in the seventeenth and Pugachev in the eighteenth century.—Tr.

for their dealings with men would never fall on any one of them individually. Otherwise it would be impossible in our times for human beings to countenance such cruel deeds as those I have witnessed today. It all comes from the fact that men think there are circumstances when they may treat their fellow beings without love, but no such circumstances ever exist. Inanimate objects may be dealt with without love: you can cut down trees, make bricks, and hammer iron without love. But human beings cannot be treated without love—just as bees cannot be handled without care. That is the nature of bees. If you handle bees carelessly you will harm the bees and yourself as well. It is just the same with men. And this cannot be otherwise, for mutual love is the fundamental law of human life. It is true that a man cannot force himself to love as he can force himself to work, but it does not follow that men may be treated without love, especially if something is required from them. If you feel no love for men—leave them alone. Occupy yourself with things, with your own self, with anything you please—but not with men. In the same way as it is harmful to eat except when one is hungry, so men can be handled without harm, and to some good end, only when one loves them. But once a man allows himself to treat men unlovingly, as I treated my brother-in-law yesterday, for instance, then there is no limit to the suffering and cruelty he may be brought to inflict on others—I have seen just such a thing happen today—and there is no limit to the suffering he may inflict on himself, as the whole of my own life has shown. Yes, that is true," thought Nekhludov. "Everything is all right now," he said to himself again and again, and felt a double joy in the refreshing coolness after the day's intense heat and in the certainty of understanding clearly a question that had occupied him so long.

***

CHAPTER FORTY-ONE

THE carriage where Nekhludov had a seat was only half full. Here were servants, factory workers, butchers, clerks, Jews, workingmen's wives, a soldier, two ladies (one young, the other elderly, with bracelets on her bare arm), and a severe-looking gentleman wearing a black cap with a cockade on it. They all sat quietly, once the first bustle was over. Some were cracking sunflower seeds, some smoking cigarettes, others had started lively conversations with their neighbors. Tarass, looking very happy, was sitting to the right of the central passage, keeping a seat for Nekhludov, and meanwhile carrying on an animated conversation with a man in a sleeveless coat who sat opposite him—a gardener on his way to a new job, as Nekhludov found out later.

Before reaching Tarass, Nekhludov stopped in the passage near a venerable old man with a white beard, also wearing a sleeveless coat, who was conversing with a young woman in peasant dress. Beside her sat a seven-year-old girl in a new sarafan[1], cracking sunflower seeds. Her hair was almost white and plaited into a little pigtail. Her legs did not reach the floor by a long way.

Looking up, the old man gathered up the skirt of his coat to make room for Nekhludov, saying in a friendly voice:

"Won't you sit here?"

Nekhludov thanked him and took the offered place, whereupon the young woman resumed her interrupted story.

She was talking about her husband whom she had just visited in the town where he worked.

"Yes, I was there all Carnival week and now I've been again, the Lord be praised, and I mean to go again at Christmas time."

"That's right," said the old man, with a glance at Nekhludov. "You must go and see him sometimes. It's easy for a young man to go astray, living in the town."

"No, Grandad, my man's not that sort. There's no nonsense about *him*. He's quiet as a young lass—and he sends me home every penny he earns. I can't tell you how glad he was to see the little girl, too," said the woman, smiling.

The little girl sat cracking the seeds and spitting out the shells; she looked with calm, intelligent eyes at the old man and Nekhludov, as though to confirm what her mother said.

"Well, if he's so wise that's better still," said the old man. "None of that sort of thing?" he added, nodding toward a married couple, evidently factory workers, sitting on the other side of the compartment. The husband with his head thrown back was pouring vodka down his throat out of a bottle, while his wife, holding a bag that had carried the bottle, was staring at him hard.

"No, my man doesn't smoke and doesn't drink," said the young woman, glad of another chance to speak in praise of her

[1]Russian peasant frock.—Tr.

husband. "There aren't many in this world like him, Grandad. That's the sort of man he is," she added, turning to Nekhludov.

"That's good," said the old man, still gazing at the factory worker, who had finished his drink and was offering his wife the bottle. She put it to her mouth, laughing and shaking her head. When he noticed that the old man and Nekhludov were looking at them, the factory worker addressed Nekhludov.

"Well, sir? Staring at us because we're having a bit of a drink, eh? When we're working, you see, nobody looks at us; but whenever we have a drop everybody's watching. I earn my money, you see, and so I drink and so I treat my wife. That's the long and short of it."

"Yes, yes, I see," said Nekhludov, not knowing just what answer to make.

"Isn't that right, sir? My wife's a steady woman. I love my wife because she sympathizes with me. Am I speaking the truth, Mavra, or am I not?"

"There, take it, I've had enough," said the wife, giving back the bottle. "And don't be gabbling like a fool."

"That's the way she is," said the workman. "She's all right most of the time, but now and again she squeaks like a wheel that needs greasing. Am I speaking the truth, Mavra, or am I not?"

Mavra laughed and waved her hand tipsily.

"There you go again—"

"Yes, she's all right for a time, but let the reins get under her tail, and she lets you know what's what. That's true. Excuse me, sir, I've had a drop and that's that . . ." he said, and putting his head on the lap of his smiling wife, prepared to go to sleep.

Nekhludov stayed a little while beside the old man, who told him about himself: he was a stove builder who had built many a stove in his day, was fifty-three and would like to take a rest but never found a chance. He had been to the city where he had started his children in business, and was now going to his village to visit his relatives. When the old man finished his story, Nekhludov rose and went to the seat that Tarass had kept for him.

"Sit down, sir, we'll put the bag here," said the gardener who was sitting opposite Tarass, in a friendly tone, and looking up into Nekhludov's face.

"It's a bit of a squeeze, but we're all friends," said the smiling Tarass in his singsong voice, and with his strong hands he lifted his eighty-pound sack as if it were a feather and put it beside the window. "There's plenty of room, and there'd be no harm in standing, either, or even in lying under the seat. This is a comfortable place, I can tell you. We won't quarrel about that," he went on, beaming good-naturedly.

Tarass used to say of himself that unless he had been drinking, he had no words, but drink helped him to find the right words and plenty of them. It was indeed true that when he was sober he was generally silent, but when he had been drinking (which happened rarely and only on special occasions), he became pleasantly talkative. He talked a great deal and he talked well—very simply, truthfully, and above all with great kindliness, which shone out of his blue eyes and gentle smile.

He was like this today. Nekhludov's presence silenced him only for a few moments. After he had arranged his sack he seated himself in his old place, folded his strong work-worn hands on his knees, and looking straight into the gardener's eyes, went on with his story. He was telling his new friend about his wife who was being exiled to Siberia, and why he was going with her.

Nekhludov, who had never heard the details of this affair, listened with interest. The story, when he came in, had reached a point where the poisoning had already happened and the family had found out about it.

"I am telling him about my troubles," said Tarass, turning to Nekhludov with heartfelt friendliness. "I've come across such a goodhearted man here that I am telling him all about it."

"Go on, go on," said Nekhludov.

"So, brother, that's how the thing came to light. Then my mother took the pancake, the one I told you about, you know. 'I'm going to the police officer,' says she. 'Wait a bit, old woman,' says my father—he's a very sensible man—'she's scarce more than a child, she can't have known what she was doing. Show her a little pity, and she'll come to her senses, maybe.' But no, sir, she wouldn't listen. 'She'll poison us like cockroaches if we keep her,' says she. So she went to the police, and the sergeant came in hot haste and called the witnesses."

"And what did you do?" asked the gardener.

"Me? I was rolling about with the pain, being sick. I was bringing up my stomach, I couldn't so much as speak. So my father harnessed up the horse, put Fedosya into the cart, and carried her off to our police station; and from there he drove her to the magistrate. As for her, let me tell you, she told the prosecutor the whole story—just what she'd told at home— where she got the arsenic and how she kneaded the dough. 'What made you do it?' says he. 'I am sick of him,' says she.

'I'd sooner go to Siberia than live with him'—she meant with *me*," said Tarass with a smile. "That was the way she made a confession of the whole business. Of course she was put in jail straight away. Father came home alone. Harvest time was just coming on and we'd only one woman to help us—that was my mother, and she wasn't good for much. So we thought, perhaps we might get Fedosya back on bail. Father went to see the magistrates, but nothing came of it. In fact, he went to five of them and was just going to give it up when he stumbled on a clerk—he was a sharp one, I can tell you. 'Give me five rubles,' says he, 'and I'll get her out.' They settled on three. So I went to pawn the linen cloth that she'd woven herself, and gave him the money. And when he'd written the document," drawled Tarass, as though he was speaking of a shot about to be fired, "—it turned out all right. I went to town to fetch her myself. When I got there I put up my mare, took the document and went to the jail. 'What is it you want?' 'So and so,' says I, 'you've got my wife here in jail.' 'And have you a paper?' So I gave him the paper. 'Wait,' says he, looking it over. So I took a seat on a bench. It was past noon. The head man comes out and says, 'Are you Birukov?' 'That I am.' 'Well, you may take her,' says he. And so they opened the gates and brought her out in her own clothes, just as it should be. 'Well, come on,' says I. So we went to the inn, I paid for putting up the mare, then I harnessed her and made a seat for Fedosya with the hay that was left. She sat down, wrapped herself up in a shawl, and we started. She never spoke a word and I kept still. As we drew near the house she asked, 'Is mother living?' 'Yes,' I said. 'And father?' 'He is alive, too.' 'Forgive me, Tarass, for my foolishness,' she said, 'I didn't know what I was doing.' 'Don't talk so much,' said I. 'Who talks much says little. I've forgiven you long ago.' And that's all that was said. When we came home she threw herself on her knees at my mother's feet. 'God will forgive you,' says mother. And father greeted her, saying, "What's the use of going over an old story? Try and be good. Now,' he said, 'is not the time for all that, there's the harvest to be gathered in. Back of Skorodnoe, on the manured field the rye is so thick, praise the Lord, that it's all tangled up; you couldn't straighten it with an iron crowbar. You and Tarass had better go and see to it tomorrow." And from that time forward she started to work with a will. She was a sight to behold. At that time we rented three *dessyatins*, and God sent us a wonderful crop—oats and rye. Sometimes I did the mowing while she bound the sheaves, and sometimes we would both of us mow.

I'm a good worker when I take hold of a job, but she goes ahead of me whatever she does. She's young and active, in the prime of her life, and so eager to work—it's hard to keep her back. When we used to come home at night, her fingers would be swollen and her hands aching, and yet she'd be out into the barn before supper, getting the binder ready for the next day. A different woman, I can tell you!"

"And did she treat you any better?" asked the gardener.

"I should say so! She clung to me as if we were one heart. Whatever it was I was thinking of, she always understood. Even mother, angry as she was, couldn't help saying, 'The old Fedosya has been charmed away: this is a different woman.' Once we were driving home, bringing the sheaves, sitting on the front of the cart side by side, and I said to her, 'Tell me, Fedosya, what made you think of doing it?' and she said, 'What made me? Why, I didn't want to live with you, I'd rather have been dead.' 'And how is it now?' 'Now,' says she, 'you're in my heart.'" Tarass paused and with a joyful smile shook his head in amazement. "When we'd finished harvesting I took the flax to be steeped and when I got home"—he paused for a moment—"there was the summons. *Appear in court*, it said. And we'd forgotten all about what she'd done."

"It's the work of the Evil One," said the gardener. "Nobody by himself would ever think of harming another human soul. I used to know a man—" and he was about to tell his story when the train began to slow up. "I reckon we're coming to a station," he said. "I'll get out and have a drink."

The conversation came to an end, and Nekhludov followed the gardener onto the wet platform.

❧

CHAPTER FORTY-TWO

WHILE still in the train, Nekhludov had noticed several elegant carriages in the station yard, drawn by three and four horses with tinkling bells on their harness. As he stepped out onto the wet, dark boards of the platform he saw a small party of people standing near the first-class carriage; conspicuous among them were a tall stout lady in a waterproof coat, wearing a hat decorated with expensive feathers, and a tall, thin-legged young man in a cycling suit, an enormous well-fed dog by his side. Behind them a coachman and several footmen holding wraps and umbrellas, who had also come to meet the train.

There was an air of wealth and calm self-confidence about the whole group, from the stout lady down to the coachman holding up his long coat. An inquisitive and servile crowd at once gathered around them: the stationmaster in a red cap, a gendarme, a thin young woman wearing Russian national costume (of the type one finds on every railway station during the summer), a telegraph clerk, and several passengers, both men and women.

In the youth with the dog Nekhludov recognized young Korchagin, the schoolboy. The stout lady was the princess's sister, to whose estate the Korchagins were now on their way. The guard, in gold braid and shiny knee boots, opened the door of the railway carriage and stood holding it open deferentially, while Philip and a porter with a white apron carefully carried out the long-faced princess in her folding chair. The sisters greeted each other and then, after some talk in French as to whether the princess should go in a closed or an open carriage, the procession made its way toward the exit, the lady's maid with her curly fringe following at the end, carrying boxes and parasols.

In order to avoid meeting them and having to say good-by all over again, Nekhludov stopped a short distance from the door and waited for the procession to pass. The princess, her son, Missy, the doctor, and the maid went out first; the old prince remained behind with his sister-in-law. Nekhludov was too far off to hear anything but a few disconnected French sentences in their conversation. As so often happens, one sentence spoken by the prince stayed in his memory for some unaccountable reason, with every tone and inflection of the voice. *"Oh, il est du vrai grand monde, du vrai grand monde,"* the prince was saying loudly and pompously, as he walked out of the station with his sister-in-law, followed by the respectful porters and railway officials.

Just at that moment, from behind the corner of the station building there suddenly appeared a crowd of workmen in bast shoes, carrying sheepskin coats and sacks over their backs. With soft yet determined steps, they went up to the nearest carriage and were about to get in when a guard drove them away. They passed on to the next carriage, hurrying and stumbling over one another's feet, and began getting in, their sacks catching against the corners and door of the carriage; but another guard noticed them from the door of the station where he was standing and shouted at them angrily. The men, who by now were already inside, hurried out again and went on with the same silent, firm steps to the next carriage—the one where Nekhludov had his seat. A guard was again going to stop them when Nekhludov told them that there was plenty of room inside and that they had better get in. They obeyed, and Nekhludov followed them in. They were about to take their seats when the gentleman with the cockade, and the two ladies, taking their attempt to settle in the carriage as a personal affront, protested indignantly and tried to turn them out. The workmen—there were about twenty of them, some old and some quite young, with wearied, haggard, sunburnt faces—began at once to push their way along the corridor, catching their sacks against the seats, partitions and doors. They evidently felt they were in the wrong and seemed ready to go on to the world's end and there sit down wherever they might be told, even on nails.

"Where are you pushing to, you devils? Sit down where you are!" shouted another guard, coming out into the corridor.

"*Voilà encore des nouvelles,*" said the younger of the two ladies, thinking that her excellent French would surely attract Nekhludov's attention. The lady with the bracelets only sniffed and made a face, and said something about the delights of sitting next to stinking peasants.

The workmen, experiencing the joy and relief of people who have escaped great danger, stopped and began to settle down, jerking their heavy sacks from off their shoulders and stowing them away under the seats.

The gardener, who had left his own seat to talk to Tarass, now went back, so that there were three seats unoccupied near Tarass. Three of the workmen took them but, when Nekhludov came up, were so embarrassed by his gentleman's clothes that they made as if to go; Nekhludov asked them to stay, himself sitting down on the arm of the seat next to the passage.

One of the workmen, about fifty years of age, exchanged surprised and even frightened looks with a younger man. It perplexed and astonished them that Nekhludov should give up his seat instead of shouting at them and driving them away in the natural way of gentlemen. They even feared that this might hold some evil consequences for them. When, however, they saw that Nekhludov meant no harm and was simply talking to Tarass, they calmed down and told a young lad who was with them to sit on a sack, insisting that Nekhludov should resume his place. At first the elderly workman who sat opposite Nekhludov drew away as far as possible and tucked in his legs for

fear of touching the gentleman, but after a while grew so
friendly that in talking to Nekhludov and Tarass he even
slapped Nekhludov familiarly on the knee whenever he reached
a point in his story that called for special attention. He told
them all about his life and his work in the peat bogs, whence he
and his comrades were now returning home. They had been
working there for two and a half months and were bringing
home their wages—which came to ten rubles only, for part had
been paid in advance when they were taken on.

They worked up to their knees in water, he said, from sunrise
to sunset, with a two-hour interval for dinner. "It's hard if
you're not used to it, of course," he said, "but after a while it's
not too bad—so long as there's enough to eat. At first the food
was bad, but after people complained it improved, and working
was easier."

Then he told them how for twenty-eight years he had gone
out to work and sent all his earnings home: first to his father,
then to his elder brother, and now to his nephew, who was looking after the family household. On himself he spent only two
or three of the fifty or sixty rubles he earned a year; they were
on luxuries, chiefly tobacco and matches. "But I'm a sinner—
I even drink a little vodka sometimes, when I'm tired," he added
with a guilty smile.

He told them, too, how the women worked at home; and how
that morning before the men had started on their journey the
contractor had treated them to half a bucket of vodka; how one
of them had died and another had to return home ill. The sick
man was in a corner of the same carriage. He was a young fellow with an ashen-gray face and blue lips, evidently worn out
by malaria.

Nekhludov approached him, but the lad looked up with such
a severe, tormented expression that Nekhludov did not care to
trouble him with questions but advised the elderly workman to
buy him quinine, and wrote the word down on a slip of paper.
He wanted to give him the money for it, but the workman said
he would pay for it himself.

"Well, all the times I've traveled about, I've never come
across a gentleman like him before," he said to Tarass. "Instead of punching your head, he goes and gives his place to you.
It seems there are different kinds of gentlefolk," he concluded.

"Yes, this is quite a new and different world," Nekhludov
was thinking, looking at the lean, muscular limbs, the coarse,
homemade clothes, and the sunburnt, kindly, weary faces. He
felt himself surrounded by a kind of people that was new to him,

with the serious interests and the genuine joys and sufferings of a life of labor.

"Here it is—*le vrai grand monde*," he thought, remembering the words of Prince Korchagin and all the idle, luxurious world of the Korchagins with its contemptible pettiness. And he experienced the joy of a traveler discovering a new, unknown, and beautiful world.

END OF BOOK II

BOOK III

CHAPTER ONE

THE gang to which Maslova was assigned had now covered about three thousand miles. As far as Perm she traveled, by train and boat, with convicts sentenced on criminal charges. Then Nekhludov succeeded in having her transferred to the "political" group; this was on the advice of Vera Bogodukhovskaya, who was herself with the politicals.

Maslova found the journey to Perm very hard, both physically and morally: physically, because crowded living conditions, filth, and horrible vermin allowed no rest by day or night; morally, because the men, as revolting as the vermin, swarmed round her and gave her no peace. Habits of cynical debauchery had taken such a hold on the women as well as on the men prisoners, warders, and soldiers of the escort, that unless a woman was willing to prostitute herself, she had to be constantly on her guard, especially if she was young. This continual state of anxiety and struggle was very hard, and Maslova was one of those who suffered most from such attacks, partly because her past life was known to everybody and partly because she was personally attractive. The determined resistance with which she met the men who annoyed her was taken as a direct insult and roused a feeling of resentment against her.

Friendship with Fedosya and Tarass brought her some comfort, however. Tarass, on learning of the molestations his wife was suffering, asked to be arrested himself so that he could protect her, and from Nizhni onward he traveled as a convict with the others.

Maslova's transfer to the party of political prisoners greatly improved her situation in all respects. To begin with, the politicals had better food and living quarters as well as gentler treat-

351

ment; next, she no longer had to suffer annoyance from men, and could live without being reminded of that past she was so anxious to forget; but the chief advantage was that she learned to know some people whose influence over her became strong and beneficial.

Whenever they came to a halting place, Maslova was allowed to stay with the political prisoners; but as she was a woman in robust health, she had to march with the criminals and so made on foot the whole journey from Tomsk. Two of the politicals also marched with her, Maria Pavlovna Shchetinina, the handsome girl with the lamblike eyes who had attracted Nekhludov's attention when he visited Bogodukhovskaya, and a certain Simonson, the dark, disheveled man with deep-sunken eyes whom Nekhludov had also noticed during that visit and who was exiled to the district of Yakutsk. Maria Pavlovna went on foot because she had given her place on the cart to a woman among the criminals who was pregnant and near her time, and Simonson because he thought it unfair to avail himself of a class privilege. These three used to set off in the early morning, leaving the other politicals to start later in the day and follow by cart; and this was the arrangement on the last day of the journey, just before they arrived at a large town where the party was to be handed over to a new commanding officer.

It was an early September morning. Snow and a drizzling rain were falling in turns and a cold wind blew in gusts. All the convicts of the party, about four hundred men and fifty women, were assembled in the yard of the halting station. Some were crowding around the chief of the convoy, who was distributing money for two days' rations to the orderlies appointed from among the prisoners, and some were bargaining with the women who had been admitted into the yard to sell provisions. The voices of prisoners counting their money and making purchases could be heard mingling with the shrill treble of the women hawkers.

Katusha and Maria Pavlovna, both wearing knee boots and short sheepskin coats, with shawls on their heads, came out of the house into the courtyard and went up to the hawkers who were sitting sheltered from the wind under the north wall of the yard and vying with one another over the sale of their goods: freshly baked pies made with brown flour, fish, vermicelli, porridge, liver, meat, eggs, and milk; one even had a roast pig to sell.

Simonson was also in the yard waiting for the party to start; he wore a waterproof jacket and rubber galoshes tied with string over woolen stockings: a vegetarian, he would not use the skin of slaughtered animals. Standing under the porch, he was jotting down in his notebook a thought that had just occurred to him: "If a bacillus were to examine a human fingernail, it would conclude that a man is inorganic substance. Similarly, men, having observed only the crust, state that the earth is inorganic substance. This is not correct."

Maslova was packing eggs, fish, rusks, and fresh white bread into a sack, while Maria Pavlovna was paying the hawkers, when a sudden stir ran through the crowd of prisoners. Everyone fell silent and began to take their places for the march. The officer came out of the building to give the last orders.

All went on as usual. The convicts had been counted, the chains examined, and the men manacled in pairs, when the officer was heard to shout angrily; this was followed by the sound of blows falling on a human body, then by the cry of a child. For a moment, everything was still. Next a dull, threatening murmur arose among the prisoners. Maslova and Maria Pavlovna went toward the source of the noise.

CHAPTER TWO

THIS is what Maria Pavlovna and Katusha saw when they drew near: the officer, a sturdy man with a fair mustache, was frowning and rubbing the palm of his right hand, which he had bruised in striking a convict on the face; he was shouting out coarse abuse. "I'll teach you"—foul abuse—"to argue"—more abuse—"Give her to the women! Now then, on with them!" he shouted.

He was insisting that one of the convicts—a man exiled by the communal decision of his village—should be manacled. The man's wife had died of typhoid fever in Tomsk and he had carried his little girl in his arms all the way from Tomsk. His plea that manacles would make him unable to carry the child so angered the commanding officer (who happened to be in a bad temper) that he gave the convict a beating for not obeying at once.[1]

In front of them a soldier was standing with another prisoner,

---

[1] An incident described by D. A. Linev in *Transportation.*—L.T.

a short, black-bearded man with manacles on one hand, who was looking gloomily at the officer from under his brows, waiting to be chained to the convict with the child. The officer again ordered the soldier to take the little girl away. A murmur arose among the prisoners and grew louder and louder.

"He's carried her all the way from Tomsk without manacles," said a hoarse voice from the back of the crowd. "It's a child, not a puppy."

"What'd he to do with the girl? It's against the law!" said another voice.

"Who said that?" shouted the officer, rushing into the crowd as though he had been stung. "I'll teach you the law! Who said that? You? You?"

"It's what we're all saying, because—" began a thickset, broad-shouldered convict. He did not finish. The officer beat him about the face with both his fists.

"So it's mutiny, is it? I'll teach you to mutiny! I'll have you shot like dogs! And I'll be thanked by the authorities for doing it! Take the girl."

The crowd fell silent. The soldier snatched the child, while another soldier manacled the prisoner, now submissively holding out his hand.

"Take her to the women," shouted the officer, readjusting his sword belt.

The child, trying to extricate her hands from the folds of her shawl, screamed at the top of her voice. Maria Pavlovna stepped forward and adressed the officer.

"Let me carry her, sir."

The soldier who was carrying the little girl halted.

"Who are you?" asked the officer.

"I am a political prisoner."

It was evident that Maria Pavlovna's handsome face and prominent beautiful eyes impressed the officer, who had noticed her on taking over command of the gang. He looked at her in silence, as though deliberating.

"You may carry her, if you like. It makes no difference to me. It's all very well for you to be sorry for them, but who'd be responsible if the man escaped?"

"How could he escape with the child?" asked Maria Pavlovna.

"Now, then—I've no time for arguing with you. Take her if you like."

"Shall I give her up, sir?" asked the soldier.

"You may."

"Come to me," said Maria Pavlovna, trying to coax the child to come to her.

But the child in the soldier's arms went on screaming and reaching out for her father, and would not go to Maria Pavlovna.

"Wait a moment, Maria Pavlovna; she'll come to me," said Maslova, taking a rusk out of her bag.

The child knew Maslova, and when she saw someone familiar holding out a rusk, allowed herself to be taken.

All were silent. The gates were opened and the gang trooped outside and formed up in their ranks. The prisoners were again counted, the baggage was loaded onto the carts, and those prisoners who were ill took up their seats. Maslova with the child in her arms returned to the women and stood beside Fedosya. Simonson, who had been watching all the time, walked resolutely up to the officer just as he had finished giving his orders and was about to climb into a trap.

"You have done wrong, sir," said Simonson.

"Go back to your place. This does not concern you."

"If I think you have done wrong, it is my concern to tell you so," said Simonson, looking the officer full in the face from under his heavy brows.

"Is the gang ready? Forward, march!" shouted the officer, paying no heed to Simonson; leaning on his driver's shoulder, he climbed into the trap. The gang moved off in a straggling column and began to march along a muddy road separated by ditches from dense forest on either side.

❖

CHAPTER THREE

AFTER six years of depraved, luxurious, pampered living, and two months spent in prison among the criminal prisoners, Katusha's life with the politicals seemed good to her, despite all its hardships. The daily marches of fifteen or twenty miles, with sufficient food and a day's rest between every two days of marching, strengthened her physically, while her new friendships opened a life full of interests such as she had never dreamt of. She had not only never met but could not even have imagined people so wonderful (so she expressed it) as her companions of the march.

"When I think that I wept when I was sentenced!" she said. "I shall thank God for it every day of my life! Now I know of things that I should never have known any other way." The principles that ruled their lives were plain and easy for her to see and, like a true daughter of the people, she fully sympathized with them. She understood that her new friends were for the people against the upper classes and, though themselves belonging to the upper classes, were giving up their privileges, their liberty, and even their lives for the people. This especially drew her admiration and esteem.

She admired all her new companions, but the one whom she particularly worshiped and loved with a peculiar, respectful, and rapturous feeling was Maria Pavlovna. She was deeply stirred by the conduct of this beautiful girl, who was the daughter of a general and spoke three languages, but lived like an ordinary working woman and gave away everything that her wealthy brother sent her; the clothes and the shoes she wore were of the commonest sort, poor in quality even, and she gave no thought to how she looked. This lack of coquetry particularly surprised and therefore attracted Maslova. She could see that Maria Pavlovna knew and was even pleased to know that she was beautiful, but far from enjoying the impression she made on men she was frightened of it and was disgusted and horrified by all love affairs. The men among her comrades who were aware of this, even those who might have been drawn toward her, no longer dared to show their admiration, but treated her as they would have treated a man. Strangers, however, had frequently annoyed her, and her strength, in which she had great pride, stood her in good stead.

"Once, in the street," she told Katusha with a laugh, "a man followed me, and to get rid of him I gave him a shaking that frightened him so much he ran away!"

She had become a revolutionary, she said, because from early childhood she had hated the way the upper classes lived, and loved the life of the common people; she had always been getting into trouble for going off to the maids' room or the kitchen or the stables, when she should have been in the drawing room. "But it was fun being with the cooks and the grooms, and our own set bored me to death. Then when I grew older I began to understand that our life was wrong. I had no mother, I wasn't fond of my father, and at nineteen I left my home and went off with a friend to work in a factory."

She had stayed at the factory for a while and then went to live in a village; later she had come back to the town and lived in lodgings where there was a secret printing press. It was there that she was arrested. Maria Pavlovna had never spoken of it herself, but Katusha found out from the others that she had been sentenced to hard labor because she had pleaded guilty to a charge of shooting, although in fact it was one of the revolutionaries who had fired in the darkness during a search by the police.

From the day that Katusha first met her, she noticed that whatever conditions Maria Pavlovna found herself in she never thought of herself but was always wanting to help others, in great matters as well as in small. One of her comrades at the time, Novodvorov, made the remark in joke that her favorite hobby was charity. And it was really so. She seemed to be wholly absorbed in finding opportunities to serve others, much as a sportsman spends his time in search of game. This sport had become a habit, the aim of her life, and she did it all so naturally that those who knew her had come to expect it of her and no longer appreciated it.

When Katusha joined the party, Maria Pavlovna felt aversion, even disgust for her. Katusha noticed this, but she also noticed how Maria Pavlovna later on tried to overcome her aversion and how friendly and kind she became. And the kindness and friendliness of this remarkable person so moved Katusha that she surrendered her whole heart; unconsciously, she accepted Maria Pavlovna's views and came to imitate her in everything.

Maria Pavlovna was in her turn touched by Katusha's devotion and began to love her. They were also drawn together by the repulsion they both felt to sexual love. One hated it because she knew all its horrors, while the other, having never experienced it, regarded it as something incomprehensible and repugnant, and offensive to human dignity.

❧

CHAPTER FOUR

MARIA PAVLOVNA's influence over Maslova was based on Maslova's love for Maria Pavlovna. Another active influence was that of Simonson, which arose from Simonson's love for Maslova.

All men rule their lives and deeds partly by their own ideas, partly by the ideas of others. The extent to which they do the one or the other is one of the chief things that differentiate men. Some people only play at thinking: their minds are like a driving wheel without a load; their acts are determined by laws, by traditions, by the ideas of other men. Some, on the contrary, base their acts on their own ideas, follow their own reasoning and bow to public opinion only on occasion, after much careful thought. Simonson belonged to the second of these types. He made up his own mind about the truth of a matter and then acted by his decisions.

As a boy, having come to the conclusion that his father's income as paymaster in a government department was dishonestly earned, he told his father that it ought to be given to the people. When his father, far from following this advice, lectured him for his foolishness, he left home and would never afterward accept one penny from him. Deciding that all the evil of the world arises out of ignorance, he became a village schoolmaster after leaving the university, and later joined the Populists. Both in the schoolroom and before the peasants he boldly put forward every cause which he believed to be just and condemned with equal boldness everything that seemed false and evil.

While he was being tried he decided that the judges had no right to sit in judgment upon him and told them so. When the judges ignored what he said and continued to hear his case, he decided that he would not answer their questions, and remained resolutely silent. He was exiled to the province of Archangel.

Here he worked out a religious doctrine, the essence of which was a theory that everything in this would is alive, and that everything hitherto called "inorganic" is part of a vast organism which no one has yet been able to comprehend. The task of man (one of the elements of this organism) is to preserve the life of all the other elements. Consequently, he considered it a crime to destroy any life whatsoever; he condemned war and capital punishment and the slaughter, by any means, both of human beings and animals. He also had his own theories about marriage: to increase and multiply seemed to him the lowest function of man, whereas his most important function was to serve what already lived. He found a confirmation of this idea in the presence of phagocytes in the blood. Celibates, according to him, were like phagocytes, whose mission it is to strengthen the weak or diseased parts of an organism. From the moment he came to that conclusion he lived accordingly, although, as a youth, his habits had been dissolute. He regarded Maria Pavlovna and himself as human phagocytes.

His love for Katusha was not a departure from principle, for it was purely platonic; he considered that such love could not hinder his activity as a phagocyte, but on the contrary would act as an inspiration to higher efforts on behalf of mankind.

Moral problems were not the only ones that he decided in this original way. He had a theory of his own about all practical matters; he had rules for the number of hours a man should work and rest, the kind of food he should eat, the kind of clothes he should wear, the proper lighting and heating of a house, and so on.

In spite of all this, Simonson was a very shy, modest man; but when he had once made up his mind nothing could shake him.

This was the man who, through loving her, won a decisive influence over Maslova. With a woman's instinct, she very soon guessed what had happened, and the knowledge that she was loved by such an extraordinary man raised her estimation of herself. Nekhludov's offer of marriage was based on generosity and knowledge of what had happened in the past, but Simonson loved her as he found her; he loved her simply because he loved her. Moreover, she felt that Simonson looked upon her as a woman above the average, different from other women, as someone of great moral qualities. Although unsure of what he understood these qualities to be, she was determined not to disappoint him and, striving after the highest she could imagine, was obliged to be as good as she knew how.

This all began in prison when, one visiting day, she noticed his kind, innocent, dark-blue eyes looking fixedly at her from under overhanging brows. It was then that she saw what a strange man he was and how strangely he looked at her; she saw his peculiar combination of sternness, emphasized by a frowning forehead and unruly hair, with good nature and child-like innocence. Later, when she joined the politicals in Tomsk and met him again, they exchanged no words, but their looks showed that they remembered each other, that each understood and was important for the other. Though they never had any serious conversation even after then, Maslova felt that when he was talking in her presence his words were spoken to her and that for her sake he tried to express himself as clearly as possible. They did not become intimate until he began marching in the ranks of the criminal prisoners.

CHAPTER FIVE

UNTIL they left Perm, Nekhludov saw Katusha only twice, when the prisoners traveled on a barge surrounded with wire netting, and again at Perm in the office of the prison. Both times she seemed reserved and unfriendly. When he asked her if she was comfortable or if she needed anything, she made evasive answers and appeared embarrassed. It seemed to him as if the hostile attitude of her earlier prison days had returned. Her depressed state of mind, which was only a result of the many annoyances to which she had been subjected by men, distressed Nekhludov. He feared that the exhausting and degrading circumstances in which she was placed during the journey might cause her to fall into her former state of inner conflict and despair which had made her so irritable with him, and to smoke and drink in the hope of forgetting herself. But he couldn't help her in any way because, during the early part of the journey, he had been unable to see her. It was only after she joined the politicals that he perceived the change—which he so longed for—that had overtaken her, and the groundlessness of his fears. The first time they met in Tomsk she seemed like her old self again. Neither sullen nor embarrassed, she greeted him joyfully and naturally, and thanked him for what he had done for her, particularly for having given him the chance to know the people with whom she was now traveling.

After two months marching in the gang, the change that had taken place in her was reflected in her general appearance. She was sunburnt and thin, and seemed older; little wrinkles had appeared on her temples and around her lips; her hair no longer fell in ringlets over her forehead but was covered with a kerchief; neither in dress nor in the way of arranging her hair nor in manner did she betray the smallest trace of coquetry. This change, which was still going on within her, made Nekhludov exceedingly happy.

Now he felt toward her as he had never felt before, and this feeling had nothing in common with either that early sense of romantic exaltation or the sensual love which he had afterward felt for her. Nor was it at all like the self-satisfaction, rooted in the sense of doing his duty, which had after the trial led him to make his offer of marriage. It was, quite simply, the same pity and tenderness that he experienced on first seeing her in the prison and which grew into a still stronger feeling after he visited her in the hospital and forgave her supposed intrigue with the doctor's assistant. (The injustice of that accusation had been fully revealed later on.) It was the same feeling, but with this difference: once it had been fleeting, now it was settled. Whatever he happened to be doing or thinking, his mood was always tender and pitiful, not toward Maslova alone, but toward the whole world.

This feeling had opened a spring of love in Nekhludov's heart, which till then had found no outlet, but now flowed out to everyone he met.

During the journey he discovered a sort of exaltation in himself that came out in an eagerness to help everyone—coachmen, soldiers, prison inspectors, and the governor himself. Meanwhile, owing to Maslova's transfer to the politicals, he had a chance of becoming acquainted with many of them, first in Ekaterinenburg where, not very closely guarded, they were kept together in one large cell; then, later on, he traveled in company with the five men and four women of Maslova's party. This intercourse with the political exiles completely changed his opinion of them.

From the very beginning of the revolutionary movement in Russia, and particularly after the first of March, Nekhludov regarded the revolutionaries with dislike and contempt. To begin with, he was repelled by the cruelty and secrecy of the methods they used in their struggle with the government, and above all by the cruel murders they committed. The overbearing self-assurance, common to all of them, was also offensive to him. But when he came to know them more intimately and saw what they had suffered at the hands of the government, often for no reason, he understood that they could not be other than they were.

Though the so-called "criminal" prisoners, too, suffered cruelty that was terrible and senseless, nevertheless there was some semblance of justice in their treatment both before and after sentence; but there was no justice at all in dealings with political prisoners, as Nekhludov had seen in the case of Shustova, and as he saw later in the case of many of his new friends. These people were like fish taken in a net. The whole catch is brought ashore, the larger fish are sorted out, and the smaller left to perish unheeded on the shore. Similarly, hundreds of people, not merely innocent but completely lacking the power to harm the government even if they had wished to, were kept imprisoned for years in places where they became consumptive or insane and sometimes took their own lives. These people were kept in prison because there was no particular reason for setting them free, and also because they might turn out to be useful as witnesses. The fate of these people—often acknowledged to be innocent even by the government itself—depended entirely on the whim of some police officer or spy or public prosecutor, magistrate, governor, or minister. If one of them happened to be restless or anxious to show especial zeal, he had some arrests made and then, following his mood, or the mood of a superior, he either set the prisoners free or kept them locked up. The higher officials acted in the same arbitrary way; everything depended on the man's ambition, or on whether he was on good or bad terms with his minister: shall he exile them to the other end of the earth? or sentence them to hard labor or death? or shall he, at the request of some noble lady, let them go?

The political offenders were treated like enemies in war and they naturally used the same methods that were used against them. Just as soldiers take their tone from public opinion, which turns their criminal acts into feats of heroism, the politicals were likewise affected by the opinions of their own circle where the cruelties they commit at the risk of liberty, life, and all that is dearest to man, are exalted as deeds of glory instead of being recognized for the evil things they really are. This accounted for the surprising fact that the mildest of men, incapable by nature of causing or even of witnessing the suffering of any living creature, could calmly plan and carry out the assassination of men; almost all of them considered murder lawful and just on certain occasions: in self-defense or as a means of promoting the general welfare. As to the great value they set on their particular aims (and consequently on themselves), this was the natural result of the concern shown by the government and of the cruel punishments they were subjected to. A high opinion of themselves was necessary to make bearable all that they had to bear.

When he knew them more intimately, Nekhludov came to the conclusion that they were neither the thoroughgoing villains some people imagined them to be, nor the heroes they were taken for by others, but very ordinary men among whom, as anywhere else, there were good, bad and mediocre individuals. Many of them had become revolutionaries because they sincerely considered it their duty to fight the evils of their time. Others had chosen that career from selfish and ambitious motives. The majority, however, had been attracted to revolutionary ideas by a longing for danger and risk, by the exhilaration of gambling with their lives—feelings common to ordinary energetic young men, as Nekhludov knew from his own experiences of war. The revolutionaries differed favorably from ordinary people in that their moral standards were higher. Abstinence, hard living, truthfulness, unselfishness, even a readiness to sacrifice their own lives for the common cause, were considered indispensable. Those among them, therefore, who were above the common run stood very far above it and achieved an exceptionally high moral quality, whilst those below the common run stood far below it and were often untruthful, hypocritical, conceited, and arrogant. That was why Nekhludov learned to have great love as well as respect for some of his new friends, though to others he remained indifferent and cold.

❧

CHAPTER SIX

NEKHLUDOV grew particularly fond of Kryltzov, a young man suffering from consumption who had been exiled and belonged to the same party as Katusha. Nekhludov made his acquaintance in Ekaterinenburg and had several talks with him during the journey. On one occasion they spent a whole day together at a halting station and Kryltzov, growing more and more communicative, told Nekhludov his whole story and explained why he had become a revolutionary.

Up to the time of his imprisonment, there was not much to tell. His father, a wealthy landowner from the south, died while he was still a child. He was an only son, brought up by his mother. He learned very easily both at school and at the university; he graduated in mathematics and was offered a university lectureship and the chance of traveling abroad; he hesitated to accept, however, for he was in love with a girl and thought of marrying her and taking an active part in local country politics. He wanted to do everything and could not make up his mind. At that time some fellow students asked him for a contribution to "the cause." He knew this was a revolutionary cause, in which at that time he took no interest whatever but, out of comradeship and vanity, and fearing to be considered a coward, he gave the money. The collectors were arrested and a note was found which proved that the money had been given by Kryltzov. He, too, was arrested, kept for a while at the police station and then sent to prison.

"The discipline in that prison was very loose," he told Nekhludov, sitting on the high sleeping bunk, with sunken chest, his elbows on his knees, with a glance now and then from his fine, fever-bright eyes. "As well as signaling between ourselves, we could walk about the corridors, share our provisions and tobacco, and we often sang songs together at night. I had a good voice. Yes. If it hadn't been for my mother, who was overcome with grief, I should have found prison life quite pleasant and interesting. It was there I met the famous Petrov, who later ended his life by cutting his throat with a piece of glass, and other revolutionaries, too. But I was not one myself. I also got to know my two neighbors, who had both been arrested over the same affair, with Polish proclamations in their possession, and were to be tried for their attempt to escape from the escort while being taken to the railway station. One was a Pole called Lozinski, and the other, Rozovski, was a Jew. This Rozovski was quite a boy. He said he was seventeen, but he looked about fifteen—small and slender, with bright black eyes, full of life, and very musical like most Jews. His voice was still breaking, but he sang beautifully. I saw them both taken to be tried. It was in the morning. At night they returned and told us that they had been condemned to death. No one had expected this. Their case was so unimportant: they had only tried to escape from the escort and hadn't even hurt anyone. And then it seemed so unnatural for a child like Rozovski to be condemned to death. So we all agreed in prison that it was only said to scare them and that the sentence would never be carried out. We were all very excited, of course, but soon calmed down and prison life went on as before. But one evening a watchman came to my door and mysteriously announced that the carpenters had come to put up the gallows. The gallows! I did not believe him at first. What gallows? But the old man was so excited that I could tell from his face that the gallows were for my two friends. I was just going to tap out a message to try and get in touch with the others, but then was afraid that those two might overhear. My companions were silent, too—evidently they also knew. There was dead silence that night in the passage and the cells. There was no tapping and no singing. About ten o'clock the watchman came again and said that the hangman had arrived from Moscow. He said this and went away. I began calling him back. Suddenly I heard Rozovski shouting to me across the passage: 'What do you want? Why are you calling him back?' I told him that he'd brought me some tobacco, but he seemed to guess something was wrong and began asking me questions: 'Why didn't we sing tonight? Why didn't anybody tap on the wall?' I don't remember what I answered, but I soon went away so as to avoid speaking to him. Yes, it was a night. I listened to every sound all night. Suddenly, toward morning, I heard doors opening and many footsteps along the passage. I went and stood at my little window. A lamp was burning in the passage. The first to go by was the inspector. He was a stout man with a great deal of self-assurance, but he looked frightened and pale as death, and walked with his head down. The assistant followed, frowning and determined, and behind him came the wardens. They passed my door and halted by the next door. Then I heard the assistant call out in a strange voice: 'Get up, Lozinski, and put on clean linen.' Yes. Then I heard the door squeak as they went into the cell. Then I heard Lozinski's steps as he crossed to the opposite side of the passage. But I could only see the inspector, pale as could be, buttoning and unbuttoning a single button on his coat and shrugging his shoulders. Yes. Then he quickly stepped aside, as though he was frightened of something. It was Lozinski who passed him at that moment and came up to my door. He was a handsome lad—you know, that fine Polish type, with a straight, broad forehead, a mass of fair, silky, curly hair, and beautiful blue eyes, full of vigor and health and youth. He stopped in front of my little window and I could see the whole of his face—a ghastly, livid face. 'Have you any cigarettes, Kryltzov?' I was just going to hand him some when the assistant, as though afraid of being late, hurriedly pulled out his own case and offered it to him. He took a cigarette and the assistant struck a match. He began to smoke and seemed to be thinking. Then, as though he had remembered something, he began to speak: 'It's cruel and unjust. I have committed no crime. I—' Something seemed to quiver in his young white throat—I couldn't tear my eyes away from it—and he stopped. Yes. Then from the corridor I heard Rozovski screaming in his thin Jewish voice. Lozinski threw down the end of his cigarette and walked away from my door. Then I saw Rozovski's face in the window. His childlike face with its moist black eyes was red and running with sweat. He was dressed in clean linen, but his trousers were too wide in the waist and he kept pulling them up with both hands, and was trembling all over. 'Didn't the doctor prescribe a herb drink for me, Anatoli Petrovich—didn't he? I'm not well. I want another sip of that herb tea.' No one answered and he looked inquiringly from me to the inspector, but I never understood what he meant. Yes. Then all at once the assistant put on his stern look again, and in a shrill, unnatural voice exclaimed: 'This is no time for joking. Come along!' Evidently Rozovski couldn't understand what was awaiting him and hurried, almost ran, ahead of the others along the passage. But a moment later he refused to move and I heard his piercing voice and wailing. I could hear a hubbub and the tramping of feet. Rozovski shrieked and wept. Then the sounds grew fainter, the door of the passage banged and everything was quiet. . . . Yes. And they were hanged. They were strangled with ropes. A watchman who saw it told me that Lozinski made no resistance, but Rozovski struggled a long time and was finally dragged to the scaffold by force and his head thrust into the noose. Yes. That watchman was a stupid fellow. 'People told me it would be horrible, but it wasn't, sir. As they were hanging their shoulders moved twice—just their shoulders. Like this'—and he demonstrated how the shoulders jerked up and then down. 'Then the hangman pulled on the rope, so as to tighten the noose, and that was the end. They didn't move any more.' No, it wasn't horrible," added Kryltzov, repeating the watchman's words and trying to smile. But the smile ended in a sob.

He was silent for some time, breathing heavily and repressing the sobs that were choking him.

"From that time I have been a revolutionary. Yes," he said. He became calmer, and briefly finished his story.

He joined the party of *Narodovoltzi*[1] and even came to be the head of a sabotage group which planned acts of terrorism to force the government to abdicate from power and call on the people to govern themselves. He went to Petersburg, Kiev, Odessa, and then abroad, and was successful wherever he went. But a man whom he trusted betrayed him. He was again arrested, imprisoned for two years, and condemned to death, though the sentence was changed to hard labor for life. While in prison he had become consumptive, and it was plain that he had not much longer to live in such conditions. He understood this, but had no regrets. He said that if he had his life over again, he would use it in the same way—that is, to destroy

---

[1] "Freedom of the people."—Tr.

the established order of things which made possible such sights as he had seen.

Knowing this man, and hearing his story, taught Nekhludov much that he had been unable to understand before.

CHAPTER SEVEN

ON the day of the encounter between the officer commanding the escort and the prisoner with the child, Nekhludov, who had spent the night at the village inn, woke late from having sat up into the night writing some business letters that had to be posted in the next town; he consequently left his lodgings later than usual and failed to overtake the gang on the road. It was dusk when he reached the village where the next halting station was to be. Having dried his clothes at the village inn, which was kept by a stout widow with an extraordinarily fat white neck, Nekhludov took his tea in a clean room decorated with many icons and pictures and then hurried to the halting place to ask permission of the officer to see Maslova.

At the six previous halts, although the officers had changed several times, he had always been refused admittance to the station; he had therefore not seen Katusha for more than a week. This strictness was due to the expected arrival of an important prison official, and now that he had passed on without so much as a cursory visit, Nekhludov hoped that the officer who had taken over command that morning would allow an interview.

Nekhludov's landlady suggested he should take her *tarantass* to the halting station, which was at the far end of the village, but he preferred to walk. A broad-shouldered young fellow with the physique of a Hercules, wearing newly tarred, strongly smelling knee boots, offered to show him the way. There was a drizzling rain, and it was so dark that Nekhludov could not see the guide three steps in front of him except when they passed occasional houses where light streamed from the windows. He could only hear the squelching of boots in the deep, sticky mud. Past the church square and down a long street of brightly lit windows Nekhludov followed behind his guide into complete darkness at the outskirts of the village. Soon, however, he could see the light of lanterns posted about the halting station. The fence surrounding the station, the dark, moving figure of the sentry, the sentry box, and a post painted with black and white stripes quickly came into sight. The sentry called out: "Who goes there?" When he understood that they were strangers, he would not even let them wait near the fence. But Nekhludov's guide was not intimidated by his severity.

"You're in a bad temper, aren't you?" he said. "Just shout, will you, and call the head man; we'll wait."

The sentry made no reply but shouted something through the gates and then stood watching the broad-shouldered young fellow scraping the mud off Nekhludov's boots with a stick by the light of the lantern.

A hum of men's and women's voices could be heard behind the fence. A couple of minutes later there came a sound of clanking iron, the wicket was opened, and a sergeant, a coat thrown over his shoulders, stepped out from the darkness into the light of the lantern and asked what they wanted. Nekhludov handed him his visiting card with a note asking the officer-in-charge to see him on personal business, and requested the sergeant to take this to the officer. This man was not so strict as the sentry, but he was extremely inquisitive. He insisted on knowing what business had brought Nekhludov and who he was, evidently hoping for a bribe and not wishing to let it escape. Nekhludov said that he had some special business and would make it worth his while to give the note to the officer. The sergeant nodded, took the note and went away. A few minutes later the gate clanked again and a line of women came through, carrying baskets, sacks, earthen jars, and covered pails made of bark, loudly chattering in their peculiar Siberian dialect. Town-fashion, they all wore fur jackets or overcoats, their skirts were tucked up high and their heads covered with kerchiefs. By the light of the lantern they peered curiously at Nekhludov and his guide, and one woman, evidently pleased to meet this well-built young fellow, affectionately showered on him a variety of Siberian oaths.

"The devil carry you off for a fiend!" she called out.

"I came to show a stranger the way," he replied. "And what did you have to bring?"

"Milk, and they have ordered more for the morning."

"Did they invite you to spend the night?" he asked her.

"Be damned to you, you liar!" she called back, laughing. "Come along and see us home."

The guide said something more that made the sentry laugh as well as the women; then, turning to Nekhludov, he added:

"Can you find your way back alone? You won't get lost, will you?"

"No, no, I'll be all right."

"After you pass the church it'll be the second house on your right, beyond the house with two stories. Here, take my stick," he said, handing Nekhludov a long stick taller than himself; then, splashing through the mud with his heavy boots, he disappeared in the darkness together with the women.

His voice, mingling with the voices of the women, could still be heard through the fog as the gate clanked and the sergeant came out, asking Nekhludov to follow him.

❖

CHAPTER EIGHT

THIS halting station, like all such stations along the Siberian road, was surrounded by a high palisade of sharp-pointed stakes and consisted of three single-story buildings standing in the middle of a yard. The largest had barred windows and was for prisoners, the second was for the soldiers of the escort, and the third, used also for administration, belonged to the officers. All the windows were lighted, giving a promise (albeit very deceptively) of something pleasant and cozy within the shining rooms. Lanterns stood gleaming in front of the porch and half a dozen more hung from the walls, lighting up the yard. The sergeant directed Nekhludov along duckboards to the porch of the smallest house. Mounting three steps, he let Nekhludov pass before him into the anteroom, which was lit by a small lamp and filled with the fumes of burning charcoal. A soldier in a coarse shirt, necktie, and black trousers, had only one of his top boots on and was using the other as a bellows for the samovar. Seeing Nekhludov, he went and helped him off with his leather coat, and then went into the inner room.

"He's here, your honor."

"Well, show him in," cried an angry voice.

"Go in through that door," said the soldier and hastily returned to the samovar.

In the adjacent room, which was lit by a hanging lamp, an officer was sitting at a table before two bottles and the remains of dinner; he had a long fair mustache and a very red face, and wore an Austrian jacket that fitted closely over his massive chest and shoulders. The warm room was filled with tobacco smoke and the strong, unpleasant smell of cheap scent.

When Nekhludov entered, the officer half rose and stared at the newcomer with an expression that was at once ironical and suspicious.

"What can I do for you?" he said and, without waiting for an answer, shouted toward the door: "Bernov, is that samovar ever going to be ready?"

"In a minute."

"I'll give you *in a minute!*" shouted the officer, his eyes flashing.

"I'm bringing it right away!" cried the soldier and came in with the samovar.

Nekhludov waited until he had placed the samovar on the table. The officer's cruel little eyes followed him out of the room as if he was taking aim where best to hit him. Then he made tea and got a square decanter of brandy and some biscuits out of his traveling case. When he had arranged these things on the table, he turned again to Nekhludov.

"Well, in what way can I assist you?"

"I should like an interview with one of the women convicts," replied Nekhludov, still standing.

"Is she a political convict? If so, that would be contrary to the law."

"No, she is not a political convict."

"Pray take a seat," said the officer. Nekhludov sat down.

"No, she is not a political prisoner," he repeated, "but, at my request, she has been allowed to march with the political prisoners—"

"Ah, yes, I know. The little brunette," interrupted the officer. "Well, that will be all right. Will you have a cigarette?"

He offered Nekhludov a box of cigarettes and, carefully pouring out two tumblers of tea, pushed one toward Nekhludov.

"Do have some tea," he said.

"Thank you, but I should like to see—"

"You'll have plenty of time for that; the night is long. I'll send for her."

"Why send for her? Can't I be taken to their room?"

"To the political prisoners' quarters? That's against the law."

"But I have been allowed to go in several times. If you are afraid that I might smuggle anything, I could do it just as well through her."

"No, sir, I don't think you could. She will be searched," said the officer, with a disagreeable laugh.

"Well, then, you'd better search me."

"I think we'll get along without that," said the officer, opening the decanter and holding it over Nekhludov's tea. "Will you allow me? No? Well, just as you like. Living as we do in Siberia, it is a delight to meet an educated man. There is no need to tell you how dreary our work is, and it's all the harder for someone who's been used to a different sort of life. People think that if a man is commanding an escort he must be an uncivilized boor; they don't seem to remember that he may have been born for other things."

The officer's red face, his scent, the ring on his finger and, above all, his unpleasant laugh, were repulsive to Nekhludov. But he was that day, as during the entire journey, in the serious and thoughtful mood that would not let him treat any human being with indifference or contempt. He now believed it to be his duty to "go all out," as he defined it. He therefore listened to the officer explaining his point of view, and then said seriously:

"I imagine that in your position there might be some comfort in easing the suffering of the prisoners."

"What do they suffer? You don't know these people."

"How do you mean? They are just like everybody else," said Nekhludov. "And some of them are innocent."

"Yes, of course, there are all sorts among them and, naturally, one feels sorry for them. Others won't overlook anything, but I try to lighten their condition where I can. I'd rather suffer myself than make them suffer. Some of our officers enforce every petty regulation, and even go so far as to shoot prisoners, but I always feel sorry for them. You'll have some more tea?" he added, pouring it out. "But what sort of woman is she, the one you want to see?"

"She is an unfortunate woman who happened to enter a brothel and was unjustly sentenced on a charge of poisoning. But she is really a very good woman."

The officer shook his head.

"Yes, I've heard of such things. There was one in Kazan—I must tell you about her. Her name was Emma. She was Hungarian by birth, but from her eyes you'd have taken her for a Persian," he went on, unable to keep from smiling at his recollections. "And what *chic* she had! Good Lord—she might have been a countess. . . ."

Interrupting him, Nekhludov returned to the previous topic.

"I am sure it lies in your power to ease the lives of these people while they are in your charge. I know that by doing so you will become much happier yourself," he said, trying to pronounce his words distinctly as though speaking to a child or a foreigner.

The officer gazed at him with sparkling eyes, only waiting for a pause that would give him a chance to go on with his story about the Hungarian woman with the Persian eyes, who had evidently become very vivid in his imagination and was taking up all his attention.

"Yes, that's all quite true," he said, "and I do pity them. But I was going to tell you about that woman, Emma. What do you suppose she did?"

"That does not interest me," said Nekhludov. "I must tell you frankly that although I myself was once a very different sort of man, I have come to loathe this kind of talk about women."

The officer looked up, disconcerted.

"Will you have more tea?" he asked.

"No, thanks."

"Bernov!" cried the officer, "take this gentleman to Vakulov and say he is to be admitted to the political cell. He may stay there till the roll is called."

❧

CHAPTER NINE

ACCOMPANIED by the orderly, Nekhludov went out again into the dark courtyard dimly lit by red lanterns.

"Where are you going?" a soldier called out.

"Cell No. 5," said the orderly.

"You can't pass this way. The gate is locked. You'll have to go around through the other porch."

"Why is it locked?"

"The sergeant locked it and went off into the village."

"Well, come along this way, then."

The soldier led Nekhludov along the duckboard to another entrance. A hubbub and a hum of voices from within could be heard in the yard, much like the sound from a beehive when the bees are getting ready to swarm. When Nekhludov approached and the door was opened, the hum grew louder and was found to be made up of shouts, curses, laughter, and the clank of chains; there hung over everything the well-remembered close, foul stench. The din of voices mingled with the clattering of chains and the terrible smell always affected Nekhludov with a moral nausea that soon turned to a physical feeling of sickness, one intensifying the other.

At the entrance to the building stood a large, stinking pail, the so-called *parashka,* and Nekhludov was met with the sight of a woman sitting on the edge of the pail; a man was standing talking to her, his pancake-shaped cap on one side of his head. On seeing Nekhludov he smiled and said with a wink:

"The tsar himself can't hold back his water."

The woman drew the skirt of her coat more closely about her and looked down in embarrassment.

The cells opened on a passage leading away from the entrance. The first cell was for families, the second for unmarried men, and at the very end of the passage were two smaller cells for the political prisoners. Four hundred and fifty people were crowded into these quarters, originally intended to hold one hundred and fifty; consequently the convicts, unable to find room in the cells, overflowed into the passage. Some were lying on the floor, others were moving about with freshly filled teapots in their hands, Tarass among them. He went up to Nekhludov and greeted him affectionately. His good-natured face was disfigured by dark bruises on his nose and under one eye.

"What have you done to yourself?" asked Nekhludov.

"Oh, nothing in particular," replied Tarass with a smile.

"They're always in some sort of brawl," remarked the soldier scornfully.

"It was all on account of a woman," said a convict, who was walking behind them. "He had a fight with Blind Fedka."

"How is Fedosya?" asked Nekhludov.

"She's all right. I'm taking her some hot water for tea," said Tarass, and entered the family cell.

Nekhludov looked in. The whole cell was crowded with men and women, some on the bunks and others underneath them. The steam from drying clothes filled the air, and there was an incessant chatter of women's voices. The second door opened into the unmarried men's cell. This was still more crowded, and the doorway itself was blocked by a noisy group of convicts in wet clothes who appeared to be either dividing something or settling a dispute. The sergeant explained that the prisoner appointed to buy provisions was paying out some of the food money to a sharper (who had won from, or lent money to, the prisoners) in return for little tickets made of playing cards. Seeing the sergeant and the gentleman, those who were nearest stopped talking and seemed annoyed at the interruption.

Among them Nekhludov noticed his acquaintance Fedorov, accompanied as usual by a pale miserable youth with raised eyebrows and a swollen face, and another still more repulsive man, a pock-marked tramp without a nose, who was reputed to have killed a comrade in the marshes while trying to escape, and then to have eaten his flesh. The tramp stood in the passage, a wet coat thrown over one shoulder, obstructing the passage-way and looking at Nekhludov in mocking defiance. Nekhludov walked around him.

Although such spectacles were familiar to Nekhludov, who had seen the same four hundred convicts in many different circumstances—in the heat, in dust clouds stirred up by the dragging of chained feet on the road, at halting places, in prison yards where during warm weather horrible, barefaced debauchery took place—nevertheless, every time he went among them and their attention was drawn to him, he felt, as now, ashamed and guilty and at the same time disgusted. While he saw that he had no right, considering the position in which they were placed, to expect them to be different, he still could not overcome his aversion. Just as he reached the door of the political prisoners, he heard a hoarse voice say:

"It's all right for them drones." This was followed by obscene swearing and a hostile, mocking burst of laughter.

❧

CHAPTER TEN

WHEN they reached the unmarried men's cell, the sergeant who had accompanied Nekhludov left him, saying that he would return before roll call. No sooner had he gone than a convict hurried up to Nekhludov, holding his chains off the ground; his feet were bare and he gave off a bitter smell of sweat. He whispered mysteriously:

"Sir, we beg you to help us. They've played a trick on the lad. They made him drunk, and today at the roll call he answered to the name of Karmanov. You must have it stopped, sir. We daren't do anything—they'd kill us." Glancing about him anxiously, he hurried away.

What had happened was this. Convict Karmanov had persuaded a lad, under sentence of exile, who was very like him in appearance, to exchange names in order that Karmanov himself would be exiled and the lad would go to the mines instead.

Nekhludov had already heard about the affair, from this very prisoner, a week before. He nodded as a sign that he understood and would do what he could, and went on without looking back.

He knew the prisoner, and was surprised by his action. They had first met in Ekaterinenburg, when the man asked Nekhludov to seek permission for his wife to join him. He was a man of middle height, an ordinary peasant of about thirty, condemned to hard labor for attempted robbery and murder. His name was Makar Devkin. His crime was unusual. Telling the story to Nekhludov he said it was not his doing but the devil's.

A stranger had called at the house of Makar's father and hired a sleigh for two rubles to take him to the next village, some twenty-five miles away. Makar was told by his father to drive; he harnessed the horse and made himself ready; then he sat down with the stranger and they drank a cup of tea. While they were drinking, the stranger told Makar that he was going to be married and that he had with him five hundred rubles which he had earned in Moscow. No sooner had Makar heard this than he went out and hid a hatchet under the straw of the cart. "I couldn't tell you myself why I took the hatchet," he said. "A voice said, 'Take the hatchet,' and I took it. We set off and went along all right. I quite forgot about the hatchet. So we went on until we were pretty near the village, about four miles away. We turned into the main road, which led up a hill. I got off and walked behind the sleigh, and then I heard 'him' whisper, 'What's the matter with you? By the time you reach the top of the hill, there'll be people about, and then there's the village. He'll get away with his money. If you're going to do it, do it now—don't wait.' So I stooped over the sleigh, as though I wanted to shake up the straw, and the hatchet seemed to leap into my hands of itself. The man turned around. 'What are you doing?' he said, and just as I swung the hatchet to strike him— he was a nimble fellow!—he jumped off the sleigh and seized my hands. 'What are you up to, you villain!' he shouted, and threw me down on the snow. I didn't resist, and gave in at once. He tied my hands with his girdle and threw me into the sleigh. Then he drove straight to the police station. I was put in jail and tried. The village commune gave me a good character and said I had never done wrong before. The people I'd worked for put in a good word for me, too. But I had no money to pay a lawyer," Makar concluded, "and so I was sentenced to four years' hard labor."

This man, now wishing to save a friend, though he knew that by speaking he was risking his life, had given Nekhludov information of a secret affair among the prisoners. If this became known, they would strangle him.

❖

CHAPTER ELEVEN

THE political prisoners' quarters consisted of two small cells, the doors of which opened into a part of the passage separated from the rest. The first to greet Nekhludov when he entered the passage was Simonson. He was crouching, with a pine stick in his hands, in front of a stove in which the draft was so strong that it made the iron doors vibrate. He did not rise when he saw Nekhludov, but only stretched out a hand and looked up from his overhanging brows.

"I am glad you've come, I wanted to see you," he said, looking Nekhludov straight in the eyes with a glance full of meaning.

"What is it?" asked Nekhludov.

"I'll tell you later. Just now I'm busy," and Simonson again turned to the stove, which he was heating after a theory of his own, based on the greatest possible conservation of heat.

Nekhludov was just entering the first door, when Maslova came out of the other. She was bent over a short birch broom, sweeping a pile of dust and refuse toward the stove. She wore a white blouse, her skirt was tucked up, and she had no shoes on her feet. A white kerchief was tied low over her forehead to keep out the dust. At the sight of Nekhludov she straightened herself; flushed and animated, she put down the broom, wiped her hands on her skirt, and stopped directly in front of Nekhludov.

"You're tidying the place up, I see," said Nekhludov, extending his hand.

"Yes, my old occupation," she answered, smiling. "You can't imagine how dirty it is here. We've scrubbed and scrubbed. . . . Well, is the rug dry?" she asked, turning to Simonson.

"Almost," replied Simonson, looking at her strangely, in a way that struck Nekhludov.

"All right, I'll come for it, and fetch in the coats to be dried. Our people are all in there," she said to Nekhludov, pointing toward the nearer door, while she herself went on to the farther one.

Nekhludov opened the door and entered a narrow cell, feebly lighted by a small tin lamp that stood on one of the lower bunks. The room was cold and smelled of damp, dust, and tobacco. The lamp threw a harsh light on those who were near it, but most of the bunks were in the dark; wavering shadows flitted along the walls.

Everybody was here except two men who had gone to fetch the provisions and hot water. Here was Nekhludov's old friend, Vera Efremovna, yellower and thinner than ever, with large, frightened eyes, and the prominent vein on her forehead. Her hair was cut short and she wore a gray blouse. Before her on a sheet of newspaper lay some tobacco which with her usual jerky movements she was rolling into cigarettes. Here was also Nekhludov's favorite, Emilia Rantzeva. She was in charge of the housekeeping, which she managed with feminine charm, even in these most trying conditions. Sitting near the lamp, her sleeves rolled up, she was busy with deft, sunburnt hands wiping and placing mugs and teacups on a towel spread across the bunk. Rantzeva was a plain young woman with an intelligent and gentle expression, and when she smiled her face was transformed and became gay and charming. She now greeted Nekhludov with one of her lovely smiles.

"Why, we thought you must have gone back to Russia," she said.

Here, in a distant corner, Nekhludov discovered Maria Pavlovna busy with a fair-haired little girl, who was prattling in a sweet, childish voice.

"How nice that you have come," said Maria Pavlovna. "Have you seen Katya? But come and meet our new guest," she added, pointing to the little girl.

Here was also Anatoli Kryltzov. Wasted and pale, he sat in another corner, bent and shivering, his feet in felt boots tucked under him, and his hands thrust into his coat sleeves. He looked at Nekhludov with feverish eyes. Nekhludov was going toward him when, on the right-hand side of the door he caught sight of a pretty, smiling girl—Grabetz by name—talking to a man with red curly hair, in spectacles and a rubber jacket, who was arranging something in a sack. This was the famous revolutionary, Novodvorov, whom Nekhludov greeted all the more hastily as, of all the political prisoners in the gang, Novodvorov was the only man he disliked. There was a glint in Novodvorov's eyes as he looked up and frowning held out his narrow hand.

"Do you enjoy this kind of journey?" he asked, with evident irony.

"Yes, there is much that is interesting," replied Nekhludov, pretending not to notice the irony, and going on to Kryltzov.

Outwardly, Nekhludov seemed indifferent, but in his heart he was far from feeling so. Novodvorov's words and his obvious desire to do and say something unpleasant discouraged the spirit of kindliness which possessed him at that time, and made him feel sad and depressed.

"Well, how is your health?" he said, pressing Kryltzov's cold, trembling hand.

"Pretty good, only I can't get warm. I've been soaked through," said Kryltzov, hurriedly returning his hand to his coat sleeve. "It's beastly cold here. Look at those windows." He pointed at the two broken panes behind the iron bars. "And how are you? Where have you been all this time?"

"I wasn't allowed in. The authorities were very strict and it is only today that I came upon an officer who has been more lenient."

"Lenient! Is he? You ask Masha what he did this morning."

Without leaving her seat in the corner, Maria Pavlovna told what had happened that morning about the little girl.

"I consider that we ought to protest in a body," said Vera Efremovna in determined accents but, as she glanced from one face to another, her eyes betrayed indecision and alarm. "Vladimir has made a protest, but that is not enough."

"What kind of a protest?" asked Kryltzov, with a grimace. It was evident that Vera Efremovna's artificial tone of voice and nervous manner had been irritating him for some time. "Are you looking for Katya?" he asked Nekhludov. "She works and scrubs from morning till night. They have cleaned the bachelors' quarters, now they are cleaning the women's room—but, of course, they can't get rid of the fleas. They're eating us alive. And what is Masha doing?" he asked, nodding toward the corner where Maria Pavlovna was sitting.

"She is toothcombing her adopted daughter's hair," said Rantzeva.

"I hope she's not going to scatter lice about," said Kryltzov.

"Certainly not," said Maria Pavlovna. "I'm being very careful. Anyway, she's quite cleaned up now. There, you see to her now," she added, addressing Rantzeva. "I'm going to help Katya, and I'll bring in Kryltzov's rug."

Rantzeva took the child on her lap, tenderly pressing her

plump little bare arms to her bosom, and gave her a lump of sugar.

As Maria Pavlovna went out, the two men who had been to fetch provisions and boiling water entered the room.

❖

CHAPTER TWELVE

ONE of the newscomers was a short, thin young man in a cloth-covered sheepskin coat and top boots. He walked with a light, quick step, carrying two steaming teapots filled with hot water and a loaf of bread wrapped in a kerchief under his arm.

"So here is our prince," he said, setting the teapot down among the mugs and handing the loaf to Rantzeva. "We've brought some wonderful things," he went on, taking off his coat and tossing it over the heads of the others into a corner bunk. "Markel bought eggs and milk. We'll have a feast today. And Rantzeva is still radiating æsthetic cleanliness," he said, looking at her with a smile. "Now, then, start the tea."

Good cheer and merriment breathed from this man's face, his movements, and the sound of his voice. The other newcomer was exactly the reverse. He was also short and thin, with very prominent cheekbones, thin lips, a sallow complexion and beautiful greenish eyes, set rather far apart. He was dejected and gloomy. He wore an old wadded coat and galoshes over his boots. He brought in two earthen jars and two round boxes made of birch bark. Putting down his load in front of Rantzeva, he nodded to Nekhludov, bending his neck stiffly and keeping his eyes fixed on Nekhludov all the while, then, reluctantly giving him his clammy hand to shake he began to take out the provisions.

Both these men came from the people. The first, Nabatov, was a peasant; the other, Markel Kondratyev, was a factory hand who had been drawn into the revolutionary movement as a middle-aged man of thirty-five, whilst Nabatov had joined it at eighteen. Chosen on brilliant examination results at a country school to continue his education at a secondary school, Nabatov left as a gold-medallist. He had supported himself all the while by teaching. He did not enter the university because, while still in the senior class at school, he decided he would go back to the people from whom he had sprung, taking enlightenment to his neglected brothers. He carried out his intention. He first became a clerk in a large village, but was soon arrested for reading books to the peasants and for organizing a consumers' and producers' co-operative league. He was kept imprisoned for eight months, then released, but placed under police surveillance. No sooner was he at liberty than he went to a village in another province and, obtaining the position of schoolmaster, renewed his former activities. He was arrested for the second time and kept in prison for a year and two months, which served only to strengthen his convictions.

After that, he was exiled to Perm, whence he escaped. Again he was arrested and exiled to Archangel. He also escaped from there, but was caught and sentenced to exile in the province of Yakutsk. In fact, he had spent half of his adult life in prison and in exile. All these adventures had not embittered him in the least, nor had they diminished his energy; if anything, they seemed to have stimulated it. He was naturally an energetic man, with a good digestion, always active, cheerful, and vigorous. He never wasted time over regrets and never looked far ahead, but applied all his mental powers, his cleverness and common sense to life in the present. When he was free he worked for the aim he had set himself—the enlightenment and unification of the working people, particularly of the peasants. When in prison he was just as practical and energetic in establishing contact with the outside world and in attempting to improve the conditions not only of his own life, but of the lives of the people about him. First and foremost, he was a social being, the member of a collective body. He seemed to want nothing for himself and could be contented with very little, but for his comrades he demanded much. He could work with his brain or with his hands incessantly, day and night, neither eating nor sleeping. He was as industrious as a peasant, intelligent, quick at his work, naturally even-tempered and polite without effort, attentive not only to the wishes but also to the opinions of others. His widowed mother, an aged, illiterate, superstitious peasant, was still living. Nabatov visited her whenever he was free. When at home he entered into her life, helped her in her work and always kept in touch with his former playmates. He smoked cheap tobacco with them in so-called "dog's feet,"[1] took part in their squabbles, and tried to make them understand that they had always been cheated and that they must make an effort

---

[1] A "dog's foot" is a kind of cigarette that the peasants smoke, made with a bit of paper bent at one end.—L.T.

to free themselves from the illusions in which they had been encouraged. When he thought of what a revolution would do to benefit the people, he always had in mind the class from which he himself had sprung, living in very nearly the same conditions as at present, only possessing more land and freed from the authority of gentry and bureaucracy. In his opinion, the revolution would not change the fundamental forms of the life of the people; in this respect he differed from Novodvorov and his follower, Markel Kondratyev. He did not believe that the revolution for which he was working ought to destroy the main framework, but only to change certain of the inner workings of the great, solid, and beautiful old structure that he loved so well.

In his religious views he was a typical peasant also. He never thought about metaphysical problems concerning the origin of all origins, or the future life. To him, as to Arago, God was a hypothesis for which, so far, he had had no use. He cared very little how the universe had come into existence, whether according to Moses or according to Darwin; this Darwinism, which seemed to be of such importance to his friends, was to him as much an intellectual game as the story of the creation in six days.

The question of the origin of the world did not interest him just because the other question, how best to live in it, was always in his mind. He never thought about a future life, having inherited from his ancestors the firm and calm belief, common to all who work on the land, that as in the animal and vegetable kingdoms nothing is lost but only changes from one form or another—manure changing into grain and grain into fowl, or the tadpole developing into a frog, the caterpillar into a butterfly, the acorn into an oak—so man also does not perish but only undergoes a change. Because he believed this, he faced death and the physical suffering that leads up to it bravely and even cheerfully; but he did not like and did not know how to talk about these things. He was fond of work and always busied himself with practical affairs, and encouraged his comrades to do the same.

The other political prisoner, Markel Kondratyev, was a man of different type. He had begun to work when he was fifteen and at the same time took to smoking and drinking as a way of stifling a dull sense of wrong. He had first known this feeling when, invited with other children of his age to a Christmas party that the manufacturer's wife had arranged for them, he and his little friends received an apple, a fig, a gilded walnut, and a penny whistle, while the children of the manufacturer were given toys which seemed to have come from fairyland and which (as he was told afterward) had cost fifty rubles. He was about thirty years old when a famous woman revolutionary came to work in the same factory; noticing his unusual ability, she gave him books and pamphlets and explained to him the causes of his condition and means of improving it. When he clearly understood that there was a chance to become a free man and to set others free from the state of bondage in which they lived, hardships and injustice seemed even worse and more cruel than before, and he longed passionately not for his freedom alone, but for revenge on those who had established these cruel social conditions and were interested in preserving them. He was told that knowledge offered this chance, and he devoted himself with all his might to acquiring knowledge. He could not fully understand how the socialist ideal was to be realized through knowledge, but he believed that as it had disclosed to him the injustice of present conditions, so it would enable him to abolish them. Moreover, knowledge would raise him in his own estimation above other people; he therefore gave up smoking and drinking, and devoted all his leisure to study.

The revolutionary who gave him lessons was struck by his capacity for absorbing knowledge on a variety of subjects. In two years he had mastered algebra, geometry, and history (of which he was particularly fond) and had read widely in belles lettres and criticism, but above all in the works of socialist writers.

The woman revolutionary was arrested and Kondratyev with her for having forbidden books in their possession. He was sent to jail and later on to Vologda. There he became acquainted with Novodvorov, continued reading revolutionary books, remembered everything that he had read, and became still firmer in his socialist views. After the term of his exile was over he organized a strike which ended in the destruction of a factory and the assassination of its director. He was again deprived of civil rights and exiled.

His views on religion were as negative as his views on economic conditions. Seeing the absurdity of the religion in which he had been reared, he made an effort to free himself— at first with certain fears, later with delight—and ever afterward, as though taking revenge for the deception practiced on his ancestors and himself, he never tired of pouring bitter ridicule on priests and religious dogma.

An ascetic from habit, he was content with little. Like any man who has labored from childhood upward and whose muscles are well developed, he could work quickly and easily; he was skillful at all sorts of crafts; however, he prized leisure above everything else, and in prison and at the halting stations he used it to continue his studies. He was now studying the first volume of Marx, and carried it about in his bag with the greatest care, like a valuable treasure. Except Novodvorov, to whom he was devoted and whose judgment on all subjects he accepted as irrefutable truth, he treated his comrades with reserve and indifference.

He had an insurmountable contempt for women and regarded them as a hindrance in all important projects. But he pitied Maslova as an example of the exploitation of the lower by the upper classes. He disliked Nekhludov for the same reason, preferred not to talk to him and never pressed his hand, merely extending his own for Nekhludov to shake.

❧

CHAPTER THIRTEEN

THE wood fire was burning brightly, the stove was hot, the tea was got ready, poured into mugs and tumblers, and milk was added. Fresh rye and wheat bread, rusks, hard-boiled eggs, butter, calf's head, and calves' feet were all spread out upon the cloth. Everyone moved toward the bunk which was used as a table and began eating, drinking, and talking. Rantzeva sat on a wooden box pouring out the tea. The others crowded around her, except Kryltzov, who had taken off his wet coat and was lying on his bunk wrapped up in a rug.

After the cold, damp march, the dirt and the disorder they had found here, and the work of getting everything in order, the hot tea and the food made them cheerful and happy. The heavy trampling of feet, the shouting and cursing that came from the neighboring cell seemed to increase their sensation of personal comfort. As though they were on a small island in the middle of the sea, these people no longer felt submerged in the degradation and misery surrounding them; they were exhilarated and excited. They talked about everything except their own predicament and their own future. Moreover, as so often happens when young men and women are brought together by circumstances, currents of sympathy or antipathy, curiously blended, had sprung up between them. Nearly all of them were in love.

Novodvorov was in love with pretty, smiling Grabetz. Though she had taken the special university course for women, Grabetz had thought very little and was quite indifferent to revolutionary ideas; but, swayed by the influences of the time, she had been somehow compromised and, as a result, exiled. Her success with men remained her chief interest in life. It had been the same during her trial, in prison and in exile. Now she was pleased that Novodvorov had become infatuated with her, and she, after her fashion, returned his love. Vera Efremovna, who fell in love very easily, did not so easily arouse this sentiment in others; yet she was ever hopeful and loved Nabatov and Novodvorov alternately. Kryltzov's feeling for Maria Pavlovna was something akin to love. He loved her as men love women; but, knowing her ideas about love, he carefully concealed his feeling under the guise of friendship and gratitude for her particularly tender care of him.

Nabatov and Rantzeva were united by a very complex bond of affection. Like Maria Pavlovna, who was a perfectly chaste virgin, Rantzeva was a perfectly chaste wife. As a girl of sixteen, she had fallen in love with Rantzev, who was then a student at Petersburg University; when she was nineteen and while he was still a student, she married him. In his fourth year he became involved in the disorders common among students at that time, was expelled from Petersburg and became a revolutionary. She also gave up her studies in medicine, followed him, and herself became a revolutionary. If she had not considered her husband to be the best and cleverest man in the world she would not have loved him, and if she had not loved him she would not have married him. But, loving the best and cleverest of husbands, she naturally looked at life through his eyes. At first he considered that the proper aim in life was to study, and she thought so, too. Then he became a revolutionary, and so did she. She could argue very clearly and plausibly that the existing order of things should not be allowed to go on, that it was everyone's duty to oppose it and endeavor to establish political and economic conditions in which every individual should be free to develop, and so on. She really believed that she thought and felt this herself, but in point of fact it amounted to thinking that her husband's beliefs constituted absolute truth. She had one desire: complete agreement, a union with his soul in which alone she could find entire satisfaction.

Parting from her husband and from her child (whom she entrusted to the care of her mother) had been unspeakably painful. But she bore it bravely without a murmur, because it was for her husband and for a cause which she had not the slightest doubt was true, since he served it. She was always with him in her thoughts and he was the only man she had ever loved. But Nabatov's pure and devoted love touched and troubled her. Being a friend of her husband, a high-minded, firm, and moral man, he tried to treat her like a sister; in his manner toward her, however, a new element sometimes appeared, which alarmed them both but at the same time gave color to their life of hardship.

Maria Pavlovna and Kondratyev were thus the only persons in the group who were not in love.

CHAPTER FOURTEEN

EXPECTING to have a private talk with Katusha, as usual, after supper, Nekhludov sat talking to Kryltzov and told him, among other things, the story of Makar's crime and his request to him. Kryltzov listened attentively, his shining eyes fixed on Nekhludov.

"Yes," he said suddenly, "I often think of us here, marching side by side with *them*—but who are *they?* The very people for whom we do it all, and yet we do not know them, we don't even wish to know them. And they are even worse—they hate us and look upon us as enemies. This is what makes it so terrible."

"There is nothing terrible in that," said Novodvorov, who was listening to the conversation. "The masses always worship power," he went on in his rasping voice. "The government has the power and they worship the government; if we were to be in power tomorrow they would worship us."

Just then an outburst of curses came from behind the wall, a dull thud of something flung against it, the clanking of chains, shouts and shrill cries. Someone had been knocked down, and someone else was shouting, "Murder! Help!"

"Listen to these beasts," Novodvorov said quietly. "What can there be in common between them and ourselves?"

"You call them beasts? And only a few minutes ago Nekhludov was telling me of an act—," said Kryltzov with anger, and went to relate the story of Makar, who was risking his life to save a friend. "That is not the action of a beast, it is heroism."

"Sentimentality, you mean," retorted Novodvorov sarcastically. "It is difficult for us to understand either the emotions of these people or their motives. What you take for generosity may be merely envy of the other convict."

"Why is it that you never want to see anything good in people?" exclaimed Maria Pavlovna excitedly.

"I can't see what isn't there."

"But why isn't it there, if a man takes the risk of a horrible death."

"I believe," said Novodvorov, "that if we want to achieve anything, the first condition is—" (Kondratyev, who had been reading by the light of the lamp, put down his book and began to listen attentively to his master) "—that we ought not to let our imagination run away with us, but look at things as they are; we should do all we can for the masses and expect nothing in return; we work on behalf of the masses, but they cannot work with us while they are inert as they are today," he went on, as though he were addressing a meeting. "Therefore it is a delusion to expect help from them until the process of their development—that process we are working for—has taken place."

"And what kind of development is that?" asked Kryltzov, growing red. "We affirm that we are against arbitrary government and against depotism, and yet would not that be the most terrible despotism?"

"Not at all," replied Novodvorov calmly. "I am only saying that I know the path that the people must travel, and can show it to them."

"But how can you be sure that it is the right path? Isn't this the same kind of despotism that produced the Inquisition and the crimes of the French Revolution? They also followed the teachings of science—the science of their day."

"The fact that they were in error does not prove that I am wrong. And then there is a great difference between the ravings of ideologists and the axioms of scientific political economy." Novodvorov's voice filled the room.

"These everlasting disputes," remarked Maria Pavlovna, when he paused for a moment.

"And what is your opinion?" Nekhludov asked her.

"I believe that Anatoli is right. We ought not to force our own ideas on the people."

"What about you, Katusha?" asked Nekhludov with a smile, anxious lest she should give an inappropriate answer.

"I think that the common people are wronged," she said, blushing scarlet. "I think they are dreadfully wronged."

"True, Katusha, very true!" exclaimed Nabatov. "The people are shamefully wronged. And this must be stopped. Therein lies our whole task."

"A strange idea to hold for the object of a revolution," said Novodvorov and fell to smoking in silence.

"I cannot talk to him," whispered Kryltzov.

"It is best not to talk to him," said Nekhludov.

❖

CHAPTER FIFTEEN

ALTHOUGH Novodvorov was very learned, and considered very wise, and although he enjoyed a high reputation among the revolutionaries, Nekhludov counted him among those revolutionaries who, falling below the average moral level, were very much below it. His mental ability—his numerator, so to speak—was high; but his self-esteem—his denominator—was immeasurably higher and had far outgrown his ability.

He was very different from Simonson. Simonson belonged to that predominantly masculine type in which action is guided by thought, whereas Novodvorov belonged to the feminine type in which thought is determined by feeling or by the need to justify acts instigated by feeling. All Novodvorov's revolutionary activities, which he talked about so eloquently and so convincingly, seemed to Nekhludov to be based on vanity and on the wish to be a leader of men. His capacity to assimilate and express clearly the thoughts of others—a gift esteemed by both teachers and students—brought him a position of supremacy at school and at the university, and he was well pleased with himself. Then, when he graduated and this supremacy came to an end, he suddenly changed his views and (as Kryltzov, who disliked him, told Nekhludov) in order to retain his leadership, from being a moderate liberal became a rabid *Narodovoletz*. His lack of æsthetic and moral principles (so frequently the cause of doubt and hesitation) procured for the leadership of a party a status which gratified his ambition. His vocation once chosen, he neither doubted nor hesitated, and was therefore certain that he never made a mistake. Everything seemed simple and unquestionably clear and, indeed, within the limits of his horizon everything *was* quite simple. All that was necessary was to be logical, as he said. His self-confidence was so gross that he either repelled or conquered. And as his activity took place before the eyes of very young people, who mistook his boundless self-assurance for depth and wisdom, the majority fell under his influence and his success in revolutionary circles became established. His aim at that time was to prepare an insurrection during which he proposed to seize the reins of government and call together a council which would then consider the program he had composed. And he was perfectly certain that this program solved every problem and would inevitably be carried out.

His comrades respected him for his daring and decision, but they did not love him. Nor did he love anyone. He looked upon all talented men as rivals; if he could, he would have gladly treated them as old male monkeys treat their young. He would have deprived them of all their powers and all their talent in order not to be eclipsed by them. He liked only those who bowed before him; thus, he was gracious to his disciple, Kondratyev, to Vera Efremovna and to pretty Grabetz, both of whom were in love with him. In theory he believed in women's rights, but at the bottom of his heart he considered all women stupid and insignificant, except those with whom he happened to be sentimentally in love (as he was now in love with Grabetz). He considered such women to be exceptional, and himself to be the only man capable of appreciating them.

The question of relations between the sexes, like all other questions, seemed to him to be solved very simply, namely by the recognition of free love. He had one nominal wife, one lawful wife (whom he had left because he had come to the conclusion that there was no true love between them), and now he was about to contract another free marriage with Grabetz.

He despised Nekhludov for "posing" (as he called it) before Maslova and especially for concerning himself with the defects of existing conditions, not holding word for word Novodvorov's views, but thinking in his own "princely" way, that is, like a fool. Nekhludov was aware of Novodvorov's opinion of him, and to his sincere sorrow knew that despite his own feelings of good will toward all men, he was returning dislike for dislike, and was quite unable to overcome his strong antipathy for the man

CHAPTER SIXTEEN

Words of command were heard from the next room. Everyone fell silent when the sergeant accompanied by two soldiers entered the room. They had come to call the roll. The sergeant counted the prisoners, pointing his finger at each one. When he saw Nekhludov, he said with good-natured familiarity:

"You can't stay after the inspection, Prince. It's time for you to go."

Knowing by experience what he meant, Nekhludov slipped into his hand a three-ruble note, which he had ready for the occasion.

"Ah, well, what can I do with you? Stay a bit longer if you like."

As he was going out, another sergeant came in, followed by a tall, thin convict with a bruised eye and a thin beard.

"I've come to see about the little girl," he said.

"There's Daddy!" cried a clear small voice, and a flaxen head appeared from behind Rantzeva's back. Katusha and Maria Pavlovna were helping her to sew a new frock for the child, making it out of an old skirt that had belonged to Rantzeva.

"Yes, here I am, daughter," said Buzovkin gently.

"She is quite happy here," said Maria Pavlovna, looking with pity at Buzovkin's bruised face. "Let her stay with us."

"The ladies are making me a new frock," said the little girl, pointing to Rantzeva's sewing. "A fine red frock," she chattered.

"Would you like to spend the night with us?" asked Rantzeva, caressing the child.

"Yes, I'd like to. I want Daddy to stay, too."

A radiant smile lit up Rantzeva's face.

"No, Daddy can't stay here. Do leave her with us," she said to the father.

"Yes, you may leave her here," said the sergeant, pausing in the doorway before he went out.

As soon as the soldiers had gone Nabatov went up to Buzovkin, and putting his hand on his shoulder, asked:

"Is it true, my boy, that Karmanov wants to exchange?"

Buzovkin's kindly, gentle face suddenly grew sad and his eyes became dim.

"We don't know anything about it. I hardly think it's true," he said. "Well, Aksutka, it seems you're to make yourself comfortable with the ladies," he added without any change of expression, and hurriedly went out.

"He knows well enough," said Nabatov. "They've already exchanged. What will you do about it?"

"I will inform the commanding officer when we come to the next town," replied Nekhludov.

No one spoke, fearing that the controversy might be renewed. Simonson, who had remained silent all the evening, lying in a corner with his hands behind his head, rose with a look of determination; walking carefully, so as not to disturb the others, he went up to Nekhludov and said:

"May I have a talk with you now?"

"Certainly," replied Nekhludov and rose to follow him. Meeting his eyes, Katusha blushed and shook her head as if perplexed.

"This is what I want to tell you," Simonson began as soon as they were outside in the passage, where the noise and the shouting of the "criminals" sounded even louder. Nekhludov frowned, but the noise seemed to make no impression on Simonson.

"Knowing your relationship with Katerina Mikhailovna," he went on earnestly and frankly, his kind eyes looking straight into Nekhludov's, "I consider it my duty—," but he had to stop, because the voices of the people quarreling and shouting sounded from just behind the door.

"I tell you, you blockhead, they're not mine!"

"I hope they choke you, you devil!" shouted another hoarse voice.

Maria Pavlovna came out.

"You can't talk here," she said. "Go in there. Vera is alone."

She led the way to a tiny cell set aside for the use of the women political prisoners. Vera Efremovna was lying on a bunk, a blanket drawn over her head.

"She has a headache. She's asleep and can't hear you, and I will go away," said Maria Pavlovna.

"Please don't," said Simonson. "I have no secrets from anyone and least of all from you."

"Very well," said Maria Pavlovna, sitting down on one of the bunks. Rocking herself from side to side as a child does, she eased herself backward and settled down ready to listen, gazing in front of her with beautiful lamblike eyes.

"Well, then, this is what I have to say," Simonson resumed.

"Knowing your relationship with Katerina Mikhailovna, I consider it my duty to explain to you my own relationship with her."

"What is it?" asked Nekhludov, who could not help admiring the simplicity and frankness with which Simonson spoke to him.

"I should like to marry her," said Simonson.

"Amazing!" said Maria Pavlovna, fixing her eyes on Simonson.

"But she will not come to any decision without you."

"Why not?"

"Because as long as your mutual relationship is not settled she cannot make up her mind."

"It is definitely settled so far as I am concerned. I wanted to do what I considered my duty, and I also wanted to make life easier for her. But I would not, on any account, stand in her way."

"That may be so, but she does not want to accept your sacrifice."

"It is no sacrifice."

"That decision of hers is final, I know."

"Well, then, what is the use of talking about it?" asked Nekhludov.

"She must know that you feel as she does."

"But how can I admit that I ought not to perform a duty when I know I ought to? All I can say is that I am not free but she is."

Simonson was silent, plunged into thought; at last he said:

"Very well, I'll tell her. You must not think for a moment that I am in love with her," he went on. "I respect and admire her as a splendid, exceptional human being who has had to endure extreme suffering; but I am disinterested, and all I want is to help her, to lighten her. . . ."

Nekhludov was surprised to notice the tremor in Simonson's voice.

"To lighten her lot," concluded Simonson. "If she won't accept your help, let her accept mine. If she consents to marry me, I shall ask to be exiled to the same place with her. Four years are not an eternity. I shall stay with her, and perhaps I can make her life less hard to bear." He paused again in agitation.

"What can I say?" said Nekhludov. "I am happy that she has found a protector in you, and—"

"That's what I wanted to know," interrupted Simonson. "I was anxious to know whether, loving her as you do and wishing for her happiness, you would consider our marriage desirable."

"Oh, yes!" Nekhludov replied emphatically.

"I want it only for her sake. I only long to comfort a suffering soul," said Simonson, gazing at Nekhludov with an expression of childlike tenderness that was unexpected in this morose-looking man.

He rose, went up to Nekhludov, and kissed him with a bashful smile.

"I shall tell her," he said and went away.

CHAPTER SEVENTEEN

"WHY, he's in love, very much in love! I should have never believed that Vladimir Simonson would fall in love like a silly boy. Amazing! But to tell you the truth, I can't help feeling that it is a pity," said Maria Pavlovna with a sigh.

"But what do you think Katusha will say?" asked Nekhludov.

"Katusha?" Maria Pavlovna paused, evidently wishing to give as exact an answer as possible. "You see, in spite of her past life, she is a woman of the highest moral character. Her love for you is good, and it makes her happy to think she can do even the negative service of preventing you from entangling yourself with her. Such a marriage seems to her to be a terrible fall for you—far worse than the whole of her own past—and that is why she will never agree to it. Yet at the same time your presence agitates her."

"So I am to disappear?" said Nekhludov.

Maria Pavlovna smiled her sweet, childlike smile.

"Yes, partly."

"And how does one disappear partly?"

"I've been talking nonsense," said Maria Pavlovna, "but what I mean to say about her was that she must see the absurdity of his rapturous love—he has never spoken of it to her, you know—and while it gratifies her, it also frightens her. You know I am not an authority in such matters, but it seems to me that it is nothing else than ordinary sexual feeling on his part, although it is masked. He says this love arouses his energy and he calls it platonic. But I feel sure that, even if it is an exceptional love, there must be something disgusting underneath—just as between Novodvorov and Grabetz."

Having started on her favorite topic, Maria Pavlovna had wandered from the main question.

"Well, what am I to do?" said Nekhludov.

"I think you ought to tell her everything. It is always better to come to a plain understanding. Talk to her. I'll call her, shall I?"

"Yes, if you please," said Nekhludov and Maria Pavlovna left the room.

A strange feeling came over Nekhludov, alone in the little cell, listening to Vera Efremovna's even breathing which was broken every now and then by moans, and to the incessant din from the criminal quarters, two doors beyond. What Simonson had told him relieved him of the obligation which he had assumed voluntarily, but which had sometimes in moments of weakness seemed difficult and distasteful. Yet he was unhappy and hurt, feeling that Simonson's offer had in a way impaired the sublimity of his own sacrifice and diminished its value in the eyes of others as well as in his own. If such a good man as Simonson was anxious to join his fate to Katusha's—his own sacrifice could never have been so great as it had seemed. Plain jealousy entered into it also, perhaps. He had grown accustomed to the thought that she loved him and it was not easy to admit that she could love another man. Moreover, it upset his plan to remain near her during the term of her exile. If she married Simonson, his presence would become unnecessary and he would have to make new plans.

He was still turning these thoughts over in his mind when the loud roar from the criminals' quarters (where something unusual seemed to be happening that day) burst in as Katusha opened the door and approached him with quick steps.

"Maria Pavlovna sent me," she said.

"Yes, I have something to say to you. Sit down. Vladimir Ivanovich has been speaking to me."

She sat down, folding her hands on her knees; she seemed calm, but no sooner had Nekhludov mentioned Simonson's name than she flushed crimson.

"What did he say?" she asked.

"He said that he wanted to marry you."

Her face suddenly puckered up as if with pain, but she said nothing and only averted her eyes.

"He asked for my consent, or my advice. I told him it all depended entirely on you. You must decide for yourself."

"Oh, why? What does it all mean?" she muttered, looking at Nekhludov with the peculiar squint that always strangely affected him. For several moments they remained silent, face to face. The glances they exchanged made many things clear to both of them.

"You must decide," repeated Nekhludov.

"But what am I to decide? It was all decided long ago."

"No, you must decide whether you will accept Vladimir Ivanovich's offer," said Nekhludov.

"What sort of a wife would I make? A convict like me! Why should I ruin him, too?"

"But if the sentence were remitted?"

"Oh, please, leave me in peace! There's nothing more to be said," she exclaimed and left the room.

CHAPTER EIGHTEEN

WHEN Nekhludov followed Katusha into the men's cell, he found everyone there in a state of great excitement. Nabatov, who was about everywhere, who knew everybody and noticed everything, had brought amazing news: he had discovered on a wall a note written by Petlin, a revolutionary sentenced to hard labor. Everyone supposed that Petlin had reached Kara long ago, but here was a proof that he had recently passed this way.

"On the seventh day of August," so ran the note, "I was sent on alone with the criminal prisoners. Neverov, who was with me, hanged himself in the lunatic asylum at Kazan. I am well and cheerful and hoping for better days."

They all fell to discussing Petlin and the possible causes of Neverov's suicide. Kryltzov alone remained silent and thoughtful, looking in front of him with fixed, glistening eyes.

"My husband told me that Neverov saw a ghost when he was in the Fortress of Peter and Paul," said Rantzeva.

"Yes, he was a poet, a dreamer," said Novodvorov. "Such people can't stand solitary confinement. Now when I was in solitary confinement, I never let my imagination run away with me, but arranged my time most systematically; that's why I could endure it so well."

"Why shouldn't you have? I was often very glad to be safe in prison," said Nabatov briskly, wishing to dispel the general gloom. "When you're free, you are afraid of everything—of getting arrested, or entangling your friends and doing more harm than good—but once you're locked up, your responsibility ends. Then you can rest. All you have to do is just to sit and smoke."

"Did you know him well?" asked Maria Pavlovna, looking uneasily at Kryltzov's altered, haggard face.

"Did you call Neverov a dreamer?" Kryltzov suddenly began; his breath was short, as though he had been speaking or singing for a long time. "Neverov was the kind of man 'the like of whom earth seldom bears,' as our doorkeeper expressed it. Yes, he was as clear as crystal, you could see through him. He couldn't lie, he couldn't even dissemble. He was more than thin-skinned—his nerves were all laid bare, as if he had been flayed. Yes, his was a rich and complex nature, not such a one as . . . But what's the use of talking?" He paused for a while, then resumed with an angry frown: "Here we are, spending our time discussing higher matters, whether we ought first to educate the people and then change the general conditions of life, or whether we had better begin by changing the conditions of life; and then we discuss the eternal question of our methods— peaceful propaganda or terrorism? Yes, we go on discussing, but *they* never discuss. *They* know their business and are perfectly indifferent whether men perish by tens or by thousands, and such men! On the contrary, their purpose is served when the best men perish. Herzen explained that when the Decembrists were eliminated the general level was lowered. Of course it was lowered. Then Herzen himself and his friends were eliminated. Now it's a man like Neverov. . . ."

"They can't exterminate us all! There will always be enough left to propagate the breed," said Nabatov, in his cheerful voice.

"No, there won't be any left, if we continue to spare *them*," said Kryltzov, raising his voice and refusing to be interrupted. "Give me a cigarette."

"Please don't smoke. It's not good for you, Anatoli," said Maria Pavlovna.

"Oh, let me alone," he exclaimed irritably, and lit the cigarette. But a fit of coughing interrupted him and he seemed to be on the point of vomiting, but he spat and continued: "No, we did not do the right thing. Instead of wasting our time on discussion, we ought to have banded together and exterminated *them*."

"But they are also human beings," said Nekhludov.

"No, they are not. Men who can do such things as they are doing are not human. . . . No. . . . It is said that some kind of bombs and balloons have been invented. Well, we ought to go up in a balloon and sprinkle them with bombs, as though they were lice, till they are all exterminated. Yes . . ." he began again, but a paroxysm of coughing seized him, he turned scarlet and blood gushed from his mouth.

Nabatov ran to get some snow. Maria Pavlovna offered him Valerian drops; gasping and with eyes closed, he pushed her away with his thin, white hand. When the snow and cold water had checked the bleeding, and he had been made comfortable for the night, Nekhludov bade them all good-by and left with the sergeant, who had been waiting for some time.

The criminal convicts had quieted down and most of them were asleep. Although people were lying both on and under the bunks and in the spaces between them, there was still not enough room for all and some were lying on the floor of the passage with their heads on their sacks and their damp cloaks thrown over them. The snoring, groaning, and sleepy muttering formed one continuous sound that seemed to come from every direction. Long rows of human bodies lay everywhere, wrapped in prison cloaks. Only a few were still awake in the unmarried men's quarters, sitting in a corner near a lighted candle end, which they blew out at once when they saw the sergeant approaching. One old man was sitting naked under the lamp in the passage, trying to rid his shirt of fleas. The foul air of the political prisoners' room seemed pure in comparison with the stinking closeness here. The light of the smoking lamp shone dimly as through a mist. Breathing was difficult. In order to pass along the corridor without stepping upon some sleeper, one had to search carefully for an unoccupied space and then, having put down one foot, look around for a spot for the other. Three men who had apparently not been able to find room in the corridors were lying on the floor by the front door, close to the stinking and leaking tub. One of them was an old imbecile whom Nekhludov had frequently noticed at the halting stations, another a ten-year-old boy. He was lying between two convicts with his hand under his cheek, resting his head on the leg of one of the sleepers.

When Nekhludov passed the gate, he stopped for some time and inhaled deep draughts of the frosty air.

CHAPTER NINETEEN

THE skies had cleared and the stars were shining as Nekhludov returned to his inn, walking cautiously over the frozen mud that yielded now and then to the pressure of his feet. He knocked at a dark window and a barefooted, broad-shouldered laborer opened the door and let him in. The drivers asleep in the living room on the right were snoring loudly. Horses could be heard chewing their oats in the yard. The spare room on the left smelt of wormwood and sweat; a mighty, rhythmical snoring and gurgling came from behind the partition; a red lamp was burning before the icon. Nekhludov undressed, spread his rug over the sofa covered with American cloth, arranged his leather pillow, and lay down, thinking over all that he had seen and heard during the day. The most painful spectacle of all had been the small boy lying asleep in the liquid which had oozed out of the tub, his head resting on the leg of a convict.

Unexpected and important as his conversation with Simonson and Katusha had been, he tried not to dwell upon it, for his position in that matter was complicated and indefinite. But the picture of the unfortunate creatures stifling in the putrid air, lying in the foul liquid oozing out of the tub, and especially the innocent face of the boy with his head on the convict's leg—those could not be driven from his mind.

It is one thing to know that somewhere, far away, men are inflicting torture upon their fellow beings, subjecting them to every kind of humiliation and suffering and degradation; it is quite another to have been for three months an eyewitness of that torture and agony. During the course of these three months Nekhludov had often asked himself: Am I mad, to see what others do not see, or are they mad who are responsible for all that I am seeing? Yet those men he was thinking of were so many, and they were doing things that seemed to him astonishing and terrible, with such calm assurance that their work was necessary, useful, and important, that it was difficult to believe them all to be mad. Nor could he believe that he was mad himself, for he was conscious of the clearness of his reasoning. This kept him in a continual state of perplexity.

What he had seen during the past three months had left this picture impressed upon his mind: From among all the men who were living in freedom, the government and the courts had selected the most nervous and the most highly excitable, the strongest, the most mentally gifted but the least crafty and cautious; these people, who were not a whit more guilty or more dangerous to society than those who remained free, were locked up in jails, exiled, sentenced to hard labor and confined for months and years in utter idleness—remote from nature, from their families and from useful work. In other words, they were deprived of all that is required for a normal and moral life. This was the first conclusion Nekhludov drew from his observations.

Secondly, these people were subjected to all sorts of unnecessary degradation: their heads were shaven, they were put into chains and shameful prison clothes, and so on. In other words, they were deprived of the main inducements which lead weak people to lead good lives: a sense of shame, regard for public opinion, and awareness of human dignity.

Thirdly, their lives were in continual danger through infectious disease, exhaustion, and ill treatment (not to mention exceptional occurrences such as sunstroke, drowning, and fire); in other words, they lived all the time in a condition in which the kindest and most moral of men are led by the instinct of self-preservation to commit (and to condone in others) cruel and abominable crimes.

Fourthly, these people were forced to live with ruffians, men debauched by evil living—and by these very institutions, particularly—men who acted like leaven in dough among those still uncorrupted.

Fifthly and finally, the principle of cruelty as a means of personal advantage was instilled into them by the most effective of all methods—namely, inhuman cruelties practiced upon themselves, the torture of women and children and old men, blows and floggings, rewards for the capture of fugitives dead or alive, separating husbands from their wives and bringing them together with other men's wives, shooting and hanging. If the government employed these methods where they suited its purpose, why should the same methods be wrong for people who are deprived of their freedom, who are in misery and in want?

These institutions seemed to have been founded for the special purpose of producing the essence of vice and debauchery impossible in any other conditions, in order that this essence might later be broadcast among the people. "It really looks as if a problem had been set: how to debauch and corrupt as many persons as possible in the shortest and surest way," thought Nekhludov, as he observed life in jails and halting stations. Hundreds and thousands of men were depraved by these methods and, when their degradation was fully accomplished, they were set free to spread over the land the moral disease they had caught in prison.

Nekhludov saw how successfully this object had been attained. In the jails of Tumen, Ekaterinenburg, Tomsk, and at the halting stations on the way, simple, ordinary men, living by the standards of Russian, social, peasant, Christian morality, lost them and formed new standards, founded on the idea that all acts of outrage, violence, and humiliation are justifiable if profitable. In the light of what was being done to them, they came to see that all the laws of compassion and respect for man preached by the church and by teachers of morals were set aside in real life, and that they also might disregard them. Nekhludov saw evidence of this in the behavior of every convict he knew—in Fedorov, Makar, and even in Tarass, who after two months of prison life had shocked Nekhludov by the immorality of his opinions. Nekhludov had discovered that tramps, when escaping into the marshes, persuaded their comrades to come with them, and then murdered them and ate their flesh. He saw a man who had been accused of this and had admitted it. Most terrible of all, such cases, far from being exceptional, recurred continually.

Only by the special cultivation of vice carried on in these institutions could a Russian be brought to the state of these tramps who (anticipating Nietzsche's recent teaching) considered everything permissible and nothing forbidden and spread this doctrine first among the convicts and then among the people in general.

The only explanation of all this was that it aimed at the prevention of crime by intimidation, correction, or "retributive justice," as it was expressed in books. But in reality, nothing of the sort was achieved and crime, instead of being suppressed, was extended. Delinquents were not intimidated but encouraged, and many of them—for example, the tramps—had gone to jail of their own accord. Instead of the correction of the vicious, there had emerged the systematic innoculation of vice. "Retributive justice" only excited the spirit of revenge where it had never before existed.

"Then why do they persist in what they are doing?" Nekhludov asked himself, and found no answer. But what surprised him most was that none of all this had happened accidentally, by mistake, but that it had been going on for centuries, with the only difference that in the old days men's noses were torn out and their ears cut off, then later they were branded and chained to iron rods, whereas now they were manacled, and transported by steam instead of in carts.

Government officials had often told Nekhludov that the conditions which excited his indignation and which they admitted to be imperfect, would be improved as soon as prisons were built in accordance with modern methods. This explanation, however, did not satisfy Nekhludov, because he felt that the things that aroused his indignation were not caused by more or less perfect or imperfect methods. He had read about improved prisons, equipped with electric bells, where execution was done by electricity (as Tarde recommended), but this perfected system of violence disgusted him all the more.

What revolted him most was that courts and ministerial offices were administered by men who received large incomes taken from the people, who spent their time reading the books of other men just like themselves and governed by the same motives, and that these men classified the deeds of lawbreakers under statutes which they themselves had framed. In accordance with such statutes, they went on sending people to places where they could no longer be seen, where they were wholly at the mercy of cruel, harsh inspectors, jailers, and soldiers, and where they perished by the million, body and soul.

Now that he had a personal knowledge of the prisons and the halting stations, Nekhludov recognized that the chief vices among the convicts—drunkenness, gambling, brutality—and even terrible crimes like cannibalism, are neither accidents nor signs of mental or physical degeneration (as certain obtuse scientists have declared to the satisfaction of governments), but that they are the inevitable result of the inconceivable delusion that one group of human beings has the right to punish another. Nekhludov saw that cannibalism begins not in the Siberian marshes, but in ministerial offices and government departments. He saw that his brother-in-law, for instance, as well as most of the judges and bureaucrats, from ministers down to policemen, do not care in the least for justice and the good of the people; all they care is to get the rubles, which were paid them for doing the things that caused all this degradation and misery. This was quite evident.

"Can it be, then, that all this simply springs from a misunderstanding? I wonder if anything can be done to secure their salaries to all these bureaucrats, even to pay them a premium, just for abstaining from their present activities?" thought Nekhludov. After the cocks had crowed for the second time, it was with thoughts like this in his mind that he fell into a sound sleep, despite the fleas that leaped around him like water from a fountain whenever he moved.

❖

CHAPTER TWENTY

WHEN Nekhludov awoke, the drivers had departed, the landlady had had her breakfast, and, mopping her perspiring fat neck with a handkerchief, she came to announce that a soldier from the halting station had brought a note. It was from Maria Pavlovna. She wrote that Kryltzov's attack had proved more serious than they had supposed. "We hoped that he might be allowed to stay here and that we might also be allowed to stay and take care of him, but this request has been refused and we are going to take him along, but we fear the worst. Could you possibly make arrangements for leaving him in the town, with one of us to take care of him? If you think it would help matters were I to marry him, I am of course willing to do so."

Nekhludov sent a lad to the posting station for horses, and packed in great haste. He had not finished his second tumbler of tea, when a three-horsed post cart, with much jingling of bells and a loud rattling of wheels drove up to the porch over the frozen mud. Paying his bill to the fat-necked landlady, Nekhludov hastily left the house, took his seat on the cart, and gave orders to the coachman to drive as fast as he could and overtake the gang. Just beyond the gates of the common pasture, he came up with the carts, laden with invalids and sacks, rattling along over the frozen mud of the high road that was beginning to be rolled smooth by the wheels. The officer of the escort had already driven ahead. The soldiers, who had clearly been drinking, were in the rear, talking cheerfully as they marched behind the carts and on both sides of the road. In each of the front carts, half a dozen of the ailing criminals sat huddled together; three political convicts occupied each of the last three carts. The last one was occupied by Novodvorov, Grabetz, and Kondratyev; the second from the rear by Rantzeva, Nabatov, and the feeble, rheumatic woman to whom Maria Pavlovna had given up her place; Kryltzov, supported by pillows, was lying on the hay in the third cart from the rear. Maria Pavlovna sat beside the driver.

Nekhludov halted near Kryltzov's cart and went toward it. One of the tipsy soldiers waved his hand to warn him off, but Nekhludov, paying no attention, went up to the cart and walked along with one hand on it. Kryltzov, in a sheepskin coat and fur cap, a scarf tied over his mouth, looked paler and thinner than ever. His beautiful eyes seemed larger and brighter. Jolting on the rough surface of the road, he lay with eyes fixed on Nekhludov. To a question about his health, he replied with an angry shake of the head and closed his eyes. He seemed to want all his remaining strength to endure the joltings of the cart. Maria Pavlovna gave Nekhludov a meaning look, which expressed all her anxiety for Kryltzov, and shouted, so as to be heard above the rattling of the wheels:

"It looks as if the officer is ashamed of himself! Buzovkin's manacles have been removed. He is carrying the little girl again. Katya and Simonson are with them, and Vera, too—she's taking my place."

Kryltzov said something that was drowned in the noise and shook his head, frowning in the effort to repress his cough. Nekhludov stooped toward him, hoping to be able to hear what he was saying. Then Kryltzov whispered, taking the scarf from off his mouth:

"I am feeling much better now. I must take care not to catch cold again."

Nekhludov nodded, as if in agreement, and exchanged glances with Maria Pavlovna.

"And how about the problem of the three bodies?" asked Kryltzov, still in a whisper and smiled painfully, with an effort. "There's no easy solution, is there?"

Nekhludov did not understand, but Maria Pavlovna explained that Kryltzov was referring to the well-known mathematical problem concerning the relative position of the three heavenly bodies, the sun, the moon, and the earth, and that Kryltzov was comparing this problem to the relationship between Nekhludov, Katusha, and Simonson. Kryltzov nodded to show that Maria Pavlovna had explained his little joke correctly.

"The solution doesn't lie with me," said Nekhludov.

"Have you received my note? Will you do it?" asked Maria Pavlovna.

"Certainly," replied Nekhludov, and, noticing a shade of annoyance on Kryltzov's face, went back to his own cart. He sat down on its sagging floor and held on to the sides as it jolted over the ruts on the rough road. He overtook the convicts in their gray coats and sheepskins, some chained and others manacled in pairs, marching in a column that stretched for nearly a mile along the road. On the far side of the road he spied Katusha's blue kerchief, Vera Efremovna's black coat, and Simonson in his short jacket and crocheted cap, his white woolen stockings tied up with leather thongs like sandals. He was walking beside the women, talking to them earnestly.

The women nodded to Nekhludov, and Simonson raised his hat very solemnly. Nekhludov could think of nothing to say and overtook them without stopping his driver. In the middle of the road, where it was not so rough, the horses could go faster; but they were frequently forced to turn aside in order to pass the rows of heavy carts that were moving on the road in both directions.

The road, deeply grooved by cart ruts, ran through a forest of pine trees mingled with larches and birches, whose bright yellow leaves still clung to the branches. Presently the forest ended, fields opened on both sides, and the gilded domes and crosses of a monastery came into sight. The clouds had dispersed, the sun rose above the forest, and the wet leaves, the puddles, the domes, and the crosses all glistened in its rays. In the blue-gray distance ahead on the right, there was a gleam of white mountains as the troika drove into a large village lying on the outskirts of a town. The street was filled with men and women, both Russian and native, in strange caps and cloaks. Peasants, men and women, some sober and some tipsy, swarmed about screaming at one another amongst shops, pothouses, inns, and carts. The influence of the neighboring town was noticeable.

Touching up the right-hand horse, the driver turned sideways on his seat so as to keep the reins on his right, and evidently anxious to show off drove through the street at a quick trot. Without reining in the horses, he drove down to the river, which was to be crossed by a ferry. The raft was at this moment in the middle of the river and was coming toward them.

Some twenty carts were already there. Nekhludov did not have to wait long. The raft, which had been taken far upstream, was now floating quickly down, carried by the swift current toward the landing. The tall, silent, muscular, broad-shouldered ferrymen, in sheepskin coats and Siberian boots, with quick, practiced movements threw the nooses over the posts, moored the raft and then, removing the bars, allowed the carts on board to drive ashore. Then they began to take the return freight, carts with restless, terrified horses, packing them closely side by side. The swift, broad river splashed against the boats of the ferry, tautening the ropes. At last Nekhludov's cart, from which the horses had been removed, was placed on the crowded raft; the ferrymen put up the bars without heeding the complaints of those left behind, cast off and got under way. All was quiet on the raft; one could hear nothing but the tramp of the ferrymen's boots and the horses' hoofs knocking against the wooden deck as they shifted uneasily from foot to foot.

❧

CHAPTER TWENTY-ONE

STANDING on the edge of the raft, Nekhludov gazed on the wide, swift river. Two images kept rising in his mind. One was the jolting head of angry, dying Kryltzov; the other was Katusha walking briskly along the road by the side of Simonson. The memory of Kryltzov, dying and unprepared for death, was painful. The memory of Katusha, who had gained the love of such a man as Simonson and was now following the firm, straight path of virtue, should have been pleasant, yet carried with it a pain that Nekhludov could not overcome.

A large brass bell was ringing in the town, and the sound came across the water. Nekhludov's driver, who stood beside him, and the other men one after another removed their caps and crossed themselves. Only one old man, short and disheveled, took no notice, but lifted his head and stared at Nekhludov, who although standing quite near had not noticed him before. He wore a patched coat, cloth trousers, and patched, down-at-heel shoes. A small bag was slung over his shoulder and on his head he had a tall fur cap much the worse for the wear.

"Why aren't you saying your prayers, old man?" asked Nekhludov's driver, putting on his cap. "Were you never baptized?"

"Whom should I pray to?" said the old man quickly and distinctly, in a determined, aggressive tone of voice.

"Whom to? Why, to God, of course," replied the driver sarcastically.

"You just show me where he is, that God of yours."

There was something so serious and determined in the old

man's expression that the driver, seeing he had a hard customer to deal with, was a little abashed; but not wishing to be worsted in front of an audience, he said quickly:

"Where? In heaven, of course."

"Have you been there?"

"Whether I've been or not, everybody knows that you must pray to God."

"No one has seen God anywhere. His only begotten Son, abiding in the bosom of His Father, He hath declared Him," said the old man, frowning sternly and speaking as fast as before.

"You must be a hole-worshiper. You pray to a hole," retorted Nekhludov's driver, tucking his whip into his belt and adjusting the harness of one of the outside horses.

Someone laughed.

"What faith is yours, grandad?" asked an elderly man standing beside a loaded cart near the edge of the raft.

"I have no kind of faith, because I believe in no one but myself," replied the old man, just as fast and with the same determination as before.

"But how can you believe in yourself?" asked Nekhludov, entering into the conversation. "You might make a mistake."

"Never in your life!" replied the old man, shaking his head vigorously.

"Then why is it that there are different religions?" asked Nekhludov.

"It's just that men believe in other men and not in themselves. When I used to believe in other men I wandered about as if I were in a swamp. I was lost, and I had no hope that I should ever find my way out. There are all kinds of faiths—Old-Believers and New-Believers, and Judaisers and *Khlisty,* the Priesters and the priestless, the Austriaks, and the Molokans and the *Skoptzy*—and every faith praises itself, so they all crawl about in different directions like blind puppies. There are many faiths, but the Spirit is one, in me, in you and in every man. So that if each man believes in the Spirit that is within him, we shall all be united. Each man will be himself, and all will be as one." The old man spoke in a loud voice and kept looking around, evidently wishing to be heard by as many people as possible.

"How long have you held this faith?" asked Nekhludov.

"Me? Oh, a long time. They've been persecuting me for twenty-two years."

"In what way?"

"As they persecuted Christ, so they persecute me. They arrest me and drag me into court, and before the priests and the scribes and the Pharisees. Once they put me in the madhouse. But they can't do me any harm because I'm a free man. 'What's your name?' they ask. They think I'm going to call myself by my own name, but I'm not. I deny everything—I have no name, no place, no country. I have nothing. I am just my own self. 'My name? A man.' 'And how old are you?' I reply, 'I never count the years, it can't be done. I always was, and I always shall be.' 'Who are your father and your mother?' 'I have no father and no mother except God and Mother Earth.' 'Do you recognize the tsar?' 'Why shouldn't I recognize him? He is a tsar unto himself, and I am a tsar unto myself.' 'What's the use of talking to you?' they say, and I reply, 'I didn't ask you to talk to me.' So they torture me."

"And where are you going now?" asked Nekhludov.

"Wherever God may lead me. I work, and if the work gives out, I beg," concluded the old man, noticing that the raft was near the opposite bank, and looking about him triumphantly.

When they had tied up, Nekhludov took out his purse and offered the old man some coins, but he refused to take them.

"I never accept that sort of thing. Bread I do accept."

"Then you must forgive me."

"There's nothing to forgive. You haven't offended me, and nobody can offend me," said the old man hoisting his bag onto his shoulder. Meanwhile Nekhludov's cart had been taken from the raft and the horses reharnessed.

"I wonder you care to talk to him, sir," said the driver to Nekhludov who, having paid the ferrymen, was climbing on to his cart again. "He's just a good-for-nothing tramp."

❖

CHAPTER TWENTY-TWO

WHEN they reached the top of the hill, the driver turned around to Nekhludov. "Where shall I take you, sir?"

"Which is the best hotel?"

"Nothing could be better than the *Sibirsk*. But Dukov's is good, too."

"Drive to whichever you like."

The driver seated himself sideways again and drove faster.

This town was like all other towns. The same sort of houses with dormer windows and green roofs, the same sort of cathedral, the same shops on the main road and even the same policemen. Only the houses were mostly of wood and the streets were unpaved. In one of the busiest streets the driver stopped his troika at the entrance of an hotel, but all the rooms were taken so they had to drive on. The other hotel had one unoccupied room, and for the first time in the course of his two months' journey Nekhludov found himself surrounded by the comfort and cleanliness to which he was accustomed. Although his room was not luxurious he was grateful for the relief from dirt and vermin encountered in two months of carts and country inns. As soon as he had unpacked, he drove to a Russian bath. Then he dressed for the city, putting on a starched shirt, trousers somewhat crumpled from long packing, a frock coat, and an overcoat, and drove to the governor-general's.

The cabby, who had been called by the hotel porter, had a big Kirghiz horse harnessed to a rattling vehicle. He drove Nekhludov to a handsome structure guarded by sentries and a policeman, which stood in a garden where the leafless branches of aspen and birch stood stark against the dark green of pine trees.

The general was indisposed and was not receiving, but all the same Nekhludov asked the footman to take in his card, and presently the man returned with a favorable message:

"You are to come in, please."

The antechamber, the footman, the orderly, the staircase, the hall with its shining parquet floor, all reminded him of Petersburg, only that it was more pretentious and less well kept.

The general, a man of sanguine temper with a bloated face, puffy eyelids, a snub nose, a knobby, bulging forehead, and a bald head, dressed in a silk Tartar dressing gown, sat smoking a cigarette and sipping his tea from a tumbler in a silver holder.

"Good morning, my dear sir. Excuse the dressing gown, but it's better to receive you in a dressing gown than not at all," he said. "I am not feeling very well and am keeping to the house. What on earth has brought you to this out-of-the-way place?"

"I followed a gang of convicts, among whom there is one who is very dear to me," said Nekhludov, "and I have come here to petition Your Excellency on her account, and also on another matter."

The general took a long whiff and a sip of tea, then extinguishing his cigarette in a malachite ash tray fixed his eyes on

Nekhludov and listened attentively. He interrupted him only once and then to offer him a cigarette.

The general belonged to the learned type of military men, who believe it possible to reconcile humanitarianism and liberalism with the activities of their profession. Being, however, by nature clever and kindhearted, he speedily recognized the impossibility of such a combination and in order to blind himself to the inconsistencies of the kind of life he was leading he had gradually become addicted to the habit of drink, so prevalent in military circles, and after indulging in the habit for thirty-five years he had become what the doctors call a "dipsomaniac." He was literally saturated with wine. Now any liquor whatever sufficed to intoxicate him, but wine had become such a necessity for him that he could not exist without it and every day toward night he was fairly drunk; but he had become so accustomed to it, that he no longer reeled or talked foolishly, and even if he did say something silly now and then, it was received as a piece of profound wisdom by virtue of the important post he held. It was only in the morning, just at the time of Nekhludov's visit, that his mind was clear enough to understand what was said to him and to give a personal illustration of the proverb he was fond of repeating: "He's tipsy and he's wise, so he's pleasant in two ways." The higher authorities knew that this man was a drunkard, but still he had had a better education than most of the other men available, and although his progress in education had stopped when his fondness for drink began, he was bold, clever, and dignified and even when intoxicated always behaved with tact. For this reason he had been appointed to this responsible and important post and had been allowed to retain it.

Nekhludov told him that the person in whom he was interested was a woman, that she had been unjustly sentenced, and that a petition on her behalf had been presented to His Majesty.

"I see . . ." said the general. "Well?"

"I was promised in Petersburg that the decision concerning her fate would be forwarded to me here some time this month."

Without taking his eyes off Nekhludov the general reached out his hand with its stumpy fingers toward the table and rang the bell, all the while puffing at his cigarette and noisily clearing his throat, yet never ceasing to listen.

"So I came to ask you to allow this woman to remain here until I receive an answer to the petition."

An orderly in uniform entered the room.

"Ask if Anna Vassilievna is up," said the general, "and give us some more tea. And what else?" he asked, turning to Nekhludov.

"My second request concerns a political prisoner who is in the same party."

"Indeed?" said the general with a meaning nod.

"He is very ill. In fact, he is dying and will probably be left here in the hospital. One of the women prisoners asks leave to remain with him."

"Is she a kinswoman of his?"

"No, but she is willing to marry him if she could be permitted to take care of him."

The general went on smoking in silence, his keen eyes fixed on Nekhludov, as if he were trying to embarrass him.

When Nekhludov had finished, the general reached for a book on the table and wetting his fingers began to turn the pages rapidly, until he found the statute relating to marriage and read it through.

"What is her sentence?" he asked, looking up from the book.

"Hard labor."

"In that case, the position of the sick man wouldn't be improved."

"But—"

"Wait a moment. Even if she were to marry a free man, she would be obliged to serve her sentence all the same. The question is, which of them has the heavier sentence, he or she?"

"They are both sentenced to hard labor."

"In that case they are both in the same boat," said the general, laughing. "He may be kept here on account of his state of health, and, of course, everything would be done to make things easier for him; but so far as she is concerned, even if she married him, she would not be allowed to remain here."

"Her Excellency is drinking her coffee," announced the orderly.

The general nodded and went on.

"Still, I will think the matter over. What are their names? Write them down here, please."

Nekhludov wrote them down.

"No, I couldn't allow that, either," said the general, when Nekhludov asked for permission to see the sick man. "I wouldn't have you imagine that I suspect you, but you are interested in this man, as well as in others, and you have money. Here everybody and everything is for sale. I have been told, 'Put down bribery'—but how can I hope to put it down, when any man will take a bribe? The lower the rank the easier they are to bribe. How am I to watch a man who is three thousand miles away? Every official is as much a little tsar in his own way as I am here." And the general laughed. "Now I am quite sure that you have seen these political prisoners and of course you didn't get in without bribery," he said, smiling. "Isn't that so?"

"Yes, that's true."

"Well, I quite realize that you had to do it. You are sorry for a certain political prisoner and wish to see him, and the inspector or a soldier in the escort accepts the bribe because he has a family to support and only gets a wretched salary. He can't help taking it. If I were in his place, or in yours, I don't doubt that I should behave in exactly the same way. But in my position I cannot allow myself to deviate from the strict letter of the law, just because I am a man and susceptible to human sympathy. I am in an official position here and have been entrusted with certain responsibilities. I must justify this trust. Well, then, we seem to have thrashed the matter out. Now tell me what is going on in the capital?" And the general talked and asked questions at the same time, evidently anxious to hear the news and also to display his own importance and philanthropy.

❖

CHAPTER TWENTY-THREE

"BY the way, where are you staying?" asked the general, as Nekhludov was about to leave. "At Dukov's? It's just as bad there as anywhere else. Come and dine with us. We dine at five. Do you speak English?"

"Yes."

"That's good! We have an English traveler here. He is studying Siberia and the exile system. We expect him to dinner this evening, and you must come, too. Don't forget, we dine at five, and my wife insists on punctuality. By that time I shall be able to give you an answer about the woman and also about the man who is ill. It may, perhaps, be possible to allow someone to remain with him."

After taking leave of the general, Nekhludov, feeling exhilarated and full of energy, went to the post office.

The post office occupied a low, vaulted room. Clerks seated at their desks were distributing letters. One clerk, with his head on one side, was stamping letters unceasingly, like an automaton. Scarcely had Nekhludov spoken his name than his large mail was handed to him; money, letters, books, and the last copy of *Vestnik Evropy*.[1] He took the things to a wooden bench and, sitting down beside a soldier who was reading a book while he waited for somebody, he opened his letters. One of them was a registered letter in a strong envelope with a bright red seal. When he opened it he saw that it was from Selenin, with an official communication enclosed. The blood rushed to his face and his heart seemed to stand still. It was the decision in Katusha's case. What would it be? Could it possibly be a refusal? Nekhludov glanced hurriedly through the letter written in a small firm hand. Then he heaved a sigh of immense relief. The answer was favorable. Selenin wrote:

My dear friend,

Our last conversation made a deep impression on me. You were right about Maslova. I went over the case carefully and saw that a shocking injustice had been done to her. But it could only be remedied by the Committee of Petitions where you entered an appeal. I succeeded in helping the matter along and am now sending you a copy of the mitigation of sentence to the address given me by Countess Katerina Ivanovna. The original document has been sent to the place of Maslova's confinement during the trial and will probably be forwarded at once to the Siberian Central Office. I hasten to write you the good news and warmly press your hand.

Yours,
SELENIN.

The contents of the document were as follows:

His Majesty's Office for the Reception of Petitions. Case No.—. Dept.—. Date—. By Order of the Chief of His Majesty's Office for the Reception of Petitions one *meshchanka* Katerina Maslova is hereby informed that in consequence of her petition His Majesty graciously condescends to grant her request and hereby orders that her sentence to hard labor be commuted to exile to some less remote place of Siberia.

It was indeed joyful and important news. Everything had ended as satisfactorily as Nekhludov could have desired for

[1] "Messenger of Europe."—Tr.

Katusha as well as for himself. It was true that the change brought new complications regarding his own relations toward her. While she was a convict, the marriage he had offered her could only be fictitious and would only have served to alleviate her situation. But now there was nothing to prevent them from living together, and for this Nekhludov was unprepared. And then, how would it affect her relations with Simonson? What did the words she had spoken yesterday really mean? And supposing she were to marry Simonson, would that be a good thing for her or a bad one? He could not unravel all these problems, so he ceased to dwell upon them. "Sometime all these perplexing difficulties will be cleared up," he thought to himself. "Now I must try to see her as soon as possible and tell her the glad news and have her set free." He thought that the copy he had in his hands would suffice; so when he left the post office he told his cabby to drive to the prison.

Although he had received no permit from the general to visit the prison that morning, Nekhludov knew from past experience that what is sometimes refused by the higher authorities can often be obtained from the subordinates, so he decided that he would at all events make an attempt to see Katusha. At the same time he could make inquiries about Kryltzov and tell him and Maria Pavlovna what the general had said.

The inspector of the prison was a tall, stout and imposing man with a mustache and side whiskers that curved around the corners of his mouth. His manner was stern, and he at once informed Nekhludov that no outsiders could be admitted without a special order from his chief. To Nekhludov's remark that he had often been admitted even in the capital, the inspector replied: "That may be so, but I do not allow it," and his tone implied: "You gentlemen who live in the metropolis think that you can surprise and impress us. But even if we do live in Eastern Siberia, we know the rules and regulations and we can teach you a thing or two!"

Even the copy of the document forwarded from His Majesty's Office of Petitions made no impression on him and he flatly refused to admit Nekhludov inside the prison walls. In answer to Nekhludov's ingenuous supposition that Maslova could be set free on the strength of this copy, he only smiled disdainfully and explained that no one could be set free without an order from his immediate superior. All that he would promise was that Maslova should be informed of the mitigation of her sentence and that she should not be detained one hour after the order for her release was received. He likewise refused to give any information concerning Kryltzov's state of health, saying that he did not even know whether there was a convict of that name in the prison. And so, having been disappointed in all his expectations, Nekhludov returned to his cab and drove back to the hotel.

The inspector's severity was chiefly due to the fact that typhoid fever had broken out in the overcrowded prison. The cabby told Nekhludov on the way that a great many persons were dying in this prison; some sort of a disease had attacked them and as many as twenty convicts were buried every day.

❧

CHAPTER TWENTY-FOUR

IN spite of his failure to get inside the prison walls, Nekhludov, his energy and confidence unabated, drove to the office of the general to inquire whether the order for Maslova's pardon had been received there. Hearing that no such paper had arrived, on his return to the hotel Nekhludov made haste to write to Selenin and to his lawyer. When both letters were written, he looked at his watch. It was already time to go to dinner at the general's.

On his way he again felt worried about Katusha. How would she receive the news of her pardon? Where would she settle? How should he live with her? What about Simonson? What was the relationship between them? He thought of the change that had come over her, and he recalled her past life. "That should be forgotten, blotted out forever," he said to himself, and again strove to change the current of his thoughts. "When the time comes I shall know what to do." And he began to think out what he was going to say to the general.

The dinner at the general's house, served with all the luxury customary among the wealthy and the higher ranks of official-dom, seemed extremely enjoyable to Nekhludov after he had been deprived for so long not only of comforts but of the actual necessities of life. The hostess, a *grande dame* of the old school, formerly a maid of honor at the Court of Nicholas I, spoke French naturally and Russian unnaturally. She held herself erect, and when she made a gesture with her hands she never lifted her elbows from her waist. Her attitude toward her husband was one of quiet and melancholy deference. Toward her guests she was gracious and attentive, though with certain shades of difference, according to their social status. She received Nekhludov like one of her own set, with that subtle, imperceptible flattery that reminded him of his virtues and gratified his vanity. She made him understand that she was aware of the unusual but honorable purpose which had brought him to Siberia and that she considered him an exceptional person. This delicate flattery, as well as the refinement and luxury about him, contributed to Nekhludov's enjoyment of his well-cooked food and the pleasure of associating with well-bred men and women of his own class. It seemed as though all he had lived through, during these last months, had been only a dream from which he had just awakened.

Besides the general's household—his daughter, her husband, and the aide-de-camp—there were three guests: an Englishman, a merchant interested in gold mines, and the governor of a distant Siberian city. They all made an agreeable impression on Nekhludov.

The healthy, rosy-cheeked Englishman spoke very poor French but had excellent command of his own language, and used it like an orator. He had traveled widely, had seen a great deal, and could talk in an interesting way of America, India, Japan, and Siberia.

The young gold merchant, the son of a peasant, wore evening dress made in London and diamond studs. He possessed an extensive library, was a philanthropist, and sympathized with liberal European ideas. Nekhludov liked him particularly because he represented a new and attractive type of the cultured European grafted onto Russian peasant stock.

The governor of the remote Siberian city was that same department director about whom there had been so much talk in Petersburg when Nekhludov was there. He was a plump and paunchy man with soft, blue eyes, a pleasant smile and thin curly hair. His white, well-kept hands were adorned with rings. The host had a sincere respect for this guest of his, because in the venal world to which he was himself accustomed he was the only man he knew who refused to take a bribe. The hostess, who was very fond of music and a good musician herself, liked him because he played the piano well and could play duets with her. Nekhludov was in such a happy frame of mind that day that he found it impossible to dislike even this man.

The jolly, lively aide-de-camp, with his shaven bluish chin, who was always offering his services to everybody, was likeable for his obvious good nature. But it was that charming couple, the general's daughter and her husband, that Nekhludov found most delightful. She was a plain, simple young woman entirely absorbed in her two children. The marriage had been a love match and had taken place only after a long struggle with her parents. Her husband was a graduate of Móscow University, an intelligent modest young man in the government service. He was interested in statistics and particularly in the native tribes, of whom he had made a study, for he liked them and hoped to save them from extinction.

Not only were all the guests attentive and amiable to Nekhludov, but they evidently enjoyed his company, finding him an original and interesting personality. The general, who came in to dinner in uniform, wearing the white cross, greeted Nekhludov like an old friend. He invited the guests to partake of the hors d'œuvres and the vodka, then asked Nekhludov what he had been doing all the afternoon after leaving him. Nekhludov told him that he had been to the post office and collected a letter informing him of the pardon of the prisoner of whom they had been speaking that morning, and that he had been to the general's office for a permit to visit the jail. The general, evidently displeased that business should have been mentioned at dinner, frowned and made no reply.

"Will you have a glass of vodka?" he said in French to the Englishman who had just come up to the table.

The Englishman, after drinking some vodka, said that he had visited the factory and the cathedral that morning, but would very much like to see the great Transportation Prison.

"An excellent idea! Then, you two can go together," said the general, turning to Nekhludov. "Write them a permit," he said, addressing the aide-de-camp.

"What hour would suit you?" Nekhludov asked the Englishman.

"I always prefer to visit prisons in the evening. Everybody is indoors then, and there is no chance for preparation, so one sees things as they really are," replied the Englishman.

"Ah, he wants to see it in all its glory! Let him, let him! When I wrote about the state of affairs they paid no attention to me. Now let them find out about it from the foreign press," said the general and took his seat at the dinner table, where the hostess was showing the guests their places. Nekhludov sat between the hostess and the Englishman. Opposite him sat the general's daughter and the ex-director.

At the table the conversation was disconnected and spasmodic. At one moment the Englishman was talking of India, at another the general was speaking disparagingly of the Tonkin expedition and then of the bribery and widespead rascality in Siberia. None of these subjects interested Nekhludov very much.

But in the drawing room after dinner, when the coffee was brought in, an interesting discussion on Gladstone arose between the hostess, the Englishman, and himself, in which Nekhludov believed that he had acquitted himself rather well. And after the good dinner, the wine, and the coffee, sitting in a soft armchair, surrounded by affable, well-bred people, Nekhludov felt more and more contented. When the hostess and the ex-director at the request of the Englishman went up to the piano and began to play Beethoven's Fifth Symphony, which they had carefully practiced together, Nekhludov felt as if he had just found out what a good man he was. It was a fine-toned grand piano, and the execution of the symphony was excellent—at least Nekhludov, who knew and loved that symphony, thought so. As he listened to the beautiful andante, he felt a tickling in his nose from suppressed tears of admiration for himself and his own virtues. Thanking his hostess for the great pleaure, from which he had so long been debarred, he was about to take leave when the general's daughter, blushing but determined, walked up to him and said:

"You were asking about my children. Would you like to see them?"

"She thinks everyone wants to see her children," said her mother, smiling at her daughter's charming artlessness. "The prince is not interested in children."

"On the contrary, I'm very interested indeed," said Nekhludov, touched by this display of overflowing mother love. "Please let me see them."

"So she is taking you to see the babies?" shouted the general from the card table, where he sat playing cards with the merchant, his son-in-law, and the aide-de-camp. "Go and pay your tribute."

The young woman, visibly excited at the thought that judgment was about to be passed on her children, walked swiftly ahead of Nekhludov, leading the way into the inner apartments. In a lofty room, with white wallpaper, lighted by a small lamp with a dark shade over it, stood two cots, and between them sat a nurse with a white cape on her shoulders; she had a good-natured face and the high cheekbones of a Siberian. She rose and bowed.

The mother bent over the first cot. In it a little girl lay sleeping peacefully. Her lips were slightly parted and her long curly hair was tumbled over the pillow. One tiny foot peeped from beneath the blue and white crocheted bedspread.

"This is my Katya," murmured the mother as she tucked the little foot in. "Isn't she a darling? She's just two years old."

"She's charming."

"And this is Vassuk, as his grandfather calls him. Quite a different type. A real Siberian, don't you think so?"

"A fine little fellow," said Nekhludov, as he stooped to look at the chubby youngster lying flat on his stomach fast asleep.

"Do you really think so?" asked the mother with a grateful smile.

Nekhludov recalled the chains, the shaven heads, the blows, the debauchery, the dying Kryltzov, Katusha and all her past, and he felt envious and longed for just such happiness as this, pure and refined as it seemed to him now.

He praised the children again and again till the mother, eager as she was to have them admired, felt her heart almost bursting with pride. When he followed her back into the drawing room Nekhludov found the Englishman all ready and waiting to drive to the jail with him, as had been arranged. Having taken leave of their hosts, old and young, they went out into the porch together.

The weather had changed. Snow was falling in large, thick flakes, and had already covered the streets, the roofs, the top of the cab, and the horse's back. The Englishman had his own carriage, so Nekhludov gave his coachman directions and then called his own cabby. As he followed him along the road over the soft snow through which the wheels churned slowly, he was oppressed by the feeling that he was being forced to perform an unpleasant duty.

♣

CHAPTER TWENTY-FIVE

IN spite of the white mantle which now covered its walls, porch and roof, the prison with the lantern hanging over the gate and the long rows of lighted windows looked to Nekhludov even more gloomy than it looked by daylight.

The imposing inspector came out of the gate, and after reading by the light of the lantern the permit that had been given to Nekhludov and the Englishman, shrugged his broad shoulders in surprise; but in obedience to the order he invited the visitors to follow him. He led them through a yard to a door on the right, then up a staircase into the office. He offered them seats, and asked what he could do for them, and when Nekhludov expressed a wish to see Maslova, he sent a warden to fetch her. He then prepared himself to answer the questions which the Englishman, with the aid of Nekhludov as an interpreter, began to put to him: "How many persons is this prison meant to hold? How many are here now? How many of them are men, how many women and how many children? How many are sentenced to hard labor, how many are exiles, and how many followed them of their own free will? How many are sick?"

Nekhludov translated the questions and the replies, hardly conscious of their significance, so agitated was he by the thought of the coming interview. In the middle of a sentence which he was translating, he heard approaching footsteps and saw the door open. As had happened many times before, the warden came in followed by Katusha in her prison blouse, her head tied up in a kerchief, and his heart sank.

"I want to live. I want a family, children of my own. I want to live like other men." These thoughts flashed across his mind, as with a quick step and downcast eyes Katusha came into the room.

As he rose and took a few steps toward her, he saw that her face was stern and hostile. It was the expression he remembered when she had reproached him. She raised and lowered her eyes, flushed and turned pale, and her fingers nervously twisted the edge of her blouse.

"Have you been told that a mitigation of your sentence has been granted?"

"Yes, the inspector told me."

"So when the document arrives you will be able to settle where you like. We will think it over——"

She interrupted him hastily.

"There's nothing to think over. I shall follow Vladimir Vassilievich wherever he goes."

In spite of her excitement she looked straight into Nekhludov's eyes and spoke quickly and distinctly, as though she had learned a lesson.

"I see," said Nekhludov.

"Well, Dmitri Ivanovich, if he wants me to live with him——" she paused, abashed, and corrected herself, "wants me to be with him, I must consider myself lucky. What else is there for me——?"

"One of two things," thought Nekhludov. "Either she loves

Simonson and has never required the sacrifice which I imagined I was making, or she continues to love me even while she refuses me for my own sake, and is burning her bridges by uniting her lot with Simonson's." He felt ashamed of himself and knew that he was blushing.

"Of course, if you love him," he said.

"Does it matter whether I do or not? I am past that sort of thing. And, besides, Vladimir Ivanovich is a different kind of man."

"Yes, of course," began Nekhludov, "he is a splendid fellow, and I think—" She interrupted him again as though she feared that he might say too much, or that she would not have a chance to say everything.

"You must forgive me, Dmitri Ivanovich, if I am not doing what you wish," she said, looking straight at him with her mysterious squinting eyes. "But this is how it had to be. You have your own life to live."

She was only saying what he himself had just been thinking, but now he felt ashamed of the thought and regretted all that he would lose when he lost her.

"I did not expect this," he said.

"Why should you live here and suffer?" she said, and smiled. "You have suffered enough already."

"I have not suffered. I have been happy and I should like to go on serving you if I could."

"We," she said, looking up at Nekhludov, "we need nothing. You have already done a great deal for me. If it hadn't been for you—" She was about to say something more, but her voice quivered.

"I am the last person you should thank," said Nekhludov.

"What's the use of trying to weigh up what we owe one another? God will make up our accounts," she said and her black eyes shone with the tears that rushed into them.

"What a good woman you are!" he said.

"I? A good woman!" She smiled pitifully through her tears.

The Englishman interrupted. "Can we get on?" he said.

"Just a moment," said Nekhludov, and asked Katusha about Kryltzov.

She pulled herself together sharply and quickly told him what she' knew. Kryltzov's journey had weakened him considerably and he had been sent straight to hospital. Maria Pavlovna was very anxious about him and had asked to be allowed to stay at the prison as a hospital nurse, but permission had not been granted.

"Shall I go now?" she asked, realizing that the Englishman was getting impatient.

"I will not say good-by. I shall see you again," said Nekhludov, holding out his hand.

"Forgive me," she whispered. Their eyes met, and by her peculiar squinting look, her pitiful smile, and the tone of her voice when she said, not 'Good-by' but 'Forgive me,' Nekhludov understood. His second supposition as to the cause of her decision was the real one. She loved him and realized only too well that union with her would ruin him. By remaining with Simonson she was releasing him, and while rejoicing that in this way she was accomplishing her purpose, she was yet mourning that she must part from him. She pressed his hand and, quickly turning, went from the room.

Nekhludov was now ready to go, but glancing at the Englishman he saw he was still busily writing in his notebook. Not wishing to disturb him, Nekhludov sat down on the wooden seat by the wall and a great weariness suddenly came over him. It was not the weariness one feels after a sleepless night of travel or excitement—he was terribly tired of life. He leaned back, closed his eyes, and at once fell into a deep slumber.

"Would you also like to see the prisoners' cells?"

It was the inspector's voice. Nekhludov awoke suddenly, very surprised to find himself in the prison.

❦

CHAPTER TWENTY-SIX

THEY went through an anteroom and then along the corridor in which, even as they passed, two prisoners were making water onto the floor. The stench of this passage made Nekhludov feel desperately sick. Escorted by warders, the inspector, the Englishman and Nekhludov entered the first part of the prison devoted to prisoners sentenced to hard labor. Seventy men were already in their bunks. These were arranged with their headrests toward one another in two long lines down the middle of the room. When the visitors entered all the prisoners sprang up, and clanking their chains stood beside their bunks, their half-shaven heads shining in the light. Only two remained lying in their bunks. One was a young man with a flushed face, evidently in a high fever, the other an old man who groaned incessantly.

The Englishman asked how long the young man had been ill, and was told by the inspector that he had been taken ill only that morning, but that old fellow had had stomach trouble for a long time. There was no room for him in the hospital, he said, as that was already overcrowded. The Englishman shook his head disapprovingly and said that he would like to say a few words to these men, and asked Nekhludov to translate for him. It appeared that besides his professed object in making the journey—to investigate the prisons and places of exile in Siberia—he also had another, namely, to preach Salvation through Faith and Redemption to the unhappy convicts.

"Tell them," he said, "that Christ loves them and pities them and died for them. If they believe this they will be saved." While he was talking, all the prisoners stood beside their bunks with their arms at their sides. "Tell them that it is all in this book," he concluded. "Can any of them read?"

There were over twenty of them who could. The Englishman took out of his bag a few bound copies of the New Testament, and several strong, muscular hands with blackened fingernails were stretched forth from under the sleeves of coarse shirts, struggling to reach the books. He left two Testaments in this room and went into the next.

The same condition of things prevailed there, the same close atmosphere and stench. A similar icon hung between the two windows, a similar tub stood to the left of the door. The prisoners were packed in just as closely. As in the first room they sprang up and stood motionless beside their bunks on the entry of the visitors. Here, however, there were three who were too ill to stand up. Two of these sat up, but one remained lying down and did not even turn his head to look at the newcomers. The Englishman made the same speech and again left two Testaments.

In the third ward four men were ill. The Englishman wanted to know why the sick men were not put all together, and was told that they themselves did not wish it. Their diseases were not contagious, and the doctor's assistant treated them and took care of them.

A voice muttered, "He has not shown his face here for a fortnight."

The inspector took no notice, but led the visitors into the next ward. As before, when the doors were thrown open, all the convicts rose and stood in silence, and as before the Englishman distributed Testaments.

They went on to the fifth and sixth wards, then to the wards of the exiles, to those of the people banished by their village communes, and lastly to those where the people who had followed voluntarily were confined. Everywhere, to right and left and all around the picture, was the same. Men, cold, sick, hungry, idle, and humiliated, under lock and key, were being exhibited like wild beasts.

When he had distributed what seemed to be the allotted number of Testaments, the Englishman made no more little speeches. Even his ardor had been diminished by the distressing sights and stifling atmosphere, and he said nothing but "I see" to anything the inspector said about the prisoners.

Nekhludov walked on with them as if in a dream, utterly dejected and weary, yet lacking the energy and initiative to refuse to go further.

❖

CHAPTER TWENTY-SEVEN

IN one of the cells, among the exiles, Nekhludov recognized, to his surprise, the strange old man he had met on the ferry. Wrinkled, ragged, barefoot, his only garments a dirty ash-gray shirt and trousers, he was sitting on the floor beside his bunk and looked sternly but inquiringly at the newcomers. His emaciated body, visible through the rents in his tattered shirt, looked feeble and wretched, but the expression on his face was even more animated and grave than it had been when he was on the raft. All the other convicts jumped up and stood at attention when the inspector came in, just as they had done in the other wards, but the old man remained sitting on the floor. His eyes glittered and he frowned angrily.

"Stand up!" shouted the inspector.

The old man did not move but smiled disdainfully and muttered:

"Thy servants are standing before thee, but I am not thy servant." Then, pointing to the inspector's forehead, he went on, "You bear the seal of—"

"What?" roared the inspector threateningly, and moved toward him.

"I know this man," Nekhludov said hurriedly. "Why is he here?"

"The police sent him because he has no passport. We ask them to keep these cases themselves, but they go on sending them," replied the inspector, looking savagely at the old man out of the corner of his eyes.

"So you, too, belong to the Army of Antichrist?" said the old man, addressing Nekhludov.

"No, I am only a visitor."

"Have you come, then, to see how Antichrist tortures people? Take your fill of it. He's got them, a whole army of them, locked up in a cage. They ought to be earning their bread by the sweat of their brows, and he has locked them up like swine. He feeds them in their idleness, so that treated like beasts they shall become beasts."

"What is he saying?" asked the Englishman.

Nekhludov told him that the old man was blaming the inspector for keeping men in prison.

"Ask him what he thinks ought to be done with men who refuse to obey the law," said the Englishman.

Nekhludov translated the question.

The old man laughed strangely, baring his teeth.

"The law!" he repeated contemptuously. "First *he* robbed everybody, taking for himself all the land and property that belonged to others, deprived them of all their rights, killed all those who resisted him, and then he wrote laws forbidding men to rob and kill. He should have made the laws first."

Nekhludov translated. The Englishman smiled.

"But ask him what ought to be done with thieves and murderers now?"

Again Nekhludov interpreted the question. The old man knitted his brows fiercely.

"You tell him to cast off the seal of Antichrist from himself, then he will know neither thieves nor murderers. Just tell him that."

"He is crazy," said the Englishman when Nekhludov translated the old man's words. Shrugging his shoulders, he turned and left the room.

Nekhludov lingered in the ward and the old man started again:

"Get on with your own business and leave others alone. Every man is his own master. The Lord knows who should be punished and who should be pardoned, but we are ignorant. Be your own master and you will need no other. Go away now!

Go away. You have seen how the servants of Antichrist feed lice with the bodies of men. Away with you, I say!"

Nekhludov stepped out into the passage and found the Englishman and the inspector standing by the open door of an unoccupied cell. The inspector explained that it was a morgue, and the Englishman, when Nekhludov had translated, expressed a wish to go in.

It was an ordinary, small cell. A tiny lamp hung on the wall and feebly illuminated the contents—a few sacks and a pile of logs in one corner, and on the bunks to the right of them four corpses. The first of these was clothed in a coarse linen shirt and a pair of drawers. It was that of a big man with a small pointed beard and a half-shaven head. The body had already stiffened; the bluish hands had evidently been crossed on the breast, but were now unclasped; the legs had fallen apart and the bare feet were sticking out in opposite directions. Beside him lay a barefooted and bareheaded old woman in a white petticoat and blouse; she had a small shriveled yellow face, a sharp nose, and a thin, short plait of hair. Then came the body of a man clothed in something purple. The color struck Nekhludov as familiar. He went nearer, and looked. A short, pointed beard, turned upward, a firm handsome nose, a high, white forehead, thin curling hair—he recognized them all but could scarcely believe his eyes. Only yesterday that face had been excited, angry, full of suffering. Now it was motionless, calm and terribly beautiful. Yes, it was Kryltzov—all that remained of Kryltzov's material existence. "Why had he suffered? Why had he lived? Does he understand now what it's all for?" The thoughts raced through Nekhludov's mind, but it seemed to him that there was no answer, that there was nothing, nothing but death. He felt faint. Without a word of farewell to the Englishman, he asked the inspector to show him the way to the yard. He needed to be alone, to have time to think over all he had seen and heard that evening. He drove back to his hotel.

CHAPTER TWENTY-EIGHT

NEKHLUDOV did not go to bed, but for a long time paced up and down his room. The Katusha business was over and done with. She no longer needed him, and it made him feel sad and rather mortified. But this was not what troubled him now. The other business on which he had embarked was not only unfinished, but tormented him more than ever, and required all his energy. The terrible wrongs which he had witnessed, particularly the sights he had seen in that awful prison today, the cruelty that had done Kryltzov to death, all forced him to think that evil was triumphant and omnipotent. He could see no possibility of conquering it, nor even of beginning to understand how it could be conquered. In his imagination he beheld hundreds and thousands of degraded men locked up in contaminated prisons by generals, prosecuting attorneys, and inspectors who were completely indifferent to their sufferings; he saw the strange, defiant old man who had denounced them all and whom they called insane; and then among the bodies of the dead he saw the beautiful waxen face of Kryltzov, who had died with his heart filled with bitterness and wrath. And the question he had so often asked himself, "Am I the madman, or are those mad who commit these deeds?" again arose in his mind with renewed force and demanded an answer.

Weary in mind and body, he sat down on the sofa by the lamp and mechanically picked up the Testament the Englishman had given him. He had thrown it on the table when he came in. "We are told that the solutions of all life's problems can be found in this book," he thought, and opening it at random began to read Matthew 18:

1 In that hour came the disciples unto Jesus, saying, Who then is greatest in the kingdom of heaven?

2 And he called to him a little child, and set him in the midst of them.

3 And said, Verily, I say unto you, Except ye turn, and become as little children, ye shall in no wise enter into the kingdom of heaven.

4 Whosoever therefore shall humble himself as this little child, the same is the greatest in the kingdom of heaven.

"Yes, yes, that is true," he thought, remembering that he himself had experienced peace and joy only in the measure in which he had humbled himself.

> *And whoso shall receive one such little child in my name receiveth me: but whoso shall cause one of these little ones which believe on me to stumble, it is profitable for him that a great millstone should be hanged about his neck, and that he should be sunk in the depth of the sea. [Matt. 18: 5, 6.]*

"What can that mean, I wonder? 'Whoso shall receive.' Receive where? And what does 'in my name' mean?" he asked himself, feeling that these words had no meaning for him. "And why 'the millstone around his neck' and 'the depth of the sea'? No, there must be something wrong there. It is not clear, not definite." He recalled now how many times in his life he had begun to read the Gospels, and how every time the absurdity of these passages had discouraged him. He went on to read the seventh, eighth, ninth, and tenth verses which deal with "occasions of stumbling," their inevitability and the punishment of mankind by "casting into hell-fire," and with the angels of "these little ones" who look upon the face of the Father in Heaven. "What a pity," he thought, "that this is not more intelligible, for one feels that it is good." He went on reading.

> *11 For the Son of man came to save that which was lost.*
> *12 How think ye? If any man have a hundred sheep, and one of them be gone astray, doth he not leave the ninety and nine, and go unto the mountains, and seek that which goeth astray?*
> *13 And if so be that he find it, verily I say unto you, he rejoiceth over it more than over the ninety and nine which have not gone astray.*
> *14 Even so it is not the will of your Father which is in heaven, that one of the little ones should perish.*

"No," he thought, "it is not the will of the Father that they should perish—and yet they do perish by the hundreds and thousands, and there is no hope of saving them."

> *21 Then came Peter, and said to him, Lord, how oft shall my brother sin against me, and I forgive him? until seven times?*
> *22 Jesus saith unto him, I say not unto thee, Until seven times: but, Until seventy times seven.*
> *23 Therefore is the kingdom of heaven likened unto a*

certain king, which would make a reckoning with his servants.

24 And when he had begun to reckon, one was brought unto him, which owed him ten thousand talents.

25 But forasmuch as he had not wherewith to pay, his lord commanded him to be sold, and his wife, and children, and all that he had, and payment be made.

26 The servant therefore fell down and worshipped him, saying, Lord, have patience with me, and I will pay thee all.

27 And the lord of that servant, being moved with compassion, released him, and forgave him the debt.

28 But that servant went out, and found one of his fellow-servants, which owed him a hundred pence: and he laid hold on him, and took him by the throat, saying, Pay what thou owest.

29 So his fellow-servant fell down and besought him, saying, Have patience with me, and I will pay thee.

30 And he would not: but went and cast him into prison, till he should pay that which was due.

31 So when his fellow-servants saw what was done, they were exceeding sorry, and came and told unto their lord all that was done.

32 Then his lord called him unto him, and saith to him, Thou wicked servant, I forgave thee all that debt, because thou besoughtest me:

33 Shouldest not thou also have had mercy on thy fellow-servant, even as I had mercy on thee?

"But can that be all?" Nekhludov suddenly exclaimed aloud. And an inner voice replied, "Yes, that is all."

And it happened to Nekhludov as it often happens to men who live a spiritual life. The thought that at first had appeared so strange, so paradoxical, even laughable, had been more and more frequently confirmed by life, and now rose before him as an indisputable truth. Now he saw quite clearly that the only sure means of salvation from the terrible wrong which man has to endure is for every man to acknowledge himself a sinner before God and therefore unfitted to punish or reform other men. It had become clear to him now that the terrible evil which he had witnessed in jails and halting places and the calm self-assurance of those who were responsible for it resulted from the attempt by men to perform the impossible. Evil themselves, they presumed to correct evil. Vicious men undertook to reform other vicious men and expected to accomplish this by mechanical means. The only result was that needy and greedy men, having made a profession of so-called punishment and correction, became utterly corrupt themselves, and unceasingly corrupted those whom they tormented. Now he knew the origin of all the horrors he had witnessed, and he also knew where to find the remedy. It lay in the answer Christ gave to Peter—to forgive everything, everyone, to forgive unceasingly, never to grow weary in forgiving. There are no men living who do not need forgiveness, and therefore there are no men living fit to correct or punish others.

"But surely it cannot be so simple?" said Nekhludov to himself. Yet he knew now with certainty, although all this had seemed strange to him at first, that it was undoubtedly not only a theoretical but a practical solution of the problem. He was no longer perplexed by the age-old question as to what should be done with evildoers. There might be some reason in the question if it had ever been shown that punishment improved the criminal and diminished crime. But when the contrary has been proved, when it has become an established fact that it is beyond the power of men to reform others, then the only rational thing to do is to abandon methods which are not only useless but harmful, immoral, and cruel.

For many centuries people considered as criminals have been executed—but have they become extinct? No; far from diminishing, their numbers have been increased by the addition of those who have been demoralized by punishments, and also of those other criminals—judges, prosecutors, magistrates, and jailers, who judge and punish men. Now Nekhludov understood that society and order still existed in general, not thanks to these legalized criminals, who judge and punish other men, but because in spite of their depraving influence men still love and pity one another.

Hoping to find a confirmation of this belief, Nekhludov began to read the Gospels from the beginning. After reading the Sermon on the Mount, which always touched him deeply, he saw in it today for the first time not beautiful abstract thoughts setting forth exaggerated and impossible demands, but clear, simple, and practical commandments, which if obeyed would establish a completely new order of things in the social life of mankind. Obedience to these commands was entirely possible, and would not only exclude all the violence that so revolted Nekludov, but would establish the Kingdom of God upon Earth, which is the greatest blessing man can hope to attain.

There were five of these commandments:

The first commandment (Matthew 5: 21-26)—that a man

must not only not kill, but he must not even be angry with his brother, or call him a fool, and if he should quarrel with any-one, he must be reconciled with him before he offers his gift to God, that is, before praying.

The second commandment (Matthew 5: 27-32)—that a man must not only abstain from committing adultery, but must even refrain from enjoying the beauty of a woman, and if he has ever been united with her he must never be unfaithful to her.

The third commandment (Matthew 5: 33-37)—that no man must seal a promise with an oath.

The fourth commandment (Matthew 5: 38-42)—that man must not only refrain from returning evil for evil, but when he is struck on one cheek he must turn the other; that he must for-give injuries and endure them with humility and never refuse to serve his fellow men.

The fifth commandment (Matthew 5: 43-48)—that a man must not only refrain from hating or fighting his enemies, but that he must love, help, and serve them.

Nekhludov sat motionless, his eyes fixed on the flame of the lamp. Recalling all the horrors of human life, he clearly pic-tured to himself what it might be if men were taught to obey these commandments, and rapture such as he had not felt for a very long time possessed his soul. It seemed that at last after long days of weariness and suffering he had found freedom and rest.

He did not sleep that night, and as happens to many a man who reads the Gospels, he understood for the first time the full meaning of words which he had read many times before and scarcely noticed. As a sponge absorbs water, so he drank in these important, welcome, and joyous revelations. All that he read seemed quite familiar, confirming and making real what he had long known but had not fully understood nor really be-lieved. Now he believed and realized completely not only that if man obeys these commandments he will attain for himself the highest possible good, but also that it is man's sole duty to do this. In this lies the only reasonable purpose of human life, and every transgression of these laws is an error that brings retribution in its wake. This was the object of all the teaching but was particularly clearly illustrated in the parable of the vineyard.

The husbandmen imagined that the vineyard into which the Master had sent them to work was their own, that everything in it belonged to them, and that their only business was to enjoy life in it, ignoring the Master and killing any who presumed to remind them of Him and of their duty to Him.

"We do the same," thought Nekhludov. "We live in the belief that we are the masters of our own lives, and that they were given us for enjoyment. That is frankly absurd. If we have been sent into this world, it is obviously by someone's will and for some purpose. Yet we have assumed that we live only for our own selfish ends and inevitably things go ill with us, as they did with the workmen who did not fulfill the will of their master. If men but follow the will of the Master as expressed in these commandments, the Kingdom of God will be established on earth and they will attain the highest good that is within their reach. *Seek ye first the Kingdom of God and His righteousness, and all these things shall be added unto you.* Here, then, is my life's work. One task is completed and another is ready to my hand."

That night a new life began for Nekhludov, not because the conditions of his life were altered, but because everything that happened to him from that time held an entirely new and different meaning for him.

Only the future will show how this new chapter of his life will end.